TRUST ME

April Joy Spring

Copyright © 2018 by April Joy Spring.

Library of Congress Control Number:		2018910886
ISBN:	Hardcover	978-1-9845-5305-8
	Softcover	978-1-9845-5306-5
	eBook	978-1-9845-5307-2

All rights reserved. No part of this book may be reproduced or transmitted in any form or by any means, electronic or mechanical, including photocopying, recording, or by any information storage and retrieval system, without permission in writing from the copyright owner.

This is a work of fiction. All of the characters, names, incidents, organizations, and dialogue in this novel are either the products of the author's imagination or are used fictitiously.

Scripture quotations marked NIV are taken from the Holy Bible, New International Version®. NIV®. Copyright © 1973, 1978, 1984 by International Bible Society. Used by permission of Zondervan. All rights reserved. [Biblica]

Any people depicted in stock imagery provided by Getty Images are models, and such images are being used for illustrative purposes only.
Certain stock imagery © Getty Images.

Print information available on the last page.

Rev. date: 10/03/2018

To order additional copies of this book, contact:
Xlibris
1-888-795-4274
www.Xlibris.com
Orders@Xlibris.com

CHAPTER 1

Thanksgiving Day, 2001

Christina Sanders, and her recently deceased husband's mother, Ruth, were watching a volleyball game between friends and family, in Christina's backyard, when she felt the familiar buzzing in her pocket. She took out her phone and flipped it open. Stopping in her tracks, her breath caught in her throat, and her heart raced as she read the bold text: "IF YOU DON'T LEAVE ALVA, MORE BAD THINGS WILL HAPPEN!"

The sounds of the volleyball game, the running, laughing and squealing kids, the barking dog chasing after them, all became muted as her whole being focused on those ten words. Nausea gripped and twisted her stomach, as sweat drenched her body.

Christina turned to Ruth and said, "I need to sit down."

Ruth immediately put her arm around Christina's waist and led her to the nearest lawn chair. Once Christina was seated, Ruth asked, "What happened? Is there anything I can get you? A glass of water? A cool washcloth?"

Christina, still processing the threat and not wanting to speak of it yet, shook her head. *Would this harassment ever end?*

Dr. Steven Dawson, Christina's colleague and good friend, since high school, noticed the sudden change in her demeanor, and watched with concern as she sat and put her head down. Alarmed, he turned to his team-mates and said, "Excuse me, I'll be right back."

Steven approached and gave Ruth a questioning look, to which she responded with a shrug.

Kneeling in front of Christina, he lifted her chin, and looked into her tear-rimmed eyes. "Hey, are you okay? Are you sick?" Remembering her near death experience a couple of months earlier with an overdose of heparin someone had slipped in her coffee, his concern was not only from friendship but medical, as well.

Christina shook her head and handed him the phone. When he read the text, worry and anger played across his face.

Standing, he called the police chief, who was just setting up a volley.

"Hey, Larry, can you come over here a minute?"

Confused and worried, Ruth asked, "What is it?"

Steven handed her the phone.

Putting her hand to her chest, Ruth said, "Oh my goodness, Christina. I had hoped all these threats were over once that crazy lady, Lula, was behind bars."

Wiping her eyes Christina sighed heavily. "Yeah, me too."

"What are you going to do?"

"I don't know, Mom."

Larry finished his volley and headed in their direction, wiping sweat from his brow with the bottom of his t-shirt. Noticing Christina's distress and Steven's anxious look, he asked, "What's going on?"

Steven handed him the phone.

"Oh man. When did you get this?"

Christina shrugged. "Just a couple of minutes ago."

Knowing that Christina was in good hands, Ruth excused herself to inform her husband of the text.

The police chief took a handkerchief out of his pocket, wiped his face, and asked, "Do you have any idea who may have sent this?"

Confused, Christina shook her head. "No. The ID number is unknown."

Larry pulled up the information on the phone, typed something and pushed the send button. A couple of seconds later, there was a *beep*. He looked at the screen. "Undeliverable."

They looked up when they heard cheering. The volleyball game was over.

Ed and Cindy joined the trio. Wiping sweat from his brow with the sleeve of his t-shirt, Ed asked, "What's going on?"

Ed worked with the Anti-Terrorist Organization, and Cindy was Christina's life long friend. The two had met during one of Ed's assignments involving the Sanders family, and had begun dating soon after. Having become friends with the police chief, Ed was kept in the loop concerning the Sanders family.

Noticing the group gathering around his mother, Brad, Christina's oldest child, left his team-mates. Squatting down in front of her, he asked, "Mom, are you okay?"

Not wanting to draw any more attention to herself or worry her son, she said, "I'm fine, now. Just felt a little woozy. Probably got overheated or something." Reaching out to push a strand of wet hair off his face, she said, "Could you go help your grandma bring out the lemonade?"

He gave her a puzzled look. "Sure, okay. Can I get you a glass?"

She nodded. "That would be great. Thanks."

When he walked away, Christina whispered to the group surrounding her, "Maybe we should just let this go for now and talk later. I don't want to worry the kids, or ruin a perfectly good day. No use getting everyone upset."

Larry nodded and returned her phone.

Steven helped her to her feet, put his arm around her shoulder and they headed over to the refreshment table.

Ed pulled Larry aside and was informed of the situation.

"So what you're saying is that there's someone else out there who wants Christina out of Alva?"

Larry sighed and nodded. "Yep. I thought when we put that crazy woman Lula, aka Ruby, in jail in Dallas for kidnapping Nicky, and wreaking havoc on the Sanders family, this would all end." Shaking his head, and rubbing his neck, he added, "Guess not."

Nicky, Christina's ten-year-old son, had been kidnapped a few weeks earlier, by a mentally impaired woman, who was convinced she would receive a substantial amount of money if she could convince Christina to leave Alva by threatening her family. Ed became involved with the investigation and subsequent apprehension of the woman. Nicky had been returned unharmed, and the woman was taken into custody. However, the man she claimed to have put her up to the kidnapping, had not been found.

Ed had grown fond of the Sanders family, and was angry that someone was continuing to cause turmoil in their lives. His tension building, he clenched his fists, wanting to punch something or someone. Instead, he took a couple of deep breaths and released them slowly, to calm the storm within.

Sighing, he said, "So back to square one."

Larry nodded, rubbing his forehead. "I still think it's someone local. Someone she knows. Maybe someone she works with."

Ed nodded. "Yeah. It's like someone knows her schedule, and knows when she's vulnerable."

Removing his ball cap and wiping his sweaty head, Larry said, "When I get back to the office, I'll start going over my list of suspects again. Surely, something will pop up."

Patting Larry on the back, Ed said, "I hope so. Christina could use a break. This has got to be wearing her down."

Nodding toward the refreshment table, Ed asked, "You want to get a drink before another round of volleyball?"

Larry grinned. "Yeah. This time, *my* team will win!"

"Oh, you think?"

"I don't think. I *know*."

Ed grinned. "I don't think you know either!"

Larry shook his head and patted Ed's shoulder. "Good one."

The two men headed to the refreshment table and asked who was ready for another game. A unanimous affirmative roar erupted from both teams.

CHAPTER 2

Janet smiled when she saw Christina's reaction to the text. A few minutes earlier she had excused herself from the volleyball game under the pretense of having to use the restroom. It was then that she used her disposable phone to send the text. *There's no way it can be traced back to me,* she thought as she hit "send". She didn't think Christina would ever leave Alva, but she could certainly make her life miserable while she was here. It was irritating to watch how everyone rallied around her—especially Dr. Dawson.

Not wanting to appear insensitive, Janet walked over and asked Christina if everything was okay, to which Christina responded with a nod.

Looking at her watch, Janet said, "It's getting late. I should be heading on home." *I've had about as much of your presence as I can stand,* she thought. *If it weren't for Linda's insistence on coming, I wouldn't even be here.*

Christina glanced at her watch as well. "Wow! The day sure has gotten away from us. Guess we'd better start cleaning up the yard."

She reached out and pulled Janet into a hug. "I'm glad y'all could come. Guess I'll see you around the hospital next week."

"Yeah. Guess I'll see you around." Janet pulled free and turned to look for Linda. Clenching her fists as she felt the anger and resentment rise within her, she walked toward the group of kids on the opposite side of the yard.

Christina watched Janet walk away. *Wow,* she thought, *that was like hugging a board.*

Feeling Christina's eyes on her, Janet shivered. *Ugh! That was awkward. If she knew how much I despise her for taking my job and Doctor Dawson, she wouldn't be so nice to me.*

Putting her hand on her daughter's shoulder, Janet said, "I hate to interrupt, but it's time to go."

Linda sighed heavily. Turning to the group surrounding her, she said, "Hey y'all, let's try to keep in touch."

They gave each other hugs and promised to keep in touch through Stacey, Christina's daughter.

CHAPTER 3

As the day progressed into evening, and people packed up their leftover food, belongings, and children, Christina felt anxiety wrapping its talons around her heart. She sensed there was safety in numbers, and now as the safety net was being depleted, her mind turned to worrisome thoughts. *How serious is this threat? If I don't comply and leave Alva, will our lives be in danger as the text implied? Who is behind all this, and for what purpose? What have I done to deserve this? Should I return to Michigan and the safety of my husband's family for the safety of my children?*

Standing at the front door, waving to her departing friends, she gnawed on a hangnail as the questions tumbled around in her head.

Steven joined her at the front door and placed his hands on her shoulders.

"What's going on in that pretty little head of yours?"

Turning to face him, she said, "Just worried. I don't know what to think about this threat. Should I just ignore it, or should I consider leaving Alva? I don't want to put any of us in jeopardy."

He pulled her into a hug and rested his chin on the top of her head.

"I wish I had answers, but I'm still trying to process that there is *still* someone out there threatening y'all." Pausing, he asked, "Are you gonna make your family aware of this threat?"

"Yes. If nothing else, I can get their prayer support."

He nodded. "You want me to call everyone into the family room?"

Disengaging from his embrace, she gave a halfhearted smile.

"Would you? I need to run upstairs a minute."

"Sure."

She called over her shoulder, "Oh Steven, just the adults. Could you ask Brad to take the kids outside?"

He nodded. "Sure."

In her bedroom, she took a few calming breaths, before grabbing a sweater and heading downstairs.

Pausing in the doorway of the family room, she noticed every chair was occupied by her close friends, as well as her deceased husband's parents, brother, sister and their spouses. She felt an overwhelming love for them as tears filled her eyes.

Hating to put a damper on such a perfect day, but needing their love, support, insight and prayer during this trying time, she wiped her eyes, squared her shoulders and went to stand in front of Steven.

The chatter subsided as all eyes turned to her.

Steven placed his hands on her shoulders as she began speaking.

"As you know, since moving to Alva, there have been threats against my family. You are aware of my episode with the heparin, and Nicky's kidnapping, and the apprehension of the woman responsible." People nodded as she looked around the room. "We thought when she was apprehended, the threats would end, but I received a text today."

She read it to them, and heard audible gasps.

David's brother asked, "What to do you plan to do?"

Shaking her head, she said, "I don't know, Robert. I was hoping we could brainstorm and come up with some possible actions."

David's sister, cleared her throat and said, "Christina, we have that condo in Dallas which sits empty most of the time. You are welcome to use it anytime you want to get away."

Christina smiled and nodded. "Thanks, Joyce. If the kids weren't in school and involved in so many activities, I would consider taking you up on that offer. Maybe when we get through the holidays, we'll give you a call and make arrangements."

Ruth, spoke next. "You know, we would love it if you and the kids came back to Michigan. If at *any* time you feel you need to get away, just let us know and we'll make arrangements."

"I'll certainly keep these offers in mind as I contemplate our next course of action."

The police chief, who had been standing in the doorway, spoke next.

"I want to assure everyone that my team will take this threat seriously, and will do everything in its power to keep Christina and the kids safe."

Cindy added, "I want to assure you that Ed and I will keep close tabs on Christina and the kids, as well." Ed nodded in agreement.

After several more minutes of discussion, her father-in-law suggested they have a few minutes of prayer before the children came in.

CHAPTER 4

After such a beautiful Thanksgiving day, the next three promised nothing but rain. Christina's family stayed in, enjoying table games, videos, baking, and eating. When Sunday rolled around, the whole gang loaded themselves and their belongings into three vans and headed to the airport in Dallas. When the two rental vans were returned, Christina parked hers and met the rest of the clan in the airport terminal. After hugs, kisses, and a few shed tears, the elder Sanders and their troupe left to board the Michigan bound plane.

The two hour drive home was quite subdued as the children mourned the departure of their relatives.

Noticing a sign for one of their favorite restaurants, Christina asked, "Hey guys, y'all want to stop at Cracker Barrel on the way home?"

"Yeah, sure," were the sullen replies she received.

Shaking her head, she said, "You know, we'll see your grandparents over Christmas, and the rest of the family when you have your mid-winter break in February."

"In February?" Stacey asked, perking up a bit.

"Yep, I made arrangements with Grandma and Grandpa. They're going to pay for our airline tickets up to Michigan."

Brad said, "Cool," and Nicky agreed.

"I know y'all are bummed about everyone leaving, but it's only about ten weeks or so before we see your cousins again. In the meantime, y'all can keep in touch through e-mail."

Parking in the Cracker Barrel lot, she turned in her seat to face her kids.

"I'll give you each five dollars to spend in the store. I know it won't make up for everyone's leaving, but maybe it'll cheer you up a bit."

Brad gave her a crooked smile. "Thanks mom. We'll be okay. It's just that we had *so* much fun with our cousins, it's going to be awfully quiet and lonely when we get home."

"I'll try to keep you busy. We have tons of laundry and dishes to do, plus general clean up. I didn't do much while everyone was here 'cause I just wanted to relax and visit. Now, however, I need to get serious about putting things back in order."

Christina couldn't see their eye-rolls, but she did hear their sighs of disgust, and couldn't help but chuckle. *Welcome back to reality, kids.*

CHAPTER 5

On her drive to the hospital on Monday morning, Christina's mind replayed memories of the weekend. It had been such a perfect time until the text came. *Who are you and why do you want me to leave? I thought all that was taken care of when that crazy lady, Lula, was arrested. Everyone thought she was the one behind all the threats and shenanigans. And now this? I thought we could go back to a normal life. I thought we were safe.*

She whispered, "God, I don't understand why You are allowing this."

The Bible verse from Proverbs, came to mind. *"Trust in the Lord with all your heart, and lean not on your own understanding. In all your ways acknowledge Him, and He will make your paths straight."*

She mumbled, "Interesting that I'm reminded of *that* particular verse. I guess it means that I am to trust You and not to worry. Easier said than done, Lord."

Pulling into a parking space, she sat in the van a few moments contemplating her next move. *I guess I could just ignore the threat and trust that God will protect us, no matter what. Worrying about it isn't going to solve anything. Sounds good in my head. Now if the rest of me cooperates, I may succeed in not worrying. Right.*

As she entered the elevator and was reaching out to press the number three button, she heard a familiar voice.

"Hey, can you hold the elevator please?"

It was Dr. Aaron Carmichael, the resident pediatrician, and Stacey's doctor. His tall, dark and handsome, middle-eastern looks and charm always made Christina's heart flutter. Even though she had seen him around the hospital, they hadn't formally met until Stacey had an emergency appendectomy a few weeks earlier. During Stacey's hospitalization and subsequent care, they had become not only colleagues, but good friends.

Aaron's wife had died in a car accident two years earlier, and he became a single dad of a five-year-old girl.

Looking up into his dark brown eyes, she said, "Oh hi, Aaron. How are you doing today? How was your Thanksgiving?"

Smiling, and reaching to push the number two button, he said, "Christina, it's nice to see you. I'm doing well, and our Thanksgiving was great! My daughter and I spent it with my parents, and they treated us to a huge meal. Sammie, enjoyed playing with her cousins, and I had a nice visit with the other adults. You?"

"My deceased husband's parents, and his brother and sister and their families, plus a few of my friends, came to share the day with us. We were blessed to have such a beautiful day."

"It *was* a beautiful day. Don't your in-laws all live in Michigan?"

"Yes, they all flew down to be with us. What a great surprise that was! I was just expecting David's folks, then, lo and behold, two rental vans showed up, and people started piling out." Chuckling, she added, "The kids were so excited, I bet their squeals of delight were heard a couple blocks away."

The elevator stopped at the second floor and the door opened. Aaron said, "Well, I need to get off here." Putting his hand in the door to keep it ajar, he asked, "By the way, how's Nicky doing?"

Christina smiled. "Considering it's only been a few weeks since the kidnapping, he's doing well. He's still having nightmares a couple of times a week, and doesn't want to venture out by himself, but other than that, he appears to be okay."

Aaron nodded. "He still in counseling?"

Christina nodded. "He meets with a school counselor a couple of times a week."

"Good. Guess I'll see you around."

He let go of the door, and as it was closing, she answered, "Yep, I'm sure we'll see each other again."

Exiting the elevator on the third floor, she headed to the Cardiac Care Unit and was greeted by Mary Kelly, the night shift nurse. After a few minutes of chit-chat, she headed to the nurses' lounge to store her belongings in a locker and don her lab coat. When she opened the metal door, she heard a clink as something fell out and hit the floor. Looking down, she was shocked to see an empty medicine vial. Picking it up and reading the label, she almost dropped it. Heparin 5cc. *Why would an empty Heparin bottle be in my locker?* She looked around to see if anyone was near. The room was empty. Sitting in the nearest chair, she thought about the implications of such a discovery. *Is someone trying to scare me by reminding me of my near-death experience? Should I tell Larry and Steven?* As she played different scenarios in her head, she heard someone call her name.

"Christina? Are you in here?"

"Yeah, I'm over here." It was Mary.

Walking over to where Christina was sitting, she asked, "Are you okay?"

Christina nodded and stood.

Reaching out to touch Christina's arm, Mary said, "I saw you come in here, and expected you to come right back out, and when you didn't, I got worried."

"I'm okay, Mary. Was just thinking about something. Guess I lost track of the time. Sorry."

"You ready to do the shift notes?"

Christina sighed. "Sure. Let's go."

After going over the three patient's charts, medications, and other pertinent information, Mary left for home, and Dr. Dawson, the attending cardiologist, came onto the floor.

After he and Christina had checked on each patient, she pulled him aside.

"Hey Steven, you got a couple of minutes?"

He smiled. "Sure. What's up?"

She showed him the Heparin bottle. "I found this in my locker this morning."

"What the…"

She sighed and shrugged. "What do you think this means?"

Frowning, he said, "Looks like it's another possible threat. Someone reminding you how easy it was to hurt you before?"

"Yeah, I took it as a warning. 'I got you before, and I can get you again' kind of thing."

"It's possible. I'm thinking you should call Larry and make him aware of this."

Glancing at the clock on the wall, she said, "I'll call him on my next break, which will be in about fifteen minutes."

Steven reached out and touched her arm. "I know this sounds a little cliché, but try not to let it worry you."

She chuckled and did a thumbs up sign. "Sure, I'll do that."

He looked around, and seeing no one, pulled her into a quick hug. "I'll see you later. Maybe after your shift, you can come by my office?"

"Sure."

When it was time for her break, she called Larry, but was told he was out on a call and wasn't expected back until later that afternoon. Loraine, his secretary, asked if it was an emergency. Christina assured her it wasn't, and asked to have him call her at his convenience.

The remainder of the day went well. The three cardiac patients were stable, and there were no new admittances. After lunch, Christina was able to clean and organize the medication room, and restock the crash cart. She wanted to see Steven, but having a cardiac catheterization scheduled, he wouldn't be available for the remainder of her shift. Once the tasks were completed, she took a few minutes to sit at the desk and think.

She had been so distracted by the Heparin bottle, she hadn't thought about a possible note...until now. She went back to the lounge and opened her locker. Removing the items: her purse, a notebook, a textbook, a clipboard, plus a few pens and pencils, and not finding anything ominous, she started replacing the items and noticed a piece of paper stuck in the clipboard. Lifting the top paper, she found a typed note which read: "What part of "Leave Alva" do you not understand? What happened before could easily happen again."

A flurry of emotions swept through her. Fear—what if this person *did* carry out the threats? Anger—how dare someone try to control her life. Worry—would her kids be spared? She stuck the piece of paper in her lab coat pocket, took a cleansing breath and headed back to the desk. She would drop by Steven's office before leaving the building and get his opinion on what she should do.

CHAPTER 6

That evening, once the kids were in their beds, Christina sat in her recliner and re-hashed the events of the day.

After she had shown Steven the note, he immediately went to the phone and called Larry, who happened to be driving by the hospital on his way back to town. He met them in Steven's office.

As he entered, Steven shook his hand, then handed him the note. Removing his hat and sitting on a chair next to Christina, Larry read it, and shook his head.

Rubbing his forehead, he said, "We really need to find this person."

Christina nodded. "You think?"

Steven, who was leaning his backside on his desk, asked, "So, what should Christina and the kids do?"

Leaning forward with his chin on his hands, Larry thought for a moment before answering.

"Since we don't have *any* idea who sent it, the only real option is to just wait it out. Unless the person slips up and leaves some kind of clue, we're... well...clueless."

Shocked, Christina asked, "What about fingerprints?"

Rubbing his chin, he said, "Well, I can have the note checked, but I doubt if anything will show up."

He held up his hands as if surrendering.

"Other than hiring a bodyguard 24/7, which would be quite expensive and invasive, there's no other option, except to be cautious and vigilant. Other than that...I don't know. I can have our patrolmen drive by your house every couple of hours, but I doubt it would be productive. The person put the note and vial in your locker, for goodness sakes. He or she probably knows your routines and schedules."

Sighing heavily, she realized her peaceful world was once again shattered by threats.

She thought about the possibility of a body guard—which took her mind to memories of movies depicting tall, dark, handsome, and well built men—kind of like Ed. Smiling, she thought, *Now if I had a guy like that....*

Steven gave her a curious look. Shaking her head, she dismissed the thought completely.

If the threats continued, or became more ominous, she would consider the option of a body guard.

Yawning, she looked at her watch and decided it was time to head for bed.

"Come on, Benji, if you want to sleep in my room." The sleeping dog thumped his tail once, opened his eyes, sighed, then closed them once again.

"Okay, I guess that means you'll be sleeping on the couch tonight." She patted his head and felt his nose which was warm and dry.

Heading up the stairs, she thought, *That's weird. Benji never misses an opportunity to sleep in my room. I hope he's not sick. I should take him in for a check-up tomorrow.*

CHAPTER 7

Christina sat up in bed, forcing her heavy eyelids open.
Did I hear something? She listened intently for a few seconds. Nothing. Closing her eyes, she tried to remember her dream before she was jolted awake by–*what*? She wasn't sure. She only remembered a fragment or two of the dream, and it didn't make a lick of sense now that she was awake. She looked at the clock. Three thirty. *Too early for anyone to be up*, she thought. *Maybe one of the kids went to the bathroom and flushed the toilet, or dropped the toilet lid, and that sound made its way into my subconscious. Or, maybe Chloe had knocked something over in her pursuit of a tasty morsel.* The cat had a nocturnal habit of hunting, and would pounce on anything that moved, whether it was edible or not. If there were ever an award for the best dust bunny bounty hunter, she would certainly be the recipient.

She waited a few more minutes, straining to hear any unusual sound. All she heard was the normal creaking and groaning of the old house settling on its foundation. She rubbed her eyes, scratched her head and sat on the side of the bed. *Maybe I should go and take a look around.* She turned on the bedside lamp, and looked around the room. *If something was wrong, surely Benji would have barked.* She listened five more minutes. Satisfied that nothing was amiss–at least nothing that couldn't wait 'till a more decent hour–she laid back down.

Yawning, she turned off the bedside lamp, fluffed her pillow and curled up on her side facing the door. Touching the cold, empty spot where her husband had once lain, she whispered, "I miss you David."

The intruder stood perfectly still, holding his breath. He still held the lamp he had bumped, and caught, before it hit the floor. He listened intently for any indication that someone had heard the commotion. After a few minutes, he breathed a sigh of relief and replaced the lamp. He had been instructed to take something small and seemingly insignificant once a week for at least a month—maybe longer. He wasn't sure what this whole thing was about, and had no desire to know. All he knew was that he was being paid to do something he enjoyed. A smile crept across his lips. It was fun rummaging around in other people's homes while they were sleeping.

He had started the home intrusions four years earlier when he was thirteen. Another boy from school had dared him to go into a neighbor's house, and steal something insignificant. He had crawled through an unlocked basement window, while the owners slept, and grabbed a horse statue before exiting. He returned it a week later. After accomplishing such a daring act, he tried it again and again.

In the beginning, he was amazed at the number of people who would carelessly leave doors or windows unlocked, or leave their house keys hidden in obvious places—like an open invitation for him to enter. He didn't bother with the inaccessible ones.

The experience was so exhilarating, it became a weekly event. Like an addiction.

After all the years, and houses, he still felt an adrenalin rush when he entered a home for the first time, but as with any addiction, the rushes weren't as intense or lasted as long. He wanted to do something more daring and dangerous.

Even though his activities were illegal, he prided himself on having a few scruples. He always returned the stolen object, and the house key once he had completed his exploration. It wasn't as if he wanted or needed the objects, it was the challenge and thrill of the hunt that kept him going.

He would never deliberately hurt any of the homeowners or their pets, but if there was the possibility of being caught, he had a backup plan in place. He always carried a vial of chloroform—which he had stolen from the local vet—and had yet to use, and tranquilized animal treats, which he had used on several occasions. He had already disposed of the Sander's dog, Benji, with one such treat thrown over the fence before the animal's last run around the yard.

Looking around the rooms for something insignificant to take, he spotted a small vase that held an arrangement of silk flowers on an end table in the front room. Moving the other items around on the table to cover the empty spot, he tucked the treasure in his jacket, looked around one last time, and spotted his next targets. He would get them in due time. Leaving the way he had entered, he gently closed the back porch door, and pocketed the key the woman had left for him in a post office box earlier that day. Walking down the driveway, and chuckling and mumbling to himself, "Piece of cake," he texted his employer: "done."

CHAPTER 8

Christina stayed home Tuesday, and caught up on the housecleaning she had been neglecting during the holiday visit. She stripped all the beds, gathered the extra bed linens from the various rooms where people had slept, and started the washing machine.

Benji was back to his normal doggy self, and followed her from room to room sniffing everything thrown on the floor, before picking a pile of bedding to curl up on. Christina almost felt guilty making him move when she had to gather his makeshift bed—almost. After the bedrooms were in order, she headed downstairs to dust and vacuum the furniture and floors. As she was moving objects around on the end table, she noticed the silk flower vase was missing. *That's odd*, she thought. Looking around the room, thinking maybe someone had moved it, she was surprised when she didn't see it. *I wonder where that went?*

The vase was the one thing she saved from David's funeral. It wasn't anything fancy, and probably cost less than five dollars, but it was a sweet memento from that sad day.

She finished cleaning and found herself looking for the vase in every room she entered. It was nowhere to be found. *How weird is that? Oh well, maybe one of the nieces or nephews liked it and took it home with them.* Rubbing her forehead, she thought, *It's not that big a deal, just weird.*

Taking a break to read the mail, she sat in her recliner and Benji jumped up beside her. She touched his wet and cool nose.

"Well buddy, guess you're alright. Must have eaten something that didn't agree with you." He sighed and laid his head on her lap.

In the pile of mail, there was an envelope from a law firm in Dallas. Thinking it was an advertisement, she set it aside to look at later. She perused through her Good Housekeeping magazine, and sipped a glass of iced-tea.

When the kids came home, the washer and dryer were still running and she was bent over the bathtub, scouring out the residue left by so many bodies. By evening, she was too exhausted to even think about cooking, so she ordered pizza from the nearby Pizza Hut. The young man who delivered it was quite charming, and she gave him a generous tip.

"Hey Brad, do you know a young man named Jamie?"

"I know a couple of guys named Jamie. Why?"

"The young man who delivered the pizza was named Jamie. He seemed like a nice kid."

"What did he look like?"

"He was about your height and weight and had red hair and blue eyes like you. In fact, he could almost be your twin. And like you, he had a nice smile and was very courteous."

"Sounds like a couple of upperclassmen. I don't know their names though. Guess I could look through the yearbook. Or you could. I need to work on my English essay when we finish eating."

"When is it due?"

"Tomorrow."

"What are you writing on?"

"How the English language has changed over the past fifty years, and it's effect on society."

She gave him a '*what?*' look and said, "I'd like to read it when you're done."

He nodded. "Okay."

"So, where's your yearbook?"

Brad brought the book to his mom and watched as she perused the pages.

"Here he is. His name is Jamie Simmons." She turned the book to face Brad. "He's a senior."

"Well, that explains why I don't know him." He stuffed the last bite of pizza in his mouth and excused himself.

"Nicky?" She called.

"Yeah Mom?"

"Did you take care of the litter box?"

"Yes ma'am. I did it soon after we got home yesterday. Man it was full and stinky! I don't think it could have survived another day. Chloe would have been doing her business on the floor for sure!"

Christina grimaced, remembering the last time Chloe had done her business in front of the dryer, and she had set the laundry basket on it.

"Thanks, Son."

He smiled and returned to eating his pizza and playing a video game on the computer.

"Stacey, thanks for folding the sheets and blankets. I'll show you which ones are ours."

"Ours? I didn't *think* we owned so many sheets and blankets! And where did all those pillows come from?"

"I borrowed some of the bedding from my friends, which reminds me, I need to return them this week."

"Whew! I was thinking we were going to open a bed and breakfast or something!"

Christina chuckled. "Maybe once you kids leave home, I'll consider that."

While the children were doing their various activities, Christina looked through Brad's yearbook more thoroughly. As she turned to the band page, memories assailed her, and she let them take her back to her own high school days.

She had loved playing the flute in the band: the camaraderie, trips, football games, competitions, and parties. Even though the popular kids called her and her fellow members, "band geeks," they had worn the label proudly.

She continued her perusal and realized that even though names and faces changed, the basic premise was the same: high school was the launching pad to the great unknown world of adulthood.

She was brought out of her reverie by Stacey's announcement that she was heading up to bed.

Nicky, looking at the clock said, "I have one more level to win, then I'll go up too."

Stacey walked over and gave her mother a hug, saying, "Good-night, Mom."

"Night, Babe."

True to his word, Nicky turned off the computer a few minutes later, hugged and kissed his mom, then headed upstairs as well.

Christina looked at her watch. 9:00. Too early for bed. She pulled out her suspense novel and began reading, then remembered the letter from the law office. She retrieved it from the stack of unread mail, tore it open, and was shocked to read that it was a formal letter written to her, and not some advertising come-on.

Dear Mrs. Sanders,

Please contact our office as soon as possible in regards to your husband's financial arrangements.

Thank you,

Mark Taylor

Law Offices of Taylor, Marshall and Campbell
8335 Diamond Blvd.
Suite 401
Dallas, Texas 75201
469-555-1234

She sat in shocked silence as she re-read the letter, contemplating the meaning.

Financial arrangements? Wonder what this is all about? His will was already taken care of. Guess I'll have to wait 'till tomorrow to find out. Good thing I didn't throw this away. She laid the letter on the end table.

At ten-thirty, hardly able to hold her eyes open, she headed upstairs. Before entering her room, she noticed the light shining under Brad's bedroom door. Knocking lightly before opening the door, she asked, "Hey, why are you still up?"

Rubbing his eyes while stretching and yawning, he said, "I was working on this paper." He held it up for her to see.

"Oh, yeah. Did you finish?"

"Thank goodness, yes! I can barely keep my eyes open and my back is getting stiff and my bottom is numb from sitting so long."

She chuckled. "May I read it?"

Blowing air out through his lips, he stood and stretched again, and handed the paper to her. "Here, you can look at it while I go brush my teeth."

She flipped through the five neatly typed pages.

Wow, I don't remember writing papers like this, she thought as she read the first page. Brad returned when she finished the second page.

"Wow, Brad, this is amazing! How long have you been working on this?"

"We got the assignment at the beginning of the year, so pretty much since then. I had to do a *lot* of research." Plopping himself on the bed, he said, "Thank goodness for the internet!"

"Yeah, I wish we had that when I was writing essays. Mind if I take this and finish it?"

He yawned. "Nah, just don't let me forget it tomorrow morning."

She gave him a hug and kiss on his cheek. "Sleep well, Son."

"Thanks, you too, Mom. Hey, before you go, I was wondering if you could tell me what went on Thanksgiving day?"

Chewing on her bottom lip, she considered her answer.

"I was thinking we could have a family meeting tomorrow night, and I'll explain everything then. It's late and we're both tired, and I don't want to discuss it right now."

He nodded slightly, then said, "Okay."

After her own bedtime preparations, she sat on the side of the bed, contemplating how much she wanted to tell the kids—wishing she didn't have to tell them anything, considering what they had been through the past several months. *Is it fair to them to keep them in the dark about the latest threats? Probably not, but how do I protect them from unnecessary worry, yet encourage them to be cautious?*

She sighed as she picked up the essay. *I just wish I had some definitive answers to all this.* She finished reading the paper, thoroughly impressed with Brad's research and presentation. *No wonder you're getting such high grades in this class,* she thought as she lay the paper aside.

That night, she dreamed of wandering through the halls of high school, wondering where her locker was, and why she was naked when everyone else was fully clothed.

CHAPTER 9

Wednesday morning, right before her alarm went off, she was jolted awake by a house shaking clap of thunder. Sitting bolt upright and realizing the house hadn't exploded around her, she laid back down and was lulled back to sleep by the steady drops of rain pelting her windows. A few minutes later, the alarm invaded her nice dream about horseback riding through a field of daisies. She scrunched her nose, remembering that even though daisies are nice to look at, their smell is akin to manure.

Once awake, and realizing that the smell lingered, she looked around the room for any signs of offensive matter, and noticed Benji sleeping at the foot of her bed, snoring slightly and farting.

"Oh my goodness, Benji!" She yelled as she woke him from his sonorous sleep, and forced him off the bed. Donning her robe and slippers, she went to the bathroom to retrieve the room spray. Benji, back on the bed with his head resting on his paws, watched as she blatantly eliminated his odoriferous gift. With a sneeze and a head shake, he jumped from the bed, and walked over to the door. Shaking her head, she escorted him from the room, down the stairs, and out to finish his business.

Pouring her first cup of coffee for the day, she looked at Benji and asked, "What in the world did you eat last night that made you stink so badly?" Looking up at her with his big brown eyes and wagging tail, it appeared he had no answer to the question. She reached down and patted his head.

"It's okay, boy. I still love you. I think we'd better keep closer tabs on what you're eating, however."

She had no idea that the tranquilized treat from the previous night was wreaking havoc with his intestinal tract.

As she drove to work, her thoughts kept returning to the letter from the law office in Dallas. *I can't imagine what that is about.*

During her first break, she called the Law Offices of Taylor, Marshall and Campbell and asked to speak with Mark Taylor.

Coming on the line, he said, "Mrs. Sanders, thank you for calling me back so quickly. I'm sure you're wondering what this is all about?"

"Well, yes. David's will has already been processed, and the financial aspects of it have been resolved, so I don't understand what this is about."

"First of all, let me apologize for not having contacted you sooner regarding this. We had a fire in our office building about a year ago, and many of our documents and files were destroyed and many were misplaced. Fortunately, we had back up files at our other office in Ft. Worth, but with the upheaval, it has taken quite some time to get everything back in order. My secretary tried calling the number we have on file, but it kept disconnecting."

"Which number do you have?"

He gave her the number.

Nodding, she said, "Oh, we switched phones and numbers when we moved to Texas in July."

"Okay, can you give me your new number, so I have it on file?"

She did.

While he was writing, she said, "So what does this have to do with David? You do realize he's been gone over two years. Why is your office involved? Our lawyers in Detroit took care of the matters then."

"Yes, and I'm sorry for your loss."

"Thank you."

"Mrs. Sanders, I was wondering if we could set up an appointment time, say, maybe next week? I will gladly explain everything then. I also have a few papers I'll need your signature on."

"Papers?"

"Yes, concerning a few financial matters."

"I'm off next Tuesday."

"Which would be better for you, morning or afternoon?"

"I prefer the morning."

"How about ten?"

"As far as I know, that will be fine. If it isn't, I'll give you a call."

"Alright then. I have you scheduled for next Tuesday morning at ten."

"You know, Mr. Taylor, you never explained what this is about."

He chuckled. "You're right, Mrs. Sanders, and I would rather not discuss the details over the phone. I promise I will explain everything when we meet next week."

She let out a disappointed sigh. "You do realize my curiosity will be in overdrive?"

He chuckled again. "Sorry about that. I can tell you that you will be pleased with the information I will share with you."

"Oh great! Now you've really piqued my interest."

Chuckling, he said, "See you next Tuesday, Mrs. Sanders."

"Next Tuesday it is."

After disconnecting, and placing the phone in her lab coat, Christina returned to the nursing station, where she was met by a smiling Sarah Stevens, the only LPN on the unit who worked swing shifts.

"Hey Sarah, you seem to be in a good mood today."

Giggling, she said, "Yes, I am."

Raising her eyebrows, Christina asked, "Any particular reason why?"

"Well, yes!" Hardly able to contain her excitement she blurted out, "I was asked out on a date for this Friday evening!"

Sarah's husband had been killed in Vietnam shortly after their second anniversary, and she had been on a handful of dates over the past forty or so years. Christina knew this was a big deal for Sarah. The woman was in her early sixties, and even though she was sweet as sugar, she was beginning to lose her girlish looks and figure, and the prospect of finding an available male in her age group was slim.

Christina smiled. "Well, who is the lucky man?"

"You remember that patient we had some time ago, Mr. Harold Wilson? He had the heart attack, and his lab slip went missing, and he had IV trouble?"

Christina thought for a moment. "Oh yes, I do recall him. Such a nice man." She couldn't help but grin. "So he asked you out?" Sarah nodded. Leaning against the counter, Christina said, "That's awesome! How did that come about?"

Sarah gave her the details, and Christina couldn't help but get caught up in the excitement of it all. Reaching out and touching Sarah's arm, Christina said, "Oh my goodness, Sarah, that is so sweet! You'll definitely have to fill me in next Monday on how everything went."

"Oh, I will!"

They were interrupted by the dinging of a call bell.

Glancing down the hallway and noting which call light was on, Sarah said, "Guess I'd better check that out."

Watching Sarah disappear into the room, and seeing the call light blink off, Christina decided it was time to make the rounds and check on the rest of her patients.

Walking down the hall, she felt the phone vibrate in her pocket. Pulling it out, she noticed a text message waiting.

She nearly dropped the phone when she read it.

WHAT ELSE NEEDS TO HAPPEN TO CONVINCE YOU THAT YOU ARE NOT WELCOME HERE IN ALVA?

Christina, feeling weak and dizzy, went back to the nurses' station and sat in the nearest chair. With shaking hands and tears streaming down her face, she called Steven. When she heard his voice, she lost control and couldn't speak except to say she needed him. He arrived at her station within five minutes, and found her in the nurses' lounge with Sarah and Sally Jean, who left when he walked in. Taking a few deep breaths to bring her emotions under control, Christina handed him the phone.

Anger played across his face as he inhaled sharply.

Looking into her terrified eyes, he knelt in front of her and said, "Oh, Honey, we'll find the person behind this, I promise."

He pulled her up to standing, wrapped his arms around her, and held her until she stopped shaking, and pulled free.

Wiping her eyes and regaining control of her emotions, she said, "Thank you, Steven for being here for me. Just knowing I have your support, is so comforting."

He reached out and pulled her in for a kiss. She was surprised at first, but found herself giving in, and allowing herself to enjoy the moment. They pulled apart on hearing a light tapping on the door.

CHAPTER 10

That evening, she called her children into the breakfast nook, and over chicken pot-pie, told them about the text she received on Thanksgiving day, purposefully omitting the information about the note and Heparin vial she found in her locker, and the text she received earlier. She was met with blank stares for a few seconds, as the full impact of what she said took hold.

Stacey spoke first. "So, you mean there is still someone out there who wants us to leave?"

Christina nodded. "Seems that way."

Chewing on her bottom lip, Stacey asked, "Why?"

Shrugging, Christina said, "I don't know."

Brad asked, "What does the sheriff have to say about this?"

Christina looked at him and sighed. "He doesn't know what to think either. He thought it was all over once Lula was arrested for kidnapping Nicky"

Brad shook his head. "What are you planning to do, Mom?"

Clasping her hands on the table, Christina answered, "Well, at this time, there isn't anything I can do. We're not moving if that's what you're concerned about. But I do want us all to be super-vigilant. That means not going anywhere alone, and having your phone on you at all times."

Nicky, with tear-rimmed eyes, asked, "You don't think they'll try to kidnap me again?"

Christina reached over and patted her son's hand. "No, honey, I don't think that will happen. The threats seem to be directed at me."

"Threats? There are other threats? I thought you said the text was the only thing." Brad said, looking confused.

"Did I say threats? I meant to say threat, singular."

Brad gave her a look that said he wasn't convinced.

She frowned and shook her head slightly. In response, he raised his eyebrows wondering what she was hiding. He'd definitely have to talk to her later.

Gathering up the dirty dishes, she asked, "Do y'all have any questions or any more concerns?"

All three kids shook their heads and mumbled, "No."

"Allrighty then, let's clean up here. Who's up for a game of scrabble?"

"I'll play with you." Stacey said.

Putting his paper plate in the garbage, Nicky said, "I'll play, but y'all always win 'cause I don't know as many words."

Christina reached over and tousled his hair.

"How about if Stacey or I help you with some of the words?"

He nodded.

"Of course, that doesn't mean you'll win." She said playfully.

Brad said, "I'm going to call Melinda. I haven't had a chance to talk to her in a couple of days."

Christina smiled and nodded. "You haven't mentioned her in a while. She doing okay?"

Brad shrugged. "Yeah. We've both been pretty busy, but we're still friends, if that's what you're wondering."

Christina shrugged. "Just asking."

Hearing his mother's footsteps on the stairs, and then the closing of her bedroom door, Brad left his room and knocked on her door.

"Yes?"

"Mom, can I come in?"

Thinking he was in bed, Christina was surprised and concerned when she opened the door and saw Brad standing there.

"What's wrong, Son?" Reaching up to touch his forehead, she asked, "You feeling okay?"

Shying away, he said, "Mom, I'm fine. I need to talk to you though."

Motioning for him to come in, and sit on the bed, she said, "Okay, so what's on your mind?" Suspecting he wanted to talk about the threats, she braced herself for his questions.

Sitting side-by-side, he said, "Mom, please be honest with me. I'm not a little kid anymore, so don't feel like you have to protect me. What other threats were there?"

She brought her hand up and began twisting a ringlet of hair around her finger, debating whether she should tell him the whole truth, or just enough to satisfy his curiosity. She decided total honesty was the best policy. He wasn't a child anymore, and if he was to be her ally in protecting his siblings and himself, he needed to know the brutal truth. No more secrets would be hanging between them.

Sighing, she said, "Alright Brad, I'll tell you."

She told him of the heparin vial, and notes that accompanied it.

When she finished, he asked, "Is that all?"

"Well, yeah, so far."

Nodding, he said. "Okay." Blowing air through his lips, he said, "I agree that we all need to be vigilant. I'll keep closer tabs on Stacey and Nicky, and will check in more often."

She nodded. "Thanks."

He continued, "I don't think we have to worry about Nicky straying very far though. After the kidnapping incident, he's been sticking pretty close to home. He seems to be afraid to even walk down to Danny's by himself."

She grimaced. "Yeah, I noticed. Hopefully, he'll get past that, and can get back to being his normal ten-year-old self."

Glancing at the clock, she said, "Hey, you need to get to bed young man."

He stood and gave her a hug. "Thanks for telling me the truth. Not knowing the whole truth really bothered me. At least now, I know what to worry about."

Smiling and shaking her head, she stood in the doorway and watched as he returned to his bedroom. She called out, "Remember, the Bible says we aren't to worry about anything. God's in control."

He turned, gave her a lopsided grin and a thumbs up sign. "Yeah, right."

As she lay in bed waiting for sleep to enfold her, Christina thought about Steven and the kiss. It had been a long time since she'd felt a man's lips on hers, and had almost forgotten how nice it felt. She had always enjoyed David's kisses, and with Steven's kiss, realized how much she missed that tenderness.

She smiled as she remembered their awkwardness when they pulled apart. The kiss had been a surprise for both of them.

When Sarah entered the room, and realized she had interrupted something, she apologized and backed out. Christina and Steven laughed, and he left with a promise to call her later.

Biting her bottom lip, she thought, *Oh, Steven, where are we going with this relationship?*

CHAPTER 11

Thursday, Christina stayed home to catch up on e-mails, write checks for bills, and chat with Lisa about their upcoming adoptions. *I sure am enjoying all these days off,* she thought as she punched in Lisa's number.

Lisa was one of Christina's high school girlfriends, and a member of the "fab four". They had rekindled their friendship when Christina moved back to Alva. Lisa, Tom and their four children, were in the process of adopting two children from Guatemala.

Christina could hear the excitement in Lisa's voice as she told of their plans.

"Tom and I will be flying to Guatemala to get the kids in January. Our kids want to wait and celebrate Christmas when Rico and Eliana get here, so I think we'll just have a small celebration on Christmas day and do the big thing once the children arrive."

"Wow, Lisa, I didn't realize things had moved along so quickly. When we talked a couple weeks ago, y'all were still waiting for some paperwork to go through."

"I know! It's definitely a God thing! The authorities and the orphanage somehow finally agreed on everything and passed our paperwork on through." Chuckling, she said, "Now Tom is hustling to get the rooms ready. He has to lay the tile in the boys bathroom, then the kids and I will do the painting and decorating. They'll be responsible for getting their stuff together and moving it to where they want it." She let out a big sigh. "It's exciting and exhausting at the same time!"

Smiling, Christina said, "We'd love to come help next week, if you need us."

"Thanks Christina, but I think more bodies might just complicate matters. Once we get everyone settled in, we want to have an open house, so everyone can meet Rico and Eliana."

"Well, count me in for helping with that, at least."

"Absolutely, girlfriend! In fact, I may have the whole gang over to help!"

After several more minutes of chit-chat, Lisa said, "You know, you haven't mentioned the incident on Thanksgiving day. What happened?"

Christina filled her in on the details of the text and the threats at the hospital. Lisa gasped. "Oh my goodness, Christina. I'll be so glad when all this is resolved. It must be so exhausting for you and the kids to always be on guard."

"Yeah, I just don't know what to do. I don't want to live in fear, but geeze, after all that's already happened, I can't help but worry. Especially for the children's safety."

"I know. Sounds like you have a good support system, though, with the police, Ed, Steven and others."

"Yes, I don't know what I'd do without them. I'll have to admit that this has really challenged my faith. I just don't understand why this is happening and what good will come of it."

Lisa sighed. "Sometimes, the answers aren't evident for a while. Just hang in there."

After a few more minutes of chit-chat, the women said their good-byes.

Christina shot a "thank you for my friends," prayer up to Heaven.

Grabbing a laundry basket, she headed up the stairs. Sorting through Stacey's clothes, she was surprised to discover a card of some kind in one of the jacket pockets. Pulling it out, she was shocked to see that it was a Tarot card—and not just any Tarot card—it was the death card.

"What the...?" She folded it, and stuck it in her jeans pocket. *I'm sure there's a valid explanation*, she thought as goose bumps popped up on her arms.

Just then, she heard the back door open and Nicky calling out for her.

"I'm up here guys. I'll be down in a minute."

"Mom?" It was Brad. She headed downstairs.

"Hey, you two. How was your day?" She asked as she hugged each boy.

Taking a sip of milk he had just poured, Nicky said, "It was good."

"Mine was okay, too," said Brad as he grabbed an apple off the counter and bit into it. "I was wondering if you could drop me off at work, though. It's looking pretty stormy out there."

Looking out the window, Christina was shocked to see dark clouds in the southern sky. "Wow! I didn't realize it had gotten so cloudy. It was clear when I let Benji out a little while ago."

"Yeah, it came up really fast. When I met Nicky at his school, I noticed the dark clouds."

Looking at the clock, Christina asked, "What time do you have to be at work?"

"In about an hour. I only work 'till eight tonight."

"Good, I have to pick Stacey up at six from play practice, then if she hasn't filled up on pizza, we'll grab a bite to eat at Dairy Queen and I'll swing by and get you."

Brad nodded. "I need to go change, do a couple of things, then I'll be back down."

CHAPTER 12

As Stacey climbed in the van after play practice, Christina noticed her daughter's subdued behavior. Surmising that the strain of school, practices and worry were taking their toll, she asked, "Stacey?"

"Yeah, Mom."

"Are you feeling okay? Any pain in your side or signs of a bladder infection?" Even though it had been several weeks since Stacey's appendectomy and following bladder infection, the nurse part of her knew there could be latent complications.

Sighing, Stacey said, "I'm feeling alright. Just tired from all the practices. I'll be so glad when this is all over. I think I'll sleep right through the Christmas break!"

Christina nodded. She'd be glad when holiday activities were over as well, and they all could rest peacefully.

"I'm gonna pick you up some vitamins, and I want you to start taking one every morning."

"Uh, okay. Why?"

"Because, you are under so much stress right now, that it can deplete your immune system and you'll be more prone to infections."

Confused, Stacey said, "Huh? You're doing your nurse-speak again." After a slight pause, she said, "So what you're saying is, I could get sick if I don't take the vitamins?"

Christina smiled and nodded. "Yes. Exactly."

Stacey shrugged. "Okay." After a few minutes, she asked, "When did you say Grandma and Grandpa will be here?"

"Grandma said they will arrive next Thursday evening the fourteenth, and leave for home the next Tuesday afternoon, the nineteenth. She also asked if it would be okay to go ahead and bring your Christmas gifts."

Stacey smiled and nodded. "Well, if they're bringing gifts, we should go shopping and get them something too."

"How about we all go to the outlet mall and shop, say, this Saturday?"

"Okay. Did you ask Nicky and Brad yet?"

Nicky spoke up from the back seat. "Hey, I wanna go too!"

Stacey jumped. "Geeze, Nicky! I forgot you were back there!"

He giggled.

Christina shook her head and smiled, "We'll see how everything works out. I'll ask Brad when we pick him up if he already has plans for Saturday."

Nicky returned to his video game and Stacey whispered, "I hope the boys can't go. It'd be fun just to have a girl's day."

Nicky spoke up, "Hey, I heard that!"

Stacey made an "oops" face.

Christina reached over and patted Stacey's leg, and whispered, "Maybe I can work on that."

"I heard that too!"

Stacey said, "I thought you were playing your video game."

"Well, I'm *not* playing it with my ears!"

Stacey and Christina burst out laughing.

When they arrived at Dairy Queen, Stacey said, "Next weekend is going to be so crazy busy. My school play is Friday night, Nicky's band concert is Saturday night, and my church play is Sunday night. Whew! Makes me tired just thinking about it all! When will we celebrate Christmas with Grandma and Grandpa?"

"I was thinking Monday evening. That way, the plays and concert will be over, and you can rest up and really enjoy the evening with your grandparents before they have to leave the next day."

Having about forty-five minutes before she had to pick up Brad, Christina decided they should eat inside the Dairy Queen restaurant. Stacey, having filled up on pizza, just had an ice-cream cone, as Christina and Nicky shared a steak finger basket.

Once home, she pulled Stacey aside. "I need to talk to you about something."

"Sure. Okay."

"Why don't we go up to your room?"

Raising her eyebrows, she said, "Uh. Okay. This sounds serious."

Once they were behind closed doors, Christina sat on the bed and patted the spot beside her. Stacey sat.

Reaching into her jeans pocket, Christina pulled out the card.

Stacey's eyes widened. Stammering, she said, "I can explain that."

"I'm sure you can."

Biting her bottom lip before replying, she finally said, "You remember when I told you Linda's mom is into Tarot Cards and stuff?"

Christina nodded.

"Well, so is Linda. She said her mom gave her a box of cards and a book on how to read them for her birthday."

Christina raised her eyebrows in surprise. *Why would a mother give her thirteen-year-old daughter Tarot Cards?*

Nervously twirling the ring on her finger, Stacey continued. "Anyway, Linda is going around the school asking kids if she can read their cards for them. Some of them have let her, and a few have become quite upset and worried about what Linda said."

Cocking her head, Christina asked, "What kind of things did Linda say?"

"A couple of kids turned over the death card, and Linda tried to cover up her shock and told them she was still new at this, and it probably didn't mean anything, but those kids are really freaked out. What could the death card mean, except death?"

Christina nodded. She was upset to think that sort of thing was going on in school.

Not wanting to over-react, she calmly asked, "So, do the teachers or principal know that Linda is doing this?"

"You mean the card reading?"

Christina nodded.

"Well, if they don't, they will soon. Linda is drawing quite a crowd around the lunch table, and it seems she's enjoying the attention."

"Have you talked to her about this?"

"Yeah, but she says I'm being silly. It's only a game."

"Do *you* think it's only a game?"

"I don't know. I know you've told me Tarot Cards and Ouija boards aren't things to be played with, but I'm not sure I totally understand why."

Christina nodded. "I'll try to explain this so you can understand. First of all, let me ask if you believe in good and evil?" Stacey nodded. "How about angels and demons?" Stacey nodded again.

"Do you know there is a constant battle raging between the angels and demons for our souls?"

"I remember reading about that stuff in Frank Peretti's books, but I never gave it much thought. I don't understand *why* the cards and game are so bad though."

"Well, the cards and game aren't evil in and of themselves, but when a person puts their faith in them and trusts in them more than God, then that's a problem. God doesn't want us to put our faith or trust in anything but Him."

Stacey cocked her head and Christina knew she wasn't being clear.

God, she prayed silently, *please give me the right words*. She took in a deep breath and let it out before continuing.

"Only *God* knows the future. Satan and his demons want us to take our focus off God and trust in people and their words. That is called deception, and believe me, Satan is the master of it. Sometimes we can convince ourselves that something is right, even when we know in our spirit that it isn't."

Stacey nodded. "So, those death cards could mean nothing after all?"

"I'm not sure I can answer that properly. Sometimes, I think people bring about tragedies by either talking about it and giving the enemy a 'go ahead' so to speak, or being so worried that they can't function, which can cause them to be careless. The enemy can't *read* our minds, but he can listen to our words and watch our actions."

"That's kinda scary."

"Yeah. It is kinda scary to think that there is an invisible force trying to destroy us. That's why I encourage you to memorize scriptures and pray a hedge of protection around yourself—and to guard your words. As I said, we don't just fight against things or people that we can *see*, we have to fight against those we can't see."

"So, what should I tell Linda?"

"What do you think you should tell her?"

Stacey gave her an exasperated look. "I hate when you turn a question around like that!"

Christina smiled and cocked her head, waiting for an answer.

Stacey sighed and began twisting a strand of hair around her finger.

"I guess I can tell her what you said about the angels and demons, and how she's gonna get in trouble with the principal if she keeps doing the Tarot Card thing."

Nodding, Christina said, "What will you do if she continues in these activities?"

Stacey's shoulders slumped. "I don't know. I don't want to lose her friendship, but I can't be a part of that stuff either! I don't want to get in trouble, too." She gave her mother a pleading look and batted her eyes to clear the tears that were forming.

Christina opened her arms and Stacey leaned into them.

"I know this is a tough thing, but please stand strong in your faith. I'll continue to pray for you and Linda, and that God would give you peace in your heart and mind." Pausing for a moment, she said, "You know, you could talk to your youth pastor as well. He may have a different perspective."

Stacey nodded. "Yeah, maybe."

Taking in a breath and blowing it out, Stacey said, "So, about that card. I took it from Linda's stack of Tarot cards."

"I gathered that. Why did you take this particular card?"

Wringing her hands together, Stacey said, "I figured if she didn't have it, kids couldn't turn it over and get all freaked out."

Christina nodded. "I see. So what happens when Linda discovers the card is missing?"

Biting her lip and looking pleadingly at her mom, she said, "Well, I'm hoping she'll just figure she lost it."

"Then what?"

Flustered, she said, "I don't know! I haven't thought that far ahead!"

Christina nodded. Speaking softly, she said, "Well, even though your intentions are noble, it's still wrong to take something that doesn't belong to you. Don't you think Linda will just get another card to replace this one?"

Stacey sighed. "Yeah. Probably."

"So what do you think you should do?"

Shaking her head, she answered, "I don't know."

Christina reached over and pulled her daughter into a hug. "I think you do know."

Pulling away and crossing her arms over her chest, Stacey said, "You don't understand, Mom! Linda and I aren't talking right now. She's being mean and is saying awful things about me!"

"Really? Like what?"

"She's telling people that I think I'm too good to be her friend, and I'm calling her a witch behind her back!" Wiping away the tears that were forming, she added, "I have never said anything bad about her, and I never said I thought I was better than her. I don't know *why* she's being so mean!" Stacey let the tears flow.

Christina knew. Sighing, she got up and brought a tissue to her distraught child. Sitting once again, she put her arm around Stacey's shoulder.

"I know this whole thing with Linda is difficult, but I just want to remind you again, that you are not responsible for what Linda does or says, no matter how hurtful. You are only responsible for your own words and actions." Stacey nodded as she blew her nose. Christina continued, "As you go through life, I'm sorry to say, there will be other people who will hurt and disappoint you. Maybe this would be a good time to think about how you will handle those people and events. Will you let them shatter you and your faith? Or will you trust God to help you through those tough times and let Him be your comforter and protector?"

"I want to *not* let it hurt, but it does. I hate being lied about and accused of things I didn't do!"

"I know. Nobody likes that. But Stacey, the truth will always come out. The people who know you won't believe the lies, and the ones that don't know you, well, they don't really count. If they choose to get to know you, then they won't believe the lies either. The main thing to remember is that you are a daughter of the King, and as a princess, your loyalty lies with Him, for He is the One that you will have to answer to."

Stacey dried her eyes. "I never thought of it that way. It reminds me of the Narnia books."

"How so?"

"Well, the kids were chosen to be the Kings and Queens of Narnia, but Aslan was still the main King, so to speak. They were loyal to him."

Christina nodded. "I guess that's a good example." After a couple of quiet, reflective moments, she said, "So what do you plan to do?'

"I guess, I'll have to give the card back, and try to explain to Linda why I took it. Hopefully, she'll be okay with it."

"If she's not?"

Stacey let out a big sigh. "I guess I'll just walk away."

Pulling Stacey close and kissing the top of her head, she said, "Why don't we pray about it and let God direct your path?"

"Sure. Can't hurt."

When they finished praying, Christina stood and pulled Stacey up for one last hug before heading back down stairs.

"I know it's tough now—this thing with Linda, juggling the play practices and school, but try to focus on the good things, because when it's all over, you're gonna miss all this."

She felt Stacey nod and mumble, "Yeah."

"Hey, why don't we go see what the boys are up to?"

Stacey wiped her eyes and blew her nose one last time, and answered, "Sure."

As Christina and Stacey walked into the den, Brad announced that he had to work re-stocking shelves at Safeway, the local grocery store, on Saturday. Nicky informed them that he was asked to spend the night at Danny's, and go with him and his family to Dallas to do Christmas shopping on Saturday. Mom and daughter looked at each other and smiled.

"When did you get invited?" Christina asked Nicky.

"When you and Stacey were upstairs. Danny called and asked me. He said since next weekend is the band concert, this is the only time they will have to go shopping."

Christina called Danny's mom, Denise, and confirmed the plans.

CHAPTER 13

That evening, Janet called her contact and asked if he would be able to do another job on Monday night, and was pleased with his response.

Linda walked in, as Janet disconnected. Looking at the bedside clock, she gave her mom a quizzical look, wondering who she would be talking to after nine o'clock. "Who was that?"

"Just some work related stuff," Janet answered dismissively. "So, you heading off to bed?"

"Yeah. I'm gonna read a few minutes in that Tarot card book you gave me. It is *so* interesting. I've got the cards and their meanings memorized, and can hardly wait to start using them!" She wasn't sure she should tell her mom that she'd been practicing on the kids at school.

"When you're ready, you can practice on me."

"Thanks, Mom. You can help me if I screw up."

Janet was pleased that her daughter seemed so anxious to follow in her footsteps.

Giving Linda a hug, she thought, *maybe the fates are in my favor after all.*

CHAPTER 14

Friday morning, after sharing a light breakfast with the kids, Christina hugged and kissed each one and headed out the door. Pulling into the hospital parking lot, and realizing she had forgotten to pray with them, she shot a quick prayer up to Heaven on their behalf.

Arriving on the CCU, Christina was surprised to see Sarah Stevens coming out of the coffee room.

"Sarah! What are you doing here?"

"Oh hi, Christina. I had to fill in for Hannah Isbell, the aid that sometimes works up here. She woke up with the stomach flu this morning, and Mrs. Ferguson called to see if I was available." With a smile that showed off her dimples, she said, "So here I am!"

"Well, I'm glad you're here. I'm not feeling up to par myself."

With concern on her face, Sarah asked, "Oh, Honey, what's wrong?"

Christina sighed, "Allergies. Now that the furnace is on, my allergies have kicked in. No telling when the duct work was cleaned out last.

Patting Christina's arm, Sarah said, "I know a good furnace guy. Remind me to give you his number before we leave."

Much to Christina's relief, the day went smoothly. The three patients on the unit were stable and under no duress, and her allergy symptoms subsided.

She and Sarah were able to spend a few minutes chatting about their lives.

"So, you still going out with..." She paused, thinking. "Geez, I forgot his name."

Sarah blushed and giggled. "Yeah. Harold and I are going out tonight. He still hasn't told me where, though. Makes me a bit nervous—not knowing."

Slapping her forehead, Christina said, "Harold Wilson. That's his name! Well, I have a feeling it will be somewhere fancy. He seems like the kind of guy that would treat a lady well."

Sarah blushed and giggled again. "I hope it's not too fancy! I haven't been on a date in years, much less gone anywhere fancy. I lead a pretty simple life."

Christina smiled and patted Sarah's hand. "I'm sure Mr. Wilson will take that into account."

When it was time to leave, Sarah gave Christina a hug, promising to tell her "everything" on Monday.

Feeling a bit jealous and lonely, and wishing she had a date, Christina decided to drop by Steven's office to see if he would be interested in joining her for dinner.

Standing outside his door and raising her hand to knock, she chickened out, telling herself that if he had wanted to ask her out, he would have. Sighing, she turned to go. The office door opened, and Steven emerged, surprise registering on his face.

"Christina!"

"Steven!"

"What are you doing here?"

She stammered, "Uhm. I uhm." Smiling, she said, "Well, I was just coming by to say hi. I haven't talked to you since this morning."

"Oh. Okay. I was just leaving. Are you heading home?"

"Well, yeah."

"Do you have time for a cup of coffee?"

She looked at her watch. "I guess so." Thinking he meant they would have a cup in his office, she took a step forward.

"I was wondering if you wanted to go to the Starbucks by the outlet mall?"

"Oh. Okay." *A coffee date was better than no date, right?*

Smiling, he said, "If you want, you could ride with me, and I'll bring you back for your car."

"Oh, thanks, but I think I should drive, then I can just head on home and be there when the kids arrive."

Turning the knob to make sure the door was locked, he nodded and they walked down the hallway side by side. "Where did you park?" He asked when they came to the end of the hallway.

"Out front," she answered.

"Okay, I parked out back. I'll see you at Starbucks in a few minutes." He gave her a quick hug and turned back down the hall.

On the way to Starbucks, she played different scenarios in her head, thinking, *Why didn't he just ask me out on a date? It is Friday night. Unless....he has a date with someone else.*

Once they were seated, Steven apologized for not having asked her sooner. "I've had so much on my mind lately, that I forgot to ask you this morning. In fact, I was going to ask you out to dinner, but time just got away from me."

"Oh. That's okay. I'm glad we can have this time together." Waving her hand, she said, "Dinner is so overrated."

He chuckled. "Well, maybe it is. I was wondering however, if you would like to go to dinner with me next Friday evening. I thought we could go to a Japanese steak house in Dallas."

Her breath caught. *I wonder if it's the same Japanese steak house that Aaron had planned on taking me to, until Nicky got kidnapped and all social plans went out the door.* She asked, "What's the name of the steakhouse?"

"Two Dragons. It's right downtown, next to some law offices."

I bet it is the same place, she thought, before replying, "I'd love to, but my in-laws will be here, and Stacey's school play is that night."

"Oh my! I forgot. I was planning on going to that. Like I said, my mind has been so preoccupied lately, I hardly remember what day it is."

She smiled and shook her head. "It's alright. If I didn't write things down, I'd forget them."

"So, can I sit with y'all at the play?"

"I'd like that!"

After sipping their coffees and chatting, Christina said her good-byes and headed home.

She stepped out of the van as the kids ran up the driveway.

Grabbing her purse, and slamming the door, she said, "Hey guys!"

Nicky ran up for a hug and Stacey and Brad ambled up after him.

"So, how was everyone's day?"

Stacey shrugged and said, "It was okay. I didn't get to talk to Linda though. It was like she was deliberately avoiding me."

Christina opened her arms and Stacey walked into them.

"I'm tired, Mom. Is it okay if I go lay down a few minutes?"

Feeling her forehead, like any concerned mother would do, and not finding it feverish, she said, "Sure honey. You look like you could use a little nap."

Stacey let out a big sigh. "If I do fall asleep, can you just let me sleep? I'll eat something when I wake up."

"Sure, Babe, you go ahead and rest. I'll set some food aside for you."

Turning to her eldest child, she asked, "How was your day, Brad?"

"No complaints. I got a message from the bike place that my new tire is in. Could I take the van and run up there?"

Handing the keys and a twenty-dollar bill to him, she said, "Sure. Could you stop at the 7-11 and get a gallon of milk and a loaf of bread?"

Nodding and smiling, he said, "Sure. No problem."

Nicky spoke up. "Can I go with him?"

Christina looked at Brad, who shrugged. Nodding, she said, "Okay. See y'all in a little while."

When the boys returned, she sent Nicky upstairs to pack a bag for his overnight adventure with Danny.

Danny showed up right as Nicky was stuffing the last bite of macaroni in his mouth.

Christina gave Nicky the usual 'mom warnings'. "It's gonna be awfully crowded at the stores, so please, stay with Danny's parents and be your normal, courteous self."

Nicky rolled his eyes and after giving her a hug and kiss on the cheek, said, "Sure, Mom."

The boys ran out the front door and down to Danny's. It seemed like those two were always running where ever they went. *Cute.* That stage would be gone soon enough and they'd be like Brad and his friends: ambling everywhere—seemingly unconcerned about time.

Stacey slept through dinner and finally came down for a glass of milk and a peanut butter sandwich around the time Christina was heading up to bed. Hugging her girl, she said, "I sure hope you can sleep tonight."

Stacey mumbled, "I don't think that will be a problem."

CHAPTER 15

Stacey woke with the sun poking her in the eye. She pulled the curtain back and saw the crystal blue sky. Hurrying through her morning rituals, she dressed and bounded down the stairs.

"Hey, Mom!" She called from the kitchen as she poured a glass of orange juice.

"Yes?" Christina answered from the den where she had been reading in her devotional book.

"What time are we leaving?"

Christina looked at her watch. Nine o'clock. "How about in an hour or so?"

"Okay. That'll give me time to eat and finish getting ready."

"Yeah. I need to go get dressed myself," Christina said, as she pulled herself free of the easy chair. Struggling to extract herself, she wondered, *Why is it called an 'easy' chair when there is nothing easy about getting out of it?*

Stacey, with a bowl of cereal in one hand and a glass of orange juice in the other came into the den, and after setting everything down, including herself, found the remote and turned on the TV. Saturday cartoons were still her favorite things to watch.

Passing her daughter on the way upstairs, Christina asked, "So did you sleep well? You look rested."

"Yep. I slept like a log." Scrunching up her nose she said, "Why do people say that? Logs don't sleep."

Christina smiled and shook her head. "Well, they do lay there and don't move. I guess that's sorta like sleeping."

Stacey shrugged.

Reaching the top step, Christina's phone simultaneously rang and buzzed in her pocket. She pulled it out and read the name—Cindy.

"Hey Cindy."

"You know, it kinda unnerves me when you do that."

"Do what?"

"When you say 'hey Cindy' before I even say hello."

Christina chuckled. "You *do* realize that I have caller ID, right?"

"Well, yeah, but it still throws me for a loop. It's like you've got ESP or something."

"Okay, Miss paranoid one, what are you calling about?"

"I was wondering if you and the kids would like to go to the movies this afternoon with Samara and me?"

"What's showing and what time?" Christina asked.

"There's that animated movie, about an ogre, that starts at one. Maybe we could grab a bite to eat first, or after."

"Well, it will be just Stacey and me. Brad has to work, and Nicky is spending the day with Danny."

"Oh, that'd be great! Just us girls for a change!"

"Stacey and I were planning to do some shopping this morning, so why don't we meet y'all at Green's for a soup and sandwich before heading over to the movie?"

"Okay, say around noonish?"

"Yep. Sounds good. See you then."

As she disconnected, Stacey called up from the bottom step, "Mom, do you know where my maroon sweatshirt hoodie is?"

"The last time I saw it, it was in the bottom of the basket of clothes in your room."

"Oh yeah. Could you bring it down when you come?"

Answering in a mock British accent, Christina answered, "Yes, your highness. Anything else I can get you before I descend the royal stairs?"

Shaking her head and doing an eye roll, Stacey mumbled, "Geez you're weird."

Christina rubbed her hands together and in her best wicked voice said, "You ain't seen nothin' yet, my pretty!"

CHAPTER 16

The shopping trip had been just the kind of diversion the female Sander's needed after such a busy and stressful week. After purchasing several gifts for the boys and grandparents, and a couple of outfits for Stacey, the gals were ready to meet Cindy and Samara at Green's pharmacy for a light lunch.

Sipping her chocolate shake, which Green's was famous for, Cindy said, "I just love this place! I'm so glad the décor hasn't changed much over the years."

Christina nodded. "Yeah, this is certainly one of the most authentic places here in town."

The girls slurped the last of their sodas, and insisted it was time to head across the street to the movie theater.

Christina couldn't help but smile as she glanced at the big Texas Theater sign hanging above the entrance. It was the original sign from the 1950's when movies became popular, and even though it was rusted through in a few places, it still had that hometown charm.

Walking to their cars after the movie, Stacey put her arm around her mother's waist and said, "Thanks Mom, for such a fun day. I love the outfits you bought me, and I'm sure the boys and Grandma and Grandpa will like their gifts too—and that movie was so fun!"

Samara piped in, "Yeah, I loved that donkey! He was like the comic relief." Everyone smiled and nodded.

Cindy added, "I was amazed at the minute details. The water and the princess's hair were so amazingly real."

Christina nodded and said, "Yeah! Cartoons have certainly come a long way in the past twenty years. Who would have thought we'd actually be watching this kind of film and enjoying it?"

Cindy chuckled. "I know!"

As they parted company, Christina felt the buzzing of her cell phone in her pocket. She pulled it out and looked at the number. Denise, Danny's mom.

She answered, "Hello Denise, are you ready to send my boy home?"

Denise sounded surprised when Christina said her name. "Oh, uh, no. I was calling to see if Nicky could spend the night again. Since the boys never got to go out on the boat a few weeks ago, Larry was wondering if it would be okay to take them out tomorrow? The weather is supposed to be perfect."

Christina, who had completely forgotten about the boat trip that was supposed to happen the weekend Nicky was kidnapped, said, "I think that would be fun for the boys. I'll be home in a few minutes. Can you send Nicky down to get a change of clothes for tomorrow?"

"Sure, I'll send him down in about...fifteen minutes?"

The women disconnected.

Stacey asked, "I take it that was Danny's mom?"

Christina nodded.

Popping a piece of gum in he mouth, she asked, "He's gonna spend the night at Danny's again?"

Christina nodded, saying, "Danny's dad is planning to take the boys out on the boat tomorrow. I forgot that they had planned that little trip a while ago."

"Oh yeah. Nicky was looking so forward to that, and then Danny got sick, and he got kidnapped. He never even mentioned it after that. I wonder why?"

"I think he just wanted to forget about that whole weekend. He may not even remember those plans."

Stacey nodded, then said, "Yeah, that was pretty traumatic for all of us. I'm not even sure I remember everything that happened that weekend."

As Christina pulled in the driveway, Nicky and Danny came running up to the van.

When she stepped out, Nicky wrapped his arms around her waist. "Thanks, Mom, for letting me spend the night again, and letting me go on the boat tomorrow."

Danny added, "Yeah, thanks, Mrs. Sanders. My grandpa said it's supposed to be sunny and warm and not very windy. My mom said to tell you that we'll be in life-jackets the whole time we're on the boat, and Nicky should bring a jacket of some kind, 'cause it may get a little chilly on the water."

Christina reached over and ruffled Danny's hair. "Thanks Danny."

He grinned and nodded.

"Okay Nicky, go pack a bag of fresh clothes for tomorrow."

A few minutes later, the boys came down the stairs, dragging Nicky's overnight bag.

"Nicky, what on earth do you have in there?"

"Just a few things I might need."

"Mind if I take a look?"

He shrugged. Looking inside, she found a change of clothes, comic books, drawing pads and pencils.

She said, "Okay. Looks like you have everything you need."

She gave him a hug and kiss and the usual mom warnings: "Listen and obey, and have fun, but be careful."

He hugged her back and said, "Yeah, I will. I promise."

Watching the boys race back down to Danny's house with their spindly legs and arms all akimbo, Christina couldn't help but chuckle. They were at that awkward age. Too young to be completely independent, but too old to be completely dependent. Because he was her baby, she particularly dreaded the time when he would cross that adolescent line. *Well, I've got at least another year or two*, she thought as she closed the door.

She poured a glass of sweet tea and headed for the family room. Sitting in her cozy new recliner, she leaned back and raised her feet, just as Stacey came in and sat across from her on the sofa.

"Mom? Can I talk to you?"

"Sure honey, what is it?"

"I was thinking about what you said yesterday, and even though I know what I need to do, and I will, I was wondering if you thought it'd be okay to put off my talk with Linda until after I'm done with the plays?"

"How do you plan to go about this?"

"Well, I was thinking that maybe I can invite her over to spend the night next week after Grandma and Grandpa leave."

"Why don't you want to talk to her before then?"

Stacey blew air out through her lips. "I guess 'cause I'm kinda scared how she'll react. I'm afraid she'll cause a scene at school and I don't want to be all upset when I'm trying to focus on my lines for the plays. It would be so totally embarrassing if I screw up a line."

"I'm proud of you, Stacey. It sounds like you've given this some thought. I agree that if Linda reacts negatively, it could affect your emotional and thinking processes." Sighing, she said, "Maybe you *should* wait 'till next week. If things don't go well, at least it'll be another two weeks before y'all are back in school, and Linda will hopefully cool down by then."

"Yeah. I hope so. I feel like I don't even know her anymore. She's turned into this negative, snarky person I don't even want to be around." She let out a big sigh. "I miss the old Linda."

Christina stood and pulled Stacey into a hug. "I know what you're going through. When I was in middle school, my best friend decided she didn't want to be my friend anymore, and started hanging out with other girls. I felt so lost and alone for a while until another girl and I started hanging out. Like I've said before, people can disappoint you."

Christina could feel Stacey's head nod up and down.

"Thanks Mom," she said as she pulled away and wiped her eyes. Glancing at the wall clock, she said, "I think I'll go on up and get ready for bed. I have some reading to do for Social Studies and I want to go over my lines for the plays. I can't believe they are both next weekend! It makes me all nervous and jittery inside when I think about it."

"Don't you have practice tomorrow afternoon at the church?"

"Yeah. We have to be there by two. It's dress rehearsal, so it'll probably run several hours."

Christina said, "I volunteered to make cookies for the meal they'll be serving around five. What kind do you want me to make?"

"I love your chocolate chip, pecan, oatmeal cookies."

"Okay, that's what I'll make."

As Stacey headed up the stairs, the back door opened and Brad walked in.

"Hey, Mom!" He called as he went directly to the fridge and poured a glass of milk. Grabbing a cookie, he headed for the family room when he heard her answer.

"Hey, Brad. Glad you're home. How was your day at Safeway?"

Before sitting down, he set his milk and cookie on the end table and leaned down to give her a hug.

"Mom, you wouldn't believe the things that happened today."

Crinkling her nose, she asked, "Why do you smell like bleach?"

Between bites of cookie and sips of milk, he began recapping his day.

"First of all, I went to the back room to check in when I noticed a stream of water on the floor. I followed the trail and discovered that the men's toilet had overflowed. Oh my goodness, it smelled so bad! I called the manager and you know what he said?"

Christina shook her head.

"He said, 'Well, Sanders, you know where the mop and bucket are. Clean up this mess.'"

Christina bit her lip to keep from laughing. "So did you?"

"Well, yeah. I put on two layers of gloves and held my breath the whole time. It was so gross!"

"Yeah. Cleaning up someone else's mess is always harder than cleaning up your own."

Brad nodded, then continued, "So, once that was cleaned up, I get a call over the intercom: 'Sanders, clean up on aisle two.' So I get my mop and bucket and, lo and behold, a kid had barfed all over the floor."

Christina couldn't help but giggle.

Brad rolled his eyes and continued, "So, I got that all mopped up. Again holding my breath, 'cause every time I did breathe, I gagged, and I didn't want to barf, too."

Christina shook her head. "Bless your heart. I hope you get some kind of compensation for that."

He shook his head. "I doubt it. Anyway, there's more."

"What?"

"After I cleaned the mop that second time and smelling like I took a bath in bleach, I headed for the checkout counter. Things went pretty good for a while, then a lady, who insisted I put her milk in a paper bag, picked it up and it tore, and yep, the milk container broke and I had a gallon of milk on the floor!"

Christina burst out laughing.

"I looked at the manager, who gave me a look that said, 'You know where the mop is.' So, once again, I got the mop and bucket. At least this mess didn't make me gag. By now, I have bleach water all over my shoes, pants and, of course, my hands and arms. I smell like a cotton-pickin' swimming pool!"

"Surely, there's nothing else."

"I wish I could say no, but there's more." He sighed loudly, finished his cookie and drank the last few drops of his milk before continuing.

"So, once again, I head back out to the counter, almost afraid of what will happen next. To my surprise, everything goes well the rest of my shift and I go out to hop on my bike to ride home, and lo and behold, my back tire is flat!"

"Why didn't you call me? I would have come got you."

"I thought about it, but, fortunately the gas station across the street has a bicycle adapter on their air hose. I pumped it up and rode home as fast as I could. I'm sure it'll be flat again tomorrow, so I'll have to get another new tire Monday after school. I just put that new one on a couple of days ago. I must have run over a nail or something."

"Whew! I'm sorry you had to go through all that, but it does make for a funny story. Someday, you'll laugh about this."

Brad shook his head. "I hope so, 'cause right now, I'm not feeling so giddy. I need to go up and shower and get these smelly clothes off."

Christina crinkled her nose. "Yeah. That's a great idea. If you want, I can throw your clothes in the washer."

"Thanks, Mom. I'll bring them down when I get out of the shower. Can you wash the tennis shoes too, or should I wash them in the tub?"

"I'm not sure. When you take them off, see if they can be washed. They may have to become your permanent work shoes."

He nodded. "Okay. I'll check. I think I'll just go on to bed. I'm exhausted."

She smiled. "Yeah. I can understand why. Did you eat dinner?"

"Yeah. I grabbed a sandwich from the deli before I came home." He gathered his napkin and glass, and before heading out asked, "I forgot to ask how your day went with Stacey."

Christina smiled. "It was fun. We met Cindy and Samara for lunch then went to see that movie about the green ogre. Schlep?"

"Oh, you mean Shrek?"

Christina nodded. "Yeah. That's it. I couldn't remember the name."

On his way to the kitchen, Brad said, "I've heard good things about that movie. I'm thinking about asking Melinda and a group of friends to go see it tomorrow afternoon."

"I think you'll enjoy it. I was amazed at how real the water looked, even though it's a cartoon of sorts."

Brad nodded. "Yeah. Computer graphics have certainly taken movies to a whole new level."

Before he disappeared upstairs, Christina asked, "So, you and Melinda still an item?"

"Yeah, sort of. She's more like a gal pal, instead of a girlfriend. We just like hanging out together."

Christina nodded. "Well, hope you sleep well. Love you."

He called over his shoulder, "Love you too, Mom."

As Christina sat thinking about Brad's day, she couldn't help but giggle. *I've got to tell Cindy about this.*

CHAPTER 17

Sunday morning felt strangely subdued without Nicky to liven things up. During the five minute drive to church, Stacey made up for his absence by chatting non-stop about her upcoming plays.

"So, Mom, is Dr. Dawson coming to my plays and Nicky's concert?"

Glancing at her daughter, she said, "As far as I know. Last time I mentioned it to him, he said he'd try to be there all three evenings."

Nodding and smiling, Stacey said, "Good. I'm glad. I like him."

Christina smiled, thinking, *Yeah, me too.*

After the service, Brad informed his mom that a group of kids *would* be going to the afternoon movie, and he would meet them there.

"What time does it start?" She asked as they headed for the van.

"Two," he answered.

"Okay. That'll give us time to get a bite to eat. Is it okay if I drop you off?"

"Yeah. I was gonna ride my bike, but the tire is flat as a pancake."

She shook her head. "Yeah, I noticed that when I got in the van this morning."

"I definitely need to go to the bike shop tomorrow. Until I get my own car, it's pretty much my mode of transportation."

"Yeah. I know. Maybe you can get a car sometime next year."

He nodded. "I hope so. It's kinda hard to date on a bicycle."

"Hey, speaking of dating, what about Melinda? Do you need to go pick her up?"

Sighing, he said, "She has some family thing to go to this afternoon, so it'll just be a group of us guys."

Christina grinned. "You know you can have the van when you need it."

He gave her a look. "Really, Mom? It's kinda embarrassing to pick up my friends in my *mom's* van."

"You've got a point there. You'll be seventeen next summer and we can get serious about getting you a car. In the meantime, we'll just have to make do with what we have."

He nodded.

"Since Stacey and I will be at the church, why don't you walk down and meet us there when the movie's over?"

He nodded in agreement. "Okay."

As they were entering the van, Stacey said, "Is it just me, or does it feel weird not having Nicky around?"

"It is weird," said Brad. "I keep expecting to see him."

Christina agreed. It did feel strange. Life could have turned out so differently if someone, besides Lula, had kidnapped him. He could be permanently missing from their lives, instead of for just a few hours. She felt a shudder go through her body.

CHAPTER 18

That evening, once everyone was safe and sound back home, they sat around the family room eating popcorn, drinking juice, and re-capping the events of the day.

"Mom," Nicky said between bites of popcorn, "Danny's grandpa's boat was awesome! It had two big sails and a cabin that had bunk beds. There was also a little kitchen and a bathroom. It was so cool! We sailed around the lake and then we stopped to do some fishing. Danny's dad caught a big ole' catfish." Making a face he said, "Those things are ugly."

"Did he keep it?" Stacey asked.

"No. He said the catfish from the lake taste kinda like dirt. Danny said that's 'cause they eat stuff off the bottom of the lake. I've had catfish before and I thought it tasted good."

Christina explained, "Well, the catfish *we* usually have come from catfish farms where they are mostly fed grains, so they don't have that strong dirty taste."

Nicky nodded. "Oh. Anyway, Danny and I did catch a couple of bass, which we did keep."

"How big were they?" Stacey asked.

Nicky put his hands up about eight inches apart. Stacey raised her eyebrows and nodded. That's pretty good. Did Mr. Snyder catch any more?"

"Yeah. He caught about six more; bigger ones."

Brad asked, "Did you bring any home for us?"

Nicky shook his head. "Mr. Snyder said he'd clean up the fish and bring it down to us tomorrow."

"That's nice," said Christina. "I remember when my dad would bring home fish to fry. Makes my mouth water just thinking about it."

"Have we ever eaten bass?" Stacey asked.

Christina shook her head. "No. We usually eat cod, perch or trout."

"What kind of fish is in Grandpa's pond?" Nicky asked.

"Those are blue gill, which are in the perch family."

"Oh, yeah. Now, those tasted good!" Nicky said, smacking his lips.

Everyone nodded in agreement. Christina looked at her daughter, who was picking a popcorn hull out of her back tooth.

"So, Stacey, how did play practice go?" Christina asked as she threw a blanket across her legs and feet.

Flicking the offensive hull off her finger, she replied, "It was great. Everyone knew exactly what to do and say. I even remembered all my lines. Now if we all do that well next Sunday night, it should be pretty awesome."

Christina smiled and nodded.

"When did you say the dress rehearsal for the school play will be?"

"This Wednesday, right after school. Mrs. Jones said she'll have pizza for us so we can practice as long as we needed to." Making a face, she said, "I'm kinda getting tired of pizza. It's like that's the universal food for kids."

Brad added, "Well, that and sloppy joes. Seems like any time there's a youth get together, there's always pizza or sloppy joes."

Christina nodded. "Even when I was a teen, that's what we were served. Weird, huh? So many years apart, but yet the same kind of food."

Taking a sip of apple juice, Nicky said nonchalantly, "I didn't know they had sloppy joes and pizza in the stone age."

Smiling, Brad gave his brother a high-five.

"Good one, bro."

"Hey," Christina said, "that's not very nice. You'd be surprised what they can make with brontosaurus meat. We called it sloppy bro instead of sloppy joe."

Stacey burst out laughing and gave her mom a high-five.

"Good come-back, Mom!"

Christina nodded and smirked.

Taking a napkin, and wiping the corners of her mouth, Christina asked, "So, Stacey, when do you think you'll be done with the practice?"

"Mrs. Jones said no later than eight. She knows we all have to get up for school the next day." Pushing a strand of hair out of her eyes, she said, "I'll be so glad when we have our Christmas break!"

Turning her attention to Brad, Christina asked, "So, did you like the movie?"

"Yeah. It was pretty awesome. I loved the donkey!"

Stacey added, "I know. He was *so* funny."

Nicky frowned. "Y'all went to see Shrek without me?"

Giggling, Stacey answered, "Yeah, but *you* got to go on a boat. Kinda makes things even, huh?"

Making a face he said, "Yeah, I guess so. I would like to see that movie though." Looking at his mom he asked, "Can you take Danny and me next weekend?"

She shook her head. "I'd love to, but it will be an extremely busy time, with Stacey's plays, your band concert, and Grandma and Grandpa being here."

Scrunching his face, he said, "Oh, yeah. Well, maybe sometime the next week? We'll be on vacation then."

"I won't make any promises, but we'll see how things play out."

He nodded. "Okay."

Looking at her three children, she felt a wave of motherly love wash through her.

God, I love these kids! Thank You for them. She thought as she felt tears begging to be released.

Stacey stood and stretched. "I'm gonna go get ready for bed. I'm pooped."

"Yeah, I think I'll head on up, too," Brad added.

They both leaned down and gave their mom a hug before leaving the room. Standing, Nicky asked, "Is it okay if I play a video game?"

"I'd rather you didn't. I'd like to just sit and talk a while. I missed you."

He sighed and sat back down.

"Anything you want to talk about?" She asked.

Making a face, he said, "Not really."

"I noticed you got a letter from Lulu...I mean Ruby yesterday. Does she still prefer to be called Ruby?" Nicky nodded.

Christina continued, "You know, I am very proud of the way you are reaching out to her. Even though she kidnapped you, and did some scary things to us, you still want to forgive her and care about her. I'm not sure I would be that nice."

Nicky shrugged. "I just feel so sorry for her. She had an awful time growing up."

Christina nodded. "What did she have to say?"

"You can read it if you want."

"No, that's okay. I'd like you to tell me what she said."

Shrugging, he said, "Okay. She wishes she could come to my band concert and Stacey's plays; her guinea pig, Sweet Pea, is getting fat and sassy; and she's on some kind of exercise program and has lost ten pounds."

"Wow! Sounds like she's doing well."

"I guess. She says everyone is nice, but she has to follow a strict schedule and isn't allowed to be alone, and they won't call her Ruby. She has to go by the name of Lulu, which she hates." Sighing and shrugging, he said, "That must really stink...to not have any control, or privacy."

Christina nodded. "Yeah. I wouldn't like it"

Nicky was silent for a moment as he chewed on a hangnail. "Do you think she'll ever get out of there?"

"Well, eventually. She has to stay in there for at least seven years for kidnapping, and putting our lives in danger—plus the ransom thing."

Nicky nodded slowly. "I know about consequences, but it just makes me sad that she has to be punished for so long. I'll be graduating high school when she gets out." Pausing and making a face, he said, "Weird."

Christina reached out and pulled him to her.

"I know, but maybe this is the best place for her right now."

He gave her a puzzled look.

"She has a clean place to stay and three good meals a day, plus she has a pet guinea pig. Sure, there are some unpleasant things, but it could have been a lot worse for her." *I personally would like her to be locked up and throw away the key!*

Nodding, Nicky said, "Yeah." After a moment, he asked, "Is it okay if I send her a Christmas gift?"

Christina forced a smile. "I'm sure it would be. I'll ask Sheriff Clifton what we will be allowed to send."

"We have to get permission to send her things?"

"Yep. There are some pretty strict rules for us to follow as well."

"Guess I never thought about that. So, can you call him tomorrow and find out, and then we can start getting things together?"

Christina nodded and stood to give Nicky a hug.

"You are an amazing kid, Nicky. God has got some awesome plans for you."

He shrugged and gave her a crooked smile.

Kissing the top of his head, and walking him to the stairs, she said, "Okay young man, you need to get up to bed. Love you. Sweet dreams."

"Love you too, Mom. See you tomorrow."

When Christina finally went to bed, she lay there thinking about everything: her kids, her job, the threats, Steven, David, her friends, the meeting with the lawyer, her life, her plans for the future. How was she going to survive and make the right decisions? After tossing and turning for what seemed like hours, she finally fell into a fitful sleep.

CHAPTER 19

When Christina entered the third floor cardiac care unit on Monday morning, she was surprised to see both Dr. Dawson and Dr. Meils standing at the nurses' station. Approaching the desk, she noticed the cardiac resuscitation cart as well as the EKG monitor sitting outside one of the patient's rooms. Steven looked up when he heard the elevator door open, and watched as Christina approached.

This can't be good, she thought. *He looks grim.*

"Good morning, Dr. Dawson, Dr. Meils."

"Hello, Christina." Steven answered without his usual smile.

"So, what happened?" She asked as she surveyed the area.

Dr. Dawson looked down, apparently too upset to answer. Dr. Meils spoke up. "Our new patient, James Perkins, just passed away."

"James Perkins? I don't remember him."

Clearing his throat and rubbing his eyes, Steven answered, "He came in around two this morning. I had him scheduled for an angioplasty in an hour, but he took a nosedive and crashed out."

She frowned, and reached out to touch his arm. "I'm so sorry, Dr. Dawson. He must have been in pretty bad shape when he came in. How old was he?"

Shaking his head, he said, "He was seventy, but didn't seem to be in too much distress. In fact, his symptoms disappeared when the medication was administered in the ER." Sighing and rubbing his eyes, he added, "The autopsy will tell us just how bad he was. I could have missed an aneurism or a more severe blockage."

Christina sighed and nodded. "Do you need me to do anything, besides clean up and prep his body for transfer?"

"No. I'll call his family and the coroner."

Wanting to reach out and hug him, but knowing it would be inappropriate, she opted to touch his arm, once again. Glancing at the night shift nurse, who was pointing to her watch, Christina nodded and said, "I've got to go, Dr. Dawson. If you need anything, let me know."

"Thanks, Christina. Dr. Meils and I will finish up here, then you can join us as we check on the other three patients."

Once she was appraised of the condition of the other patients, signed the paperwork for the deceased patient, and sent her team to prepare the body for presentation and transfer, Christina joined Dr. Dawson.

Mr. Perkins' family had congregated at the nurses' station, while she and the two doctors were assessing the last patient.

Once the body was ready for presentation, Christina entered with the grieving widow, children and grand-children. Not wanting to intrude, Christina stood by the door as they all said good-bye to their beloved one.

After several minutes, Christina gave them directions to the hospital's administrative office where they would fill out paper work and be directed to the next person in a long line of people, before they could lay their loved one to rest.

The remainder of the day held no new crises, thus freeing her up to do a little organizing and cleaning around the station and nurses' lounge. Thankfully, the only ominous and threatening items lying about were used Kleenexes. Carefully picking each up by its corner, she deposited them into the waste can.

Anxious to hear about Sarah's date on Friday evening, Christina was disappointed when she didn't see her on the unit. Curiosity was nibbling at her mind, like a mouse in a box of crackers.

After informing the next shift of the three patient's conditions, she gathered her belongings and headed for the elevator. Feeling her phone buzzing in her pocket, she stopped outside the elevator and answered it.

She was pleased to hear Steven's voice on the other end.

"Hey Christina, can you come by my office before you leave?"

"Sure. I can't stay long though, as I need to be home when the kids arrive."

"Okay. See you in a few?"

"On my way."

I wonder what that's about, she thought as she entered the elevator and punched the number one button.

CHAPTER 20

Standing with her hands on her hips, Janet looked around the clean and decorated living room, and felt a sense of pride and accomplishment. *Linda will be happy to see the Christmas decorations out, and the tree up.*

Walking out the front door on her way to school, she had turned and said, "Mom, Christmas is two weeks away, in case your forgot."

Janet had decided then to use her day off to do that very thing. Up until then, she hadn't felt in any kind of festive mood, and wanted to skip the whole holiday scene—and would have—had it not been for Linda. Once she started decorating however, her mood lightened, and she found herself singing familiar Christmas tunes, along with the radio.

She sat on the floor and began sorting through the box of tree ornaments, smiling as memories flooded her mind and heart. Her favorite ornaments were Linda's hand prints in round pieces of plaster. She rubbed her finger over the smooth indentations of the first one, and recalled the moment it had been placed there.

Janet looked at the stack: one for every year–which reminded her that she needed one for this year. *I wonder, now that Linda is a teenager, if she'll still be wiling to make one. I hope so. I'd like one for every year until she turns eighteen.*

As Janet was returning the last empty box to the closet, Linda walked in the door, and without speaking a word, went to her room, and slammed the door.

Uh oh, Janet thought, *wonder what happened? Should I go in, or just give her space until she calms down?* She chose the latter, and went to the kitchen to prepare dinner.

Glancing at the clock on the stove, and knowing there would be several hours before the intruder would enter Christina's home, Janet felt anxiety tapping at her heart. She knew there was a possibility of something going wrong, and let a few scenarios play out in her mind. If her guy was as careful as he indicated, there should be no problem. *But...*There was always that little word that made her feel insecure.

If the boy did get caught, he didn't know her name, and the number she used was from a disposable phone. As many times as she told herself those facts, there was still that niggling feeling that something could go wrong, and she would be implicated. Leaning against the counter, and massaging her forehead, she called on every cosmic energy available to help the boy succeed.

CHAPTER 21

Christina tapped on Dr. Dawson's door before entering. Standing, he greeted her.

"Hi, Christina. Thanks for coming by."

Stepping into the room, she asked, "So what's up?"

Shrugging, he said, "To be quite honest, I just wanted to see how you are doing."

She smiled and shook her head. "Honestly Steven, every time you ask to see me, I get butterflies in my gut and am afraid it's something serious."

He smiled sheepishly. "Sorry."

She put her hand up dismissively. "It's okay. My problem, not yours. Just letting my paranoia and insecurities seep through."

He pointed to the chair opposite his desk and she sat. Leaning his backside against the desktop, he looked down at her, making her feel uncomfortable—like she was about to be interrogated—she squirmed in her seat, and rubbed her neck.

"Steven, could you please sit down? I don't like looking up at you. Makes my neck hurt."

"Oh, sorry." He pulled a chair over and sat opposite of her.

"So how are you really doing?"

"I guess okay. Getting ready for the super busy weekend coming up."

"Oh, yeah. You told me your in-laws are flying in, and the kids plays and concerts are taking place."

"You haven't changed your mind about coming to the plays and concert, right?"

Smiling and shaking his head, he said, "No, no! I wouldn't miss them for the world."

"Good. I know the kids would be so disappointed if you didn't show up." *And so would I*, she thought.

"Well, I wouldn't want to disappoint the kids." *And you either*, he thought.

She glanced at her watch. Standing, she said, "Steven, I really need to get home. I'd love to sit and chat, but my mother-duty calls."

He reached out his hand and pulled her into a hug—which caught her off guard.

"I just want you to know that I'll be around if you need anything."

"Uh, okay. I appreciate that." Releasing herself from his hug and cocking her head, she looked up at him. "Are you okay? You seem a little—uhm, emotional."

Leaning back on his desk and crossing his arms, he smiled and nodded. "Yeah, I'm fine. Just concerned about you and the kids." Clearing his throat, he added, "I guess losing my patient this morning kinda made me think about the whole life and death thing. What's really important."

She smiled and nodded. "I see." *But I don't have time for a philosophical discussion right now*, she thought as she turned to head for the door.

"Christina?"

"Yes?"

On a sigh he said, "Be careful."

Cocking her head, she answered, "I always try to be."

Walking to her van, she thought, *What was that about? He sure was mysterious—like he wanted to say more, but was afraid to. Does he know something I don't? And if so, what? Wonder if I should have told him about the meeting I have with the lawyer. It's not really any of his business, but I'm sure he'd like to know. Maybe I'll tell him once I know what it's all about.*

CHAPTER 22

Arriving home a few minutes before her children, she was able to retrieve the mail and let Benji out. Glancing through the pile of advertisements and catalogs, she was pleased to see an envelope with the return address of her friends, Linda and John, from Michigan. She tore it open and found a letter, photograph, and Christmas card enclosed. Feeling a little guilty, she realized she hadn't sent any Christmas cards out—yet. *I've still got a couple of weeks,* she thought. *I could just send them to a few of my friends.*

So many events had occurred over the past several months, she wasn't sure where she would even start. *Besides,* she thought, *the people I care about, and who are in my circle of friends and relatives, already know what has happened, via phone or e-mail, so why bother? Well, Mom would say, it's the thought that counts.* She read the letter and studied the photograph. Such a happy, healthy-looking family. The kids had grown into attractive teens, and John and Linda looked pretty much the same as she remembered them. *Maybe next year, I can get my act together and send out cards and photos.*

She heard Benji bark and went to let him in just as her children entered the back door.

"Mom?" She heard Stacey call.

"I'm letting Benji in." She called back as the excited pooch ran past her and headed for his other favorite humans.

Entering the kitchen, she watched as each child grabbed something cold to drink, while Benji ran from one to the other, demanding attention. Glancing at the clock, she asked, "Stacey, do you have play practice tonight?"

"Amazingly, no. Mrs. Gibson is having the scenery group finish up the last bit of painting and stage preparations."

Christina nodded. "Good. You could use a break."

"Yeah, I don't have any homework either, so I'm not sure what to do with my time!"

Christina smiled and raised her eyebrows. "I'm sure I can find *something* for you to do."

Stacey did an eye-roll. "Actually, I do have a book I want to finish, but I could help you fix dinner if you want."

"Oh, that would be nice. You can make the salad."

Stacey smiled and nodded. "Okay. When?"

"How about in an hour?"

"Sure. I'm gonna go call Carmen."

"Hey, how's Carmen doing these days?" Christina asked as she sipped her glass of tea.

"She's good. Her older sister is coming home for the holidays."

"That's nice. You know, we should invite them over for dinner sometime."

"That'd be fun. They seem like such a funny family—especially her older sister."

"Funny?"

"Yeah. They're always teasing each other and telling jokes. At least that's what Carmen says. I haven't been around them that much."

Christina nodded. "Well, you go ahead and call Carmen. I'll call you when it's time to fix the salad."

She turned to her youngest son, who was pouring food in the animals' bowls. "Hey, Nicky. How was your day?"

He looked up at her and grinned. "It was great! We had our Christmas party in the lunchroom and every kid got a bag of gifts from the teachers. We played games and sang songs, and had cake and ice-cream. It was pretty cool."

Christina raised her eyebrows and smiled. "Wow! I forgot your party was today. What did you get?

"We all got pencils, markers, cool notebooks—you know, school stuff."

Nodding, she said, "Were y'all supposed to take gifts?"

Nicky shook his head and took a sip of milk. "Nah. Some of the kids did give each other gifts, but most of them didn't. I'm gonna give Danny his on Christmas day."

She nodded. "Okay. I was afraid I had forgotten to get a gift for you to give. Which reminds me, I do want to give your teachers something."

"Well, we have a few more days."

"What do you think we should give them?"

He crinkled his nose. "I don't know. Soap or a candle or something like that."

She smiled. "Okay. I'll think about it."

Giggling, he said, "Danny is gonna give our science teacher a can with those snakes that pop out!"

Christina looked surprised. "Why your science teacher?"

"Mom, he is so uptight about everything. He knows if a pencil on his desk is missing, and freaks out if anyone sits in a different chair. One time we all switched seats to see what he would do, and he told everyone that if they didn't get back in the right seats by the time he came back from the office, he would count everyone absent."

"Oh my goodness! I didn't realize he was so...strange."

She said, "I mean, I kinda got that impression when I met him, and he was wearing a bow-tie, and seemed very nervous talking to us parents, but..."

"Yeah. Anyway, it should be pretty funny seeing his reaction."

Christina couldn't help but smile as she pictured the scene in her head.

Calling Benji, Nicky headed upstairs.

Brad, who had been leaning against the counter chuckling, spoke up, "So Mom, how was your day?"

"Hey, I was just gonna ask you that."

Grinning, he said, "You first."

She gave a condensed version of her day at the hospital and her appointment for the next morning.

"What do you think those guys will tell you?"

She shook her head. "I haven't the foggiest idea." Patting his arm, she said, "So, your turn. How was your day?"

Just as he opened his mouth to speak, there was an ear-shattering trumpet blast coming from upstairs.

Grabbing her chest, Christina went to the bottom of the stairs and yelled up, "Nicky!"

"Sorry Mom."

"Next time give us a warning. I almost had a heart attack!"

"Is it okay if I practice a few minutes?"

"Yes, but please close your door."

"Yes, Ma'am."

Shaking her head, she turned back to Brad who was laughing.

"You should have seen your face, Mom! I thought you were gonna pass out!"

Letting out a sigh, she said, "I almost did!" They both giggled.

Shaking her head and rubbing her temple, she said, "Of all the instruments in the band, why he had to choose the trumpet, I'll never know."

Sighing, she said, "So where were we?"

"I was telling you about my day."

"Oh yeah. Continue please."

"We had a pop quiz in Algebra as well as American Government. I aced the Algebra, but the Government one threw me for a loop."

"So, did you pass it?"

"Well, yeah. Barely. I really don't like that class, so I don't tend to do as well."

"It's not gonna affect your GPA is it?"

Shaking his head, he said, "No. Not at this point. I will definitely have to step it up if I plan to get an A, however."

"Do you think you can pull it off?"

Nodding, and taking a sip of his apple juice, he said, "Oh yeah. Now that I don't have to do any more research papers for English, I'm pretty sure I can focus more on Government." Grinning, he added, "After all, if I'm gonna run for President someday, I need to know all about the American Government."

She gave him a shocked look. "You want to run for President someday?"

Shaking his head and chuckling, he said, "Nah. I just thought I'd pull your chain."

She punched him in the arm. "I think I've had enough shocks for today, thank you very much."

Rubbing his arm, he said, "Sorry, Mom."

She pulled him into a hug. "You know, if you *did* run for President, I'd vote for you."

"Good to know."

"So what else happened today?"

Leaning against the counter, he finished telling about his day.

"The coach is gonna let us have a pizza party tomorrow. I need to bring a bag of chips and some dip."

"I think both of those are in the pantry."

"I'd better get them now, or I'll probably forget."

Suddenly the trumpet noise stopped and she breathed a sigh of relief. Understanding the need to practice didn't negate the irritation it caused.

Pulling the salad fixin's out of the fridge, she called up to Stacey.

Once dinner was eaten, and the kitchen was clean, she called the children into the family room and told them of her planned trip to the lawyer's office the next morning. Christina answered their questions to the best of her ability, and seemingly satisfied, the kids headed up to bed. She noticed Benji sitting by the back door.

"Okay Buddy, I'll let you out one more time."

When he finished his business and barked to come in, she noticed a dog cookie in his mouth.

"Hey, Benji, where did you get that?"

She reached for the cookie, and he immediately chewed it up.

"Maybe Nicky gave it to you. Well, okay, let's go to bed."

Wagging his tail, he followed her up the stairs.

Later that night, as everyone slept peacefully, the intruder entered once again. He replaced the flower vase, and instead of staying on the first floor as he usually did, he tiptoed up the stairs. and stood in the hallway. Heart pounding, hands shaking, and knowing he was taking a great risk, he forced himself to take a few calming breaths before descending the stairs. Once downstairs in the front room, he felt his mind and body relax. *That was fun. Too bad all the doors were closed. I would have enjoyed watching them sleep.* Walking into the den, he spotted the treasure he desired to take. As he exited the house, he texted his employer: done.

CHAPTER 23

When Janet woke Tuesday morning, and read the text, she breathed a sigh of relief. *I wonder how long it will take for Christina to notice the items missing? I wish I could ask her without sounding like I know about it. Maybe I could say, "Hey Christina, have you heard anything about the break-ins around town? From what I hear, the guy just takes things and gives them back."* Smiling, she thought, *Well, maybe I'll do that sometime later, after the boy has done a few jobs. By then, she should be showing signs of paranoia.*

When her alarm sounded the first time, Christina found waking to be quite a task. Her eyes kept closing, and she would be jarred awake by the snooze alarm. After the second snooze alarm warning, she sighed and pulled herself out of bed.

She had had several nightmares during the night, and try as she might, couldn't remember a single one. She just remembered waking up and feeling frightened. Benji was sound asleep, and didn't seem to sense any danger, so she assumed everything was okay.

Stretching and yawning, she said, "Benji, it's time to go downstairs." The sleeping dog didn't even stir. Frowning, she walked over and patted his belly, calling his name once again. He thumped his tail once, and drifted back to sleep.

"Well, okay. I guess I'll let you sleep."

Leaving the bedroom door open, she went to the kitchen and made a pot of coffee. *Surely, he'll come down in a minute when he hears the kids.*

Thoughts of Benji dissipated as she drank her coffee, until Nicky asked where he was.

Frowning, she asked, "He hasn't come down yet?"

Nicky looked around. "I haven't seen him."

"He was up on my bed. Why don't you go check on him?"

Nicky returned a few minutes later with an obviously groggy dog.

"He's acting weird, Mom. I think he may be sick or something."

She called the dog over and touched his warm, dry nose.

"If he's not any better when I get back from Dallas, I'll take him to the vet."

Rubbing Benji's ears, Nicky asked, "Do you have to wait that long?"

Benji yawned and lay down at Nicky's feet.

Christina looked at the dog, then up into her son's worried face.

"Nicky, I have to go to Dallas. I'll be back by early afternoon. I'm sure Benji will be fine 'till then."

Burying his face in Benji's neck fur, he said, "I sure hope so, Mom."

Nicky pulled gently on Benji's collar and led him to the back door. The sleepy dog followed slowly, went out and did his business, then stood by the door until Nicky let him back in. He then went to his bed on the floor in the corner of the family room, and after walking in a circle three times, laid down with a big sigh, and closed his eyes.

With tear-rimmed eyes, Nicky said, "He better not die before you get back!"

Not knowing what was wrong with the dog, she couldn't *exactly* promise he wouldn't, but she said what most mothers would say to assure their children, "I'm sure he'll be back to his normal self in a few hours. He just needs to sleep off whatever it is that's bothering him."

Brad spoke up and said, "Yeah, Nicky. He'll be okay. He's acted like this before and snapped back by the afternoon."

"Yeah," Stacey added, "Remember last week when he was so sleepy?"

Nicky scrunched his face and nodded. "I hope you're right."

Looking at his mom, he asked, "You promise you'll take him to the vet if he's not better?"

Christina held up two fingers in the universal girl-scout promise sign.

"I promise."

Nicky nodded, gave Benji one more hug and stood. Walking over to his mom, he hugged her and gathered his backpack and walked to the back door. His siblings did the same before joining him. Christina watched out the front window as they disappeared.

She went over, knelt and laid her hand on Benji's head. She felt tears sting her eyes as she prayed over him. Glancing at the clock, she quickly cleaned up the breakfast dishes, brushed her teeth, checked her make-up and headed out the door.

Having mapped out her route the previous evening, she knew which roads to take to avoid traffic and construction, thus arriving earlier than she had anticipated. After parking in a complex across from the building that held the lawyers' office, she spotted a coffee shop next door and headed in that direction, where she was able to finish a cup and peruse the Dallas newspaper before her appointment. Glancing across the street, next to the parking garage, she noticed the red, black and gold Two Dragons restaurant sign. *So there it is,* she thought. *Looks nice…and expensive.* Glancing at her watch, she replaced the newspaper, tossed her coffee cup, freshened her lipstick and headed over to the building next door.

Entering the glass doors into a massive foyer surrounded by tinted windows, she was reminded of a futuristic building she had once seen on a movie. The reception counter was sitting in the middle of an area flanked by black leather couches and chairs, glass coffee tables and a variety of tropical plants. Walking to the counter, she was aware of the clicking sound her heels made on the polished marble floor.

"May I help you?" The receptionist asked as she watched Christina approach.

Feeling slightly intimidated, Christina cleared her throat and said, "Yes. I'm here to see Mr. Mark Taylor."

The young woman, who appeared to be in her early twenties and model beautiful, with her blond hair pulled up into a bun, long eyelashes that framed cerulean blue eyes, french-manicured nails, and flawless skin, typed something on the computer, then looked up at Christina and smiled. "You are Mrs. Christina Sanders?"

"Yes, Ma'am."

"Mr. Taylor is expecting you. His office is on the fourth floor, suite 401."

Christina looked around for an elevator.

Smiling, and showing flawless white teeth, the receptionist said, "The elevators are around that corner."

Christina nodded and said, "Thank you." As she walked away, the thought flitted through her mind, that the young woman was almost too perfect…*like an android from a science-fiction movie.* Glancing around and noting that the people entering and exiting the building, as well as the space surrounding her, were also flawless, she felt like she *was* on a movie set. Feeling gooseflesh rise on her arms and nape of her neck, she click-clacked her way to the elevator, thankful when it arrived and took her to her destination. *I'm almost tempted to remove my shoes on the way out,* she thought as the elevator doors opened to a nicely carpeted hallway. *I don't want to draw any attention to myself, and end up transformed into a perfectly replicated android.* She chuckled at the absurdness of the thought.

As she reached up to tap on the door, with the law office names and logo, it opened. She was greeted by a handsome, fifty-ish looking man with a head full of salt and pepper hair, and clear blue eyes—which reminded her of Steven—which made her think of the whole cloning, robot thing again. She shivered and those ridiculous thoughts vanished.

Taking her hand, he said, "Mrs. Sanders?"

"Yes."

"I'm Mark Taylor. We spoke on the phone."

"Yes, Sir. It's nice to meet you."

"Come on in to my office."

As they walked across the carpeted waiting area, he said, "So, did you have any trouble finding us?"

"No sir. I've been in this area before, and remembered the building."

"Well, good. Did you miss the rush-hour traffic?"

Nodding and smiling she said, "Yes. Thank goodness!"

As he opened the door, she was surprised to see Ed, Tom and a heavy-set man stand as she entered.

She was dumbstruck. *What are they doing here?*

Ed, sensing her confusion, walked over, took her hand and led her to a leather chair opposite a large mahogany desk.

He whispered, "I know you're wondering why we're here, but it'll all be explained in a few minutes."

Walking behind the desk, the lawyer asked, "Can I get you anything? A soda, water, coffee?"

Shaking her head, she said, "No, thanks."

"Alright then. Why don't we get started?" He motioned for the other men to sit.

Everyone sat as she cocked her head, and glanced at Ed.

"I take it you already know Tom and Ed?"

She nodded.

"Well, this is their boss, Henry Steil."

He reached over and took her hand in his.

"Mrs. Sanders, it's so nice to finally meet you. I didn't know David personally, but I heard he was a good man. I'm so sorry for your loss."

She felt tears sting her eyes and quickly batted them away.

"Thank you, Mr. Steil. He *was* a good man."

After a few seconds of silence, Mark cleared his throat, and said, "I'm sure you're wondering what this is all about?"

She nodded slightly.

"Well then, let's get down to business."

Opening a large manilla folder, he turned it to face her.

"Mrs. Sanders, there are a lot of papers here filled with legalese, as we call it, and I'm not going to bore or confuse you with that. I will, however, show you a few papers which you may be unaware of."

She cocked her head and frowned.

Shuffling through the papers, he pulled one out and laid it in front of her.

CORONER'S REPORT was printed in large bold letters at the top. She gave him a confused look.

"I already know about this." She pushed the page back at him. "David died from the injuries he sustained in the automobile accident. Why are you showing me this?"

"I know this is going to come as a shock to you, Mrs. Sanders, but we have evidence that points us in the direction of a murder investigation."

"What? Murder? You think David was murdered? How? Why?" She looked over at Ed, who nodded.

Tears stinging her eyes, she asked the lawyer, "Who would do such a thing?" As a tear ran down her cheek, she looked at Ed and asked, "Ed, did you know about this?"

Shaking his head, he answered, "I was just recently informed."

She sat for a minute, reigning in her emotions and composing her thoughts. Looking up at the lawyer once again she said, "I thought you said I'd be happy with the news. I'm not happy. Confused, for sure. But happy? No. So, I'm assuming there's more to this meeting than what you have presented so far?"

Mark Taylor nodded. "Yes, there is. I showed you the coroner's report because you needed to understand the *real* reason your husband died. He did indeed die of complications from his injuries, but upon further examination and toxicology reports, there was evidence that he had an overdose of morphine and blood thinners in his system."

"Morphine? Blood thinners? Like Heparin?" Shaking her head in disbelief, she asked, "How could that have happened? I know the Doctor who cared for him, and I doubt he would have administered anything like that to David."

"We don't know exactly how it happened, or when, but we suspect that one of the EMTs gave it to him on the way to the hospital. We have checked the names and backgrounds of all, but one. He seems to have disappeared."

Shaking her head, she said, "Disappeared? How is that possible?"

Ed said, "Remember we're talking about terrorists. They will go to extreme measures to accomplish their mission. They've been known to infiltrate all kinds of businesses...including EMT work. These are intelligent and highly motivated individuals with one common goal."

Shaking her head, Christina said, "I'm still confused. Why would anyone want to kill David? He was a decent, loving, kind man who loved his family. He was a computer programmer for goodness sakes!" When those words came out of her mouth, she put her hand up to her lips, as the implications hit her.

Looking at Ed and Tom, she said, "You told me he was working for the government to help find terrorist cells." The men nodded.

"So, this has something to do with that?"

Again they nodded.

Panic filling her voice, she asked, "What? What was he *really* doing that would get him killed?"

Henry Steil, who's looks reminded her of a walrus, cleared his throat before answering. "Mrs. Sanders, our agency here in Dallas was informed that David had been tracking a sleeper cell in Detroit, which had Dallas connections. We became involved when it was confirmed that your husband had been killed and his family had moved here to Texas. We were concerned that there may have been overlooked information left in David's files, which could have put you and your children in danger."

Pointing to Ed and Tom, he continued. "That's why I had these two gentlemen go through your computer files. We had to make sure there were no loose ends."

Glancing at Ed and Tom, she asked, "Did you find anything useful?"

Henry nodded. "Actually, they did. I'm not at liberty to tell you what it was, but rest assured, you and your children are safe."

Looking at Mr. Steil, she asked, "So, why am *I* here? You said we aren't in any danger, but if you haven't caught the guy that supposedly killed David, how can you know for sure? I'm still getting threats, for goodness sakes! What if those are related?"

Ed said, "Christina, our ATO office has been monitoring the airwaves for any chatter mentioning David or your family's name. Nothing has surfaced for the past couple of years. We're pretty confident that that part of the threat is over. As far as the threats you're receiving now, I still think it's someone you know who is just out for some kind of revenge."

Biting her bottom lip, and twisting a ringlet of hair around a finger, she said, "Well, I hope you're right about the terrorist threat, but I still can't figure out why anyone would want revenge. As far as I know, I haven't done anything to warrant revenge."

Shaking his head and shrugging, Ed said, "It is a mystery for sure. One I hope will be resolved soon."

She sighed and nodded.

The lawyer spoke up. "Because David worked for the government, and died while serving, you and the children, will receive a substantial compensation."

She gave him a confused look. "Substantial compensation? What does that mean?"

"It means that you and your children will be well taken care of for the rest of your lives."

"Huh?"

"Here, let me show you." He reached in his desk drawer and pulled out another folder. Opening it, he presented a piece of paper for her inspection.

Taking it from him, she inhaled sharply when she read the contents.

"Oh my goodness! It's a check for fifty thousand dollars!"

She looked up at the smiling lawyer and asked, "What does this mean?"

"It means, that every year, you will receive a check like this." She started to protest and he put a hand up. "I know, it doesn't make up for your husband's death, but it is one of the ways our government can help relieve the strain of being a widow. You can choose whichever month you want to receive it. We just chose this month because this is the time everything came together."

"Wow! I'm speechless. I'm not sure what I'll do with all this money."

Ed spoke up, "You have three children that will eventually go to college, and a house that needs some major repair work, plus Brad will need a new car, and you will have to replace your van before too long. I'm sure it will all be put to good use."

"Well, if I add this to the money David left us, and the money I make at the hospital, that'll be way more than we need to survive!" Looking at the lawyer she said, "I almost feel guilty taking so much money from the government."

He raised his eyebrows. "Really?"

She smiled. "I said almost."

That elicited a chuckle from the other men.

After a moment's silence while she processed the information, she said, "I don't want the kids to know about this yet. I think it would confuse them. I was wondering if I could have it directly deposited in a saving's account?"

The lawyer nodded. "You can go ahead and take this one, then have your bank get in touch with me and we'll set that up."

She handed the check back. "I'll talk to the bank manager, and see what he suggests and I'll have him get back to you. In the meantime, hold on to it. I don't want to carry it around or have one of the kids find it. This is a lot of information to process."

Nodding, the lawyer took it and placed it in an envelope. "I'll hang on to it until I hear from you or your bank."

She nodded. "Thank you."

The men stood. Mark reached out for her hand. "Mrs. Sanders, I wish we could have met under different circumstances, but, hopefully, this hasn't been a totally negative experience."

She smiled and shook her head. "Well, it certainly was a surprise. I never suspected that David had been deliberately killed, and I certainly didn't expect such a large compensation. I'm still in shock."

Handing her the manilla envelope, he said, "Once the shock wears off, I would like for you to read through these papers, sign and return them, please. If you find you have more questions, please feel free to call me. I will try my best to resolve any issues."

She took the envelope.

"Thank you." Turning to the other three men, she added, "And you too, gentlemen."

Henry said, "Mrs. Sanders, if I receive any further information regarding your husband, I will let you know."

She nodded.

Ed walked over to the door and held it open. "Christina, would you like me to walk you to your van?"

Looking up at him, she smiled. "Yes, that would be nice."

As they walked, she told him of the new threats.

Shaking his head, he said, "Man, that stinks."

"Yeah."

"Maybe the person who is doing this, is just trying to keep you unhinged."

Nodding, she said, "Yeah, maybe. If so, it's working. I don't know whether I should be worried, or if I should just ignore them."

Sighing, and rubbing the nape of his neck, he said, "Geez, I don't know what to tell you. I guess it's better to err on the side of caution. Do the kids know about these latest threats?"

"Brad does. It's difficult to keep *anything* from him these days. He's keeping close tabs on Stacey and Nicky."

As he opened her van door, he asked, "How's Nicky doing anyway?"

"Okay, I guess. He still won't venture off alone. Not even to Danny's. And, he has nightmares about once a week."

"Hopefully he'll get past that."

Nodding, she said, "The school counselor works with him once or twice a week for an hour. He says Nicky's reaction is normal and he'll eventually outgrow it."

"Kids are pretty resilient. Nicky's got a loving family and a good support group at church and school."

Stepping up into the van she said, "Yeah, that's better than some kids."

As Ed began to close the door, she said, "Hey, Ed, I was wondering if you and Cindy wanted to share Christmas with us? My in-laws are coming Thursday and we'll be doing our family one that following Monday, but on Christmas day, we'll be alone."

He smiled and nodded. "I'll be free, as my family celebrates on Christmas Eve. I'll ask Cindy."

"Good! I'll talk to Cindy too. Thanks again, Ed, for being here today and being a good friend."

"Hey, you're welcome. Please keep me informed about any more threats."

She nodded, closed the door and drove away.

CHAPTER 24

As Christina drove home, she couldn't help but think about the money, and what she could or should do with it.

The house needed so many repairs, that she could easily spend the fifty thousand on it alone. *I would love to put in central air, which would involve duct work, and an air-conditioning system, and then I might as well get a new furnace, and insulation in the walls, and, oh yes, new windows. And that roof. When was the last time it was checked or updated? I could get rid of the wallpaper in all the rooms, and put up drywall, and the kitchen needs new cabinets, and why not a tile floor and counter-tops? Then there are the bathrooms. Oh my, those need everything new as well. Yep, the money could go fast, but then again, if I'm getting the same amount every year, I could space out the projects. I'll have to make a list of all the things we want and need, and prioritize them.*

She glanced at the clock on the dashboard. 12:30. *No wonder my stomach is growling.* She pulled into the next fast food place and ordered lunch.

As she continued the drive home, her thoughts returned to events of the morning—and Benji. Recalling his odd behavior, she thought, *Oh my goodness, I hope he's alright!* Worry started nibbling at her heart and mind. The past couple of weeks, he seemed to be a bit off key. Some days he seemed fine, then other days, like today, he would just drag. *I think I'll take him to the vet this week. It's about time for an annual check up anyway. Something is just not right.*

Janet texted her accomplice during her lunch break..
What have you taken so far? When are you going again?
She received the text: *Took flower vase/family picture. Christmas vacation next week. Maybe after New Year.*
She responded: *Okay, be in touch.*

She was getting the hang of reading and sending texts. When she first began, every word was spelled out, which took a while—now, she short-handed the words, and was amazed at how quickly she could send a message.

Texting her accomplice was much better than calling and talking. She didn't want to take the chance of him recognizing her voice. The first time she had communicated with Jamie via phone, she had used a Mexican accent. Hopefully, that was disguise enough.

CHAPTER 25

Walking in the door, Christina was surprised and pleased when Benji came running to meet her—tail wagging, and tongue hanging out.

Bending down, grabbing his face and massaging behind his ears, she said, "Well, Benji, seems you've made a full recovery. You need to go out?"

Hearing the word 'out', he immediately headed to the back door. As she waited for him to finish his business, she heard her phone ringing—in her purse—in the kitchen. She ran to get it, but missed the call by seconds.

She looked at the caller ID—Mom.

She immediately called back and heard a busy signal.

Benji barked, signaling the completion of his business. Opening the door, she nearly dropped the phone when it rang in her hand.

"Hello, Mom."

"Well hi, Christina. I called a minute ago and almost left you a message, but thought I'd chance another call."

"I know. My phone was in my purse and I couldn't get it out in time."

"Oh, that's alright. I just called to let you know, we'll be arriving in Dallas on Thursday at two o'clock. We'll just rent a car and drive on down to Alva if that's alright with you."

As she talked, Christina walked to the front door to retrieve the mail. "Sure Mom, but I can come get y'all. I don't have to work that day."

"Well, that's sweet, but you know how dad likes to have his own car in case he wants to go somewhere, and you aren't available."

Christina smiled. "Yes, I remember. So y'all will be arriving here around five?"

"That sounds about right. Once we land, get our luggage, and get the rental car and drive there, it'll be about three hours."

"That's fine. I'll have dinner ready. Looking forward to seeing y'all again. The kids are so excited that y'all will be here for their activities."

"Did you tell them we want to have Christmas before we leave?"

"Oh yes! And they can hardly wait!"

A moment of silence passed before Ruth asked, "Is everything okay with you, Christina?"

"Yes, Mom. Everything is fine. I have some interesting news to tell you when you get here."

"Good news, I hope."

"Well, yes and no. I don't want to go into it right now."

"That's fine, Honey. We'll talk when we get there. We'll see you in a couple of days then. Love you, and give the kids hugs and kisses for us."

"Love you, too, and I'll let the kids know the plans. I'll be praying for a safe trip for y'all."

Wanting desperately to call Cindy and tell her of the meeting with Ed and the lawyer, she glanced at her watch and realized her friend would still be working. She had a couple of hours before the kids arrived, and decided to use that time to relax and read. After pouring a glass of iced-tea, and settling into the recliner, her eyes were immediately drawn to the empty spot on the shelf where their family picture had sat since they moved in—the last one taken before David had died. She was sure it had been there the previous night, as she always said goodnight to it before heading up to bed. *Where in the world is that picture?* She asked herself, as she stood and walked over to the shelving unit.

Maybe it fell. She looked beside and behind it—nothing.

Returning to her chair, she thought, "*Huh. I wonder what happened to that picture? Did I move it? I don't remember moving it. Maybe one of the kids moved it, or took it to their room. I'll have to ask when they get home.*

Scanning through her "Better Homes and Gardens" magazine, she was captivated by the beauty of the homes and decorations presented. Looking around the room, she thought, *Someday, this house will look that beautiful.*

She had to admit that they were all in better spirits this year than the previous one, following David's death. When the kids had helped put up the tree and a few holiday decorations the weekend before, they had laughed, shared stories of previous Christmases, and cleaned up without complaining. Sighing, she thought, *Maybe next year we'll start with another clean slate. Hopefully, we're all past the worst of the grieving process.*

Continuing on that train of thought, she surmised it wasn't just David's passing that had upset their lives. In the past year, they had moved from Michigan to Texas—which she hated to admit had been stressful on all of them. The children not only left the only home they knew—plus all their friends and family—they had to adjust to the strange climate and dialect of Texas. Even though there had been a few incidences of screaming, tears, threats and throwing things over the issue of moving, she had stood firm and had ultimately won because—well—she was the parent. Only time would tell if she had made the right choice for her family.

Feeling guilty about subjecting her children to the emotional trauma of moving, she was more distressed at having inadvertently put them and herself in harms way.

I think any one of those events would put a damper on anyone's spirits. Maybe, eventually, the old Christmas spirit would return. Next year, I'll make a better effort at getting everyone in a festive mood. Right now, I'll just appreciate the small steps in the right direction.

She laid her head back and closed her eyes and soon was asleep, but was jolted awake by a frightening dream: *it was dark and someone was in her house.* Opening her eyes, she was relieved to find it still daylight. The dream had seemed so real. *Was it a warning? A premonition? Or just a subconscious fear being played out in her mind? Geez, I hope it's just a bad dream!*

Glancing at the wall clock, and realizing her children would be arriving soon, she pulled herself out of the chair, and headed to the kitchen hoping to find something for dinner. Opening first the pantry, then the refrigerator, she felt like Old Mother Hubbard discovering her cupboards and refrigerator were bare. A happy thought came to her: *I won't have to worry so much about grocery bills anymore. That extra cash will come in handy when stocking up for my three growing children.*

Running up the driveway and into the house at a speedy clip, Nicky ran past his mother on a quest to find his beloved pet. Benji, upon hearing his young master, headed towards the kitchen as fast as his little beagle legs would carry him. He and Nicky met in the hallway. Christina, hearing a loud crash, a dog's yelp and a boy's yell, ran in to see what had happened, stopping short and gasping at the sight before her. Nicky, trying to stop, slipped on the rug which caused him to catapult over the dog, who had slid into the rug, causing him to become entangled in it. Nicky, trying to stop his descent, grabbed at the coat rack, which fell, unloading it's winter garb on his head.

Once she determined that both parties were uninjured, she covered her mouth and stifled a giggle. She was joined by Brad and Stacey, who had no problem expressing their feelings. Brad, wiping laughter tears from his eyes, reached out a hand to his little brother, while Stacey helped untangle the dog, and Christina picked up the coats.

Chuckling, Christina said, "You know, Nicky, you could have just asked me how Benji was."

Nicky rolled his eyes. "Yeah, and miss all this?" Squatting, he pulled Benji onto his lap. "Well, he does look and act better. I guess it was just a weird bug or something."

Christina reached down and tousled his hair. "Hey, that reminds me, did you give Benji any treats yesterday?"

"No."

She looked at Stacey and Brad who shook their heads.

Standing and brushing the dog fur off his pants, Nicky asked, "Why are you asking?"

"When he came in last night, he had a dog cookie in his mouth. It didn't look like the brand we normally get. I tried to get it, but he gobbled it up."

"Hmm." Nicky said, scrunching his face in thought. "I don't know where he could have gotten it. We ran out of treats a couple of days ago. Unless, he had it buried."

Christina shrugged. "Well, if it had been buried, no telling how long it was in the ground. The bacteria from the ground could have made him sick. Guess we'll have to keep a closer watch on what he's doing outside."

Stacey said, "Mom, I saw the neighbor kids behind us throw a chicken bone over the fence once. Thank goodness, I was outside and got to it before Benji. I told them that dogs can't have chicken bones, and asked them to not give him any more. They promised they wouldn't, but they may have given him a dog cookie."

Christina nodded. "Now that's a possibility. I don't know those neighbors, so I'm not sure I want to confront them." Sighing, she said, "Like I said before, let's all keep a better watch on what he eats."

Sitting around the dinner table, she brought up the subject of the missing picture and frame.

Each child denied knowing its whereabouts.

After eating, Christina received a call from Cindy, and leaving the kids to finish cleaning up the dinner dishes, she went upstairs to chat.

"Hey girlfriend!" Cindy said in her usual, exuberant manner.

"Hey yourself."

"I just talked to Ed, and he said he saw you today, but he wouldn't tell me where or why. He said that I needed to talk to you. So....what's up? Are you meeting my man on some covert rendezvous?"

Christina giggled. "Hang on." She stuck her head out the bedroom door and listened, satisfied with the sound of her three kids in the kitchen.

"Alright. I just had to make sure the kids weren't in hearing distance."

"Ooh, sounds like this may be intriguing!"

Christina giggled again. "Well, it kinda is."

She re-capped her conversation with the lawyer and Ed's partners, and the fact that they were treating David's death as a murder.

"What? David was murdered? How? Why?"

"Those were my questions too. They seem to think because of David's involvement with the ATO, he was targeted."

"Wait. Who is 'they'?"

"The anti-terrorist-organization, and I guess other government officials."

"So what does all this mean? Are you and the kids gonna be safe?"

"Ed's boss, Henry Steil, said the children and I are in no danger, now that David has been eliminated." Inhaling sharply, Christina added, "Wow, that sounds so awful!"

"Yeah it does, but at least you and the kids will be alright."

"It's bad enough I'm still getting threatening notes from someone."

"Wait. What threatening notes?"

"I haven't told you about the latest ones, have I?"

"Well, no. I only know about the Thanksgiving Day one. There's more?"

Christina sighed. "Yeah. I found a note and an empty heparin bottle in my locker at work last week and another threatening text yesterday."

"Oh, Honey! How come you didn't tell me before now?"

"I kept meaning to, but every time I'd think about calling, something would come up. Besides, Larry thinks that whoever is doing this is just trying to rattle my cage."

"What do you think? Or feel? Do the kids know?"

"Right now I'm just frustrated, 'cause I don't know whether to take this seriously, or just treat it as idle threats. If I think about it for too long, I get really angry. How dare someone treat us, or me, like that!" Blowing air out through her teeth, she continued, "Stacey and Nicky know about the Thanksgiving one, but only Brad knows about the other ones."

"Man, that stinks!"

"You think?"

"Well, if it's any consolation, Ed and I will keep our eyes and ears open. Someone, somewhere, knows something. It's just a matter of time before the truth comes out."

Christina sighed. "Yeah. We can hope whoever it is will grow tired of this nonsense and quit." Pausing a beat, she said, "On a lighter note, I do have some exciting news!"

"What would that be, and does it involve a handsome cardiologist?"

"First off, it doesn't involve Steven. Secondly, it does involve the government."

"Okay, now you've got me really intrigued."

"The lawyer handed me a check for a huge amount of money, saying it was kind of a compensation for David's service to his country."

"Huh? You mean his working for the ATO?"

"Yep. Because he was killed in the line of duty, so to speak, the government decided to pay the kids and I a compensation fee."

"Do you mind if I ask how much?"

"I'll tell you, as long as you promise not to tell anyone...especially Samara."

"Well, yeah. Okay. Why not Samara?"

"I'm not telling the kids about the money. I think it would confuse them and change them somehow. They could become greedy or prideful, and I don't want that."

"So if Samara knows, she might accidentally let it slip. Okay."

"Are you sitting?"

Cindy mumbled, "Yep."

"Fifty thousand a year for as long as I'm alive!"

"What? Get out of town! Seriously?"

"I'm not kidding! I was just as shocked as you."

Christina went on to explain her plans for the money.

When she finished, Cindy blew out air between her teeth. "Whew! Well I hope you don't forget about us poor folk."

"Oh, Cindy. If I ever get uppity, you have my permission to just shoot me!"

"If you *do* get uppity, I *will* shoot you, permission or not!"

Their conversation was interrupted by Nicky's voice calling up the stairs. "Mom?"

"I'll talk to you tomorrow, Cindy. Love you!" Closing the phone, she called down the stairs, "Yes, Nicky. I'm in my room."

Instead of coming upstairs, he called from the bottom step, "Stacey wants to know if you want to play a game of CLUE with us?"

She opened the door and stepped into the hallway.

"Sure. I'll be down in a minute. Go ahead and set it up."

CHAPTER 26

Rolling over and slamming her fist onto the alarm button, Christina peeled one eye open, and realized her room was pitch black. Her heart did a triple beat. *Why is it so dark?* She had been afraid of the dark for as long as she could remember and always slept with a nightlight. Sitting up, she looked at the clock, concerned they may have lost power—but then realized her alarm wouldn't have gone off if they had. *The night light must have burned out,* she surmised. Benji, hearing his mistress stir, stood, stretched, shook himself and yawned—completely unfazed by the darkness.

Christina stood, and flicked on the ceiling light switch.

"Ow! That's too bright!" She quickly turned it off and was plunged into total darkness again. Turning towards the bed, she stubbed her right pinkie toe on the bed leg, and let out an expletive. Reaching out, she knocked the alarm clock off the nightstand and yelped as it landed on her already throbbing toe. A couple more expletives escaped from her lips, before she finally found the lamp and clicked it on.

"Ah, that's better!"

Sitting on the side of the bed, she pulled her foot up to take a look at her abused toe. It was beginning to turn purple.

"Ah geez! I hope I didn't break it!" Sighing, she stood and told Benji, "Guess I'd better go get an ice-pack and a light bulb. Come on boy, I might as well let you out too."

Wagging his tail, he was more than happy to accompany her to the great outdoors—after she stopped at the freezer for an ice-pack, and turned on the coffee maker. Standing on the patio in her white velour robe, she had received from David the Christmas before he passed, and her fuzzy pink slippers, she felt a chill as she realized the moisture coming down was freezing as it hit the pecan tree branches.

Speaking her thoughts to God or any angelic being who may have some kind of weather changing power, she said, "Well, shoot! I'd sure appreciate it, if you'd make this pass before tomorrow. I don't want David's parents to be delayed because of bad weather!" Pulling her robe tighter around her neck, she called for Benji.

As she opened the door, he paused and shook himself, leaving wet, icy droplets all over the bottom half of her robe and the tops of her slippers.

Shaking her head, she mumbled, "Thanks, Benji."

After wiping down the wet dog, and her clothing, with a bath towel, she headed to the kitchen for a nice steamy cup of coffee.

Entering the kitchen, she slipped and landed on her bottom, in a puddle of brown liquid.

"Really?" She said, as she watched the brown liquid pour from the bottom of the coffee-maker onto the floor and realized she was actually happy it was coffee and not something worse—like backed up sewage.

Trying to rise, her slipper caught in the hem of her robe and she fell to her knees, thus soaking more of the liquid into her white fluffy robe, turning it a nice shade of tan.

Laughing, she sat on the floor and watched as the remaining few drops drained from the coffee-maker. Stripping off the robe and slippers, she stood and went to the counter to see what had caused the coffee mishap. There was a large crack in the glass carafe.

Dropping the carafe into the recycle can, she said, "Well, that explains that."

Looking up to the ceiling, sighing, and shaking her head, she said, "Okay, God, you've had your laugh. Can we *please* have no more surprises?" Not hearing a reply, she shook her head. "Not answering, huh? I'm gonna take that as a 'maybe'." She bent down and picked up her soaked, coffee-stained robe and her slippers. Chuckling, she said, "Well, Benji, I'd best go put these in the washer or I'll have a tan robe instead of a white one."

He wagged his tail in agreement. On her way out of the laundry room, she grabbed a basket of clean towels.

As she was placing the towels in the linen closet, in the upstairs hallway, Brad came out of the bathroom.

"Mornin' Mom." He said on his way back to his room.

"Hey Brad. It's raining ice outside."

"Raining ice?"

"I mean, it's raining and turning to ice."

"Oh. Sleeting. You think we'll have school?"

"I didn't think about that. Can you call or text someone to find out?"

"Sure, or I can check the school's website. It'll have information there."

"The school has a website?" Christina asked, placing the last towel on the shelf.

"Yeah. They just implemented it this year. Neat, huh?"

"Yeah. That's good. Should make things easier."

Brad shrugged, "I suppose. I don't have to make a bunch of phone calls to find out what's happening."

Christina nodded. "I wish we had something like that when I was in school. I really like this new technology."

Brad nodded and smiled, "Yeah, me too."

A few minutes later, Brad knocked on her bedroom door.

"Mom?"

"Yeah. Just a minute." She pulled on her scrub pants and top. Opening the door, she said, "So, what's the word?"

Grinning, he said, "No school!"

Nodding, she said, "Well, okay. I still have to get into work, however, so I guess you're in charge of things around here 'till I get home."

Hearing Stacey and Nicky's alarms go off simultaneously, she said, "I'll tell Stacey, and you tell Nicky. Maybe y'all can sleep in a while."

CHAPTER 27

Slip-sliding out to her van, which was parked—thank goodness—in the garage, and almost landing on her bum twice, she crawled onto the driver's seat, blowing out the air she had held captive during her little jaunt. Putting on her seat-belt, she said a quick prayer of protection as she backed out of the driveway onto the icy street. Not a soul was in sight. Usually there were people out jogging, walking dogs or heading off to work, or places unknown. But this morning, she had the road all to herself. Turning on the wipers, she was irritated at how ineffective they were at removing the quickly forming ice. She pushed the defrost button and the window washer fluid button and was relieved when the ice began sliding off to the sides with the wipers.

As she turned the corner to the next street, she almost slid into a van that couldn't seem to stop, thus sliding right through the stop sign. Glancing in her rear-view mirror to make sure the van and driver were safely through the intersection, she proceeded on to her destination. She couldn't help but chuckle as she watched the inexperienced drivers swerve and spin, barely missing her van and other adventuresome vehicles, as she made her way to the hospital. She had to completely stop as one vehicle did a one-eighty and ended up facing her. After a few tense seconds, the driver was able to turn his car in the right direction, and ever so slowly proceed to the next street.

In Michigan, this kind of weather was expected and prepared for, but here, in Texas? The *best* thing to do, was wait it out in the comfort of ones' home—unless of course you had to go to work.

Pulling into the hospital parking lot, she glanced at the dashboard clock. A trip that normally took her five to ten minutes at the most, took almost a half-hour. *Good thing I left early*, she thought, as she carefully stepped from the van. *It'd be my luck to slip and fall and slide under the van, unable to crawl out. I can read* the headlines now: Woman found frozen under her van in hospital parking lot.

Chuckling as she entered the front door, she was surprised when she bumped into Janet who was bending over wiping the slush from her shoes. Christina reached out and grabbed Janet's coat before she took a nose-dive.

"Janet! I'm sorry! I wasn't paying attention to where I was going."

Janet stood, straightening her clothing. Frowning and giving Christina a look that could freeze an inferno, she said, "Obviously."

As both women headed to the elevator, Christina said, "Nasty weather, huh?"

Janet nodded. "Yeah. Thought I'd never make it here in one piece."

Christina chuckled. "Yeah, me either. One car in front of me spun completely around and another van slid right through a stop sign."

"I slid through a couple of intersections myself. Good thing there aren't very many people out."

Christina nodded. Pushing the number three button on the wall, she asked, "So where are you working today?"

"I'll be on the CCU with you."

"Really? Did someone call in?"

Looking straight ahead to avoid eye contact, Janet frowned and said, "Hannah Isbell, the aide, called in sick this morning, and, of course, Mrs. Ferguson called me. So, here I am."

Nodding, Christina said, "Well good. There were only three patients on Monday when I left, so unless there were more admittances, it will be a relatively peaceful day."

Janet rubbed her forehead, and said, "I could use peaceful."

"Me too." Christina said, thinking, *Especially after this morning.*

Sitting in the viewing room, David, Christina's deceased, but spiritually alive husband, smiled as he watched his wife's morning play out. It had indeed been a trying one. He chuckled as Christina's angel, Michael, walked behind her on the slippery driveway, keeping her upright. She had no idea how many times she had almost fallen. Michael then flew in front of her van as she maneuvered through the sliding and spinning vehicles, pushing vehicles right and left to assure her safe passage. *Poor Michael, he's really getting a workout this morning,* David thought, right before he felt Jarrod's—his own guardian angel—presence.

"Hey, Jarrod."

"Hey, David. How's the family?"

"They're doing okay. Michael sure has been working hard though. There's an ice storm hitting the Dallas area right now."

Nodding, Jarrod said, "Ah yes. I can see that."

Standing next to David he said, "I hate to pull you away, but Father has a job for you to do."

"Do you know what or where?"

Jarrod shook his head. "You will have to speak to Him yourself."

David immediately left Jarrod's presence and was in the presence of God.

Jarrod occupied the seat that his companion had vacated and continued to watch the events of Earth play out. Watching the billions of screens before him, he said, "Silly little humans. I don't know what Father sees in you. You are like blind little ants, running here and there, totally unaware of what is taking place." Looking at the entire room of screens at once, he was aware of the tiny dots of light scattered about. He smiled. "Except for you. You know."

Turning from the screens and heading to the door, he was intercepted by David. "Okay my friend. We have an assignment."

CHAPTER 28

Christina felt strangely tense and apprehensive as she stood next to Janet, listening to Dr. Dawson's assessment and protocol for his three patients. Janet stood with shoulders back, spine straight and lips pursed together. Once they had exited the locker room, listened to the night report, and waited for Dr. Dawson to begin his rounds, Janet had spoken not a word to Christina.

When both women were at the desk, Christina said, "So, Janet. You okay this morning?"

Janet gave her a look that could paralyze a lion. "Yes."

"You seem a bit preoccupied."

"Do I now? Maybe I have a lot on my mind."

Biting her bottom lip, Christina said, "Well, if you want to talk about anything, I'll be around."

Janet nodded, closed the file she had been writing in, and turned to walk down the hall.

Christina thought, *Geez, wonder what's going on with her? She kinda scares me sometimes.*

Sarah approached the desk. "Hey, Christina."

Looking up from the file she was reading, Christina answered, "Hey, Sarah. So glad you're back! How was your date?"

Sarah smiled. Looking around to confirm their privacy, she giggled and said, "It was fabulous!"

Christina patted the chair next to hers. "Come, sit, tell me about it."

"Well, Harold arrived in a black Mercedes, handed me a dozen red roses, and took me to that restaurant at the top of the GM building in downtown Dallas."

Christina put her hand over her heart. "Oh my."

"Yeah." Giggling, Sarah continued, "At first all I could think about was how much this had to cost! He must have sensed that 'cause he said, "Sarah, don't you worry your little head about the price-tag on all this. Trust me. I have plenty of money to take care of it."

Christina said, "Oh my! What does that mean?"

Sarah continued with a far off look in her eyes, "We had steak, wine, and dancing. Oh Christina, I've never felt like such a princess! Even when my husband was alive, we were too poor to do anything like that."

Christina shook her head and exhaled. "I never would have pictured Harold as a romantic."

Sarah giggled. "Me neither! I thought he was just a hay-seed farm boy. You know what he told me?"

Christina shook her head.

"He said he owns three oil wells out in west Texas, and they are all productive. He said his boys and grand-kids will have a nice inheritance when he passes on."

"Where does he live?"

"Oh my, Christina, that's the amazing part! He took me to his house after dinner, which is on the south-side of Dallas in a little farming area named Palmer. He owns a thousand acres of farm land, a dozen horses and about two-hundred cattle. His house reminds me of one of those Spanish Villas they show in the movies. It is gorgeous! My little house could fit in one of his bathrooms! I ended up staying the night in one of his guest rooms which would rival any fine hotel suite! And, to top it all off, he had butlers and maids, and his own personal chef!"

Christina giggled and grabbed Sarah's hands. "Wow, Sarah!. Sounds like you had an awesome weekend. So when's your next date?"

Before she could answer, a cardiac alarm went off in one of the rooms. Glancing at the monitors, Christina saw what all doctors and nurses dread—flat lines. She hit the code-blue button, grabbed the patient's chart, and she and Sarah headed to the room in question. Janet met them at the door with the crash cart.

Christina immediately went into hyper-nurse mode in which all her energy and concentration was directed towards the patient in front of her. She did a quick visual assessment, noting the body position, color of skin, lips and fingertips, and whether there was visual breathing or alertness. The patient before her, a 61 year-old morbidly obese female was showing no signs of life. As Christina listened for heart and breath sounds, Janet prepared the patient and cardiac cart for resuscitation, and Sarah took a blood-pressure and breath count, which were absent. She looked up at Christina and shook her head. No words were spoken until Dr. Dawson and Dr. Meils appeared, then the preliminary reports were given and the women stepped back as the doctors took charge. Dr. Dawson started giving orders and all five of them rolled the woman on her side to insert a board under her chest to make CPR more effective. Because of the woman's size, Dr. Dawson climbed on top of her and began cardiac compressions. Janet administered drugs, as Christina prepared the electric shock paddles. Sarah stood by to hand any needed items to any of the attending medical staff. After almost fifteen minutes of unsuccessful attempts to gain a stable cardiac rhythm, Dr, Dawson, whose shirt was sweat-drenched, finally called the time of death.

Glancing up at the room clock, he said, "Time of death, ten-fifteen." Except for Dr. Dawson's heavy breathing, the room was eerily silent.

Finally, Dr. Meils broke the silence. "Good job, ladies. I just wished we'd had better success." Looking directly at Christina, he said, "Would you please prep the body to transport to the morgue, and I'll notify the family."

Dr. Dawson, taking one last look at his patient as he crawled off and straightened his clothing, whispered, "I'm sorry, Carol. I hope you're dancing with the angels now."

He gave Christina a sad look and left the room.

Janet and Sarah picked up the discarded papers, syringes, medication bottles, and linens on and around the bed and crash cart, while Christina removed IV's, monitor patches, and other various wiring and tubing from the still warm body. All three women carried their tasks out in silence. Preparing someone for the next phase of their journey from life to eternity, was always a solemn, reflective time. Christina's thoughts returned her to her parents and David, Sarah's to her young husband, killed so long ago in Vietnam, and Janet to her mother who had died giving birth to her youngest sister, and that same little sister who died shortly after. Each woman had lost someone dear to them, and each death thereafter brought their thoughts to the inevitability of their own demise. *What really waited on the other side of life? What happens to the people left behind?*

As Christina was sitting at the desk, having just finished all the paperwork for Mrs. Nelson, Janet walked up and let out a lungful of air.

"Well, that was certainly unexpected."

Massaging her temples, Christina said, "Yeah. And so close to Christmas. That poor family."

Janet nodded. "Yeah."

Christina sighed. "Dr. Dawson called a few minutes ago and said to ready the body for transport to the morgue downstairs."

Janet looked confused. "How come? Isn't the family coming?"

"He said he talked to the oldest daughter, and she said because of the weather, there was no way anyone could make it here. They all live in the Dallas area."

Nodding, Janet said, "Okay, I guess that makes sense. I'll go get everything ready."

"Thanks. I'll have the paperwork and chart ready as well."

Once Mrs. Nelson's body was on its way to the morgue, the two nurses sat at the desk, taking a well-deserved coffee break.

Taking a sip, Christina said, "Man, this tastes good!"

Janet smiled—the first one of the day. "Yeah. I needed this."

"Janet?" Christina ventured, "You okay? You seem a little off-kilter today."

Frowning, Janet nodded, and set her coffee cup down. Sighing, she said, "I'm worried about my girl. Seems she's having some trouble at school."

Christina thought, *Oh. It probably has to do with Stacey.*

"I don't mean to be nosy, but what's going on?" Christina asked, taking a sip of coffee.

As Janet opened her mouth to speak, the PA system announced a Code Orange. Both women looked at each other. A Code Orange meant there was a major accident with many injured, and possible casualties. The announcement came again. "Code Orange. Any extra hospital staff is to meet in the ER."

Sarah and Sally Jean came running up to the counter. "What's going on?"

Christina shook her head. "I'm not sure, but I imagine it's a bad car accident. The roads have got to be brutal."

Looking at Sarah and Janet, Christina said, "Sally Jean and I can take care of the two patients up here, why don't you two go down and see if you're needed?"

Sarah nodded. "If I'm not needed, I'll be back up as soon as possible."

"If you do need to stay, don't worry. Fortunately, both patients are stable for now."

Both women headed towards the elevator.

Christina called out, "Hey Sarah, if you get a chance, can you text or call me and let me know what happened?"

"Sure."

Christina called home to check on the kids and give them a list of chores to do. Their grandparents would be arriving tomorrow evening, and she wanted to make sure the house was clean and in order.

She busied herself with chart reading, and chatting with the two cardiac patients on the floor, all the while wondering what was going on downstairs.

I wish Sarah would let me know, she thought, just as the phone buzzed in her pocket.

She read the message: 10 car pile-up on I-35. Many injured. Will be a while.

Oh my goodness, she thought and shot up a prayer for all the people involved.

Sally Jean approached the counter. "Heard anything from Sarah?"

"Yeah, I just got a text. She said there was a ten car pile-up on I-35. She may be a while."

Sally Jean put her hand up to her mouth. "Oh my goodness! I hope no one died. That would be horrible, right before Christmas and all."

Christina nodded. "Yes, indeed it would be."

When three-o'clock rolled around and still no sign of Sarah or Janet, Christina sent a text to each lady: "Shift change soon. Will come down to ER to see if I can help. She received an "Okay." from Sarah.

Once the evening shift was appraised of the patient's conditions, and the situation in the ER, Christina left to offer her assistance.

When the elevator door opened onto the first floor, Christina gasped. There were people everywhere, standing, sitting, lying, milling about. She looked around for someone who seemed to be in charge and headed in that direction.

"Excuse me. I'm Christina Sanders, an RN from the CCU, is there anything I can do to help?"

The woman, who's name-tag read Gina Anderson, RN, handed her a pen and clipboard with paperwork on it.

"Here. Please go find these people and have them sign this paperwork."

Christina flipped through the papers and found there to be a dozen or so needing signatures. She walked the hallway and waiting room, calling names until she found each one.

Realizing she was going to be quite late returning home, she called Brad and explained the situation.

"Stay as long as you need, Mom. I've got everything under control here. I'm heating up pizza and Stacey made a salad. We'll save some for you."

She smiled and sighed. "Thanks, babe. I'll be home as soon as I can."

Returning the phone to her pocket, she heard her name being called.

She turned and saw Sarah approaching.

"Christina, I'm so glad you made it down here. What a mess, huh?"

Blowing out air, Christina said, "Yeah. I guess I didn't know what to expect." Waving her hand, she added, "Certainly not this."

"Yeah. I don't think we've ever had anything as bad as this."

Returning the clipboard to the nurse in charge, Christina asked, "Any casualties?"

"Unfortunately, yes. An elderly couple. Their car ended up between two semis. They were killed instantly. Then there was a car full of young people on their way home from college. The driver, a girl, died, and the other three are in critical condition. Their little car ended up under one of the trucks."

Christina shook her head. "Oh those poor parents! I can't even imagine how devastated they are."

"The sad thing is, they are from Sherman, north of Dallas, and can't even get here until this storm subsides. Maybe tomorrow."

Christina felt tears sting her eyes as she tried to imagine how she would feel if she were in that situation.

Once the injured people had been evaluated, the families informed, and tensions eased, Christina, Sarah, and Janet left the ER. They rode up in the elevator together to the CCU to retrieve their personal belongings before heading home.

Sarah said, "Wow! That was awful. In all my years working here, I can only recall one other incident that was similar to that."

"When was that?" Christina asked.

"About thirty years ago, a tornado went through an area north of town. Wiped out all fifty mobile homes close by, and a couple of farms lost barns and buildings as well. There were a lot of injuries and a few casualties. It was a terrible time for this town, but everyone pitched in and helped those poor, unfortunate people."

Stepping out of the elevator first, Christina said, "I remember Mom and Dad talking about that. They said their church helped house some of those folks, until they found other living arrangements. I was just a little girl, when it happened."

Sarah continued, "It was quite a mess for a while. Debris was scattered for miles. But even among all that tragedy, there were stories of miracles. One little baby, who had been ripped out of his mother's arms, ended up in a field a mile away, uninjured."

The three women entered the nurse's lounge and headed for their lockers.

Smiling and nodding as she opened her locker, Christina said, "Wow! That *is* a miracle."

Turning the knob on the door, Sarah said, "Another family, who's dog had been taken, found it's way back home a few days later. Even though several pets were never recovered, there were many who returned home."

Putting her purse over her shoulder, Christina asked, "You said there were a few casualties. Do you remember anything about them?"

Janet stood in front of her locker, gathering her belongings, listening as the two women conversed.

Frowning, Sarah said, "There was a young woman and her baby who were trying to escape in a pick-up truck, and a couple of young men, and a toddler, but I don't recall if there were others."

Closing the locker door, Christina said, "Tornadoes are weird like that. They can jump around, or carve paths right through an area and not even touch something a few feet away."

Placing her hand over her heart, Sarah said, "I know! I've never experienced one personally, and hope I never do, but fortunately, I have a storm cellar, if there ever is a threat."

Christina said, "Yeah, those are great. It's too bad more folks don't have them, especially since our town is in a tornado alley."

"Do you have a storm cellar?" Sarah asked.

"No, but we have a basement, which is kinda unusual around here."

Closing her locker door and replacing the lock, Sarah said, "Huh. That's interesting. Not very many homes around here have basements. Something about the limestone layer under the dirt."

Janet, who had been silently listening to the conversation finally spoke.

"I was in that tornado, when I was a child."

The other two women, so involved in their conversation, had forgotten Janet was present. They turned to face her.

"Really? Tell us about it." Christina said.

Janet shook her head and practically ran out the door towards the elevator.

"Now my curiosity is piqued," Sarah said, as she too headed for the elevator.

"Yeah, mine too," Christina added as she headed to the nurses' station. "Guess we'll have to wait 'till later to get the rest of the story."

Placing her belongings on the counter, Christina said, "I'm gonna check on things, then I'll be ready if you want to wait and ride back down with me."

"Sure. Okay. Take your time. I'm not in any hurry." Reaching the elevator soon after the door had closed, Sarah reached out and punched the call button. Sarah thought about Janet's behavior. *She's a strange one,* she concluded.

Janet wiped her eyes as she entered the elevator. *I hadn't thought about that tornado in years!* As she rode the three floors down, she recalled the event as if it had happened yesterday.

She had been around twelve-years-old when she, her brothers, and little sister were in the field, helping their daddy pick cotton. They had been so involved, that when a storm blew in, they were taken by surprise. They barely had time to grab the bags, load them in the truck and head back to the safety of the ranch.

She grabbed her two-year old sister as everyone else exited the truck and ran towards the open door of the cellar, which was only a few feet away. One of the ranch hands was shouting something, and she turned to look behind her in time to see the truck being lifted off the ground and spun around. She felt something hit her head, and as she fell, her sister landed a few feet away and ran towards her daddy. A day later, after waking up in the hospital, Janet learned that the little girl had been picked up and swept away in the tornado on her way to the cellar. Janet's daddy had run out and pulled Janet to safety just seconds after the toddler had been swept away. Her brothers told her later that he had held her and sobbed, afraid he would lose her as well.

The hurt and devastation in her father's eyes after that made her wish time and again that she had been taken instead of her sister. The child's body was recovered the next day in a field about two miles from the ranch. Janet remembered wondering, as she stood over the casket, how she could possibly be dead when there wasn't a mark on her little body.

CHAPTER 29

Thursday morning, the people of Alva were blessed with a clear blue sky, and warmer temperature. There was enough ice left on the trees and bushes however, to give off diamond-like reflections in the morning sun.

When Christina let Benji out for his morning routine, she was awestruck by the magnificent beauty, and wanted to share it with the kids, and as they entered the kitchen, she immediately sent them outside. Their "oohs, and ahhs" made her smile.

Being their last day of school for two weeks, and the fact that their grandparents would be there in the afternoon, the kids were in a state of excitement—talking and laughing and asking questions.

Christina interrupted their chatter by asking if each one had their room in order, and if the upstairs bathroom was cleaned. When they all nodded, she mentally checked those items off her list.

Looking at the clock, Christina said, "Y'all need to get a move on. I'll drop you off this morning, because I need to go to the grocery store and do a couple of errands." Grabbing her purse and van keys, she added, "The weather man said it would be nice this afternoon. Y'all want to walk home?"

Brad said, "Sure. I'll go by and get Stacey and Nicky."

Looking at his siblings, he said, "Y'all wait for me."

They nodded.

Christina said, "You know what? Benji and I will walk down to the elementary school and get Nicky, and you and Stacey can just come on home. I could use the exercise, and I know Benji would love it."

Chewing his last piece of toast, Brad said, "Okay. So Stacey, just wait on the front steps and I'll come by."

She nodded. "I'll be there."

Nicky asked, "So where do you want me to meet you, Mom?"

"I'll meet you at the front entrance."

He smiled and nodded. "Danny will probably be with me, too."

"That's fine."

Clapping her hands together, Christina said, "Okay, y'all go finish up and let's get out of here in about half and hour."

It's gonna be a good day, she thought, as she put the dishes in the dishwasher.

CHAPTER 30

After dropping the kids off, and picking up a few items from the grocery store, Christina decided to stop at Mary's Clothes Garden to see Cindy, and check out the pre-Christmas sale items.

When she entered the shop, Cindy let out a squeal of excitement and rushed over to give her friend a hug, catching Christina off guard and almost knocking her down.

"I didn't know you were coming by!" She said excitedly.

Re-arranging her sweater that had gotten bunched up in the hug, Christina chuckled and said, "I didn't either, until a minute ago, when the van just magically pulled into a parking space in front of the store."

Cindy giggled. "Well, I'm glad it did."

Noticing the outfit Cindy was wearing, Christina said, "Cindy, you look like a Christmas elf!"

Cindy twirled. "I do, don't I? You like my twinkling necklace and earrings?"

Making an 'I don't believe it' face, Christina said, "On purpose?"

Cindy rolled her eyes. "Well, yeah. It *is* almost Christmas, and I wanted to get into the spirit of things."

Christina nodded. "Well, that certainly is spirited. So where are the wonderful sale items you were telling me about?"

Cindy grabbed her friend's hand and pulled her to the sale racks at the back of the store.

While looking through the items, Christina asked, "So, did you have a chance to talk to Ed? Are y'all planning to come over Christmas day?"

Cindy nodded. "Yep. We're looking forward to it. We got some of the neatest gifts for the kids!"

"You don't have to come with gifts."

Cindy gave her a look. "Why not? It *is* Christmas after all."

"Yeah, but I don't want you to feel obligated."

Cindy put her hands on her hips. "Christina! Obligated? Really? Did you forget who you're talking to?"

Christina shook her head and shrugged. "Sorry. I just know that money is tight and…"

Cindy shook her head. "Thanks for your concern, but it's okay. I have a special Christmas account that I've been putting into all year. I have more than enough to buy a few extra gifts."

Christina nodded. Pulling a bright red sequined dress with a plunging neckline, and a barely-over-the-bottom hemline off the hanger, she held it up to herself and asked, "Me?"

Cindy burst out laughing, "Actually, I was thinking of getting that one for myself."

Christina gave her a look that said, *"Really?"* Shaking her head, she returned the dress to the rack, thinking, *It wouldn't surprise me to see Cindy in a dress like that. If I tried to pull it off….well, the word indecent comes to mind. Cindy, however, could make it look amazing.*

"So how are you and Ed doing these days?" Christina asked as she perused the sale rack.

Pulling a few outfits off the racks and holding them up for Christina's appraisal, Cindy answered, "We're doing really well. He calls every evening and we re-cap our days."

"How does Samara feel about him?"

"She thinks he's awesome. She told me the other day that she would *love* to have a boyfriend like Ed. Her words were, 'He's so hot, and so totally nice.'"

Smiling, Christina said,. "Well, she's right on both accounts."

Cindy giggled. "I know! Right?"

Taking a few outfits into the changing room, Christina continued conversing with Cindy about the upcoming weekend. She would try on an outfit, then step out to get Cindy's opinion.

"So, my in-laws will be here this evening, sometime."

Cindy, nodding her approval of the pant-suit that Christina had on, asked, "Is it awkward having them around without David?"

Shaking her head, Christina answered, "Not really. I guess because they've been such an integral part of our lives, I can't even imagine life without them."

"If you and Steven end up together, do you think that would be a problem for them?"

"I have thought about that, and I don't think it would be a problem. But I'm not gonna cross that bridge 'till I get there."

Cindy smiled. "So, are you and Steven getting serious?"

Christina smiled and shook her head. "Maybe. Still too early to tell."

As Christina went back in the dressing room, Cindy said, "If Ed asked me to marry him tomorrow, I'd definitely say yes."

Wearing a cute little black dress, Christina said, "I think that would be awesome! You deserve a good man like Ed."

Cindy gasped. "I love that dress on you! You have got to get that!" Looking at the price-tag, she added, "With my twenty-per-cent discount, this would only cost you twenty-five dollars! And yes, I do deserve a guy like Ed. I've been waiting my whole life for someone like him."

Christina smiled. "I could use a little black dress and it *does* look good on me. I will get it. My Christmas gift to me!"

While returning the rejected items to the racks, Cindy asked, "So, any more threatening notes?"

Christina shook her head. "No, thank goodness. Wouldn't it be nice if they stopped all together?"

"Yeah, it would." Looking around the store and seeing no one else, Cindy asked, "You got a few minutes for a cup of coffee?"

Glancing at her watch, Christina said, "Sure. I have a little time before I have to get home and finish getting the house in order. I also told Nicky I'd meet him after school and we'd walk home together."

As they sipped their coffees, Christina told her friend about the previous day's events.

Cindy couldn't help but laugh as Christina recalled her mornings trials. "I've had mornings similar to that, but nothing as bad as yours!"

Shaking her head, Christina said, "When I'm in the middle of it, I get so frustrated and angry, but once it's over, I can usually laugh about it. Which reminds me, I need to stop at the hardware store and get a new carafe. I had to drink instant coffee this morning." Making a face, she continued. "Yuck! I ended up pouring it out. I don't want to go another day, without my coffee."

Cindy nodded and said, "Yeah. I can't imagine starting a day without coffee!" Setting her empty cup on the table, she said, "I heard about that accident out on I35. It was pretty bad, huh?"

Christina sighed, "Yeah. An elderly couple and a college-age girl died. It breaks my heart to think how devastated the families are...so close to Christmas and all."

"Yeah. That is sad."

As Christina was leaving the store, Cindy called out, "Hey, Ed and I will be at the plays and band concert. Wouldn't want to miss any of them."

"Thanks, Cindy. I'll save you seats."

CHAPTER 31

Unloading the groceries, and carrying them into the kitchen, Christina had an unsettling feeling—like something just wasn't right. *Is someone in the house? Am I being paranoid?* Looking down at Benji, who didn't seem the least bit anxious, she chalked her feelings up to pre-holiday jitters. *Surely, Benji would let me know if someone is in the house...wouldn't he?*

Looking through his binoculars, from his perfectly concealed hiding place, Jamie watched as the Sanders family left for the day.

During one of his jaunts around the neighborhood, he had noticed the pecan tree and the partially built fort within its branches behind Christina's house. Taking a chance that no one was watching, he had climbed up and sat in the fort for quite some time watching people around the neighborhood tending to their business. It had given him a feeling of power—like he could decide their fate if he wanted to. If he had a gun or bow and arrow, and was so inclined, he could pick them off, one by one. But he didn't have those weapons, and wasn't interested in doing something like that anyway. He didn't even like to go hunting, which angered his dad, who enjoyed killing things.

He had decided the previous night to return the photograph he had taken on the last heist. It just didn't feel right to have it, especially since he had broken one of his own rules about taking items that had special meaning. *Besides,* he reasoned, *it would be a nice thing to do before Christmas.* His dad had always told him, "What goes around, comes around," and he didn't want any bad Karma coming his way.

That morning, after deciding to skip school—like his dad would know or care anyway—he had ridden his bike over to the alley behind the Sander's house, climbed up, and perched himself in the tree.

Once the Sanders family left, he let himself in the back door. Benji barked a few times, but all he had to do was scratch the dog behind the ears, and give him a cookie, reminding the animal that he was indeed a friend.

After replacing the picture frame, he walked through the empty house, wishing he could live there, instead of the shack he shared with his dad. After exploring, and picking up another item, he returned to his post to watch for Mrs. Sanders.

Realizing she wasn't returning right away, and beginning to feel the bite of the cold air through his jeans, he decided he might as well go back home.

He couldn't see Christina's reaction when she found the returned picture anyway––which he would have loved to witness—so he had no reason to stay. Maybe someday, he'd be able to afford video equipment to put it in the houses, so he could see how the folks reacted to his little games.

The feeling of unease continued as Christina put the groceries away. She felt anxious as she took a step down the basement stairs, to the laundry room, to get clothes out of the dryer, and froze on the first step.

What is going on? She wondered, as her hands shook and her heart raced. *Is someone in the basement?* She set the laundry basket down and went back to the kitchen. She had a mental argument with herself about what she should do. Her emotional side wanted to call someone—the sheriff—to come take a look. The rational side just said to suck it up and go downstairs. She gave in to her emotional side.

After asking to speak to the Sheriff, he came on the phone line.

"Sheriff Clifton."

"Hey, Larry, this is Christina Sanders."

"Hey, yourself. What can I do for you?"

"Well, I know this sounds silly, but considering what we've been through lately, and the continuing threats, I was wondering if you could come by. I'm feeling quite anxious, like maybe someone is in the house or has been. It's probably nothing, and my imagination is running wild, but I just can't shake this feeling."

"Are you by yourself?"

"Yes."

"Why don't you go sit in your van until I get there? Make sure you lock the doors."

She nodded, and said, "Okay."

"I'll be there in about five minutes."

"Good. Like I said, it's probably nothing."

Gathering his keys and donning his hat, he said, "It may be, but it doesn't hurt to err on the side of caution. Besides, I could use a break."

"Thanks, Larry." She said, as she grabbed her van keys, and called for Benji to follow.

True to his word, he arrived within five minutes. She met him at the back door.

"Could you check in the basement first?"

He nodded and walked cautiously down the stairs, keeping his right hand on the butt of his gun. Christina stood at the top of the stairs.

After a few minutes, he returned. Shaking his head and shrugging, he said, "No one down there. Nothing seems to be out of place either."

Christina breathed a sigh of relief. "I just couldn't bring myself to go down there."

He nodded and smiled. "Well, I'd rather you be safe than sorry."

She nodded.

"How about I check out the rest of the house?"

"Okay." Biting her thumbnail as she followed him through the kitchen, she asked, "Have you ever felt like something just wasn't right?"

"Yeah. A few times. I never underestimate those gut feelings, because most of the time, they *are* correct."

When they entered the family room, Christina inhaled sharply.

"What?" Larry asked, looking around for an intruder.

Again, Larry asked, "What?" as he watched her walk over and pick up a picture frame from the bookshelf.

Holding it out for him to see, she said, "This picture wasn't here this morning. I thought it was missing. How did it get here?"

"Maybe one of the kids moved it?"

She chewed her bottom lip considering that explanation.

"I don't think so. I asked them about it when it went missing a week or so ago, and none of them knew anything about it. Makes me wonder how it ended up here."

"Well, when the kids get home ask them about it. If they don't know, then maybe we should consider the possibility of someone else messing with your stuff."

She nodded in agreement. "It's probably nothing. Just my paranoia surfacing."

After checking the rest of the house, and finding nothing amiss, Larry left and Christina returned to her chores. She only had a few hours to get the house in order, so she could truly enjoy her in-laws visit without having to worry about cleaning.

CHAPTER 32

As Brad walked up the sidewalk to the middle-school building, he spotted Stacey and Carmen sitting on the steps. Carmen had her arm around Stacey's shoulder, and it looked as if Stacey was crying.

Approaching cautiously, he called out, "Hey girls!"

The girls stood and Stacey wiped her eyes.

"Hey, Brad." Carmen said as she adjusted her back pack.

Looking at Stacey, he asked, "What's wrong Stacey?"

She shook her head. "Nothing, really."

He frowned and looked at Carmen who shrugged and said, "She and Linda got in a fight."

Looking at Stacey, he said, "We can talk on the way home."

She nodded and reached out to give Carmen a hug.

"I'll see you tomorrow afternoon."

"Yep. What time are we supposed to be here?"

"Four. The play starts at six."

Carmen giggled. "I'm so excited and nervous. This is the first play I've ever been in."

Stacey smiled. "You'll do great!"

The girls hugged once more, and said their good-byes.

Walking side by side, Stacey told Brad about the confrontation with Linda.

"I don't know what's gotten into her. She's certainly not the Linda I used to know."

Brad nodded. "Yeah, sounds like, since she got those Tarot cards, she has turned quite bratty."

Looking up at her brother with tear-rimmed eyes, she said, "I miss the old Linda. I mean, I'm glad she's come out of her shell and made new friends and all, but I just hate her snarky attitude. She acts like I'm her enemy, and she hates me now. I don't get it!"

Brad put an arm around his sister's shoulder. "I know. Hopefully, she'll come around and realize what a great friend you are, and will want to start over."

Stacey nodded. "Yeah, maybe. If not, I guess I'll just have to let her go and focus on Carmen and other friends."

"Well, at least you have Carmen to turn to."

Sighing, Stacey nodded.

CHAPTER 33

After locking the back and side doors to the house, Christina put Benji's leash on, and headed out the front door, closing and locking it as well. *I hardly ever had to lock my doors, when I lived in Michigan. Of course, I lived in the country and no one was threatening us,* she thought, as she looked back at the two-story Tudor-style house.

Benji, being so excited about going for a walk, pulled on his leash hard enough to make himself choke and cough. After a couple of times, he finally gave in and walked beside Christina, sniffing and peeing on every tree and bush along the way. By the time they reached the school, his bladder was empty, and although he continued hiking his leg, not one drop could be squeezed out. Christina chuckled.

As she approached the school, Nicky and Danny jumped up from the front steps, where they had been sitting, and with backpacks bouncing, ran to greet her. Benji was so excited, he disengaged his leash from Christina's hand and ran to meet his young master and friend.

"Benji!" she called, to no avail. He was on a mission. Reaching the boys, he jumped up and slathered each face with doggy kisses. Christina laughed as the boys yelled, squealed, and giggled with delight and disgust.

The group stopped at Danny's house to drop off his backpack and ask permission to stay until dinner.

"Hey, Mom, what time will Grandma and Grandpa be here?" Nicky asked before he and Danny headed upstairs.

Christina sighed, *how many times have I answered that question?* "They said around five, but it may be around six or seven. Depends on the weather, traffic and when their plane took off and landed. Grandma said she'd call when they landed in Dallas."

"Oh. Okay. Are we gonna wait to eat dinner with them?"

"I'd like to."

"I don't know if I can wait that long, 'cause I'm starving!"

Christina chuckled. "You want a snack to tie you over?"

"Sure. What do we have?"

"How about I cut y'all up an apple with peanut-butter?"

Both boys nodded.

As the boys were heading upstairs with their snack plates, Brad and Stacey walked in the door.

"Hey, you two. Want an apple and peanut-butter?" Christina asked as she disposed of the apple cores and rinds from the previous ones.

Walking over to give their mom a hug, they said simultaneously, "Sure!"

"So, how was your day?" She asked as she sliced and slathered the apple pieces with peanut-butter.

Brad said, "Today was pretty much a wasted day. Most of the teachers just let us hang out or play games during class. My algebra teacher gave us this math quiz that had us adding, subtracting, multiplying, and dividing numbers, until we ended up with the same number we started with." Nodding, he added, "It was pretty cool, actually."

Stacey said, "Yeah. My day was pretty much the same." Brad gave her a look that said, "tell Mom about Linda." She shook her head and frowned, as if to say, "not now." He shrugged.

Washing, then wiping her hands on a paper towel, Stacey said, "Mom, Carmen told me that the college girl who was killed the other day in that car accident, was a friend of her sisters. She *had* planned to ride home with them, but Carmen's folks came and got her instead. She could have been killed or hurt! Carmen said her sister is pretty upset about it all."

Pulling her daughter into a hug, Christina said, "Oh, I'm so sorry to hear that. This is a terrible time of year to lose someone."

"Yeah. The funeral is Saturday. Carmen and her family are going, and she asked if I could go too, but I told her my grandparents would be here."

"Do you *want* to go?" Christina asked.

Pulling away from her mother's embrace and shaking her head, Stacey said, "No. Not really. I don't know any of those people and I'd rather be here with Grandma and Grandpa."

"Okay. If you change your mind, I don't think your grandparents would mind."

Shaking her head, Stacey said, "I don't think I'll change my mind."

Nodding, Christina said, "Okay, it's settled."

Swallowing a bite of apple, Brad wiped his mouth and said, "Mom?"

"Yes, Brad."

"My boss asked if I could come in for a couple of hours to stock some shelves." Looking at the clock, he said, "I should be back by six or seven. What time did you say Grandma and Grandpa will be here?"

Sighing, and thinking, *If I have to answer that question one more time, I think I'm gonna lose it!*

She said, "As far as I know, around that time. I haven't heard from them yet."

"It's getting pretty chilly out there. Do you mind if I take the van?"

"No, that's fine. I don't plan to go anywhere else today."

Giving her a hug, he said, "Thanks. I'm gonna change, then I'll be taking off."

"How was your day, Mom?" Stacey asked as she put her plate in the dishwasher.

"Well, it was kinda weird."

"How so?"

"You remember that picture of us that we took the Christmas before your dad died?"

"Yeah."

"Remember I couldn't find it?"

Stacey nodded.

"Well, it's back on the shelf in the family room."

Stacey gave her a shocked look and asked, "How'd it end up there?"

Christina shrugged. "I was hoping you or your brothers might know."

Stacey shook her head. "I haven't got a clue! The last time I saw it was a couple of weeks ago, when I was dusting. Of course, I was so used to seeing it, that I didn't even notice when it went missing."

"Yeah. Funny how our minds work. I'll have to ask your brothers about it."

"Also, remember that vase with flowers that seemed to have vanished? Well, it's back in it's usual place as well."

Stacey nodded. "Wow, that's weird. Maybe the house is haunted and the ghosts are playing hide-and-seek with our stuff."

Christina grimaced. "Well, I don't think that's possible, but it does make me question my sanity."

Not seeming the least bit concerned, Stacey gave her mom a hug and said, "I'm gonna go up and change into my fuzzy jammies."

Christina nodded and said, "I'll get dinner started."

CHAPTER 34

As Brad was backing out of the driveway, Christina's cell phone rang. Her mother-in-law informed her that their plane had just landed. Christina glanced at the clock.

"That's great, Mom. We are so anxious to see y'all."

"Us too, Honey. If all goes as planned, we'll see you in a couple of hours."

"I'll have supper ready." When she disconnected, Christina yelled up the stairs to Stacey and Nicky that their grandparents would be arriving in a couple of hours. She heard affirmative remarks in reply.

While peeling and slicing the potatoes for dinner, she let her mind wander back to the morning's events, and felt her face flush, as feelings of embarrassment washed over her. *Larry must think I'm such a wuss.*

She mentally argued with herself.

Why should I feel embarrassed? What if there had been someone in the house? We're not given intuitive feelings for nothing. Larry didn't seem to mind coming over. Better to be cautious and safe than foolish and dead, right? Dead? Geez, oh Pete! I'm freaking myself out! I'm sure there's a logical explanation for all of this. I just wish I knew it!

Her thoughts were interrupted by two boys running down the stairs.

"Mom?" Nicky called.

"Yes?"

"Is it time for Danny to go home?"

Christina looked at the clock. "I think so. His mom said to send him home before dinner."

Danny spoke up, "Thanks, Mrs. Sanders. Is it okay if I come over tomorrow?"

Christina nodded. "Maybe for a little while. Nicky's grandparents will be here and Stacey's play is tomorrow evening, so we'll be pretty busy in the afternoon."

He nodded, and lightly punched Nicky on the arm. "I'll call you tomorrow."

Nicky walked him to the front door and watched, until he disappeared from view.

Entering the kitchen, he asked, "What are we having for dinner?"

"Beef stew."

"Sounds good. You want me to set the table?"

Christina smiled and nodded. "That'd be great."

"Hey, Nicky?"

"Yeah?" He answered as he gathered the plates from the cupboard.

"Remember that picture of our family that went missing a couple weeks ago?"

"Yeah. The one that was on the shelf in the family room?"

Christina nodded.

Nicky shrugged. "What about it?"

"Well, the strangest thing happened today."

Setting the plates down and returning for the silverware, he asked, "What?"

"I found it back on the bookshelf in the family room. Do you know anything about that?"

Shaking his head, he said, "Nope. Did you ask Stacey and Brad?"

"I asked Stacey and she didn't know anything about it either."

Making a face, he shrugged and said, "Well, that just leaves Brad. If he doesn't know how it got there, then I'm guessing it was aliens."

Christina giggled and shook her head. "You know, that would make sense. They probably sneak in while we're sleeping and re-arrange things."

Nicky nodded. "Yep. Those sneaky aliens!"

Christina thought, *I'd rather it be aliens than ghosts. At least I could see an alien.*

CHAPTER 35

Janet was putting a chicken in the oven when Linda walked in the front door, dropped her backpack on the floor beside the sofa, and, with an audible sigh, plopped down on the sofa.

Janet, wiping her hands on a towel as she approached her daughter, asked, "Why the gloomy face?" *Oh no, not more drama. I don't have time for this nonsense, but I guess I'll have to do my motherly duty and at least pretend to be interested.*

"I hate my life!"

Janet sat and took her daughter's hand in hers, thinking, *so, what thirteen-year-old doesn't hate their life?* "So tell me why you hate your life."

Linda shrugged, let out another large sigh and laid her head on her mom's shoulder.

"I don't know. Nothing in particular, everything in general."

"That's pretty vague. Ya think you could narrow it down a bit?"

Janet felt Linda's shoulders shrug. "I guess. Mostly, I miss Stacey."

Janet felt herself tense. *I thought Stacey Sanders was a thing of the past.* "So are you and Stacey still not talking?" hoping the answer was a resounding 'yes'.

Pulling her legs up into a crossed position and turning to face her mother, she paused before speaking. "I know you don't like Stacey and her family, and it would probably make you happy if I never spoke to her again, but *I* don't want to lose her friendship."

Janet clenched her jaw and thought, *I wish the Sanders family would just go back to Michigan, so we can go back to our normal life.*

Pushing the raven colored hair out of her daughter's face, Janet asked, "What about the new friends you've made?"

Grabbing a pillow and holding it to her chest, Linda said, "*Nobody* can compare to Stacey. Even though I've been mean and said bad things to, and about Stacey, not once has she been mean back. The other girls, however..."

Janet made a "continue" sign with her hand. "The other girls, what?"

"I heard them in the bathroom today. They didn't know I was in one of the stalls, and they were talking about me and calling me names."

"Names? Like what?" Remembering some of the names she had been called as a teen.

"Witch, liar, spoiled brat. Just to name a few." She wiped tears away with her shirt sleeve.

Janet reached out, but Linda scooted further away—not wanting any contact yet.

"Oh, Honey. I'm so sorry. Kids can be so cruel." *I think I know a spell I can cast on those mean little girls!*

"Are you sure Stacey wasn't with them?"

Letting out a frustrated moan, Linda said, "Mom! Weren't you listening? I said those were the girls that have been hanging around me!" Hitting the pillow, she let out a growly sound. "You want me to *hate* Stacey as much as you do, so you're trying to make her out to be mean and cruel!"

Janet put her hands up. "Sorry. I've never said I hated Stacey, and didn't want you to be friends with her." *I've certainly thought it though.* "I was just hoping you'd branch out and find new friends."

Biting her bottom lip, Linda asked, "So, if I make up with Stacey and we become friends again, you'll be okay with that?"

Stifling her anger, and forcing a smile, Janet said, "Sure, Honey. If that makes you happy."

Linda tossed the pillow on the floor, and reached out for a much needed hug.

Patting Linda on the back, Janet said, "Why don't you cut up some potatoes and I'll make a salad."

Taking in a deep breath, Linda asked, "What is that yummy smell?"

"It's roasted chicken with your favorite garlic marinade."

"Thanks, Mom. Just what I needed after such a yucky day." Gathering up her backpack, she said, "I'm gonna change into my pj's and I'll be right in."

Janet nodded. As she cut up the vegetables for the salad, thoughts—mostly unpleasant—coursed through her mind. *Out of all the girls in middle school, why did Linda have to attach herself to Stacey Sanders? It's not like she's all that special. She's rather plain looking and has an average intelligence, and she's not all that popular. What is it that is keeping Linda enamored? Surely there is some kind of spell or potion or something that I can use to dissuade this friendship.* Her train of thought was interrupted when Linda walked in. She'd definitely visit those thoughts later.

"By the way, Mom, the house looks great! I'm so glad you decorated."

Janet smiled and said, "You know how every year I have you make a plaster cast of your hands for the tree?"

Linda nodded, warily. "You're not going to make me do another one are you?"

"Well, I'd like you to do them until you leave home, but this could be the last one, if you want. You're a teenager now, and I doubt your hands will change much after this year."

Linda shrugged. "Okay. I guess one more won't hurt."

Janet reached out and pulled her girl into a hug. "Thanks."

CHAPTER 36

Ellie Sterling rose from her chair and felt a stabbing pain in her sternum. Grabbing her chest, she sat and calmly took inventory of her symptoms. Her heart was racing and occasionally skipping beats, the pain came in waves, and she felt light-headed and nauseous. *Time to call 911,* she heard her inner voice say. The phone was in the kitchen—a good twenty steps away. *Now I wish I had one of those cell-phones,* she thought as she carefully stood. Slowly making her way to the kitchen, and bracing herself against the pain, she mentally made a list of whom she should call: Margaret, her daughter, and Christina Sanders. *Why should I call Christina?* she asked herself, and heard a reply that sounded like Burt's voice. *Just call her and let her know what's happening.*

Christina's parents had been friends with Ellie and Burt Sterling, and now that Burt and Christina's parents, the Nichol's, were gone, Ellie was alone. She had re-connected with Christina several Sunday's ago, when Christina and her children had attended the church service, and Christina had called and checked on Ellie several times after that meeting.

After dialing 911 and giving the pertinent information, she called Margaret, her only child, and was put through to her voice mail. She left a short message. "Margaret, it's Mom. I think I'm having a heart-attack. I called 911 and will be going to the hospital. Call me there. I love you."

She then dialed Christina's number.

"Hello?"

"Christina dear?"

"Yes. Ellie? Are you alright?" concern filling her voice.

"Well, honey, I think I'm having a heart attack. I called 911 and they're on their way. I was wondering if you could meet me at the hospital?"

"Of course, Ellie. I'll be there. Do you want me to call Margaret?" She heard sirens over the phone line.

"No, I already did."

"Sounds like they're there. I'll be praying for you."

"Thanks, dear." The line went dead, and Ellie looked around her kitchen, and out into the living room. She and Burt had lived in the house for nearly fifty years, and even though small compared to what the young people bought these days, it had been sufficient and comfortable. She knew in her spirit that this would be the last time she would see it, and felt a nostalgic sadness wash over her.

After Burt passed, and in preparation for this day, she had sorted through and disposed of unnecessary items, cataloged and separated the family heirlooms, and organized the family photos. Margaret would be pleased. After Burt's funeral, Ellie had overheard her daughter tell a friend that she dreaded going through all of her mother's belongings when she passed.

Ellie looked around and sighed. She was ready for whatever happened.

Her cat, Elijah, jumped onto her lap and kneaded her chest and purred. He was such an affectionate creature, and she hoped he would be okay after she passed on. She snuggled him close and cried. "I'm not sure I'm ready to leave you, but if it's my time to go, I know God will take care of you." He looked up into her eyes and rubbed his head on her cheek, then jumped down, and ran to hide under the bed when he heard knocking and strange voices at the door.

CHAPTER 37

Christina called for Stacey and Nicky to come downstairs. "I just got a call from Ellie Sterling."

"Who's that?" asked Nicky.

"She's the little old lady from church we met that first Sunday we went there."

"Oh yeah." Nicky said.

"What did she want?" Stacey asked.

"She thinks she's having a heart-attack and is on her way to the hospital."

"Oh, no! So why'd she call you?"

Christina shook her head. "I don't really know, but she wants me there, so I'm going to head on over. Grandma and Grandpa will be here in about an hour or so. I may be back, I may not." Looking at Stacey first, then Nicky, she asked, "Can you handle everything 'till I get back?"

They both nodded. "Isn't Brad coming home soon?" Stacey asked.

Christina slapped her hand on her forehead. "I can't go to the hospital. I don't have a car! I'll call Cindy and see if she can take me. I don't want to wait until Brad gets home."

Christina glanced at the clock. Brad should be home in an hour or so, and he can come get me." Sighing, she said, "This is *not* good timing."

"I'll say!" agreed Stacey.

CHAPTER 38

Cindy pulled into the parking lot, dropping Christina at the door. just as the ambulance pulled into the emergency bay area.

"You sure you don't want me to wait?"

"I don't know how long I'll be, and besides, Brad can come get me."

Sighing, Cindy said, "Okay, but call me if you need me."

"Thanks Cindy. I appreciate this."

Standing in the doorway, she watched as the EMTs whisked Ellie into a triage room. Putting her hand over her heart, Christina thought, *Oh my, she looks so pale and fragile.*

Walking over to the admitting desk, she cleared her throat to get one of the attending nurses' attention.

"Excuse me."

"Yes?"

"Could you please inform Mrs. Sterling that Christina Sanders is here?"

Nodding, she said, "Sure. Are you a family member?"

Shaking her head, Christina said, "No, just a friend."

The nurse nodded, and continued on her way to the curtained off area.

Walking to the waiting room, with her head bowed in prayer, she was surprised when someone grabbed her by the shoulders.

"Huh?" She said, startled as she looked up into the face of Dr. Dawson.

"Hey, you almost walked into that door!" He said, nodding toward the door a few inches from her nose.

"Oh. Thanks for rescuing me. I was praying for Ellie and wasn't paying attention."

"Who's Ellie? And why are you here?"

"Ellie is a dear little lady from church who just came in by ambulance. She called and asked me to be here with her."

Nodding, he said, "Oh, she must be the patient I'm on my way to see.

"Oh, okay. You'd best get going. I'll talk to you later."

He gave her a quick hug and said, "Are there any other family members here?"

She looked around the empty waiting room. "Not yet."

"Okay. I'll let you know how she's doing in a few minutes. Do you have any of her family's phone numbers?"

Shaking her head, she said, "No. I hope the hospital has her daughter's phone number."

"I'm sure someone will contact her."

Walking away, he turned and said, "I'll see you in a few minutes."

She nodded. "I'll be here."

After two cups of coffee and perusing a couple of year old magazines, she stood to stretch when Steven appeared.

Approaching him, she asked, "So, how is she?"

Shaking his head and frowning, he said, "It doesn't look good. I'll be surprised if she makes it through the night."

Christina felt tears sting her eyes. Looking around and seeing no one, Steven pulled her into a hug and rested his chin on her head—her arms' encircled his waist, as her face pressed against his chest.

"So, it was a heart-attack?" She asked softly.

She felt his head nod. "Yes. A pretty severe one at that, and there is definite weakness on her left side which indicates a stroke."

Pulling away, she wiped her eyes and sighed. "Can I see her?"

Nodding, he said, "Yeah. She's mildly sedated, but conscious."

One of the ER nurses approached them.

"Sorry to interrupt you, Dr. Dawson."

Breaking from the embrace and turning to face her, he said, "It's okay. What can I do for you?"

Handing him a clipboard and pen, she said, "I need you to sign off on these medications."

Nodding, he took the pen and scribbled his name while asking, "Say, did you get in touch with Mrs. Sterling's daughter?"

Smiling, the nurse said, "Yes, and she's on her way."

Christina and Steven replied in unison, "Good."

As the nurse returned to her station in the ER, Christina turned to Steven and said, "I'm gonna go check on Ellie."

"I'll go with you, then I need to go get some paperwork done in my office."

Entering the cubicle, Christina inhaled sharply as she took in the frail and slightly blue-tinged woman on the bed, the IV bags. and all the monitoring equipment. The continuous beeping of the cardiac and IV monitors were the only sounds in the otherwise deathly quiet room. For an instant, her mind took her back to David's room. Steven, noticing the change in her demeanor, put his arm around her shoulder, bringing her thoughts back to the present. Reigning in her emotions, she approached the bed.

"Ellie?" She whispered, as she covered the cool, limp hand with both of hers.

Ellie turned her head towards the voice and opened her eyes, which were remarkably clear.

"Christina, dear. You came."

With tears threatening to overflow, Christina said, "Yes, Ellie. Was there a particular reason you wanted me here?"

Blinking as if to clear not only her vision, but her mind, Ellie said, "Well, I wasn't sure if I could hang on 'till Margaret arrived and I didn't want to be alone." Swallowing, and licking her parched lips, she said, "I have a favor to ask of you."

Patting Ellie's hand, Christina said, "Well, I'm glad you thought of me. I wouldn't want you to be alone either."

Ellie sighed and smiled. Taking a deep breath and releasing it, she said, "About that favor?"

"Yes?"

"I have a cat named Elijah."

Christina's heart sank. *Oh no, not a cat! I don't want another cat!*

To Ellie, she said, "Yes?"

Feeling Christina's hands tense, Ellie blinked her eyes rapidly to keep the tears from forming before saying, "He's an old cat, and it would be okay to put him to sleep, but if you *could* find him a nice home to finish out his days, that would be appreciated."

"Ellie, you're talking as if you aren't going back home."

Ellie smiled. "Oh. I don't think I will, honey. Burt has been with me all day, and is waiting for me to come to him. I'm waiting for Margaret to come so I can say good-bye."

Christina felt tears well in her eyes. Looking around the room, she asked, "Is he here now?"

Ellie smiled and looked towards the corner of the room. "Yes. He's over there, smiling and waving at me." Christina and Steven turned their heads toward the corner, and saw nothing.

"Ellie, would Margaret be able to take the cat?" *Oh please say yes!*

Turning her face to the ceiling, Ellie said, "Margaret and I had that conversation about a month ago, and she made it very clear that she didn't want him. She is allergic to cats, and doesn't even like them."

Christina nodded. "I see."

"He has enough food and water and litter for a couple of days, but he'll need care after that."

Ellie yawned. "I'm sorry, but I'm so tired. I can't seem to keep my eyes open."

Dr. Dawson patted her hand. "It's the medication, plus your body's been through a lot of stress. We'll let you rest."

Christina squeezed the bird-like hand. "Ellie, don't worry about Elijah. I'll see to it that he's taken care of."

Closing her eyes and giving in to sleep, Ellie mumbled, "Thank you, dear."

Steven excused himself and headed to his office, as Christina stepped outside the room to call home. As she began punching in numbers, a woman with the same body structure and intense blue eyes as Ellie, approached the desk and inquired of Ellie's whereabouts. After introducing herself as Margaret, Ellie's daughter, Christina walked over and explained the situation concerning her mother. Giving Christina a hug, and promising to keep her informed of her mother's condition, Margaret followed the nurse into Ellie's cubicle.

Christina then finished punching in the numbers to call the home phone. Stacey answered after two rings.

"Hey, girl. Are the grandparents there yet?"

"Nope, not yet, but Brad just walked in."

"Oh, good. May I speak with him?"

Brad came on the line, "Hey Mom. Where are you?"

Christina explained the incident with Ellie and asked if he could please come get her.

"I'll be there in a few minutes. Want to meet me at the front door?" He asked, grabbing the keys he had just laid on the counter.

"Sure. Thanks."

Brad arrived within ten minutes. Christina shivered as she climbed in and stuck her hands in front of the heater vent.

"Man, it's cold out here!"

"Yeah. Good thing the van is nice and warm." As they drove the short distance home, Christina told Brad about Ellie.

"Oh, man! I'm sorry, Mom." Shaking his head, he said, "So many deaths this week. Hopefully, the week will get better."

After entering the garage and turning off the van's engine, they heard the beep-beep of a car horn in the driveway.

Brad and Christina exited the van, and were walking towards Grandpa Dan and Grandma Ruth, when Stacey and Nicky came running out the back door.

CHAPTER 39

Once the grandparent's luggage was unloaded and taken upstairs, everyone met back in the dining room for a wonderful beef stew dinner.

As they ate, they talked about the plane trip down.

Sipping his tea, Grandpa said, "Our trip down was pretty uneventful, except for some turbulence over Indiana."

"What kind of turbulence?" Nicky asked.

Grandma answered. "According to the pilot, there were some strong winds and thick snow, but it only lasted a few seconds."

Swallowing a piece of stew meat, Stacey said, "I'm glad! I think that would be pretty scary."

"Well, I was certainly doing some heavy praying!" Ruth said with a smile.

"So, Stacey, you ready for the play tomorrow night?" Dan asked, wiping up gravy with a biscuit.

Stacey made a face. "I guess as ready as I'll ever be, Grandpa."

Clasping her hands together, Ruth said, "I'm looking so forward to this whole weekend! I get to see *two* plays and a concert, which is more than I've seen this whole year!"

Nicky said, "There's gonna be a surprise at the end of our concert!"

"Really?" Christina asked. "You never told me that."

He gave her a look. "Well, if I *told* you, it wouldn't be a surprise."

"You just told your grandparents." She said defensively.

"Well, yeah. But I didn't tell them what the surprise is."

Christina chuckled. "Okay. Guess we'll all be surprised then."

Grinning and nodding, Nicky said, "Yep."

The time passed quickly as each family member caught up on the latest events in their life. When they finished dinner, and began clearing off the table, Christina said, "I'll do the dishes tomorrow. Let's go into the family room."

They continued their conversations until midnight approached, and eyes got heavier and yawns became more frequent. Christina suggested they all head up to bed, except Brad, who prepared his bed on the couch.

Christina's cell phone rang as she reached the top of the stairs. Not recognizing the number, and wondering why someone would call so late, she let it go to voice mail. After changing into her pajamas, she listened to the message.

"Hi Christina, it's Margaret. Ellie's daughter. Mom just passed a few minutes ago. I knew you'd want to know. I know it's late, but if you want to call me back, it's okay. Or we can wait and talk tomorrow. Thanks for being here with mom. It meant a great deal to her."

Christina sat on the edge of the bed and let the tears fall. She hadn't known Ellie all that well, but just the fact that another dear soul from her parent's generation had passed, made her sad and even more aware of how quickly time was passing. As she crawled into bed, Steven called.

"Did Margaret call you?" He asked.

"Yeah. Just a few minutes ago. Did Ellie go peacefully?"

"Yes, she did. She even had a smile on her face."

Christina was silent for a moment picturing the event.

Concern filling his voice, Steven asked, "You doing okay?"

Sighing, she said, "Yeah. I didn't know Ellie all that well, but she seemed like a dear, sweet lady. How's Margaret doing?"

"She's actually holding up pretty well. I think she had mentally and emotionally prepared herself, and it wasn't quite as shocking as some deaths are. Did you know Margaret?"

"No. My parents were friends with Ellie and Burt, but Margaret was already grown and married by then. I was still in high school, so I knew *of* her, but I had never met her."

"I see. I wondered what the connection was."

After a moment, he asked, "Did your in-laws arrive safe and sound?"

"Yeah, soon after I got home this evening. We've had a nice time chatting about stuff. We were just heading off to bed when I got the call. Do you know about the funeral arrangements?"

"No, but I heard Margaret say something about cremation."

"I don't think I've ever attended a cremation service."

"Me neither. I'm not sure how it would be handled. Guess we'll find out soon enough. Say, I know you're tired, so I'm gonna go for now. Do you have to work tomorrow?"

"No. I asked Janet if she could fill in for me, and she agreed."

"That's good. I'll call you tomorrow and discuss plans for tomorrow night."

Yawning, she said, "Okay. I'll talk to you then."

CHAPTER 40

Janet was jolted awake by the insistent buzzing of her alarm clock. She had another nightmare. This one, similar to the others, involved being chased by a large bat-like creature through a maze of dark tunnels. Just as the creature was closing in on her, the alarm rang. She chuckled and said, "I was literally saved by the bell!" Climbing out of bed and heading to the bathroom, she wondered why she was having so many nightmares—and so similar. It seemed like every dream she had over the past several months had an ominous undertone—something dark and scary pursuing her.

Standing under the hot shower, she let her mind wander back to the conversation she had with Linda. From what her girl said, it seemed as if her classmates had turned against her. When Janet had questioned about the origins of this angst, Linda had reluctantly told her it all began with the Tarot cards. She recalled their conversation.

"Oh, honey. I didn't give you those to use so carelessly. They are to be used to help people—like a tool of sorts."

"I *was* trying to help people!" Linda had insisted.

"But, Linda, there's no way you could possibly understand and relate the interpretation of the cards. It takes years of studying and practice to read them correctly."

"How can that be? They pick a card and it's pretty evident what it means."

"I know it seems that way, but there's more to it. Have you read the books I gave you regarding interpretation of the cards?"

Linda made a face and shook her head. "I read some of them, but not all the way through. They're kind of boring."

Janet sighed and nodded. "Tell you what. You stop taking the cards to school and I'll help you learn how to interpret them. We can practice together. It's been a while since I've used them, and I could use a refresher course."

Linda had seemed satisfied and went to bed in a much better mood.

While rinsing her hair, Janet thought, *Maybe thirteen is too young to entrust her with such knowledge. After all, it does take maturity and discipline to give an accurate reading.* Turning the water off and reaching for a towel, she thought, *I wish I could read Christina's cards. It would be interesting to see what they predict.*

Christina. Why do I let her get under my skin? What is it about her that irritates me so...besides everything?

Before leaving for work, she wrote Linda a note explaining that she would be there for the performance. Even though Linda had a small singing part with a group of girls, it was still important to show support. That's one thing she could do for her daughter that her parents were unable to do for her.

Driving the few miles to work, she let her mind wander back to her childhood.

Her parents were referred to as migrant farm workers, or gypsies, because they would travel from farm to farm, hiring on as laborers. It wasn't unusual to see whole families, including toddlers, out in the fields picking cotton, beans, or other vegetables and fruits. When a child grew up in that environment, hard work was as natural as breathing—unlike today where they would be considered abused, or exploited.

When she and her two brothers were school-age, her mom would enroll them in the local school, but their attendance was sporadic. When the crops needed planting, hoeing, or harvesting, every available body needed to be present. In the summer of her tenth year, her whole life was turned upside down, and school became a thing of the past.

She and her mother had been hoeing a field of beans when her mother bent over and screamed in pain. Janet, ten at the time, ran to her side.

"Mama, what's wrong?"

"I'm gonna have a baby, honey. You need to help me to the tent over there."

Janet looked around for her daddy, but he was nowhere to be seen. She helped her mother to the tent, and stayed by her side as she gave birth to her little sister. Her brothers came after it was all over, and didn't understand what had happened. Janet tried to explain, but her little ten-year-old mind could barely comprehend it herself. Her mother had talked her through the delivery and clean up, but even Janet knew something wasn't right when the bleeding didn't stop. She called out for help, but no one was around. Her brothers had taken off to the other side of the field, and her daddy hadn't returned. Her mother lay with the new baby suckling at her breast and went to sleep. A few hours later when her daddy finally came back, her little sister was screaming, and her mother was dead.

Pulling into the hospital parking lot, Janet shut her memories down. She had to focus on work, and not painful memories she couldn't undo anyway. Besides, they'd return. They always did.

CHAPTER 41

When Linda woke the first time the next morning, the room was dark and chilly, and she could hear running water in the bathroom. Rolling onto her side and bringing the covers up under her chin, she thought about the events of the past few weeks, and what her mother had said the previous evening. *Maybe she's right. I should stop taking the Tarot cards to school. It's only a matter of time before I get caught, and then I'll be in big trouble.*

Feeling tears sting her eyes, she recalled the mean comments of her friends. *Maybe I should stop being friends with those girls. True friends don't say mean things behind your back.* Then she felt a pang of guilt as she recalled her own negative comments about Stacey. She whispered, "I'm sorry Stacey. I miss you so much!"

She heard the front door close and the sound of her mother's car coming to life. Rolling over, and re-adjusting the blankets and pillow, she fell back to sleep, wondering how she could regain Stacey's friendship.

The next time she woke, the sunlight was peeking through her curtains and into her eyes. Stretching and yawning, she smiled. *It's going to be a good day! Tonight's the play, and I'm gonna apologize to Stacey and be friends again.* She jumped out of bed and headed to the bathroom.

Walking back to her room, she stopped in front of her mother's door, and debated whether she should go ahead and get those tarot card books, or wait for her mom to give them to her—which could take days.

I could start reading them, since I have nothing planned until it's time to leave for the play. She opened the door and walked in, and was immediately assaulted by a strong patchouli incense odor, which caused an instant sneezing reaction, and flooding of her nostrils. Grabbing a tissue out of the box by the bed, she sneezed a couple more times and blew her nose. She left the door open to dissipate the smell and give her sensitive sinuses a break.

She had never visited her mother's room as an uninvited guest, and felt a mixture of excitement and fear. The room was dark and foreboding with its gray walls and carpet, and black curtains and bedspread—a complete opposite of her rainbow themed room. Standing in the middle of the room, she let her eyes wander. There were books and papers in piles all around the room, shelves filled with books, knickknacks and bottles containing—well, she wasn't sure what they contained. *A true witches lair. What? Where had that thought come from? My mom is not a witch—or is she?* She shook her head and cleared her mind of such thoughts. There seemed to be some kind of order in all the chaos. *I bet my mom could find anything she wanted to in this mess*, she thought as she lifted a couple of papers from a pile by the bed.

Locating the desired books, she reached for them, and spotted a leather bound notebook lying in the middle of her mother's bed. Curiosity getting the better of her, she picked it up, opened it, and began reading. The first page had the previous day's date and she realized it was a journal. She sat on the edge of the bed and continued reading—instantly captivated.

Today, L informed me that a few of her so called friends were saying bad things about her, reminding me of my own experiences as a teen. Kids can be so cruel. I wanted to hurt those girls for hurting L, but I know that's not the right approach. I'm thinking about casting a spell that would give them a taste of their own medicine.

L's wanting to re-establish her friendship with S S. Ugh! Of all the girls in that school, why does she have to pick S? It's bad enough that I have to work with C, but now S may be re-entering our lives! I've tried several spells to get rid of the S family, but something keeps them from working! It's so frustrating. I wish they'd all go back to Michigan!

Linda stopped reading for a minute, and thought about her mother's comments.

Spells? I wonder what kind of spells? Why does she hate the Sanders family? She flipped through the pages, and stopped at an entry dated a week earlier.

I'm missing my brothers today. Not sure why. I hope they're doing alright. Maybe I should call them. It's been several years since I've spoken to either of them. I wish they'd reach out to me, but I guess that old saying, 'out of sight, out of mind' is true. They probably don't think of me at all.

Linda stopped again. *Brothers? I didn't know she had brothers. Why hasn't she told me about them? I thought she was an only child. She's never really talked about her past, come to think of it. I guess I never really cared enough to ask—till now. I wonder what other secrets she's keeping from me?* She continued reading, her curiosity piqued.

With her stomach growling, and nothing else of interest jumping out from the pages, she closed the book and placed it back on the bed. Straightening the covers, she looked around the room, grabbed the books, and closed the door, wondering how she could address the subject of her uncles without revealing that she had read the journal.

She glanced at the clock and quickly dressed for school, grabbing a granola bar on her way out the door.

CHAPTER 42

When her shift ended, and the evening staff had been appraised of the two cardiac patient's status, Janet gladly left the CCU and headed towards the elevator, grateful that the uneventful day was over. Boarding the empty space, she glanced at her watch and thought, *I have a couple of hours before I need to be at the school. That'll give me time to shower, dress, and stop for a burger and fries for Lee Lee before the play starts.* Lee Lee. That was her nickname for Linda. She had called her that off and on since she was an infant. Her given name was Linda Lenore, so Lee Lee just seemed to be a natural nickname. As Linda aged, Janet used the name less frequently. Linda expressed her dislike of the nickname, complaining that it sounded babyish.

Walking into the house, Janet was immediately hit by the strong odor of Patchouli. Knowing her bedroom was the only place it could have come from, she walked over and threw open the door and looked around. Everything was as she had left it. *Hmm.* She thought. *I wonder if Linda came in here? She has never entered uninvited before. Why would she do that now?* Closing the door, and walking back to the kitchen, she spotted the two books on the table. Picking them up and reading the titles, she realized that Linda *had* gone into her room to retrieve them. It was then that Janet decided her room would be off limits. She had secrets she didn't want anyone to know—especially her daughter.

As she showered and dressed, she replayed the incident in her mind and chuckled. *What if there had been a burglar in my room? What would I have done? Thrown a book or two at him? I should probably be a little more cautious about how I react to things—at least carry some kind of weapon before I go barging into an unknown situation.*

CHAPTER 43

"Mom?" Brad called as he dropped the van keys on the kitchen counter, after dropping Stacey off at the school.

"Upstairs!"

He ran up the steps, and found her in the bathroom, applying mousse to Nicky's hair to make it spike in the front.

"Hey, after dropping Stacey off, I noticed there were a lot of cars in the parking lot. I think it's gonna be really crowded tonight. We may want to leave pretty soon."

Looking at her watch, she said, "Okay, but the play doesn't start for another hour."

Shrugging, he said, "Yeah, but if we have to save a whole row of seats..."

Sighing, she said, "Alright. Go inform your grandparents we'll be leaving in about fifteen minutes."

Nodding, he ran back down the stairs and found his grandparents in the den.

"Nicky, go get your shoes and socks on and meet us downstairs."

"Okay."

True to her word, Christina had the family loaded and driving out of the driveway fifteen minutes later.

Hearing her cell-phone ring, she handed her purse to Brad and asked him to answer it.

"Mrs. Murray wants to know if you could save three more seats—for Tom, Eleanor and Tommy?"

Nodding, she said, "Sure."

Ruth said, "I can't help but feel a little nervous for Stacey, this being her first big play and all."

Christina smiled and nodded. "I know. I've had butterflies all day. I can only imagine how she feels!"

Dropping her in-laws and boys off at the door, Christina went to park the van and almost collided with Janet as they were vying for the same parking spot. She chuckled, and waved Janet on in, as she drove two spaces down and pulled in.

"Hey, Janet!" She called, as she exited her van.

I almost got away! Janet thought as she turned and waited for Christina.

Approaching Janet, Christina said, "Hey, I'm glad I caught you. I just wanted to thank you again for filling in for me today. Anything happen that I should be aware of?"

Janet shook her head, "Nope, nothing exciting happened. In fact it was a very boring day."

"Same two patients, I presume?"

Janet nodded. "Both are scheduled to go home in a day or so."

Christina nodded. "Hey, you sitting with anyone?"

Janet hesitated, sensing what was coming next. "No, just myself."

Smiling, Christina said, "Well, why don't you sit with us?" Chuckling, she said, "We're saving a whole row, so I'm sure we can squeeze in one more."

Janet nodded. "Okay." *It would be rude to decline*, she thought. *I don't want her to know how much I detest being around her. Not yet, anyway.*

After entering the front door, and receiving their programs, Nicky ushered them to their seats. The auditorium was about half full and Christina whispered to Brad, "Glad you told us to get here early. We may not have been able to save all these seats."

Nodding in agreement, he looked around the room, and spotted a group of friends. Waving, he excused himself to go greet them.

Christina introduced her in-laws to Janet, and after a little chit-chat, Janet excused herself, and took the bag of food she had purchased for Linda.

As the time drew near for the play to begin, and Steven hadn't arrived yet, Christina debated whether she should call or not. *What if one of his patients has crashed? If he doesn't arrive once the play begins, I'll slip out and call.*

As the lights were being dimmed, Steven slipped into the seat next to Christina. After waving a greeting to everyone, he whispered in her ear, "Sorry I'm late. I had a conference call with a couple of cardiologists in Dallas."

She nodded. "I'm glad you're here."

As the curtain opened, he reached over and took her hand, holding on to it for the remainder of the play—which didn't go unnoticed by Janet.

The play, was about a little doll—played by Stacey—who fell out of Santa's bag, and her adventures before she finally ended up with the little girl she was meant to be with. There was just the right amount of humor and drama, and the audience seemed to enjoy every minute of it. All in all, everything went smoothly with nary a line skipped, and the music and dances were performed with ease.

Stacey is definitely a drama queen, Christina thought as she watched her daughter take the stage for a final bow.

During the curtain call, an incident occurred that would have the town buzzing for weeks to come. As Stacey took her bow, and the audience stood cheering and clapping, the principal walked out and stood in front of the microphone. It took several seconds to get everyone's attention.

He cleared his throat and said, "Excuse me."

The lights in the auditorium brightened, and the room became eerily quiet, except for a few random whispers.

"I'm sorry to interrupt, but one of our fire alarms has been set off, and I need everyone to evacuate the building in an orderly fashion, so that our fire department men can get in and search the building. If there are any volunteer firemen in the audience, or anyone else who would like to help, we would appreciate your assistance, as this is quite a large building. Please meet at the front of the auditorium for instructions. Again, I'm sorry for the inconvenience, and it may be nothing, but we need to be cautious. Thank you for attending, and thank you for your cooperation."

When he finished speaking, people gathered belongings and family members and headed towards the doors.

Samara, who had been sitting with her friends across the room, came running up to her mother, and said, "Mom, Jenny asked if I could spend the night at their house. Is that okay?"

Looking over to Jenny's mom who was nodding her head, Cindy gave her daughter a hug, and said, "Oh, okay. I'll call you tomorrow."

She watched as Samara joined her friends, confident she would be safe.

Ed looked at Cindy and said, "I'm gonna see if I can help."

She nodded and squeezed his hand.

Steven said, "I'd like to come along, too."

Looking at Tom, Ed asked, "You want to come with us?"

Tom nodded, and after giving Eleanor and Tommy hugs, went with the two men.

Christina called out. "Hey, I'll take the ladies to my house, so come by when you're finished." The men nodded and waved.

"Geez, what next?" Christina mumbled under her breath. Stacey, with her long light brown hair bouncing freely behind her, and Linda, with her raven hair bouncing in a pony tail, came running up to them.

Breathless, Stacey said, "Mom! Can you believe this?"

Christina, shaking her head, reached out, pulled her close and answered, "Not really. Weird, huh?"

Stacey nodded.

Linda said, "I didn't see or smell any smoke, so I think it's a false alarm, but our teacher said it's better to be careful than careless."

Janet reached out and pulled Linda into a hug.

"I'm glad you're okay."

Linda shrugged.

Looking around the almost empty auditorium, Nicky said, "I guess we'd better leave."

Christina turned to her friends. "My van can hold eight people, so I think we can all fit in, if you want to just ride with me. That way, we can leave the vehicles for the guys."

Cindy and Eleanor nodded.

Eleanor said, "We might as well; they have the keys anyway. It would be too bothersome to track them down for the keys."

Brad said, "Mom, a few of us guys want to stay and help, too. The more people looking for the source of the fire, the better it'll be."

She nodded and gave him a hug. "Make sure you let Ed or the other guys know you're here, so one of them can bring you home."

Nodding, he said, "Yeah, I'll go find them." Giving his mom a hug and peck on the cheek, he turned to go. "See you later."

Turning to her friends, Christina said, "Okay, ladies and gents, you ready to head out?"

They all nodded, except Janet who said, "Linda and I will head on home. Thanks for letting me sit with y'all," while thinking: *Even though watching you and Dr. Dawson holding hands and laughing and whispering made me sick to my stomach!*

"Janet," Christina said, "You are more than welcome to come over, too."

Shaking her head, she said, "Nah, that's okay. We need to get on home." *I need to get my emotions under control, otherwise I may say or do something we'll both regret,* she thought, as she turned to go.

Stacey walked over, and surprising Linda, gave her a hug. "Your song sounded so awesome!"

Linda smiled and said, "Thanks. You did an amazing job too."

Grinning, Stacey asked, "Maybe we can get together over the holidays?"

Linda smiled and nodded. "I'd like that." She returned the hug and with her mother's prompting, turned to go.

"See you later!" She called over her shoulder before disappearing through the doorway.

Christina cocked her head. "That was really nice of you Stacey."

"Huh?"

"You know, giving Linda a hug and saying nice things to her. I'm proud of you."

Shrugging, she said, "Oh, yeah."

Christina nodded. "Well, I'm glad you two are resolving your issues."

Once home, Tommy, Nicky and his grandpa—being the only males in the group—went into the family room and turned on the TV, surprised to see the school incident being discussed.

The ladies, after preparing cups of coffee, tea and cocoa, sat around the dining room table, discussing the play and how well it went. Stacey, who was with them, said, "I'm just glad the fire alarm didn't go off during the play. That would have been awful!"

"I agree," said Cindy.

Ruth, after taking a sip of tea, said, "I sure hope it was a false alarm."

No sooner had the words come out of her mouth than she and the other ladies felt the floor shake. "What was that?"

Then they heard Grandpa Dan yell, "Oh, my goodness! Ruth, ladies, get in here!"

They immediately went to the family room. "What is it?"

Tommy ran to his mother's arms. Nicky said, "There was an explosion at the school!"

"What?" Christina asked.

"The lady news announcer was talking in front of the school, and all of a sudden, there was a big explosion! It knocked her down and the camera must have been dropped because the picture went all crazy!"

The announcer came on the TV screen, said they had lost contact with their correspondent, and would keep the audience appraised of the situation, as it unfolded.

As this was occurring, Cindy, Eleanor and Christina's phones all rang simultaneously.

Each lady grabbed theirs and answered. Their men were checking in.

Christina heard sirens and yelling in the background as Steven explained that the fire had started in the science lab where there were flammable liquids and chemicals.

He said, "When the fire made contact with them, well, that caused the explosion."

"Geeze! Anyone hurt?" Christina asked.

"Too early to tell yet," He said.

"Is Brad with you?"

"What? Brad? He's here?"

Christina said, "Yeah, he and his friend Eric decided to stay and help. Have you seen them? What about Ed and Tom?"

"When we left y'all, we sorta split up to look in different hallways and classrooms. I didn't see Brad. I'll go look for him and the other guys."

"Wait, Steven. Let me ask Cindy and Eleanor where the men are. They're on the phone with them now."

After talking to the women, she said, "Tom is in the auditorium, and Ed is in the gymnasium. Neither one has seen Brad. Please find him and call me back!"

"I will. Try not to worry. I'll call you, as soon as I find him."

They disconnected, and she shot a prayer up to heaven.

"Mom?" Stacey said, "What's going on?"

Christina with tear-rimmed eyes and trying to hold her emotions in check, answered, "Steven said there was a fire in the science lab which caused an explosion. The firemen are getting it under control."

"Was anyone hurt?" Ruth asked.

"I don't know. Steven didn't know either. He was in another area. Did Ed or Tom know if anyone was hurt?" she asked Eleanor and Cindy.

Both women shook their heads.

Eleanor said, "Tom was running in that direction when I hung up."

Cindy nodded and said, "Yeah, so was Ed. Guess we'll know more in a little while."

Nicky, with worry etched on his face asked, "Where's Brad?"

Christina, rubbing her forehead said, "I don't know. I tried calling his cell phone, but he's not answering, and the guys haven't seen him."

Nicky went to his mother and put his arms around her waist.

"Can we pray?"

Christina nodded. Everyone joined hands and stood in a circle as Dan led a prayer of protection for Brad and the other people putting their lives on the line to stop the fire.

A few minutes later, Christina's cell-phone rang. It was Steven.

"Christina, I found Brad."

"Is he alright?"

"Well, he's injured, but it doesn't look too serious."

"Injured? What do you mean 'not too serious'?"

"He and his friend Eric were walking by the lab when it exploded. They were thrown into a wall and got hit by flying glass and debris. They're shook up, but they'll be fine. I'll ride in the ambulance to the hospital with them. You can meet us there if you want."

Christina, not even realizing that she'd sat down, stood and said, "Ambulance? I'll be there in a few minutes." When she disconnected, she was hit with a barrage of questions.

Explaining the situation while donning her jacket, and grabbing her purse and keys, she headed to the back door.

"I'd like to go with you," Ruth said.

Christina smiled and nodded.

"Sure, Mom. Dad, can you stay with Nicky and Stacey?"

He nodded. Eleanor and Cindy gave her hugs.

Eleanor said, "We'll just wait here for Ed and Tom."

Cindy said, "Call me later. I don't care what time it is. I want to know how Brad is doing."

Christina nodded, and after giving Stacey and Nicky a hug, left with Ruth.

The ride to the hospital was quiet as each woman replayed the last hour's events in their minds, and prayed for safety, healing and peace.

Pulling into the emergency parking lot, Christina was surprised to see how full it was. She found a space in the back of the lot, then she and Ruth headed for the ER bay, and watched as an ambulance, emptied of its patients, drove off with sirens blaring. *Off to pick up more victims*, thought Christina as she approached the admitting desk.

Introducing herself, she was informed that Brad hadn't arrived yet. One of the women at the desk said, "The ambulance that just left will be bringing two young men in."

"I wonder if Eric's mom knows?" She asked Ruth.

"Maybe you should call her."

"Yeah. Even if she knows and is on her way, we can wait together."

Ruth nodded.

Christina made the call and was surprised that Eric's mom, Erica, didn't know about the explosion, or the condition of her son.

"I'll be there in a few minutes!" She had said as she disconnected..

"It's a good thing I called her." Christina said, as she paced around the waiting room.

Christina had been so focused on her own situation, that she hadn't noticed the chaos surrounding her. When she finally stopped to look and listen, she was surprised by the number of injured people. The ER was set up to care for about a dozen patients, and it looked as if it had reached its limit. *Where had they all come from?* She thought about volunteering to help, but needed to be available when Brad came in. The medical staff seemed to have everything under control, as there were no life-threatening injuries that she could see.

People were milling about, and she could hear bits and pieces of conversations, moaning and coughing. She watched as firefighters and police went from patient to patient asking questions trying to make sense of the whole event. She looked around for the police chief, and saw him talking to one of the firemen lying on a gurney with an oxygen mask on—obviously suffering from smoke inhalation.

She was headed that way, when she heard an ambulance pull in.

She motioned for Ruth to follow, and they both headed for the ER admitting area. She watched as Steven helped Brad and Eric into wheelchairs, then ran over to them.

She leaned down to hug her son.

"Oh, Brad! Are you okay?" Pushing his blood stained red hair out of his blue eyes, and noticing they were bloodshot, she did a quick assessment of the rest of his head, and found several gashes which were oozing blood.

"I'm okay, Mom. Just a few cuts and bruises."

She glanced over at Eric, who had blood smeared across his face and running down from under a bandage over one eye. She went over and hugged him as well, saying, "Your mom is on her way."

He nodded and she saw a tear escape from under the bandage, and run down his cheek.

"Excuse me, ma'am. I need to get these boys into the triage."

"Sure." Backing away, she called out, "I'll see you in a few minutes."

Brad put his hand up in a wave.

Steven walked over and put his arm around her shoulder.

"He's a tough kid, Christina. He'll be okay."

Nodding, and wiping tears from her eyes, she said, "Yeah. Thanks for finding the boys, and riding in with them."

He pulled her into a hug. "I'm just glad no one was killed. The fire following that explosion was pretty intense."

"What was in there to cause such an explosion?"

Shrugging, he said, "I'm not really sure. Someone said there were a few gas tanks in the corner."

"Why would a middle-school lab have gas tanks?"

Steven shrugged again. "I'm sure we'll find out."

Ruth watched the interchange with Christina and Steven, and felt tears sting her eyes. Although she was pleased that Christina had Steven for support, she felt a little pang of jealousy on David's behalf. In her head, she knew feeling jealousy was irrational, as David had been gone for two years, but the mother part of her had difficulty releasing it. She had a mental argument with herself, and brought her emotions under control, before approaching her former daughter-in-law.

Christina and Steven both looked towards the doors as they heard someone say, "I'm Mrs. Smith. Is my son Eric here?"

Christina walked over and met the distraught woman. She was holding a toddler in her arms, and was surrounded by her husband and three other children.

"Mrs. Smith, I'm Christina Sanders, Brad's mom."

"Are the boys alright?" She asked, close to hysteria.

Christina reached out and touched the distraught woman's shoulder.

"They just had some cuts and bruises. I haven't talked to the doctor yet, but they didn't look too bad when they came in."

Handing the toddler girl to her husband, Mrs. Smith asked, "What happened?"

Christina put her hand on the woman's trembling arm and led her to a nearby chair. Sitting next to each other, while Mr. Smith stood close by with the children, Christina said, "There was an explosion in the middle-school. Seems someone had started a fire in the science lab during the Christmas play, and then pulled the fire alarm. Once everyone had been evacuated, the lab exploded."

"How did our boys get hurt?"

"They had volunteered to help search the building, and were in the hallway next to the lab, when it exploded."

"How could you let them go, knowing there was a fire?"

Christina swallowed and cleared her throat. "The principal had called for volunteers, and the boys wanted to go. I guess I didn't think it was serious because we didn't see or smell any smoke. We were hoping it was a false alarm, a prank."

With anger in her eyes, the woman said, "Obviously, it wasn't a prank!"

Sighing, Christina said, "No, it wasn't."

"Eric should have called me. I would have told him to just come home."

Christina nodded. "I'm sorry. If I could undo this, I would."

Squinting her eyes and chewing on her bottom lip, Mrs. Smith said, "I guess I'm not really mad at you. I'm just worried about my boy."

Christina nodded and patted the woman's hand. "Me, too."

CHAPTER 44

Watching the events unfolding on Earth in the viewing room, and realizing his family was in danger, David asked permission to intervene on his family's behalf. Once granted, he arrived in time to divert Brad and Eric's entry into the lab, by whispering in Brad's ear that they needed to check the bathroom at the end of the hall. That's where they were headed when total chaos broke loose. He had stayed with them, from the time of the explosion until their arrival at the hospital. He knew they would be fine physically, but there was quite a spiritual battle going on between the angels and demons, and he wasn't sure if one or more of those slimy beings would turn their attention on the boys. If they had, he knew he couldn't do battle with them himself, but he could call on Jarrod and the guardian angels to intervene.

He walked over and shook hands with Brad's and Eric's angels.

"Hey, guys. I'm glad you're here watching over the boys."

They both nodded.

Brad's angel, Argus, spoke, "There's a lot of turmoil in the spiritual realm right now." Looking down at Brad, he said, "I'm sorry your boy was hurt, but we were instructed to send as many demons back to where they came from, as we could. When I saw you arrive, and knew you'd be with the boys, I knew it was time for us to go to battle."

David nodded. "I wondered why you disappeared when I arrived."

Joshua, Eric's angel said, "I heard one of the demons say that your family was on their target list, and they weren't finished yet."

"Target list? What does that mean?" David asked.

Joshua shook his head. "I think it means they want to destroy your family somehow."

"Why?" David asked.

Argus, reaching out and putting his hand on David's shoulder said, "Because Father has great plans for them, and the demons know this. They want to stop them any way they can."

"What plans?"

Argus shrugged, "Only the Father knows."

"Will they succeed?"

Argus shrugged again. "Humans *do* have free will and it will be up to them to decide what path they will take."

David said, "So, what can we do in the meantime to protect them?"

"We have to be diligent. Remember, we can only act if they give us permission. Their words have great power."

"Permission?"

Argus shook his head at David's lack of understanding. "When a human prays and asks for God's help, He gives us the 'go ahead' to intervene. When you were on Earth, did you not pray and ask for help, and things beyond your ability and understanding began occurring?"

David nodded.

Patting David's back, he said, "You, my friend, still have so much to learn about the spiritual realm."

David sighed. "Yep."

When the doctor entered the room, the spiritual beings became silent as they watched and listened.

CHAPTER 45

Dr. Carmichael approached Brad's bed and held out his hand.
"Hi, Brad. I'm Dr. Aaron Carmichael."

Brad extended his hand. "Oh yeah. You're Stacey's doctor, right?"

Aaron nodded and smiled. Looking through the chart, he asked, "How are you feeling?"

Brad rubbed his head, "Well, right now I've got a killer headache and I'm beginning to feel every one of those cuts and bruises."

Aaron nodded. "I've ordered some pain medication that will help. I'm going to order a CT scan of your head and we may keep you overnight for observation."

"Okay. Have you talked to my mom yet?"

Shaking his head, he said, "No. I was waiting for your lab results and I wanted to examine you first."

Pulling the curtain for privacy, he had Brad remove his gown and did a preliminary exam.

"Your lungs are clear and even though you have many cuts and bruises, there are only a couple of them on your head, deep enough to cause concern. I'll give you a round of antibiotics in your IV, to thwart any possible infection."

Patting Brad's leg, he asked, "Do you have any questions or concerns?"

Brad shook his head. "Not about me, but is Eric okay?"

Smiling, Dr. Carmichael said, "I'm going to check on him right now, and I'll let you know."

Before he disappeared behind the curtain, Brad called out, "Hey, can I see my mom now? I know she's gotta be worried sick."

Nodding at the nurse in the room, Dr. Carmichael said, "Sure. I'll send for both moms."

Brad listened as Dr. Carmichael checked Eric, giving him the same information he had received.

Alone with his friend, Brad said, "Looks like we'll be spending the night here."

"Yeah, hopefully we'll be in the same room."

"I'll ask."

Dr. Carmichael, after leaving the boys, entered the congested waiting room. Walking over to the anxious parents, he said, "Christina, and Mr. and Mrs. Smith, will you come with me?"

Ruth said, "I'll stay with the children if you'd like." The three older children stayed with Ruth, while the toddler stayed in her daddy's arms. While the children watched a TV program, Ruth called her husband and informed him of the situation with the boys.

The parents followed, as he led them to an empty office, and apprised them of the boy's conditions, and his intention to keep them overnight for observation.

CHAPTER 46

Once the boys were settled in their room, hospital aids came and took them to the CT department. By the time they returned an hour or so later, Eric's dad had left with the other children, and his mom, Erica, had stayed behind.

While the boys were gone, the women used that time to become better acquainted.

Christina hadn't realized that Eric came from a racially mixed family until she saw them all together. His mother was blonde, blue-eyed, and fair skinned, and his dad was a complete opposite with his dark skin, hair and eyes. The children from that union were beautiful—a nice combination of both races.

Christina, noticing her mother-in-law yawning, asked, "Mom, would you like to go back to the house?"

"Well, I *am* a bit tired. It's been a very long day."

Patting her arm, Christina said, "If you want, you can take the van. Now that the crisis has passed, and we know the boys will be fine, we can all relax a bit."

"Why don't you come home, too? I'm sure Brad will be well cared for. He'd probably rest better, knowing that you're home in your own bed. After all, wouldn't you be more comfortable at home than here in a chair?"

Nodding and sighing, Christina said, "Yeah. You're right, but the mother part of me wants to stay close to my baby."

Ruth smiled and nodded. "Of course you do, but Brad isn't a baby anymore, and it might embarrass him to have you hovering over him, especially since he's only got cuts and bruises."

"Well, you may be right. Let's wait and see what the CT scan shows, then I'll decide."

Nodding again, Ruth said, "Okay, but either way, I would like to go home. I don't think I'm up to sitting in a chair all night."

It was going on midnight when Dr. Carmichael came in with the good news that the boy's CT scans were normal. There was an audible sigh from everyone in the room.

"So, can we go home?" Brad asked.

Looking at the almost empty IV bags that held the antibiotics, and pointing to them, he said, "When those are empty, you can go."

Looking at Christina and Erica, he said, "I'll need you to sign the discharge papers."

Both women nodded. Looking at the teens, he said, "I want to see you both in my office on Monday or Tuesday. If there are any signs of infection, fever, redness, yellow or green oozing from the wounds, call me ASAP."

Both boys answered, "Yes, Sir."

He turned to the women, "Ladies, I'll send the nurse in a few minutes to remove the IVs and bring the discharge papers. I'm sure the boys will be fine, but don't hesitate to call me, if there are any concerns."

Erica said, "Thank you, Dr. Carmichael." Christina smiled and nodded in agreement.

Turning to Erica, Christina said, "I'm glad we finally met. I'm sorry it was under such stressful circumstances though."

Erica smiled and pulled Christina into a hug. "I'm glad we met too. I'm sorry I was angry with you, and implied that this was your fault."

"Well, I did allow the boys to go. I'm just thankful they weren't hurt any worse than they were."

Nodding, Erica said, "Could we get a ride from y'all? I don't want my husband to have to get the other kids out, being it's so late and all."

"Sure. I have room in my van. I'll be glad to drop y'all off."

CHAPTER 47

Even though Christina hadn't fallen asleep before three-o'clock, she woke at her usual six-o'clock time. The house was dark and quiet. Benji followed her to the bathroom, then downstairs to check on Brad. He had given his room to his grandparents, and was sleeping on the couch in the family room. She placed her hand on his forehead, which felt warm, but not feverish. As she turned to go, he whispered, "Mom?"

"Yes, Brad."

"Could you bring me a cup of water?"

Smiling and patting his arm, she said, "Of course. You need anything else? A pain reliever, perhaps."

Stretching and wincing, he said, "Yeah. That's a good idea. I'm gonna go pee first."

Once he was settled, she returned to her bed and fell into a deep sleep, not waking again until around ten.

When she entered the kitchen, Ruth handed her a cup of coffee, and asked, "Did you sleep well?"

Stretching, yawning, and rubbing her eyes, Christina said, "Yeah. I think maybe a little too well. I'm having trouble waking up."

"Well, it was a stressful day, and very late night. I'm glad you were able to sleep in."

"Did you and Dad sleep alright?"

Ruth nodded. "Yes we did. Dan is such a deep sleeper, he didn't even know when I came to bed, and once my head hit the pillow, I don't remember anything, 'till I woke this morning."

"Good. After such a busy day, I was concerned how well y'all would sleep."

Looking towards the family room, Christina asked, "How's our boy?"

Ruth smiled, "He seems to be doing alright. He says he's very sore though."

Just then, Nicky entered the room. "Mom, do you think we'll still have the band concert tonight?"

Christina considered that for a moment. "I would imagine so. Your concert is at the elementary school, so I don't know why it would be canceled. Probably wouldn't hurt to call your principal, which I'll do right after breakfast."

Nodding and shrugging, he said, "Okay." Taking a plate that held pancakes and bacon, he returned to the family room, where his grandpa and siblings were watching TV.

Once breakfast was eaten, Christina asked her in-laws to meet with her in the dining room. Sitting around the large oak table, she told them of her meeting with the lawyer and proposed money situation.

Ruth looked shocked. "You mean, you'll be getting paid by the government, on top of David's life insurance policy?"

Nodding, Christina said, "Yeah, we should be set for the rest of our lives."

Taking a sip of coffee, Ruth said, "You could stop working, if you wanted to."

"I could. However, I really *like* working in the CCU and my part-time hours fit into our schedules nicely." Smiling, she said, "I suppose if, or when, I choose to quit, I can without any guilt feelings."

Dan asked, "Do the kids know about this?"

"Know about what?" Brad asked as he entered the room.

Looking like a deer caught in headlights, Christina stammered, "Uh, we were just discussing financial matters."

Looking at his grandparents, who were smiling and nodding, Brad frowned, wondering if there was more to the discussion than they were letting on.

"Okay." Walking over to his mom, he said, "Could you check the bandage on the back of my head? It feels weird."

Christina inspected the bandage, and found it to be caked with blood and partially detached from the wound. "I need to change it and secure it better. You must have dislodged it, while you were sleeping."

Turning around, he said, "I'll go get the supplies and be right back."

When he left, she looked at her in-laws and blew out air. "That was close. I don't want them to know about the money yet."

Ruth cocked her head. "Why?"

"My gut feeling tells me it isn't the right time. First of all, I don't think they'd understand, and I don't want them to become greedy or boastful." Shrugging, she added, "You know how kids can be, sometimes."

"What are your plans?" Dan asked.

"I'll talk to the banker and set up separate savings accounts for each of us." Waving her hand, she added, "Plus, some of the money will be used to upgrade this house."

Brad returned and handed the bandage items to his mother, who carefully cleaned and re-dressed the wound, noting that one of the stitches had come loose. *I'll have to keep an eye on that.*

Putting an arm around his waist, and looking up into his bruised, stitched and scraped face, she asked, "You doin' okay?"

He nodded and smiled. "Yeah. Sore, achy, and very tired, though. I think I'll lay back down and take a nap."

Christina nodded and said, "That's a good idea. Your tiredness is probably due to a combination of the injuries, stress and medication."

Ruth said, "Brad, why don't you go up to your room? It'll be quieter and you'll probably sleep better in your own bed."

Nodding, he said, "Thanks, Grandma. I will."

When he left, the adults continued their conversation concerning the money situation while the other two kids played a game of scrabble.

Christina's phone rang. It was Cindy.

Answering, Christina said, "Oh man, Cindy! I forgot to call you!"

"That's okay. How's Brad and his friend?"

"They're okay. Just a bunch of scrapes, bruises and a few deep cuts that required stitches."

"Are they still in the hospital?"

Christina stifled a yawn, "No. We came home around midnight last night."

"Good! Is the band concert still on for tonight? Ed and I would like to attend, if it is."

"I need to call the principal to find out, then I'll let you know. I'm pretty sure it's still on. That school wasn't involved in the fire, so I don't see why not."

"Yeah. That's what I was thinking, but Ed said they may cancel it because of fear that whoever set the first fire, might set another one."

"I didn't think of that," Christina said. "I hope that's not the case!"

"Yeah. That would be awful!"

Christina asked, "Say, has Ed or the sheriff got any leads on who may have done this?"

Cindy said, "They're thinking it was a teen-age prank that got out of control, but they're continuing to investigate."

After a pause, Christina said, "Well, I hope it doesn't happen again."

"Me, too." Cindy said on a sigh. "Well, I'll talk to you later."

Looking in the desk drawer for the principal's number, Christina said, "Yep. I'll call as soon as I know anything."

CHAPTER 48

Once the breakfast dishes were washed and put away, and the kitchen was back in order, Christina excused herself to call the principal. She heard a recorded message that said the concert would still be on.

Walking towards the family room, she called, "Hey, Nicky!"

"Yeah, Mom?"

Standing in the doorway, she said, "The band concert is still on. The principal said they have volunteers going through the school to check for anything abnormal. He says he's pretty sure everything will be okay."

Smiling and nodding, Nicky said, "Cool! Can I borrow your phone to call Danny?"

She handed him the phone.

Stacey said, "Mom, when Nicky's through with the phone, can I call Linda? Is it okay if I ask her to come to the concert with us?"

Taking a mental head count, she said, "Sure. We'll have room for her in the van. Tell her we can swing by and get her around six."

"Why so early? Doesn't the concert start at seven?"

"Nicky needs to be there an hour earlier, so I thought we could drop him off and grab a quick dinner at McDonald's, before heading back to the school."

Standing with his hands on his hips, Nicky said, "Hey, I wanna go to McDonald's too!"

Christina, shaking her head, reached out to tousle his hair, "You will be having pizza at the school."

"Oh, okay." He said, handing the phone to Stacey.

CHAPTER 49

"Mom?" Linda called from the other side of her mother's bedroom door. Janet was in the middle of reading an important passage in her spell book, and didn't want to be disturbed, but if she ignored Linda, the girl would just keep knocking.

"Yes, Lee Lee?"

"Stacey called and asked if I could go to the elementary school band concert with them?"

Janet stopped reading, took a breath, and let it out slowly.

"Do you want to go? I thought you and Stacey were fighting."

"Well, we were, but maybe this will help us be friends again."

"Lee Lee, come in and talk to me. I don't like the door between us."

Linda opened the door and stepped in shyly—afraid of what her mother may say.

Janet, patted a spot on the bed beside her. Linda sat.

"So, you want to re-establish your friendship with Stacey?"

Linda nodded.

"I see. I was kinda hoping you were finished with her...as a friend."

Linda gave her a confused look. "Why would you think that? I never said I wanted to lose her friendship *forever*!"

Janet held her hand up. "Okay. I just thought you had made different friends and Stacey was out of the picture."

Linda shook her head. "Well, those friends I had were the ones saying bad things about me. As far as I know, Stacey has never said anything bad about me."

"Well, not to your face. Obviously, she doesn't agree with your belief system."

"My belief system?"

"You know. Casting spells, reading Tarot cards, using nature's energy to help us."

Linda frowned. Her mom had a point. "Well, we don't have to agree on everything to be friends, do we?"

Janet considered this. "No, but when there are such major differences, it makes it quite challenging to maintain a relationship."

Linda sat for a moment, contemplating what her mom had said. Shrugging, she said, "Guess I'll have to see how it all plays out. In the meantime, can I go to the concert?"

Really? Janet thought, rubbing her eyes and running her hands through her hair. "Alright. What time will they pick you up?"

"Stacey said around six. They're gonna stop at McDonald's for a bite to eat before the concert."

Looking at her watch, Janet said, "Well, you have a couple of hours. Why not do a load of laundry and pick up your room?"

Linda smiled and leaned over to give her mom a hug.

"Thanks, mom. You're the best! Oh, and Mom, could you please stop calling me Lee Lee? I prefer Linda."

Janet sighed. "Sorry. I'll try to remember that."

CHAPTER 50

After disconnecting with Linda, Stacey approached her grandmother. "Grandma?"

Ruth looked up from her needlepoint. "Yes, Stacey."

"Can I ask you a question?"

"Of course! Come sit by me."

Stacey told her about of the conflict she had with Linda and the Tarot cards, then asked, "Do you think Tarot cards are bad?"

Ruth took a moment as she thought about how to answer the question. "Well, I'd like to hear your opinion first."

Stacey shook her head. "Why do grown-ups always do that?"

Ruth crinkled her brow. "Do what?"

"You know, turn the question around. What do *I* think?"

Ruth smiled and nodded. "Well, I did it because I truly want to know what you think about Tarot cards before I just bombard you with my own thoughts and opinions."

Stacey nodded. "Okay, I guess that's fair." Scrunching her face, and biting her bottom lip she said, "I don't really know that much about Tarot cards, but Mom says they're not to be trusted."

"Not to be trusted?"

"Well, I think she means we can't believe everything that they show."

Ruth gave her a questioning look.

Stacey continued. "Like if someone turns over the death card, does it *really* mean they or someone close to them is gonna die? Or can it mean something else will die—like a dream or desire?"

Reaching up and twisting a ringlet of light brown hair around her finger, Stacey continued, "How can a person really predict what will happen to another person?"

Ruth nodded. "Only God holds each individual's future in His hand."

Stacey nodded. "Yeah, that's what I want to tell Linda. I know she means well, but I don't think what she's doing is…right."

Ruth reached out and stroked Stacey's face.

"You know, to be so young, you sure have a lot of wisdom in that noggin' of yours."

Stacey smiled. "Thanks, Grandma."

After a few seconds, she said, "So, Grandma, you never really said what you think about this whole thing with Linda, and what I should do." Chuckling, she added, "And please, don't ask me what I want to do!"

Ruth sat back and thought a moment before replying.

"Have you said anything to Linda or about Linda that would hurt her feelings?"

Stacey shook her head. "No. I was very careful about what I said, 'cause I know how things can get twisted, and made so much worse. I still like Linda and I don't want to deliberately hurt her. I just don't agree with what she's doing, or how she's going about it."

Ruth nodded. "Well, that's a plus. Most girls your age would want to fight back and hurt the person that's hurt them. I'm amazed and proud of you for not falling into that trap."

Stacey cocked her head. "Trap?"

"I think the enemy wants Christians to act and react meanly and selfishly, so those who aren't believers will think our faith isn't real. That's why so many folks label Christians as hypocrites."

"Hypocrites? I've heard that term, but I'm not sure what it means."

"People who *say* one thing and do the opposite."

"Oh yeah. I remember the pastor speaking about that a few Sundays ago."

"As far as maintaining a friendship with Linda, if you can stand firm in your beliefs and not be swayed by hers, I think you can still be friends. I'd be on guard however, because the enemy has a way of twisting lies to make them sound true.

We can be in the world, just not of the world."

Stacey made a face. "Huh?"

Ruth chuckled. "We have to live here in this world until we die and go to heaven, but while here, we have to keep our spiritual mind in tact, and try not to participate in things that we know in our spirit aren't from God. Being wise as serpents and gentle as doves."

"How do I do that?"

"By reading your Bible, asking questions from those who are older and wiser, and attending church and other classes that help you understand God's word."

Stacey nodded.

Ruth continued, "When you asked Jesus to be Lord of your life, He gave you His Holy Spirit to guide and give you spiritual insight. You can tap into that power through prayer."

Stacey leaned over and gave her grandmother a hug. "Thanks, grandma."

Ruth pulled her into a hug as well and felt tears sting her eyes. "You are so much like your dad," she whispered.

As Stacey turned to walk away, Ruth asked, "Did you talk to your friend, Carmen, today?"

Leaning against the door jamb and facing her grandmother, she said, "Yeah. Her family went to the funeral for that girl who died in the accident. She didn't know the girl, but just seeing her family and the girl's family and friends all crying—well, it just made her feel so...sad."

Ruth gave her a sympathetic look and nodded. "Yeah, losing a child at any age is difficult. So much living left undone."

Stacey sighed. "I don't understand why God allows people to die before they've lived a long life." Bunching her fists, she added, "Sometimes I get so mad at Him when I hear about babies or kids dying, and even for taking my daddy. Why would He do that? Why cause so much pain and suffering for those left behind?" With tear-rimmed eyes, she asked, "Why doesn't He take the bad and evil people, instead of good people like my dad and that girl?" She gave her grandmother a pleading look.

Wiping tears from her own eyes, Ruth opened her arms and Stacey came into them. Patting Stacey's back and stroking her hair, Ruth said, "Oh, baby, I wish I had answers to those questions. I ask them myself sometimes. I only know that God is outside of time and He can see the past, present and future, and He has His plan all worked out." Putting her hands on the sides of Stacey's face, she said, "Even though death is hard on us left behind, if a person has a relationship with God, they truly *are* in a better place, and we can take comfort in that. I miss your dad too, but I know he's busy working for God, and he doesn't have to suffer any physical or emotional pain, and he doesn't have to worry about anything. Someday, we'll all be back together...forever."

Stacey wiped her eyes and nodded. "I know all that in my head, but sometimes my heart hurts."

"I know, sweetheart. Mine does too. Unfortunately, that is part of the human condition."

Sighing, and standing once again, Stacey said, "Thanks, Grandma. I love you."

"Oh, thank you, and I love you to the moon and back!"

Christina, having listened to the interchange from the doorway, wiped tears from her eyes. Clearing her throat to make her presence known, she walked in.

"Hey, you two! I was wondering where y'all were."

"Hey, Mom. Grandma and I were just talking."

Christina looked at them both and nodded. "About?"

Shrugging, Stacey said, "Oh, just stuff."

Not wanting to press the issue, Christina nodded and said, "Good. Wanna help me cut up veggies for the soup I'm making for lunch tomorrow?"

"Sure!" they both said together, which elicited a giggle from all three women.

Walking into the kitchen, Stacey asked, "Hey, Mom. Where's Grandpa and Nicky?"

"I sent them to the store to get some biscuits, animal food, and cat litter. Chloe's canned food is just about gone and Benji needs more doggie cookies."

Looking towards the stairs, Stacey said, "Brad's been sleeping a long time."

Christina looked at the clock. "Only a couple of hours. I'll wake him in an hour or so, so he can shower and dress for the concert."

"When the guys get back, why don't we make sandwiches. I know we had a big, late breakfast, but I'm starting to get hungry now."

"That sounds good," Ruth said, as she began slicing potatoes for the soup.

CHAPTER 51

"Sheriff Clifton?" Ed asked, as he approached the desk in the police department.

"He's in a meeting with the fire chief right now," answered Loraine, the police chief's secretary. "They've been in there quite a while. I'll let him know you're here. Mr. Florres, right?"

Ed nodded. Soon after announcing Ed's presence, the door to the Chief's office opened, and two men appeared, shaking hands and saying their good-byes.

Larry Clifton looked over at Ed and nodded, then signaled for him to come into his office.

Reaching his hand out for a shake, he asked, "So, Ed, what brings you by today?"

"I just want to know how the fire investigation is going. I see the fire chief was here. Any leads?"

Sitting, Larry said, "Well, unfortunately, no. There are no witnesses that have come forward, and any evidence we may have gathered was destroyed in the fire. Whoever did this was either lucky, or had some knowledge about arson."

Ed nodded, and steepled his fingers. "Have there been any fires like this in the past?"

"Not in the twenty-five years I've been here. Well, unless you count the court house fire, but that was because of a lightning strike, so...no, not like this. Guess there's always a first time for everything."

"Yeah. I hope it doesn't start a trend."

Nodding and sighing, Larry said, "Yeah. If whoever got away with it this time thinks he can get away with it again...well, that would be bad."

"Yep. So, do you think it was a teen-age prank, or deliberately planned and executed."

Leaning back in his chair and steepling his fingers, he said, "I'm not sure what to think. I hope the former, but I suspect the latter."

Nodding, Ed said, "Well, y'all were lucky it was confined to the science lab and didn't spread elsewhere."

"Don't I know it!"

"Will the repairs be done by the time the kids have to be back in school?"

"The fire chief, and the contractor I spoke with, seem to think so, barring any unforeseen circumstances."

"Hey, while I'm here, I was wondering if you've had any luck tracking down Christina's tormentor."

Rubbing his forehead, Larry said, "Unfortunately, no. Do you know if she's had any other unusual events occur?"

"Cindy said that Christina felt like someone had been in her house. She had a picture that disappeared, then reappeared."

Nodding, Larry said, "Oh yes. I went over one day to check that out. Nothing seemed amiss, and she told me of the mysterious occurrence with the picture." Shaking his head, he said, "I just hope she doesn't get so paranoid she sees boogeymen behind every shadow."

Ed smiled. "Well, I can't imagine Christina being like that, but if I'd been through everything she's been through in the past few months, I might get a little paranoid myself."

"I guess you're right. She has been through a lot. I'll try to be gentle and patient with her."

Standing and reaching out his hand, Ed said, "Well, thanks, Larry. If anything comes up, feel free to call me. I'd like to be kept in the loop, if that's alright with you."

Nodding and returning the handshake, Larry said, "Sure. I can always use another set of eyes and ears around here."

CHAPTER 52

Janet leaned against the headboard of her bed thinking about the fire at the school, and wondering if Jamie had anything to do with it.

She recalled her first encounter with him, and how their business relationship had blossomed from that.

One Sunday morning, at the Enlightened Ones meeting place, as she was hanging her coat, she overheard a conversation between Jamie and his friend.

The friend asked, "Hey, you still breaking into people's houses?"

She heard Jamie reply with a shush sound. "Don't talk so loud." Whispering, he said, "Yeah, I am. It's so cool! You should come with me sometime."

The other boy whispered back, "That does sound like fun. Let me know when you go again, and I'll sneak out, and meet you."

"Okay. I've been thinking about doing something a little more risky."

"Oh yeah? What?"

Jamie paused, then said, "I'm not sure yet, but I want it to be spectacular. Something that will bring some excitement to this boring town."

"Yeah? I've been thinking about doing something, too."

Before Janet could hear the rest of the conversation, Linda had come up and asked what was taking so long.

During the service, Janet began forming a plan. *If I can get the boy to break into Christina's home, and re-arrange, or steal a few things, that would at least keep her on edge. Who knows? If she's tormented enough, she may decide to go back to Michigan. It's a long shot, but if I do nothing, she'll stay here for sure.*

The next Sunday, she had sidled up to the boy and his dad at the refreshment table, and introduced herself and Linda.

Nodding, he said, "I'm Jack, and this is Jamie."

Looking nervous and fidgety, Jamie nodded a greeting.

After the service, Janet and Jack chatted a little longer, and she was able to get his and Jamie's phone numbers—in case she needed some help around her house. *Jack was a handyman, and Jamie enjoyed mowing lawns—and breaking into houses. Perfect.*

She called Jamie's phone the next day, and propositioned him. He had balked at first, and demanded to know who she was, but when she threatened to report him to the sheriff for breaking into homes, he relented.

After laying out the plan before him, they agreed on the terms. Things had gone as planned...until now.

Now this.

Was the spectacular thing he wanted to do, the school fire? If I ask him, and he admits it, then what? Who knows, maybe it was that other kid. Maybe it was neither of them. Maybe I should re-think this whole thing. Do I hate Christina enough to put my own life at risk?

CHAPTER 53

Once the soup was in the pot, Christina went upstairs to wake Brad. When she opened the door, she heard his deep resonant breathing.

Wow, he's in such a deep sleep, maybe I should let him sleep a little longer. She tip-toed over and felt his forehead: Warm and damp. Retrieving the thermometer from her room, she placed it on his temple. 99.8. *Not high enough to cause concern.* It wasn't uncommon for a body to run a low grade fever during a repair phase. She gently closed the door and went back downstairs.

Grandpa and Nicky entered the back door as she reached the last step.

"Hey, you two! How was your trip to town?"

Nicky said, "It was fun! Grandpa bought me an ice-cream sundae from Dairy Queen."

Stacey walked in and said, "Hey, that's not fair!"

Dan, who had his hand behind his back, reached in a bag and pulled out a chocolate covered sundae. "See, sweetheart, we didn't forget about you."

"Oh, thank you, grandpa!" She said as she reached for the sundae. Christina put her hands on her hips. "So, Mom and I don't rate?"

Grandpa smiled, then handed the bag to Christina. "I almost didn't get y'all anything, because I know you're watching your girlish figure." Winking at Nicky, he continued, "But Nicky talked me into getting you sundaes, too."

"Oh, thanks guys." Christina said as she took the bag.

"Yes, thank you honey." Ruth said as she reached in and took her mostly liquid sundae. Looking at Ruth, Christina said, "Guess this will ruin our appetite for lunch."

Ruth chuckled and nodded. "Yep. Guess we'll just have to wait and eat lunch at dinner."

Giggling, Nicky asked, "Then when are we gonna eat dinner? At breakfast? Then breakfast would be lunch, then lunch would be dinner." Pausing, he added, "This could get really confusing!"

Christina smiled and shook her head.

Sitting and eating their sundaes in the den, they were surprised when Brad came stumbling in.

Christina watched with concern as he rubbed his eyes and forehead.

"Did you sleep well, son?"

"Yeah. I'm so dopey, and I've got a killer headache. Can I take another pain pill?"

Christina stood and walked over to him, reaching up to feel his forehead.

He didn't feel any warmer. Looking at her watch, she said, "Seeing how those pills knock you out, and the concert starts in about three hours, maybe you should just take some aspirin."

He nodded, grimacing with the movement. "Yeah, okay. I don't want to miss the concert."

"Brad, there's a sundae in the freezer for you." Dan said, scraping the bottom of his cup to get the last drop of chocolate.

"Thanks, Grandpa, but I'm not hungry for anything right now. I think I'll take a hot shower. Hopefully, that and the aspirin will get rid of this headache."

Christina said, "Brad, let me look at your scalp."

He turned and she examined the stitched area. It looked swollen and felt warm to the touch. "Is this hurting?" she asked as she lightly pressed it.

"Ow!" He said, pulling away and putting his hand up to the back of his head.

"Geeze, Mom!"

"I'm sorry, honey. I'm just a bit concerned that it still hurts so much and it looks swollen. I wonder if all the glass was removed."

"I'm sure Dr. Carmichael got it all."

Christina sighed. "Probably. Why don't I get those aspirins and you head on up to the shower?"

He nodded and followed her to the kitchen.

When they were out of hearing, Ruth whispered to Dan. "Brad's color doesn't look good. I'm worried about him."

Dan nodded in agreement. Stacey, overhearing the comment, looked at Nicky who's eyes were furrowed with worry.

When Christina returned, she was frowning. Ruth asked, "What's wrong, honey?"

"I'm worried about Brad. If he isn't better by Monday, I'm taking him in to see Dr. Carmichael. No telling what was in the lab when it blew up. There could have been some bacteria, or weird chemicals that could make him sick."

Ruth frowned. "I guess that's possible, but it was a middle school lab and not some research lab. I kinda doubt if there would be anything dangerous."

Christina smiled and nodded. "Yeah, you're right. Guess I'm just being a bit paranoid." Sighing, she said, "It's only been a day. He'll probably be better tomorrow."

Stacey and Nicky said in unison. "Yeah, Mom. He'll be okay tomorrow." They looked at each other and giggled.

Standing, Christina said, "We need to get ready to leave, especially if we're gonna pick Linda up on the way."

Stacey and Nicky raced up the steps and returned a few minutes later with Brad. All were scrubbed and dressed. The women freshened up their make-up and hair as Dan waited patiently.

After dropping Nicky off at the school, Christina and the gang headed to McDonald's for a quick dinner, even though their appetites had been squelched by the sundaes.

CHAPTER 54

Nicky joined his band friends as they tuned their instruments with a cacophony of sounds. There was nervous chatter about the fire and explosion in the middle-school, and concerns that it could happen again at their school.

As they took their places to practice their Christmas concert music, all the while, blowing, tooting and banging their instruments, the principal walked out on stage, cleared his throat and waited for silence.

"Students, I know that many of you are concerned about the possibility of an incident like the one that occurred last night, but let me assure you that you will be safe. The police and fire departments have been all over this building and are confident that there are no dangerous items on the premises." He stopped and looked at the group of wide-eyed children and thought, *Please, dear God, let me be speaking the truth.*

"So kids, do your best, and I know this will be an amazing performance. Thank you." As he turned to leave, Nicky stood and began clapping his hands, and was soon joined by the rest of the band members.

The principal smiled, and nodded, then exited the stage.

The Sander's family, along with the same people who had attended Stacey's play the previous evening, sans Janet, filled a row of chairs. In spite of a few squeaks and squawks, the band performed well. After the final note of Jingle Bells, the overhead lights dimmed, plunging the audience into darkness, resulting in a few gasps of surprise. Soon after, small battery-operated candles started flickering to life on the stage, as the band members held them up. The audience sat in reverential silence, as Nicky stood and played Silent Night on his trumpet. When the song ended, Christina was in tears. She was thinking how very proud David would have been. Little did she know, he was standing on the stage beside Nicky, telling him that very thing.

Brad, Stacey and Linda stood, and with great enthusiasm, hooted, hollered and clapped, encouraging everyone else in the audience to follow suit. The lights in the auditorium illuminated, and the band members bowed in unison. Nicky walked off the stage, and returned with a brightly colored box containing a gift certificate for a free meal at the local Black-Eyed-Pea restaurant. Amidst cheering and clapping from his fellow band members, he handed the box to his instructor, who opened it, held up the certificate, and thanked the band members. He then thanked the audience for attending and wished everyone a safe and blessed holiday.

Looking around the room, Christina spotted Brad and Eric with a group of friends. They seemed to be doing well, despite the fact that they both would grimace and rub their necks occasionally, causing her to surmise that they both had headaches—which in an odd way, eased some of her worry.

Being an RN, and a mother, her mind would often take her to worrisome places when the children were sick or injured: *Would this bronchitis turn into pneumonia? Would a bump on the head lead to brain damage? Are the growing pains really leukemia in disguise? Would the deep cuts on Brad's head lead to meningitis?*

I'm being an overly concerned mom, she thought, as she resumed her conversation with her friends.

After congratulating Nicky on his fine performance, Ed gave Christina a hug and invited the group to join him and Cindy for dinner.

Hugging Cindy, Christina said, "Oh thanks for the invite, but we already ate before the performance."

Looking at Ed, Cindy said, "That's okay. We're planning on attending Stacey's play at the church tomorrow evening, so why don't we plan to meet before hand, or after, and have dinner together then?"

Touching Cindy's arm, Christina said, "Oh, I hope you don't feel obligated to attend her play. You've been so supportive of her and Nicky already!"

Steven walked over to shake Ed's hand. As the men talked, Cindy turned Christina away from them and scolded her saying, "Christina! We count it an honor, not an obligation, to be able to attend her play! Besides," she whispered, "it's a good reason to go out with Ed...again!" Giggling, she added, "Three nights in a row! A girl could get used to this!"

Christina smiled and shook her head. "Cindy, you're a hopeless romantic."

CHAPTER 55

Once home, Christina made hot cocoa for everyone and they sat around the family room, recapping the evening.

"Nicky, I didn't realize you could play the trumpet so well," Stacey said, adding, "I mean, when you practiced at home, you didn't sound that good."

"Stacey!" Christina said.

"I'm just sayin' he must have been practicing at school to be able to play so well."

Nicky grinned. "Thanks, Stacey. And yes, I was practicing a lot at school. I didn't want to sound like a dork, when I played."

Taking a sip of her cocoa, Ruth said, "Well, Grandpa and I are very proud of you. It just goes to show that, when you want something bad enough, you'll do whatever you need to do to achieve it."

Christina smiled. "I know your dad would be so proud of you."

Nicky nodded. "Oh, he is! I could *see* him standing right by me, telling me he was proud of me."

Christina inhaled sharply and felt tears sting her eyes.

"Well, if it is possible for him to cross the spiritual and physical realms, I'm sure he would. I, personally, have felt his presence once in a while."

"Me, too!" stated Stacey, emphatically.

Nicky and Brad both nodded in agreement. Brad said, "I know, I've seen and talked to him and he's talked to me, as well."

"Grandma, do you ever see or hear Daddy?" Nicky asked.

Ruth, with tear-rimmed eyes said, "I have! I didn't say anything about it because I thought it was my imagination working overtime, but now that you guys have said you've seen and heard from him, I think maybe what I experienced was real."

Nicky grinned. "When did you see him, Grandma?"

She wiped her eyes, set her cocoa down and began her story.

"I was in my garden picking tomatoes, remembering how much your dad liked my salsa. I started crying, and had to sit down. I was crying out to God, asking why He had allowed David to be taken, when I suddenly felt a presence. I opened my eyes, and standing before me was David."

Leaning forward with her chin on her hands, Stacey asked, "What'd he look like, grandma?"

"He looked just like he did before he died. I reached out to touch him, but he wasn't solid. He *looked* solid, but he wasn't. That's why I thought maybe I was having an awake dream. I even thought I may have passed out, and was just imagining it." Wiping her eyes once again, and clearing her throat, she continued. "I was shocked, of course, and asked him if he was real and what he was doing there. He explained that the Father...God, had let him come to comfort me. He wanted to reassure me that he was *indeed* in a better place. He said that heaven was even more beautiful and amazing than any of us could imagine."

"Wow!" Nicky said.

Ruth nodded, "Yeah. Anyway, he said to tell you all he loved you and would keep close tabs on you, and then he just faded away."

"When did this happen?"

"Back in August. That's when the tomatoes started ripening."

Christina asked, "Anyone else want to share about their experience?"

Brad, Stacey, Nicky and Dan shared stories about when and how David had appeared to them, or when they heard his voice of encouragement.

After listening, Stacey said, "So I guess that means that when people die, they *are* able to cross over the supernatural line."

"Only if God allows it." Ruth added.

Sighing, Stacey said, "Well, when I die, I'll ask God if I can come visit y'all."

Christina's eyes widened as fear gripped her heart and she said, "Well, by the time you die, many of us will be there with you." Nodding and looking around the room, she added, "Maybe."

Christina, not wanting to think about the possibility of her children dying before her, stood and said, "Well, will you look at the time?" Yawning and stretching, she added, "I'm tired. Everyone ready to head up to bed?"

Dan and Ruth glanced at each other and nodded. Stacey gathered the cups and mugs and headed for the kitchen.

"Thanks, Stacey." Christina said as she walked over to Brad who was rubbing his forehead with his fingers.

Nicky announced that he would let Benji out, and called the dog to follow him.

Concern filling her voice, Christina asked Brad if he still had a headache.

"Yeah. It's starting up again. It never completely went away, but it was bearable. Now, it feels like a vice is squeezing my brains out!"

"Let me see the back of your head. He leaned down and she felt the tender spot. It felt hot to the touch, and had increased in size.

"Does it still hurt when I touch it?"

"Ow! Yeah. Worse than before."

"Monday morning, we're going to see Dr. Carmichael."

Sighing, he said, "Yeah, I think that would be a good idea. I asked Eric if his head was hurting like this and he said no. Of course, his gash wasn't as deep as mine."

"Yeah, even though he had practically the same ones, his were pretty superficial." Patting Brad on the shoulder, she said, "I'll go get you a couple of pain relievers and an ice pack. The cold will relieve some of the swelling and help numb the pain."

Standing, he said, "Yeah, I could use something."

CHAPTER 56

Around two o'clock, Christina was wakened by a strange sound, then she heard Brad calling for her. She threw off the covers, donned her robe, then ran down the stairs and into the bathroom. She found Brad sitting on the floor with his head over the toilet.

Rushing in, she said, "Brad, honey! Are you okay?" She reached out to touch his shoulder and realized he was shaking and sobbing.

Between sobs and dry heaves, he said, "Mom! I think my head is gonna explode! It hurts so bad and I can't stop throwing up!"

Wetting a washcloth with cold water, and wiping his face, she asked, "How long have you been up?"

"I don't know. Seems like a long time. I couldn't fall asleep right away, and when I finally did, I was wakened by this horrible headache and I threw-up on the couch. I ran in here and have been throwing-up ever since."

"Oh honey, I'm sorry. Why didn't you call me sooner?"

"I couldn't. It all happened so fast, I couldn't even think straight." He was overtaken by another stomach spasm. Retching over the toilet bowl, he produced nothing but saliva and bile.

Grabbing his head, he cried out in pain, and fainted.

Christina grabbed his head before it hit the toilet or the floor. Easing him down, she called out, "Mom! Dad! I need your help!"

Placing Brad's head in her lap, she felt his forehead. It felt like it was on fire. She began to pray.

She heard footsteps running down the stairs to the bathroom, and when Dan appeared, she yelled, "Call 911!"

He ran back up to the bedroom, found his phone and dialed.

Ruth found the thermometer, and after re-wetting the washcloth, placed it on Brad's head.

Christina, reading the thermometer, almost dropped it when she saw the numbers. "Oh my goodness, Mom! It's at 106. Please go fill a bag with ice and bring it here! I need to cool his head down or he's going to have a seizure!"

Stacey and Nicky, wakened by all the commotion, came to the bathroom rubbing their eyes. "What's going on?" Nicky asked when he noticed Brad on the floor.

"Brad's sick. We're taking him to the hospital."

Stacey, with worry etched on her face asked, "Is he gonna be okay?"

Christina, not wanting to unnecessarily worry her children, said, "Of course. The doctor will give him some medicine and he'll be fine." Praying in her head, *Okay, David, please ask favor from God on behalf of your son.*

Ruth returned with the ice bag, and Christina placed it on Brad's head. Dan walked in, announcing that the ambulance would soon arrive.

"Please go turn the porch lights on, Stacey."

Within ten minutes, with lights flashing, the ambulance pulled in the driveway. Dan, Ruth, Stacey and Nicky met them at the front door, and directed them to where Brad lay in his mother's arms.

As they loaded the unconscious boy onto a stretcher, the Sheriff arrived.

"Christina, what's going on?" He asked, motioning her to join him in the hallway.

"I think he may have meningitis. He's been complaining of a headache since the explosion, and his temperature has spiked, plus he's been vomiting for a while."

Nodding, he instructed the EMS workers to get the boy to the hospital ASAP—as if they wouldn't already.

Christina ran to her room, threw on some clothes and headed downstairs. Ruth met her in the hallway, fully dressed as well.

"I'm going with you."

Christina smiled and nodded. "Thanks."

Standing with her arm around her little brother's shoulder, Stacey said, "Mom, tell Brad we love him and are praying for him."

Rushing over and hugging them tightly, she nodded and said, "I will."

Dan stood behind the children, resting a hand on each shoulder. Looking at Christina, he nodded. No words needed to be exchanged.

Ruth drove the short distance to the hospital, as Christina bowed her head and prayed every prayer and scripture she could think of on behalf of her son.

Arriving a few minutes after the ambulance, Christina jumped out of the van as soon as it stopped and ran into the ER. Ruth found a parking place, and soon joined her.

Christina, with shaking hands and voice, filled out paper work and answered questions. She appreciated Ruth's presence as a calming factor, given the intensity of the situation.

She paced around the waiting room, as Ruth sat silently with her head bowed and her hands folded.

Feeling a rush of cold air as the Emergency Room doors slid open, she was surprised and pleased to see Steven rushing towards her. He pulled her into a hug, and she once again felt warmth and comfort in that embrace.

"So, what happened?"

"First of all, why are you here?"

"One of the ER nurses, who knew we were dating, gave me a call. I came as soon as I could."

Nodding, she said, "I think Brad may have meningitis."

Looking shocked, he said, "Why? What's going on?"

Walking over to chairs, close to, but not next to Ruth, who had her eyes closed in prayer, and was unaware of their presence anyway, Christina explained the progression of symptoms since the accident two nights earlier.

"So, you think this has to do with the explosion?"

"Well, yeah. The gash on the back of his head from the shrapnel, was quite hot and swollen. I wonder if there is still debris in it, or if something was in the lab that would cause such a reaction."

"Have you talked to Eric or his mom to see if he's having any symptoms?"

Christina shook her head. "No, but Brad talked to him tonight after the concert, and he said he hadn't had any severe headaches so far. His injuries weren't as extensive as Brad's, however."

Steven nodded. "Yeah, Brad was closer to the window when the explosion occurred. It would only seem feasible that he would be hit with more shrapnel."

A few minutes later, Dr. Carmichael appeared. Ruth stood and joined Christina and Steven, as Aaron explained the situation.

"After examining Brad and reviewing his symptoms, I've come to the conclusion that we're dealing with meningitis."

Christina's eyes grew large, and she inhaled sharply, as the words echoed in her brain and landed in her heart, solidifying her worst fear.

"I haven't got all the blood work back yet, and, right now, he's having a CT scan done, but I want to keep him overnight. Depending on the lab results, and CT scan, I may need to put him in a medical coma—if the scan shows there is swelling in his brain."

Christina began to shake. Ruth batted away tears.

Steven tightened his grip around Christina's shoulders.

Dr. Carmichael reached out and took Christina's hand. Looking her in the eyes, he said, "We will do everything we possibly can to get Brad through this. If, at any time, I feel his needs exceed our capabilities, I will send him to Children's Hospital in Dallas."

Christina nodded.

"When can I see him?'

"As soon as he gets into a room, and is settled." Noticing her misery, he said, "It shouldn't be long."

"Dr. Carmichael?" A nurse said as she approached the group.

He turned. "Yes?"

"Here's the blood report and CT results you asked for."

Nodding, and taking the papers, he thanked her and began scanning the pages.

Sighing and frowning, he said, "Christina, I hate to be the bearer of bad news, but Brad does indeed have meningitis. We will need to do a blood culture to determine exactly what bug we're dealing with, but in the meantime, I will order a medication to put him into a coma, and I need to reopen the head wound for it to drain and relieve some of the pressure."

Batting back tears, and trying to control her speech, she asked, "How long do you think he'll be in a coma?"

Shaking his head, he said, "I don't know. Patients vary in their response to the medication and other treatments."

"I thought you gave him antibiotics already. How can he have an infection?"

Shrugging and shaking his head, he said, "We gave him a broad spectrum antibiotic, but it may not have been a strong enough dose. I'll have a culture run, and will see which antibiotic will work for him."

Nodding and biting her bottom lip, she said, "Thank you, Aaron. Please let us know when we can see him."

"Sure, I will. I'm sending him down the hall to the ICU." Reaching out, he shook Steven's hand, and patted Christina and her mother-in-law on their shoulders. He headed down the hall, then stopped and turned, "Oh, Christina, you'll probably need to sign more papers authorizing the implementation of the medical coma and surgical procedure."

She nodded and headed to the nurses' station.

CHAPTER 57

"Mom!" Linda called from her bedroom.

"In the laundry room!" Janet called back as she put a load of jeans in to wash.

Linda appeared in the doorway holding the phone in her hand.

"I just talked to Stacey, and she said they had to take Brad to the hospital last night."

Janet felt fear clutch her heart. "Why? What happened?" Sitting in a chair at the kitchen table, unsure if she could trust her legs to do their job, and feeling her hands begin to shake, she held them together as her daughter sat across from her, and explained the situation.

"Well, Stacey said that after the explosion, Brad had been complaining of a headache. Everyone blew it off 'cause that was kinda normal after getting hit in the head with something." After taking a sip of chocolate milk, she continued. "Anyway, it got worse and worse, and he woke up throwing up and crying 'cause it hurt so bad. Stacey said, he said it felt like his head was going to explode! Then he passed out."

Janet put a hand up to her chest to keep her heart from beating out of it.

"So, is he at the hospital now, or did they take him to Dallas?" She asked her daughter.

Chewing on a hangnail, Linda said, "Her grandpa just talked to Mrs. Sanders, and told Stacey that Brad was in the ICU at the hospital here! If he gets worse, they'll send him to Dallas."

Shock and worry filled Janet's being. "ICU? Why there?"

Sighing, Linda said, "Well, Stacey said she heard her mom through the phone say something with "itis" on the end of it. Not sure what it is, but she thought maybe it was an infection in his brain."

"Meningitis?"

"Yeah, that's it! I knew it was a long word. I've never heard of that. What is it?"

Blowing air out, Janet said, "It's an infection in the brain."

Linda gasped. "Oh! That sounds serious!"

Nodding, Janet said, "It is."

"Do people die from that?"

"Some have." Noticing the fear, worry, and tear-rimmed eyes of her daughter, Janet added, "Not everyone does. If it's caught early enough, the person can recover."

"Will he be a vegetable?"

Shocked, Janet said, "What?"

"You know, will he have brain damage?"

Rubbing her eyes, Janet said, "Highly doubtful. Most people who recover are fine."

Sitting up straighter, Linda said, "You said most. What about the other ones?"

"Well, sometimes...rarely though, people will have some brain damage."

"Oh my goodness!" Linda said as tears filled her eyes. "I really like Brad! I don't want him to be brain damaged or die!"

Janet reached over, patted Linda's hand and said, "He'll be okay. They caught it pretty early." Looking her in the eyes, she continued, "Besides, the doctors at the hospital are about the best around. If they can't help him, they'll send him to Children's Hospital in Dallas."

Wiping her eyes and blowing her nose in a napkin, Linda said, "I hope you're right, Mom."

Smiling, and hoping to lighten the mood, Janet said, "Hey, have I ever been wrong?"

"Well..."

"Okay, don't answer that!"

Standing, Janet said, "You keep in touch with Stacey, and I'll call the hospital and see if I can get any other information. I have a couple of friends in the ER."

Linda smiled and said, "Thanks, Mom."

Cocking her head, Janet asked, "For what?"

"Well, for just listening and caring."

Janet's heart did a triple beat. *If she only knew my part in all this, she wouldn't be so apt to thank me. I've gotta make sure she never finds out.*

CHAPTER 58

Nicky and his grandpa sat side by side on the couch, looking at the TV, but not really watching it—both lost in their thoughts and prayers for Brad.

After a few minutes, Nicky said, "Grandpa?"

Muting the TV, Dan said, "Yes, Nicky."

"Why did God make my daddy die?"

Shocked by the question, Dan took in a deep breath and released it.

Turning to face Nicky, he said, "Well, Nicky, God didn't make him die. He died because of all the injuries he had from the accident. There were too many for his body to handle."

Nodding, Nicky said, "Yeah, my mom said that." Sighing, he continued his train of thought. "But if God is the giver and taker of life, it must mean He took my dad, right?"

"Many folks have debated that over the years, but if I understand the Bible correctly, God *allows* certain things to happen. He doesn't necessarily cause them to happen."

Nicky gave him a confused look.

"Do you remember the story about Job and how Satan asked permission from God to test Job's faith by inflicting different kinds of pain on him, emotional and physical?"

"Yeah. His kids were all killed, and all his livestock and servants. Then he got sores all over his body, and his friends were kinda jerks to him, and his wife said 'Curse God and die!' Which I thought was kinda mean, too."

Dan chuckled. "Yeah, it was pretty mean. Anyway, God didn't make those things happen to Job, but He allowed them to happen, to prove Job's faithfulness."

Nicky thought about that a moment, then asked, "So when bad things happen, like when I was kidnapped, God allows Satan to do them?" He paused and scrunched up his face. "How do we fight against that?"

Dan sighed. "Well, I know prayer is a great tool to use against the enemy. That, and Bible verses."

"You think praying will stop him?"

Nodding, Dan said, "Well, if God has a greater purpose for someone and wants them to go through a trial, I think our prayers can help keep them safe and, maybe, take some of Satan's powers away."

"So...God allowed Ruby to kidnap me, so I could learn a lesson?" With tear-rimmed eyes, he added, "I don't understand what lesson He wants me to learn! I've thought about it a lot, and I just don't know."

Dan reached out and pulled Nicky close to his side.

"I think sometimes the lesson isn't necessarily for the person going through the trial, as it may be for those around him or her, watching them go through the trail."

Nicky pulled away and looked at his grandpa. "So, maybe it wasn't a lesson for me to learn?"

Dan nodded.

Sighing, and leaning back into his grandpa, he said, "Well, if it was for me, I didn't get it, but if it was for someone else, then I guess I'm okay with that."

Dan smiled. "Well, your behavior and testimony concerning the event could have impacted someone's life in ways you can't even imagine...like Ruby's. If it wasn't for you, she wouldn't have someone to love her unconditionally."

Scrunching his face, Nicky nodded and said, "I hope so, 'cause I don't want to go through anything like that again!"

"Well, Son, there may be different trials you will go through, throughout your life, that will test your integrity and faith...but, hopefully, no more kidnappings!"

"Integrity? What's that?"

"Integrity is being honest and trustworthy, no matter what. Like, if you tell someone you're going to do something, you do it, no matter how you feel. God wants us to be honest and dependable, even if it's uncomfortable."

Nicky scrunched up his face as he thought about being trustworthy and honest.

"Have you gone through a lot of trials, Grandpa?"

Nodding, he answered, "Yes, Nicky, I certainly have."

"Can you tell me about them sometime?"

Nodding and pulling Nicky close, kissing the top of his head, he said, "Someday I will, but I think we have enough to deal with right now. Why don't we say a prayer for Brad?"

"Yeah, and make that 'ole devil leave him alone!"

CHAPTER 59

By the time Brad was settled into his room, Cindy and Ed had arrived. Surprised at their presence, because of the early morning hour, Christina asked how they knew to come.

"Your mother-in-law called me." Cindy said with a shrug. "Ed decided to stay the night on the couch, so when I told him about Brad, he wanted to come too."

Smiling, she gave each one a hug and turned to thank her mother-in-law.

"Thanks, Lord knows I'm in need of some emotional support."

Dr. Carmichael approached the group and cleared his throat.

"Christina, Brad is settled in, if you want to see him."

Motioning to the group, Christina asked, "Is it okay if they come in as well?"

He thought a moment, then said, "It's a pretty tight space in there. How about just three of you at a time?"

Christina looked at Cindy and shrugged. Cindy understood that she and Ed would have to wait. Taking Ed's arm, Cindy said, "We'll be out in the waiting lounge."

Christina made a face. "Sorry."

Cindy put her hand up as if to wave off the comment.

Dr. Carmichael turned to Christina.

"You need to understand that Brad is in an induced coma, and because of that, he has a respirator, several IV bags hung, a catheter, and cardiac and respiratory monitors, plus an EEG machine to check his brain activity."

Christina's eyes began to tear up. Holding on to Ruth's and Steven's arms for support, and blinking back tears, she nodded and said, "Okay. I'm ready."

Hearing about the condition of her son, and actually seeing it involved two totally different brain processes. When they walked into the room, the first things that grabbed her attention were the rhythmic shushing sound of the respirator, and the beeping of the heart monitor. Looking at her son, her brain took her back to the familiar scene of David's room, and she felt the room spin and dim, and her legs go limp. If Steven hadn't been holding her arm, she would have surely hit the floor. He and Ruth caught her, and helped her to a nearby chair. Steven put her head down between her knees as Ruth rubbed her back, and Dr. Carmichael waved a small vial of ammonia under her nose. Coming back to full consciousness, she sat up, rubbed her eyes, and said, "Thanks guys."

Blowing out a lung-full of air, she said, "Wow! I didn't expect that reaction! Guess my mind and body did a shut down."

Looking over at Brad, Steven said, "It certainly looks worse than it is."

Nodding, Ruth said, "Yeah. I wasn't expecting it to look so...awful."

Dr. Carmichael walked over and checked the monitors and IVs. He then bent down to check the catheter bag. "Everything seems to be in working order."

Patting Christina's arm, he said, "You can stay for a few minutes, but I suggest you go home, and rest a while. Brad's stable, and he isn't aware of your presence." Giving her arm a light squeeze, he added, "You have two other kids to think of."

Christina frowned. *How dare he tell me to leave my son!* To him, she said, "Thank you for your concern, Aaron, but I'd rather stay here. My in-laws can take care of the other two kids." Turning to her mother-in-law, she said, "Right, Mom?"

Ruth answered with a nod, wishing she could stay as well, but knowing it wouldn't be wise.

Aaron nodded. If it was his daughter, Sammy, in the bed, he wouldn't want to leave either. "I'll have the staff find a cot for you, and arrange the room so you can stay."

Nodding and rubbing her eyes, Christina said, "Thanks, Aaron. I'd appreciate that."

After walking over to stroke and kiss Brad's head, Christina and Ruth went out to talk to Cindy and Ed.

Crossing her arms over her chest, Christina said, "I really appreciate y'all coming to support us, but we'll be okay. Brad's resting well, and he's in very good hands."

Cindy hugged Christina. "He'll be okay too. There are a lot of people rooting for him, and as the word spreads, there will be many more."

Christina gave her a tired smile and nodded. "Thanks."

"Can Ed and I just peek in?"

"Sure. Let me warn you, it looks pretty scary."

Cindy gasped when she saw Brad lying on the bed, surrounded by paraphernalia designed to keep him alive.

Touching her friend's back ever so lightly, Christina said, "See? Looks awful, but fortunately he's not aware of anything."

Cindy nodded. "Yeah." Pulling Christina into a hug, she asked, "You want Ed and I to take Ruth home?"

Looking at Ruth, who seemed to have aged a bit, Christina asked, "You look so tired, Mom. Are you okay with them dropping you off, or can you drive back home?"

Ruth sighed and nodded. "I can drive home, but if they'd follow me, I'd like that."

After good-nights were said, Steven pulled her into another hug.

"You okay?"

"I guess. It's hard to be okay, when my son is lying in a hospital bed in a coma."

"Can I get you anything?"

Sighing, she said, "Why don't we sit quietly while the nurses get my bed ready?"

They walked into the waiting room and sat. She leaned into him and closed her eyes.

She must have dozed off, because she was aware of Steven's voice urging her to wake up.

"Honey, the room is ready for you. Let me help you."

Putting his arm around her shoulder, he led her into the room, helped her onto the cot, and waited, as she drifted off to sleep. Kissing her on the forehead, he checked on Brad before heading to the couch in his office. He had a busy day ahead, and needed at least a couple hours of good sleep.

CHAPTER 60

When Ruth pulled the van into Christina's driveway, Ed flashed his lights, and he and Cindy went back to her house.

Looking at her watch, Cindy said, "Geeze, it's five o'clock. I don't know whether to go back to bed, or stay up."

"I'd say go back to bed. I, however want to stay up a while and read up on meningitis. I'm not familiar with it, and I want to know what Brad is dealing with."

Cindy yawned, stretched and said, "Yeah, okay. I am going back to bed. Hopefully, I won't sleep the day away."

After giving her a quick hug and kiss, Ed went to the kitchen table, turned on his laptop computer, and pulled up information regarding meningitis.

Reading the symptoms, (headache, nausea, vomiting, fever, seizures, brain swelling), he wondered if perhaps there had been something potentially deadly brewing in the lab, and the explosion set it free—or perhaps, Brad's meningitis was simply the result of injuries sustained. *Besides,* he reasoned, *what deadly thing would be lurking in a middle school lab?* He closed the computer, and laid on the couch, letting his mind ruminate over the past few months events, before falling into a deep sleep.

CHAPTER 61

Stacey woke from a nightmarish dream in which she and her brothers were being chased by a large dog-like creature. She had lost track of Brad and was calling for him when she woke. Sitting up in bed, and rubbing her eyes, she whispered, "Please, God, heal my brother."

She heard a light tapping on her bedroom door.

"Yes?"

"Stacey? Can I come in?"

It was Nicky. "Sure."

Looking around the room, he said, "I thought I heard you talking to someone."

"Yeah. God. I was just praying out loud."

Nodding, he said, "Yeah, I've been doing a lot of that, too."

She patted her bed, and he sat. Sighing, he said, "I don't understand why all this stuff is happening to us. Do you think it's because God's mad that we moved here instead of staying in Michigan?"

Stacey scrunched her face. "I never thought about that, but I don't think so. I think there may be more going on than we can see."

"Huh? Like what?"

"I think there may be a spiritual battle going on."

"Spiritual battle? Why?"

Sighing, she said, "I don't know why, except maybe to test our faithfulness. Remember how Job was tested in the Bible?"

"Yeah. Grandpa and I were just talking about that." Pausing a moment, he asked, "Why us?"

Frowning, she said, "I don't know. Why was Job tested?"

"Because Satan wanted to prove that he wasn't really as dedicated to God as he appeared to be?"

Nodding, Stacey said, "Yeah. Maybe Satan doesn't think we're as dedicated as we claim to be, and he wants to break us down. Make us angry at God, and turn away from Him."

Nicky, scrunching his face, said, "Well, I am kinda mad at God for taking Daddy, and letting me be kidnapped, and now this thing with Brad."

Reaching out to take her brother's hands, Stacey said, "Yeah, me too."

Nicky asked, "Do you think our anger is giving Satan more power?"

"I suppose that's possible. I think it makes him happy when we humans get mad at each other, but especially when we get mad at God."

Sighing, Nicky said, "Yeah, I guess we ought not be mad at God. Grandpa said that God sets things up, and is in control at all times. He also said that God can see the past, present, and the future, and His plans are already laid out. We just have to trust that He will do what is best for us, no matter what happens."

With eyes full of concern and tears, Nicky whispered, "But what if Brad dies?"

Stacey shrugged and sighed. "I guess I'd rather him die than live with brain damage." Picturing Brad, in her mind's eye, lying in a bed, unable to move made her cringe.

"I can only imagine how awful it would be to not be able to do the things I once did. I would rather die than live like that."

Pulling his hands free, and wiping the tears that threatened to fall, Nicky said, "I don't want him to die!"

Tears streaming down her face, Stacey said, "Me neither, but that's not for us to decide. No matter what happens, we can't let Satan win."

Wiping his eyes and reigning in his emotions, Nicky nodded.

"Stacey?"

"Yeah?"

"What are you gonna do about your play at church tonight?"

Sighing, she said, "Well, I was thinking about that. Since I'm the only one that can play Mary, I guess I'll just have to go and do it." She gave a crooked smile. "The show must go on!"

Nodding, he said, "Yeah. The show must go on."

CHAPTER 62

When Christina wasn't dozing on the cot next to Brad's bed, she was praying and thinking. Her family had been through so much the past couple of years and she couldn't help but wonder if they had been targeted by demonic forces, and if so, for what reason? To test their faith? To test someone else's faith? She was trying to be strong, but as she watched her unconscious son depending on a respirator for oxygen, and fed through IVs, she couldn't help but wonder what could possibly be good about this. Her mother's heart grieved with the possibility of losing him to death or to a life of mental and physical incapacitation. Her mind and body were so tired of all the stress. As tears streamed down her face and sobs shook her body, she sensed a presence, and felt a warm embrace. The tears and sobs subsided, and she relaxed, knowing beyond a shadow of a doubt that everything would work out. How they would work out was beyond her knowing, but she knew that no amount of worry or anxiety would change the outcome. Faith and trust were her two allies that she would have to lean on, during this trying time.

CHAPTER 63

Later that morning, as Christina stood by the bed watching the nurse change Brad's IV, he opened his eyes and looked at her. She gasped and squeezed his hand, feeling a slight response from him, before he drifted back into unconsciousness.

The nurse, busy with the IV, didn't notice the exchange, and was surprised by Christina's sudden outburst.

"Oh my goodness!" She whispered excitedly, "He opened his eyes and looked at me, then he squeezed my hand!"

The nurse gave her a skeptical look, thinking she had imagined it.

Looking at Brad, who was sleeping peacefully, she asked, "Are you sure?"

Christina frowned. "Of course I'm sure! While you were changing the IV, he opened his eyes, looked at me, and squeezed my hand!"

"Well, that's unusual. The doctor hasn't started the medication to wake him yet. I'm surprised he's responsive at all."

Christina bit her lip. She wanted to scream. Instead, she said, "Well, that may be, but I know what I know."

The nurse cocked her head and nodded. How could she argue with that?

"Okay, Mrs. Sanders. If he does something like that again, please let us know."

Nodding and squeezing Brad's hand again, she said, "I will."

After the nurse left, Christina sat and bowed her head in prayer.

"Thank you, God. I needed that reassurance. I know he'll be okay now."

Her cell phone rang. She dug through her purse and found it.

"Mom?" She heard Stacey's voice on the other end.

"Hey, good morning, sweetie! How are you this morning?"

"Good morning to you. I'm okay. How's Brad doing?"

Christina told her the good news.

"Oh, my goodness! Does that mean he'll be waking up soon?"

"I don't know. I do believe it's a sign from God letting us know he's gonna be okay though."

"That's awesome!" After a pause Stacey said, "Mom, my church play is tonight. I have to be there. I'm the only one who can play the role of Mary."

Christina sighed. "Oh, honey, I'm sorry I forgot about that. Of course you need to be there."

"Will you be there?"

"I wouldn't miss it. What time do you need to be at the church?"

"At four. We'll practice, then have pizza. I doubt if I'll be able to eat though. I'm already nervous."

"You'll do great, honey. I know you know your lines backwards and forwards."

Stacey nodded and sighed. "Yeah, I just hope I don't have any brain farts and forget them."

Christina chuckled. "I doubt that'll happen." Pausing she asked, "Is Grandma up?"

"Yes. You want to talk to her?"

"Yes, please."

Christina paced in the hallway, as Stacey called for her grandmother.

"Christina is everything alright?" Ruth asked as she came on the line.

Smiling, Christina told her mother-in-law about Brad's progress.

"Oh my!" Ruth said, "That *is* good news."

"I know! I had just asked God for some kind of sign that he'd be okay, and that happened! I don't feel so worried anymore."

"Have you talked to the doctor yet?"

"No, he should be in soon though." Pausing, she said, "Mom, Stacey has her play tonight and I need to be there. If I can't get anyone to sit with Brad, could you come stay with him so I can go to the play?"

Without hesitating, Ruth answered, "Of course, honey. In fact, I was just thinking that I would run up there in a little while and let you come home to shower and change."

Christina sighed. "That would be nice, Mom. I feel a bit rumpled."

Ruth chuckled. "How about you call me after the doctor comes, and I'll head on over?"

Christina nodded. "Sounds like a plan."

"Oh, by the way, you got a call from a lady named Margaret. She said her mom's memorial service will be tomorrow at ten at the First Baptist Church. I hope it was okay, but I explained the situation with Brad, and assured her that if you could be there, you would, but you may not be able to attend. She said she understood and said to thank you again for caring, and volunteering to take Elijah."

"Thanks, Mom. I doubt if I'll go, given the circumstances. I'll give her a call. I'm hoping she can bring Elijah over, since I haven't been able to go get him."

The women disconnected and Christina walked to the nurses' station to inquire about Dr. Carmichael's schedule.

"He should be here in a few minutes, Mrs. Sanders. He usually does his rounds before seeing his office patients."

Christina nodded and smiled. "I'm gonna grab a coffee before heading back to the room."

"Would you like us to have the kitchen bring you a breakfast tray?"

Smiling, she said, "That would be nice."

She peeked in at Brad once more before heading down the hall to the coffee bar. Walking back with the cup in hand, her mind took her back to the day David had died. She had been walking back to his room with a cup of coffee when the alarm sounded. She was hit with the possibility of the same scenario, and had to stop, catch her breath, and calm her spirit before continuing. Thankfully, no alarms sounded, and she returned to find Brad still sleeping peacefully. She stepped out of the room to call Margaret.

Sipping the coffee and absently perusing through an old magazine the nurse had brought in, she was startled when she heard someone clearing their throat. Looking up, and seeing Dr. Carmichael standing in the doorway, looking like he had stepped out of a GQ magazine, her breath caught. She hated that he brought that kind of reaction to the surface, but he was a beautiful specimen of a man with his thick dark hair, dark eyes and eyelashes, and his well-toned body.

Bringing her emotions under control, she said, "Oh, hi, Aaron. I mean Dr. Carmichael."

He smiled his million dollar smile and said, "You can call me Aaron."

She could feel the blush creeping up her neck to her face. Nodding, she said, "Right."

Walking over to Brad, he said, "The nurses said you spent the night here." She nodded.

"Did you get any rest?"

Running her fingers through her hair and rubbing her eyes, she shook her head and said, "Not really."

"I imagine it's difficult to rest when the nurses are always coming in and out of the room."

She grimaced. "Yeah, seems like I'd just doze and someone would be in taking Brad's vitals, or adjusting and changing his medication."

He bent over, and putting his stethoscope on Brad's chest, listened for a moment before lifting the sleeping boy's eyelids and checking the pupils' reaction time with a flashlight.

He turned to face Christina. "His vitals are stable, but I think we'll keep him under one more day. I'll order another CT scan to check on the swelling, but it seems he's going to get through this pretty quick."

"So the antibiotics are working?"

Nodding, he said, "Yes. Very well, it seems. The first culture came back as staph, but I had the lab run blood cultures to check for other bacteria, as well. I should be getting those results tomorrow. It takes a good twenty-four hours to grow anything."

"How do you know it was staph?"

"It grew rapidly in the culture tube and I was able to see it under the microscope. Another day or so of antibiotics and he should be good as new. His fever is steadily dropping, so that's a good sign."

She let out a big sigh. "Thank you. That's good news."

"He was a lucky young man. We were able to catch the meningitis before it did any damage."

Chewing on her thumbnail, she asked, "So you're sure he won't have any brain-damage?"

He smiled and shook his head. "I can assure you, he won't have any brain-damage."

Smiling and nodding, she said, "I just needed to hear you say that."

Taking her hand in his, and looking into her eyes—which made her heart race, and her knees weaken, he said, "Christina, why don't you go home for a while and rest? Brad is in good hands here, and since he's sleeping so deeply, he isn't even aware of your presence."

Pulling her hand free and walking over to Brad's bed, she said, "My mother-in-law is coming in a few minutes so I can go home and freshen up, and I was planning to go to Stacey's play at the church tonight. My mother-in-law said she'd come sit with Brad."

"Don't you think your mother-in-law would like to see Stacey's play too?"

Making a face she said, "Yeah, I suppose so, but I'm not sure who else could sit with Brad."

Leaning against the door jamb, he said, "Christina, Brad will be fine for the few hours you will be at the play. If anything changes, I have your number in my phone, and I can let you know immediately. I know you're worried. You're his mom. But honestly, your daughter needs you and her grandmother there, more than Brad needs you here."

Rubbing her hands over her face, she wrestled with the idea. Looking up, she said, "My head knows you're right, but my heart doesn't want to leave Brad alone. What if he wakes up and no one is here?"

Shaking his head and softening his voice, he said, "Christina, he isn't going to wake up until I order the drug to wake him up. Please go and be with the rest of your family."

Sighing and nodding, she said, "Okay. I'll call my mother-in-law to come get me."

After one last glance at Brad, he patted Christina's shoulder on the way out. "Remember, I'll call if anything changes."

"Thanks." After finding her cell phone, she called home.

CHAPTER 64

"Mom!" Stacey called, as Christina walked in the back door. Christina opened her arms, as Stacey walked into them.

"I'm so glad you came home. Is Brad okay? Is he awake yet? Are you coming to my play?"

"Whoa, babe. First of all, Brad is doing okay. Still asleep. The doctor says he should wake up in a day or two. And yes, I'm coming to your play. I wouldn't miss it for the world." She felt Stacey sigh and relax.

Looking at her watch, she asked, "What time did you say you have to be at the church?"

Stacey pulled away and said, "Four o'clock. The play starts at six."

"Well, it's two now, so I'm gonna go hop in the shower, then we can have a few minutes, before I drop you off at the church.

Smiling, as she ran up the stairs to do her own prepping, Stacey said, "I'll see you in a few."

Ruth, who was leaning on the kitchen counter watching and listening to the exchange, patted Christina's arm as she walked by.

"I know you feel torn between Brad and Stacey, but you're doing the right thing. Stacey was so worried that we wouldn't be there for her play."

Sighing, Christina said, "Yeah, this is certainly *not* how I had planned the weekend to go."

Letting out a sigh herself, Ruth said, "Well, I'm glad we're here. I'd hate for you to go through all this alone."

Christina reached out and hugged her mother-in-law, feeling the sting of tears as they threatened to overflow. Blinking rapidly to disperse them, she said, "The hardest thing is to wait, and not know the outcome. I know Dr. Carmichael said Brad would be okay, but can he really know for sure? I know how fast something can go wrong. We've been through so much these past couple of years, I just want some normalcy. Is that too much to ask?"

Patting Christina's back, Ruth said, "I know this has been difficult for you, and I wish I could make it better—to assure you that everything will be okay, but unfortunately, only God knows the outcome. That's why we have to trust Him to get us and those we love through the tough times."

Wiping her eyes, Christina said, "I'm trying to stay strong in my faith, but it's getting more and more difficult. I'm getting tired. Seems like one crisis passes and another one begins." Grabbing a tissue from a box on the counter and blowing her nose, she continued, "I've hardly had time to catch my breath."

Nodding, Ruth said, "I wish I had some great insight or words of wisdom, but the only thing that comes to mind is the verse that reminds us to trust in God, even when we don't understand."

"Yeah, that verse keeps popping up in my mind too—especially lately. 'Trust in the Lord with all your heart, and lean not on your own understanding. In all your ways acknowledge Him, and He will direct your paths.' Now, if I can put that into practice."

Nodding, Ruth said, "Easier said than done, sometimes."

On a sigh, Christina added, "Don't I know it." Patting Ruth's arm, Christina turned to head upstairs.

Stopping on the first step, she turned and said, "Thanks, Mom, for listening, and for being here."

"I wouldn't want to be anywhere else." She whispered to Christina's disappearing back.

After dropping off Stacey, Christina called the ICU to check on Brad. No change. During the drive home, she thought of Eric and wondered how he was doing, and if he knew about Brad. When she pulled the van into the driveway, she sat for a few minutes, and called Eric's mom and brought her up to date on Brad's situation,

"Oh, my goodness, Christina! I had no idea he had gotten worse. We just saw him a couple of nights ago, and he seemed fine."

"I know. The change came on so suddenly, and intensely. He had been complaining of a headache, and I had planned to take him to the doctor on Monday, but then he passed out, and it was kinda downhill from there."

"Yeah. Eric had a headache for a couple of days, but seems better this evening. Even though their injuries were similar, I don't think Eric had as many deep gashes as Brad."

"Have you checked them today to make sure there is no drainage or swelling?"

"I did a few minutes ago, and everything seems to be healing nicely. I plan to call in the morning to make an appointment this week, just to make sure before Christmas gets here."

"Good idea. It's hard to believe that Christmas will be here in a few days! We were planning to celebrate with my in-laws tomorrow, but I guess that'll have to wait until Brad wakes up."

"Oh, Christina, I wish I could help in some way. Do you need anything?"

Christina smiled. She hardly knew the woman, and here she was, offering her help. "Thanks, Erica, but with my in-laws here, I think we'll be okay."

After disconnecting, Erica went to inform her family of Brad's condition. Her son, Eric, began making phone calls soon after.

CHAPTER 65

Stacey's play went on without any glitches: no skipped lines, missing props, or costume malfunctions. Stacey portrayed the part of the modern-day Mary with such aplomb, she earned a standing ovation, at the end of the performance. Christina and her entourage decided it would be a fitting end to a successful evening, by meeting Ed and Cindy at the new Dessert Palace in the outlet mall. As everyone recapped the events of the evening, Christina slipped away to the restroom, to call the hospital.

"ICU, Desiree Mitchell speaking."

"Hi, Desiree, this is Christina Sanders. Brad's mom."

"Oh, hi, Mrs. Sanders. I just checked on Brad and he's sleeping peacefully."

"Well, I assumed so, since I hadn't heard from anyone, but I just needed to make sure."

Christina could sense the nurse smiling.

"Rest assured, Mrs. Sanders, that we will call you immediately, if anything changes. In the meantime, enjoy your time away."

"Thank you, Desiree. I should be returning in about an hour or so."

"Okay. We'll be here."

As Christina returned the phone to her purse, she breathed a sigh of relief and shot a thank you prayer up to heaven.

She was so thoroughly enjoying the conversation, laughter and taste of the decadent hot fudge cake, she didn't hear the buzzing of her phone in her purse. As they began donning coats and saying good-byes, Cindy's phone rang loud and clear.

Pulling it out of her purse, she frowned as she read the unfamiliar number and answered, warily.

"Hello?"

Christina paused, and looked at Cindy when she heard her gasp and say, "She's right here. Let me hand the phone to her."

Christina's heart skipped a coupe of beats as she took the phone. *Who in the world would be calling her on Cindy's phone?* Realization hit her like a semi truck—the hospital.

Taking the phone, she put it up to her ear, and with a surprisingly calm voice, said, "This is Christina Sanders."

"Mrs. Sanders, this is Desiree Mitchell from the ICU. You need to come to the hospital right away."

"Okay. Why? Is Brad okay?"

"We'll explain more when you get here, but I will tell you, he had a seizure."

"I'll be right there. I'm only a couple of blocks away."

Handing the phone back to Cindy, she said, "I need to get to the hospital. Brad's had a seizure."

Looking at Stacey and Nicky, she said, "Cindy could you stay with the kids 'cause I'd like to have Mom and Dad take me to the hospital." She wanted—no, needed them to be with her in case the worse-case-scenario took place.

"Mom? We'd like to come too!" pleaded Stacey.

Christina hugged both kids and said, "I know, but you can't be in there anyway, and someone needs to go home, and take care of the animals."

Letting out large sighs, the siblings nodded.

Even though unspoken, they both knew the real reason for their mom's reluctance to have them accompany her. If Brad had indeed taken a turn for the worse, she didn't need them underfoot. She would need all her resources to deal with that crisis.

As the Sander's kids watched their mother and grandparents leave, Samara, who had been standing by her mother, walked over and placed a hand on each of their shoulders.

Ed broke the silence and intensity of the moment by clearing his throat and saying, "Well, we best get going." Looking around and noting the waitstaff clearing tables and sweeping floors, he added, "I think they're closing up."

CHAPTER 66

As soon as the van rolled up to the hospital entrance, Christina hopped out, and ran to the door, calling over her shoulder, "I'll see y'all in the ICU!"

Running down the hallway, past the Emergency Room, X-ray, CT, MRI departments, and various other offices and labs, she entered the ICU wing at the east end of the hospital, stopping in Brad's doorway. She saw Dr. Carmichael, and a couple of the ICU nurses hunched over the still body of her son. Gasping and expecting the worst, she grabbed the door frame for support. Dr. Carmichael turned to face her, and noticing her pallor, was concerned she may pass-out. He walked over, put his arm around her shoulders, and pulled her into the room—his expression unreadable.

"Christina, he's okay. The seizure was minor and, even though his heart stopped for a few beats, there was no permanent damage."

She looked up at him wide-eyed. "Heart stopped?"

Seeing the fear in her eyes, he led her to the bedside and said, "I'm not sure what caused the seizure or cardiac arrhythmia, but the EEG shows no more unusual activity, and his heart activity has returned to normal."

Reaching out, taking her son's limp hand, and looking up into Dr. Carmichael's dark brown eyes, she asked, "How many is a few beats?"

"About two minutes."

"What? Two minutes? That's a long time with no oxygen to his brain. Do you think he has any brain damage?"

"I know it seems like a long time, but I've had patients oxygen deprived for longer and with no apparent side effects. He's young and healthy, so I doubt he'll suffer any, as well. We'll know more when he wakes up."

"So when will that be? Maybe he's been under too long."

Nodding, he said, "I've discontinued the meds that are keeping him sedated. Hopefully, he'll be alert by morning. In the meantime, we'll continue to monitor his progress."

Hearing commotion at the door, she looked over to see her in-laws speaking to one of the nurses.

Dr. Carmichael motioned them into the room and explained Brad's condition.

Tears filling their eyes, they quietly approached the bed.

Ruth asked, "How do you know for sure there is no brain or heart damage?"

If this were his little girl lying in the bed, he'd wonder the same thing. Clearing his throat, he answered, "I trust the machines are accurate in their interpretation of the information. According to them, everything is back to normal."

Nodding, but not thoroughly convinced, Ruth turned her attention back to Brad.

Dan asked, "So, you think he'll wake up tomorrow?"

"That's our hope." After a few moments of silence, Dr. Carmichael said, "Well, I suggest you all go home and rest. It appears as if there will be no further changes."

Christina shook her head. "Yeah. That's what you said last time and he ended up with a seizure and cardiac arrest." Looking up at him with determination in her eyes, she added, "I'm not leaving his side until he's ready to be discharged."

Nodding, he said, "Alright then." Glancing at Dan and Ruth, he added, "Maybe your in-laws would like to go home?"

Not thoroughly convinced that Brad was out of the woods yet, Dan furrowed his eyebrows, and looking at Ruth, said, "Maybe in a little while."

Seeing the determination on their faces, Dr. Carmichael nodded, glanced one more time at Brad's monitors, patted Christina's arm and left the room.

The three adults gathered around Brad's bed, joined hands and began praying for physical and mental safety as his unconscious mind began it's long swim to the surface of consciousness.

CHAPTER 67

When Brad's heart stopped, he immediately became aware of several things: his limp body and the hospital staff frantically working over it, his dad, and several ethereal beings surrounding the bed.

"Dad!" He exclaimed as he ran or floated—he wasn't sure—to David's open arms.

David enfolded him and kissed his neck. "Son, it's so nice to be able to hug you!"

Brad, looking down at their ethereal bodies asked, "How is this possible?"

David smiled, as he disengaged. "Weird, huh?"

Brad nodded, as he scanned the room and floated towards the body on the bed.

"Is that me?"

David nodded.

"How can I be there and here?" As he asked the question, realization hit him and his eyes widened. "Am I dead?"

David shook his head. "Not yet."

"Not yet? Does that mean I *will* die?"

David smiled and nodded. "Sometime son, but not today."

Brad watched the flurry of activity. "Do they know that?"

David chuckled. "They will in a few minutes, when your soul returns back to your body."

Brad gave him a confused look. "How can this be happening, and why is this happening, and who are all those people standing around?"

David made a "get lost" movement with his head and the group of angelic beings left, except for Jarrod and Brad's angel, Argus.

David introduced the two angels, and explained their presence.

"Jarrod is my guide and Argus is yours."

Argus reached out to shake Brad's hand.

"So are you the one I saw that night on the football field?"

Argus smiled and nodded. "Humans don't usually see us, but Father wanted you to be aware of my presence, so it would put you on the road to further study and discovery."

"Discovery?" Brad asked, looking at his dad, then Argus.

David said, "Sometimes, we humans have to experience something traumatic to make us curious enough to do research, thereby building our faith."

Brad nodded. Looking at his earthly body, and feeling a person pass through his spiritual one, he asked, "So why am I *here*?"

"Father has a message for you," Argus answered.

"Father...as in God?"

The angels and David nodded in unison.

"What message?"

Argus took Brad's hand, and said, "Only He can tell you." With that explanation, Brad was immediately whisked from the hospital room, up through the ceiling, remaining floors, and the roof. Brad felt himself being pulled along at an alarming rate, and was helpless to do anything, so he relaxed and enjoyed the ride. Argus had a tight grip on his hand, and he was pretty sure he wouldn't let it go, until they reached their destination—*which was where? Heaven?*

"Dad!" He called back over his shoulder.

"Yeah?"

"When will we get there?"

David smiled. Brad had asked that same question on many a road trip.

David gave his standard reply, "Soon."

Within seconds, they all stopped, and stood in a large, empty, cathedral-like room—reminding Brad of the few magnificent Catholic sanctuaries he had visited in person, or via media presentations. Argus released Brad's hand, motioned him forward, and backed up, joining David and Jarrod who were both lying prostrate on the marble-looking floor.

Brad ascended the long stairway in front of him, and stood before an impressively sized and adorned throne. Raising his eyes, he gazed upon a giant sized version of...Santa?

He inhaled sharply. *God wasn't supposed to look like Santa, was He?*

The Being chuckled and spoke. "Don't be alarmed, Brad. I only look like this because this is what you pictured me to look like. I can appear in any form that is suitable to the one before me. My true form is too incomprehensible for the human mind. You'd be surprised to know how many people think of me in this form."

Brad stood mute with his mouth hanging open. *This is God, and He's actually speaking to me!*

With each step towards Brad, God shrank until He stood before Brad—human sized.

Pulling Brad into a hug, He said, "It's so good to see you! I've been keeping an eye on you since you were conceived, because I have great plans for your life."

Shocked into silence, all Brad could do was nod and return the hug. It felt so real—all warm and tingly. *Is this a dream? A figment of my imagination? It certainly feels real, but the mind can play tricks on a person, making the unreal seem real—right?*

God chuckled again, reminding Brad once more of his perception of Santa. Pushing Brad at arm's length, He said, "What you're experiencing is real, Brad. Not a figment of your imagination. Your body is back on Earth being resuscitated, and your soul is here in the Heavenly realm."

"How can I be in both places?"

"Ah. Good question. Most people in your situation ask the same thing."

Shrugging, He said, "I'm not through with your earthly body yet, so I'm keeping it alive until I return your soul to it."

Brad gave Him a worried look. God smiled. "You won't have any brain damage, I promise. In fact, when you return, you will be completely healed and will live a very long life."

Brad nodded and thought, *I can't believe I'm actually talking to God...the creator of all the universe and beyond. Why in the world would He choose me to carry out one of His plans?*

Smiling, God said, "Follow Me."

Brad obeyed. They passed by the three prostrate beings on the floor.

Noticing them, God said, "Thank you, but you three may stand."

Following God as they entered an adjacent room, Brad glanced over his shoulder, in time to see his dad and the two angels stand, nod, and smile at him.

Walking down a long hallway, Brad thought, *I wonder where He's taking me?*

God immediately answered. "We're going to a place I call the Viewing Room. There, you can see people and events from all over the world. I can keep track of each of my creations with just a glance."

How does He do that? Brad asked himself.

God smiled. "I am God, after all. You'd be shocked, baffled, amazed and frightened at all the things I can create and do in the blink of an eye. I'll have to admit that even though mankind is my greatest creation, they do frustrate me the most. They—I'm speaking generally of course, because there are a few exceptions—get so involved with their earthly activities that they forget to acknowledge My existence. They don't even think about the fact that I keep their hearts beating, and their lungs breathing, and their brains functioning. I could, at any time, pull the plug, but because of my love and compassion for them, I keep giving them chances." Looking at Brad and reading his thoughts, He continued, "I know you're wondering why I would allow babies and children to die and let the criminals live. People have questioned that since the beginning of time. Let Me say that I do understand the questions, but because I can see events outside of time, only I can deem who lives or dies, and the consequences or blessings from those events."

Brad was speechless. Even if he had a question, he knew God would answer it before he even voiced it.

God stopped suddenly, causing Brad to bump into Him.

"Oops! Sorry, Sir. I was looking around, and not paying attention."

God chuckled, a rosy, dimpled-cheeked, perfect white teeth under a perfectly white beard, twinkle in his eye and bowl full of jelly kind of chuckle. Brad smiled and shook his head. *He must think we humans are pretty awkward and amusing.*

Putting His arm around Brad's shoulder, He said, "I do find humans to be quite amusing at times. Their limited knowledge, and their desire to control events—present and future—and their stubbornness in trying to do it all on their own without asking or considering My will, is what amuses, baffles and frustrates Me." Shaking His head and sighing, He added, "I just wish they'd ask Me for help or wisdom, which I'd gladly give, but they just keep stumbling through life. I gave them free-will so they could choose wisely, but alas, many of them don't."

"Guilty as charged," Brad said, adding, "I mean about the whole not asking and trusting stuff."

"Well, all humans are guilty at some time or another in their lives. That's why I sent My son to give them a second chance, or a way out—so to speak. I've even sent an instruction book, but again, many people will choose to either ignore it, read and ignore it, or misinterpret it for their own selfish gain. Fortunately, there are those who will read it and try their best to follow the teachings—like your mom and dad, and your grandparents. Unfortunately for the human race, the righteous are becoming less and less in number."

"Why?"

Sighing and frowning, God said, "Because they are advancing in technology—which by the way, I taught them—and are so preoccupied with their physical well-being, that they don't think they need a God they can't see. They've made many other things their gods."

"Like what?"

"Work, sex, TV, video games, food, looks, things...the list could go on, but you get the idea."

Sighing, Brad said, "Again, I've been guilty of some of those behaviors." Pausing, he said, "I'm sorry."

God pulled him into a hug. "I know. That's one reason I've chosen you to carry out some of My plans. I know that you're reliable, strong in character, and truly want to please Me."

Nodding, Brad said, "Yes, I do want to please you."

After a moment of silence, God turned to face the opposite wall. On it were about a million computer screens. Brad inhaled sharply.

"What the....? That wasn't here a few seconds ago!"

Smiling and nodding, God explained, "Oh it's always been here, but I just revealed it to you. This isn't exactly what it looks like, but this is what your mind can comprehend."

"Wow! This reminds me of one of the scenes from a movie I watched recently."

"I know. That's why I presented it in this form."

Awestruck, Brad turned in circles, taking in the incomprehensible number of screens. "So, where's my mom?"

Instantly, a screen came forward and showed Christina jumping out of the van, and running into the hospital entrance.

Brad's eyes widened. "What about Stacey and Nicky?"

Again, the screens came forward and he watched his two siblings, entering Ed's car, each looking miserable.

Brad's eyes widened. "Wow! That's amazing! So You come here and see what we're up to?"

"Well, I don't need to come here, because I already know, but your dad and other earthly souls come here to check on their families."

"So...what is it You want me to do?"

Waving a hand, the computer screens disappeared and they were left standing in the center of a large, empty, brightly-lit room, which Brad noticed had no source from which the light came—it just was.

Placing His hands on Brad's shoulders and looking him squarely in the eyes, God laid out His plan.

Awestruck, and speechless, all Brad could do was nod. God pulled him into a hug and said, "It's time for you to go back. It's been such a pleasure visiting with you. I will see you again, after many of your human years. For Me, it will be an instant."

Brad felt himself being pulled backwards—away from God. He started fighting against it, yelling, "I don't want to leave You."

God smiled, waved and said, "Remember to trust Me, even when things don't make sense."

With that, Brad was returned to his body. Inhaling deeply, he sat up and surprised everyone in the immediate area. Looking around, he said, "Heaven is real! I just came back from there! Where's my mom?"

Dr. Carmichael, who had been bent over Brad, listening for breath and heart activity, got his head bumped when Brad sat up. Reaching up to rub the area, he said, "Whoa, young man! Settle down. Your mom will be here soon."

Looking into the eyes of the man before him, Brad whispered, "Dr. Carmichael, I met God, and He looked like Santa!"

Smiling and nodding, and laying a hand on Brad's chest to gently push him back down, and thinking the boy was hallucinating, he said, "It's alright, son. You're back with us now. I'm going to give you something to help you relax and sleep a little while. When you wake up again, your mom will be here."

Nodding at the nurse, who pushed a syringe full of liquid into the IV cannula, and watching as Brad's eyelids grew heavy, Dr. Carmichael couldn't help but wonder if what had just occurred was a true out-of-body experience, or just some sort of brain-chemical reaction. He had read and heard of accounts given by people who had similar experiences when their hearts stopped, but had never witnessed it firsthand—until now. Brad mumbled, and Dr. Carmichael leaned down, thinking he heard Brad say, "I want to go back."

CHAPTER 68

After her in-laws had left the hospital, and a nurse had brought her fresh blankets and pillows, the beeping noise of the monitors began lulling Christina to sleep. Her eyes flew open when she head Brad whisper, "Mom?"

Throwing off the blankets, and knocking her pillows on the floor, she jumped up, and went to stand by her son's bedside.

"Yes, Brad. I'm here."

Still a bit bleary-eyed, but trying to focus on his mother's face, he said, "I'm thirsty. Can I have a drink, please? What time is it?"

"Of course!" Grabbing a cup, pouring fresh water in, and adding a straw, she offered it to him. Glancing at the clock, she said, "It's three a.m."

He tried sitting up, but the effort seemed to exhaust him.

"What day?"

"It's Monday morning."

"How long have I been asleep?"

"Since Saturday night."

"What happened?"

"I'll explain everything to you when you're more conscious. Do you want to sit up a while?" He nodded, grimacing as he shifted his weight.

"Here, let me raise the head of the bed."

Sipping on the water, as his eyes focused, he felt the tendrils of sleep ebbing away, and said, with a surprisingly clear and strong voice, "I went to Heaven and met God. I also saw Dad, and met his and my guardian angels."

Christina's breath caught, and thinking she must have misheard him, whispered, "What?"

Brad repeated his statement and added, "How long was I gone?"

Christina pulled a chair next to the bed and sat, feeling that familiar weakness creeping into her legs.

"Wait, you met God?"

Brad smiled. "Yeah. He looked like Santa!"

Christina shook her head. "Santa? Really? Huh. That's kind of how I pictured Him."

Taking a sip of water, Brad said, "He said a lot of people picture Him like that." Wiping his lips on the sleeve of his gown, he asked, "So, how long was I gone?"

"Gone? As in, how long your heart stopped?"

Brad nodded.

"According to Dr. Carmichael, your heart stopped for two minutes."

Shaking his head, he said, "That's all? Geeze, it seemed like hours."

Taking a few calming breaths, because her heart had started galloping like a racehorse at the mention of God and heaven, she said, "So, tell me what heaven was like."

Brad told her of his experience from the time he left his body until he returned. "Oh, Mom. It was so...so...I can't even think of words that are adequate. Magnificent, just doesn't do it. Even if I could combine a few awe-inspiring words, they wouldn't even touch what I saw and felt."

"So did you see the Pearly Gates and Saint Peter, and were the streets really gold?"

He chuckled. "Well, I didn't see the gates or Saint Peter, but yes, the streets and buildings did appear to be made of some kind of see-through iridescent gold. It gave off a glow, but I couldn't see where the light was coming from. Like...it just...was." Shaking his head, which caused a grimace, he added, "I don't think there's anything on Earth that could or would compare to it, except on film." Pausing as he contemplated the idea, he said, "I guess film geeks could come up with something comparable." Sighing, he added, "If God called me back, I'd be ready to go." He saw the shock in his mother's eyes and quickly added, "I don't want it to be anytime soon! Besides, God said I would have a long, productive life, so you don't need to worry."

She sighed. "Good. I really like having you around." Gently rubbing his forehead with her fingertips, she asked, "What assignment does God have for you?"

"I know this is gonna sound weird, but I don't remember what He said. Hopefully, it'll come back to me. I'd hate to think I went through all that, and won't be able to carry out the assignment."

Christina patted his arm. "I'm sure He'll let you know when it's time. If He said it, we can believe it." When she saw a shiver pass through him, she reached down for his blanket and tucked it under his chin, then felt his forehead, which seemed warm, but not feverish. "So how are you feeling otherwise?"

"Amazingly good. My head still hurts a little, but I'm *so* ready to get out of this bed and go home!"

"I'll let the nurse know you're awake and she can tell Dr. Carmichael. Maybe he'll let you go home tomorrow, if you continue to improve."

Taking a sip of water and nodding, Brad said, "When you get back, I'd like you to catch me up on everything."

"Will do."

The ICU nurse returned with Christina and began to assess her patient's vital signs, and noted other pertinent information.

He retold of his out of body experience, and her response was less than enthusiastic—almost condescending.

Patting his hand, she said, "Well, Mr. Sanders, it sounds like you had quite the vision. Sometimes patients report such incidences when their hearts stop. It's probably just due to the lack of oxygen and the body's chemical changes. I think our subconscious mind takes us to a safe place, so to speak, until our body recovers from the trauma its experiencing."

Brad gave her an exasperated look. "So, I take it you don't believe in out of body experiences?"

She nodded, slightly.

"Do you believe in heaven?"

Shaking her head and giving him a terse smile—as if he were an uneducated oaf—she said, "Well, no. I think once we die, that's it. That's why I think we should live life to the fullest. This is all we have, and if we don't enjoy it, then it's our loss."

"So you probably don't believe in Hell either? What about people who have a terrifying experience? Like, if they see demons and visit Hell instead of Heaven?"

Smiling pleasantly, she answered, "Well, obviously those people are suffering from some kind of guilt or phobia, and their subconscious is trying to resolve them of it. Punishing them one last time, so when they wake up, they will not feel so guilty."

Brad gave her a "what?" face and said, "Okay, but I know what I experienced, and I do believe in heaven and hell, and we do get a taste of them from time to time so we *can* have another chance to redeem ourselves."

Shaking her head, and continuing to smile, she patted his hand once more and said, "Well, we're all welcome to our beliefs."

After she left the room, Brad whispered, "That was weird. I've never met anyone who doesn't believe in life after death."

Christina nodded. "I've met a few, and it still boggles my mind when I hear them explain their version of life and death." Sighing, she added, "It all seems so...so...I don't know, hopeless, I guess."

Nodding slightly, Brad said, "Yeah. I guess it makes sense if you don't believe in God. You can do whatever you want to do, with no feelings of guilt. Kinda like being your own judge...your own god."

"I can't help but wonder what happened in her life to lead her into that kind of reasoning."

Shrugging, Brad said, "Maybe she never went to Sunday School or church. Maybe her parents believe that way, and she never had the chance to hear or learn about God, and His love and forgiveness."

"Maybe."

"Mom, I need to use the bathroom. Can you help me up or should I call the nurse?"

Smiling, and placing her finger on her cheek, she said, "Let me see...I'm your mother, and a nurse myself, and I'm pretty fit yet. Yeah, I think I can help you."

Grinning and shaking his head, he said, "Thanks."

After hanging his IV and catheter bags on a pole, she helped him push the contraption to the bathroom.

Walking out, he complained about the catheter and wondered when it would be removed.

Her reply was, "Probably first thing in the morning."

Sighing, he said, "It's not only uncomfortable, it's embarrassing."

Once his toileting was completed, and he was back in bed, and asleep, she stepped out of the room to make a call to her in-laws. As the phone rang, she made a mental list of others she wanted to contact.

Her mother-in-law picked up after the second ring, and, sounding groggy, asked, "Christina, is Brad doing alright?"

Smiling and stifling a yawn, Christina said, "Yes, Mom. He even woke up and talked to me. He said he went to heaven and talked to God, and get this, he said God looks like Santa!"

Ruth chuckled. "Well, that's how I would picture Him."

Christina shared more about Brad's experience, yawned, looked at her watch and said, "Geeze, mom, I didn't realize it was so early. I'll call you back later and give you an update. In the meantime, I'm gonna try catching a few winks."

Ruth yawned and said, "Yes, that sounds good. Sleep well, dear."

Deciding it was too early to call her friends, she returned to her son's bedside, fluffed her pillow, laid down, pulled up the blanket, and immediately fell into a peaceful sleep, not waking until she heard the morning hustle and bustle of the hospital staff.

CHAPTER 69

Walking out of the bathroom in Brad;s room, Christina jumped, when she heard the door bang into someone, who let out an audible grunt. She was shocked and pleased to see that it was Dr. Dawson.

"Steven! I'm sorry. I wasn't expecting anyone to be there."

Rubbing his elbow where the door had hit, he smiled and said, "It's Okay. I don't think anything is broken."

She rolled her eyes and walked into his arms.

"How's our boy?"

Glancing over at her sleeping son, who, in spite of his gangly arms and legs, and on the cusp of manhood, was looking quite angelic.

"He's doing well." Placing her hand on Steven's arm, she said, "Why don't we get a cup of coffee, because I have something interesting to tell you." He nodded, and followed her to the lounge area. Sitting across from each other, she told him of Brad's experience.

His response was what she expected. Neither shock nor alarm, but a calm contemplative nodding of the head.

She asked, "You've dealt with life and death situations. Have any of your patients told you stories like that?"

Nodding, he said, "Yeah, more than I ever imagined possible. Those stories solidify my belief in a life after death." Leaning forward and taking her hand in his, he added, "Too many similarities to brush them off as coincidence."

Taking a sip of her coffee and setting the cup down on the end table, she said, "I think sometimes God pulls back the curtain and allows us to see the supernatural realm. At David's funeral, the kids and I saw him waving at us, and I've conversed with him in my dreams."

He rubbed his chin as he mulled over her statement, then leaning forward, and in a hushed tone so no one else could hear, he said, "I know this is gonna sound weird, but every now and then, I sense a presence and have caught glimpses of people who have passed on, out of the corner of my eye. I've never experienced an out of body experience, but like I said earlier, I believe it is possible."

Nodding, she said, "I'm so glad you think that way. I've never told anyone, but when I passed out and nearly died a few months ago, I was floating above my body and watched as everyone scurried around me."

He raised his eyebrows in surprise.

"I even saw you riding in the elevator beside me. For a long time, I just thought I had been dreaming, but now, I know it was more than that." Shaking her head, she added, "I never made it all the way to Heaven, and I can't say I saw Jesus, or God, but I was able to see angelic beings."

"What did they look like?"

Taking a deep breath, and releasing it slowly, she said, "Well, the ones I saw had a human form, but I could see through them. They seemed to have a pale blue glow about them, and even though most of them were beautiful, there were almost as many ugly gargoyle-looking ones. I sensed those were demons."

"Huh."

"Yeah. One of the beings standing near me said he was my guardian angel, and assured me that I would be alright." Sighing, she said, "That's all I remember."

Nodding, Steven said, "That's cool. I guess you can take comfort knowing that God isn't finished with you yet."

Smiling, she said, "Yeah, I just wish I could see His plan, because it's a little disconcerting going through these trials, and not knowing what to expect or what's expected of me."

Steven looked at his watch and stood. "I'm sorry, but I've gotta get going. I'll drop by after rounds. Hopefully, Brad will be awake by then."

Looking up at him, she said, "I think I'll stay here a few more minutes and finish my coffee."

Nodding, he leaned down and kissed the top of her head. "See you later."

As she watched him disappear down the hall, she immediately missed his presence. Sipping her cooled coffee, she let her mind wander.

Where is this relationship headed? Am I letting it move too fast? Am I closing the door on other opportunities? Where does Aaron fit in all this? I've noticed how he looks at me, with his smoky brown, puppy dog eyes and I can't help but feel a twinge of desire. Oh, God, please clear my heart and head, and direct my path toward what You want me to do.

Entering the hospital room, Christina noticed the curtain was drawn around Brad's bed. Wondering what was happening, she stopped and listened, hearing a verbal exchange between a female voice and Brad's.

The perky female voice said, "So, Mr. Sanders, it's nice to see you awake. Are you ready to take a little walk to the bathroom, then around the hall?"

She heard Brad grunt, then say, "Sure. I feel a bit dizzy, though."

"Here, let me help."

Christina pulled the curtain aside, in time to see her son stand and take a step.

Grinning, he said, "Hey, Mom! I'm up."

"I see that! Good for you. Feeling okay?" She noticed that the catheter had been removed, and he was wearing his sweat pants.

"Just a little dizzy, but otherwise okay."

Holding on to Brad's arm, the nurse said, "Good morning, Mrs. Sanders. My name is Patty Whitaker. I'm from the rehab center down the street. Dr. Carmichael asked me to come and assess Brad's physical status."

Smiling, and looking at Brad, she said, "So far, so good."

Nodding and smiling back at the petite brunette, Christina said, "Yeah, he got up around three-o'clock this morning to go to the bathroom. He did pretty well then. You think he'll go home today?"

"Maybe. He seems more alert and stronger than I expected."

In the doorway of the bathroom, Brad stopped and said, "Thanks, Patty, but I can handle it from here."

She smiled and released his arm. "I'll be waiting."

She and Christina stood outside the bathroom door and chatted. Patty had graduated the previous June from Baylor University with a BS in Physical Therapy. She was from the little town of Milford, about twenty-five miles northeast of Alva, and until she was able to survive on her own, lived with her parents.

Christina said, "I have relatives who live in Milford. Do you know the Jennings?"

Patty's face lit up. "Carl and Sadie?"

"Yes. That's my aunt and uncle."

Patty said, "We attend the Methodist Church together. Their daughter, Olivia, was one of our youth leaders, when I was a teen."

Nodding, and smiling, Christina said, "Wow, what a small world. I haven't seen or talked to them in a while. They had planned to come on Thanksgiving, but Sadie came down with the flu."

"Oh, that's too bad. I really like that family. Olivia's one of the elementary school teachers, right?"

Nodding, Christina said, "Yeah, third grade, I believe."

Just then, Brad walked out of the bathroom. Grabbing Brad's arm, Patty said, "You okay, buddy? You're all sweaty."

Sighing, Brad said, "I'm a bit shakier than I expected. I'd like to lay back down a few minutes, before we walk around the hall, if that's okay."

Helping him back into bed, Patty said, "Sure. Why don't I come back in about an hour? You can eat some breakfast and rest a bit."

"Thanks, Patty," Brad said as he crawled under the covers on his bed.

With Patty gone, Brad turned his attention to his mother.

"I guess I'm weaker than I thought." Sighing, he said, "Whew, that was exhausting!"

Christina chuckled and said, "Well, you have been inactive for the past couple of days, It's gonna take a little while to regain your strength."

Nodding, he said, "I'm gonna do what I can to expedite that."

Breakfast trays arrived, and mother and son enjoyed bowls of oatmeal and applesauce as they revisited the events of the past several days.

Between bites, Brad asked, "So, how's Eric doing?"

"I talked to his mom yesterday, and she said he was doing well. I told her of your little set-back, and she said to tell you they're praying for you."

Brad nodded. "Aww, that's nice. Does the Sheriff have any idea how all this came about?'

Christina sighed and rubbed her eyes. "Well, not really. He and Ed are working on it."

Setting his empty glass of milk down, he said, "Ed? Is the ATO involved? Do they think it's terrorist related?"

Shaking her head, Christina said, "No, the ATO isn't involved, just Ed. He thinks it's just some teenage prank gone bad."

"I asked God about that, and He said He allowed it to happen because He has a greater plan."

"A greater plan?"

"Yeah, He wouldn't say anything else about it, except that I'd understand someday."

Standing and gathering the trays and garbage, Christina said, "So can you tell me anymore about your visit to Heaven?"

Smiling and nodding, Brad said, "Yeah, I keep getting little flashes of memory. I think if I remembered everything I saw and heard at one time, my head would explode."

Christina listened intently, as Brad described the viewing room.

CHAPTER 70

Christina's friend, Lisa, woke with a strong impression that she needed to call Christina. She had a dream about an explosion at the hospital, and her grandma, who had been dead for three years, and Christina were a couple of the injured people. *Weird*, she thought. *Why would I dream of my grandma?* Before leaving her warm bed, she turned on her side and prayed a hedge of protection around the hospital and Christina. Only then, did she feel her spirit relax, and sensed her prayer had made a difference.

As she enjoyed breakfast with her children, her eight-year-old son, Adam, announced that he'd had a scary dream about a big explosion and fire.

Pausing with her coffee cup half way to her mouth, and feeling gooseflesh pop up on her arms, she asked, "What kind of explosion and fire?"

Scrunching his face and thinking, he said, "I'm not sure, but it was in a tall building."

His twin brother, Aaron said, "The only tall buildings around here are the courthouse and the hospital. Was it one of them?"

Shrugging, Adam said, "Maybe. I just remember that there were a lot of people walking around, and I could see fire and flashing lights and someone said it was an explosion like the school one. Weird."

Fourteen-year-old Sarah said, "At least it wasn't a plane crash." Both her brothers gave her a startled look. "I'm just sayin,' with mom and dad's trip down to Guatemala coming up in a couple of weeks to adopt our new siblings, it's good you didn't get some kind of premonition or something. Maybe your mind is still processing the explosion at the middle school. That was pretty traumatic."

Reaching over and patting her son's hand, Lisa said, "I think your sister is right. Sometimes, the mind works out our fears, and worries and such, as we sleep." *At least I hope that's all it is and not some kind of warning,* she thought as she finished her coffee and listened to her children's chatter. Unaware that Christina was in the hospital with Brad, Lisa looked at her watch, and thought, *I'm gonna call Christina in an hour or so. Give her time to wake up.*

CHAPTER 71

By the time Dr. Carmichael had made his rounds on the pediatric floor, and headed for Brad's room in the ICU, Brad had eaten breakfast, walked around the nurses' station, showered, and dressed for the day.

Dr. Carmichael couldn't contain his surprise, when he saw Brad sitting on the edge of the bed wearing sweatpants and a t-shirt, instead of the hospital gown he'd been wearing the previous two days.

Walking over to shake Brad's hand, he said, "Well, Brad, don't you look chipper today?"

Chipper? Who says that anymore? Taking Dr. Carmichael's hand, he said, "I'm feeling quite, hmm…chipper today, sir."

Aaron smiled his million dollar smile, and Christina felt her heart kick against her ribs.

"The nurse and physical therapist both say you are doing very well. If you hadn't been in a coma, and near death just yesterday, I would be tempted to let you go home, but alas, you gave me reason to keep you one more day for observation."

Brad's shoulders slumped. "Oh, man, I was hoping I could convince you to let me go, but when you put it that way, I guess you've got a point."

Aaron chuckled. "I will move you out of the ICU however, and put you on the pediatric unit."

"Pediatric unit? Really?"

"Brad, there's only two other kids there, and it would be easier to have all three of my patients in one unit."

Brad nodded and sighed. "Okay. How old are the kids?"

"Both are toddlers. They won't even know you're there, and it's only for one more day and night, if all goes well."

Brad rolled his eyes and nodded in surrender.

"Alright, but Mom, don't let anyone come visit me in the pediatric unit."

She bit her bottom lip to keep from smiling. He had reacted in a typical teenage fashion. She held two fingers up in a girl scout pledge.

"I promise to not let any of your friends visit, but is it okay to let mine?"

Shrugging, he said, "Yeah, I guess so."

After checking his patient from head to toe, Dr. Carmichael reached out to shake Brad's hand again.

"I'll get these orders signed, and you will be on your way in a little while."

After returning the handshake, Brad pulled his feet back up on the bed and under the covers.

"Thank you, sir."

Dr. Carmichael patted Brad's foot, and nodded. Glancing at Christina, he smiled and winked. "I'll see you two later."

She was speechless. He not only had a killer smile, he winked at her. David used to wink at her.

Brad, noticing his mom's reaction, asked, "Mom? You okay?"

She shook her head and said, "Yeah, I think so.

After a short nap, Brad woke and said, "Mom?"

"Yes, Brad." Christina stood and walked over to the bed,

"I want to go home today because we're supposed to have Christmas with Grandma and Grandpa. Aren't they leaving tomorrow?"

Christina patted his hand.

"We can celebrate when you get home tomorrow. Grandpa called the airline, and was able to change the flight to Thursday."

"Oh, thank goodness! I was so worried that we'd miss our Christmas time with them."

Christina shook her head. "Not to worry. Everything's been taken care of. You just focus on healing."

"But, Mom, I am healed. God said I would be when I came back, and I am. I feel great!"

"Be that as it may, you still have earthly protocols to follow. When Dr. Carmichael dismisses you, after he sees your complete recovery, then we can truly rejoice over your healing."

Christina's phone buzzed. Lisa.

Smiling and stepping out of the room, Christina said, "Hey girlfriend. I was planning to call you later. How are y'all doing?"

Lisa said, "Well, I haven't talked to you since the school fire, so I wanted to catch up on Brad's progress."

"Oh Lisa. I'm so sorry I didn't call and tell you. Brad's been in the hospital for the past couple of days."

"What? Is he okay? What happened?"

Christina brought her friend up to date on Brads condition.

"So, he'll probably go home tomorrow," she said in conclusion.

"Wow! Wish I'd known. I could have been holding y'all up in prayer. Are your in-laws still here?"

"Yes. They had planned to go home tomorrow, but with all that's happened, they decided to stay until Thursday."

"Well, good. I had the weirdest dream about an explosion and fire."

She told Christina about her and her son's dreams.

"That is weird that you both would have such similar dreams. Huh. Well, hopefully, they won't come true."

Sighing, Lisa said, "Yeah." After a few more minutes of conversation, the ladies disconnected.

Christina had just replaced the phone in her purse when the nurse came in with a wheelchair, to take Brad to the pediatric unit.

CHAPTER 72

As Janet worked Christina's shift, she listened intently for any news about the school explosion, and Brad's condition. When she overheard one of the nurses comment about his admittance to the ICU, her heart skipped a couple of beats.

"So, Sally Jean, would you mind running down to the ICU, and ask Christina how Brad's doing?"

Sally Jean cocked her head. "Uhm, okay. You want me to tell her anything?"

Janet shook her head. "Well, just tell her we're concerned and that everything up here is running smoothly. Only two patients."

Sally Jean shrugged. "Okay. You want me to go right now?"

Janet looked at the clock. Noon. "Sure. While you're gone, you might as well take your lunch break."

Sally Jean smiled. "I was hoping so. I got this new novel I want to start reading." She held it up for Janet to see.

"What's it about?" Janet asked, reaching for the book.

"Oh it's one of those vampire series. I just love this new author. I could imagine her books becoming movies someday."

After reading the cover and returning it to Sally Jean, she said, "When you're finished, may I borrow it?"

Sally Jean smiled. "Sure! I can bring the first two in tomorrow. Will you be here tomorrow?"

Janet nodded and sighed. "As far as I know, unless Mrs. Ferguson found someone else. I just hope I don't have to work Christmas Day."

"Yeah, that'd be a bummer." Leaning on the counter, Sally Jean said, "My family is getting together on Christmas Day, and having dinner and exchanging gifts in the afternoon. What are your plans?"

Janet sighed. "Well, it'll just be me and my daughter. I'm hoping we can just stay in our pajamas, order pizza and watch movies all day and evening."

"Oh yeah, I forgot you have a girl. How old is she again?"

"She just turned thirteen."

Sally Jeans eyes opened in surprise, and she made a face. "Ooh. I remember thirteen. So much changed that year. I started my period, broke out with acne, got and lost my first boyfriend and got my first D in algebra. Not very pleasant memories. I hope your girl does better."

Janet grimaced. "Yeah, me too."

"Anyway," Sally Jean said on a sigh, "guess I'd better head on downstairs and check on Brad."

"Thanks. Just text me the information."

Sally Jean nodded, turned and did a finger wave as she and her flouncy ponytail headed down the hall to the elevator.

After checking on the two patients, Janet sat at the desk and contemplated her next move. Brad's injury complicated things. Christina would be emotionally vulnerable—a perfect time to amp up the threats.

Rubbing the back of her neck to release the building tension, she began to mentally peruse her options.

An idea would form, and she would examine it and either toss it, or put it in her mental file. She had been sitting about ten minutes when her phone buzzed. Taking it out of her pocket and checking the screen, she saw a message from Sally Jean: B mved to ped floor. ok. May go hm tmrow.

So Brad's out of ICU and in the pediatric unit. That's an amazing recovery time for someone who had meningitis. Interesting. The kid must have some strong life energies working for him.

CHAPTER 73

Christina was surprised when she looked up from her laptop computer and saw Sally Jean standing in the doorway.

"There y'all are! I went to the ICU, and they said Brad had been moved to the pediatric floor."

Closing the computer and standing, Christina said, "Hey, girl!"

The young aid walked over, and gave Christina a hug.

"Hey, yourself." Looking at Brad, she said "Hey," to him as well, and walked over to introduce herself.

Thrusting out her hand, she said, "I'm Sally Jean. I work with your mom in the CCU."

Smiling, he said, "My mom's told me about you. Nice to finally put a face with a name."

Sally Jean cocked her head and looked over at Christina.

"I hope she only said good things about me."

Christina smiled and nodded.

Grinning, Brad said, "Of course she did!" Conscious of his appearance, he ran his hands through his disheveled hair. *Geeze, she's cute. Wish I were a few years older, or she was a few years younger.* He felt heat rise to his neck and face, knowing he must be blushing.

Giggling, Sally Jean said, "Whew! So when did you arrive here?"

"Here? As in this room, or here as in Alva?"

Again Sally Jean giggled, which made his heart begin to trot. It was a sweet, melodious, genuine giggle.

"In this room, silly."

"I just got here a few minutes ago."

"Are you doin' okay? When will you go home?"

Nodding, he said, "I'm actually doing great, and will probably go home tomorrow."

Smiling and nodding, she looked at Christina.

"Janet wanted you to know that everything is okay up on the unit, and we only have two patients, and they're doing well."

"Thanks for the info, Sally Jean. You want to join us for lunch?" Right as the words left her mouth, an aide came in with their lunch trays.

"Oh, thanks, but I'm gonna eat in the cafeteria, and start reading a new novel I got yesterday."

Brad asked, "What are you gonna read?"

Sally Jean pulled the book out of her jacket, and handed it to him.

Examining it, he said, "Hey, I've heard of this series. Guess vampirism is the newest craze now."

"Yeah. Kinda creepy, but somehow romantic at the same time."

Chuckling, nodding, and handing the book back, he said, "I'm not really into that kind of stuff, but I have friends who are."

She nodded, then sighed.

"Well, guess I'd best get going, so y'all can eat, and I can get started reading."

Christina pulled Sally Jean into a hug.

"Thanks for dropping by. You're our first visitor to this room."

Sally Jean giggled, and on her way out, said, "Hey, why don't I stop by on my way home today?"

Brad's smile broadened.

"That'd be great! See you later."

"Yeah, see ya!"

Christina turned to look at Brad, who had a silly grin on his face.

"What?" He asked.

Biting her bottom lip, Christina shook her head, thinking, *Ah, teenage infatuation. How cute.*

CHAPTER 74

Grandma Ruth, who had been doing needlepoint in the family room while Grandpa Dan read the newspaper and the kids played a game of spades, jumped when she heard the doorbell ring.

Nicky, who had been sitting across from his sister on the floor, jumped up and headed for the door.

"I'll get it!" A few seconds later, he called out, "Hey, Grandma, the guy here says you gotta sign something before he can give us our mail."

Pulling herself out of the easy chair, she said, "Okay, I'll be right there."

Dan and Stacey joined them at the door.

The man in a Federal Express uniform handed her an envelope.

Handing her a pen, and pointing to a spot on his clipboard, he said, "You need to sign right here."

She did, and he turned to go.

Examining the envelope, and seeing that it was from a bank in Dallas, she turned to Dan and whispered, "I wonder if this is the check Christina told us about?"

Nicky gave Stacey a questioning look, then asked, "What check?"

Realizing her mistake in revealing that information, Ruth covered it by saying, "Some kind of reimbursement check."

Cocking his head, Nicky asked, "What's reimbursement?"

Stacey spoke up. "It's when you pay for something, then decide you don't want it, and you send or take it back, and you get your money back. Right, Grandma?"

Ruth nodded. "Right."

Shrugging, and turning to head back into the family room, Nicky said, "Oh, okay."

Ruth gave Dan a thumbs up sign.

"Good recovery," he whispered.

After placing the envelope on top of the refrigerator, so inquisitive little eyes couldn't find it, Ruth called Christina.

Christina was happy to hear her mother-in-law's voice, and told her of the room change,

"Well, good. Dan and I will bring the kids in a little while for a visit. They're anxious to see you and Brad."

She then informed her of the envelope's arrival.

"Oh, good! I was hoping it'd get deposited before Christmas. I'm assuming, of course, that it *is* indeed a copy of the check I was promised."

As they waited for the family to arrive, Christina handed Brad her laptop, and encouraged him to document his experience.

CHAPTER 75

When he wasn't typing, Brad spent the afternoon walking around the unit, and acquainting himself with the toddlers and their mothers. Christina watched from his doorway, as he volunteered to read to the restless little ones, while their moms took a much needed break. She smiled as she watched him interact with the little two and three-year old children—a boy and girl—both in for pneumonia, and confined to their beds.

The near-death experience had changed him somehow. He seemed more confident and peaceful, and an inner joy radiated from him, when he talked to the staff and others in the area.

Around three-o'clock, the grandparents and siblings walked onto the floor. The kids ran up to greet and hug their brother as the grandparents greeted Christina.

"Wow, he looks good," Ruth whispered as she gave Christina a hug.

"I know! He said God told him he'd be completely healed, and I believe he has been."

Brad walked over and gave his grandparents a hug and said, "Dad said to tell you hi, and he's really enjoying being in Heaven. He said not to worry about anything, because God's got everything under control."

Ruth's eyes immediately teared up. Catching her breath, she said, "So Brad, I think we'd all like to hear about your trip to Heaven."

Once Brad had shared his experience with them, they all sat in shocked silence, while they processed the information.

"So, God really looked like Santa?" Nicky asked with a giggle,.

Brad nodded. "Yep. He said He could take on any form or character to present Himself to us humans. He said I had pictured Him as Santa, so that's the form He took."

Twirling a strand of hair around her finger, Stacey said, "I never thought about what He would look like, but I guess that comes pretty close to what I'd expect."

"Well, according to God, a lot of people think that. Maybe that's where the whole idea of Santa came from. Someone's interpretation of God."

Grandpa Dan spoke up, "Well, I'm not sure I'd go that far, for the simple fact that Santa isn't real."

Nicky and Stacey looked at their grandpa in shock.

"What? Santa's not real?" Nicky said, doing a fine interpretation of a confused child.

Dan was caught off guard and started to backtrack, when the kids started giggling.

Between giggles, Stacey said, "Gotcha, Grandpa! We know Santa isn't a real person, but he represents the spirit of Christmas."

Brad said, "Yeah, those who don't want to believe in Christ needed something to believe in, so Santa fit that something. It's sad really, to think how much emphasis we put on gift giving and getting, that we forget the true meaning of Christmas. After my visit with God, I'm looking at things in a whole different light."

"I know I've been guilty over the years, of getting caught up in the whole commercial spirit of Christmas instead of the spiritual side. I need to be reminded every now and then as to why we celebrate it and our purpose as Christians...to know Him and make Him known."

After a few minutes of contemplative silence, Christina said, "I have something I'd like to discuss with y'all."

All eyes turned towards her. She explained the situation with the cat.

Wide-eyed, Stacey said, "I forgot about the cat. I don't think Chloe will like it. She's pretty temperamental and territorial."

Nicky added, "Yeah. I'm thinking Benji will drive it crazy wanting to play, and if he's old, he won't like that."

"What's his name, again?" Stacey asked.

"Elijah," Christina answered, as she chewed on a hangnail.

"That's a weird name for a cat," Nicky said.

Nodding, Christina agreed and wondered why Ellie had chosen that name. Maybe Margaret would know. "I asked Margaret to bring him over tomorrow morning. I guess we can keep him, until we find another home."

"But, what if we can't find him a home?" Nicky asked.

Sighing, Christina said, "Well, I guess we'll have another cat, and everyone will have to adjust. I can't bring myself to take him to a shelter or have him put down."

Understanding their mom's dilemma, Stacey and Nicky nodded.

Dan spoke up, "Maybe you could get the word out amongst your friends and church family. Maybe one of them would be interested in an old cat."

Nodding, Christina said, "Good idea, Dad."

After sharing the evening meal with Brad, thanks to the hospital cafeteria, the elder and younger Sanders family went back to the house, leaving Brad and Christina alone once more.

Watching his mom typing on her laptop, Brad was filled with an overwhelming love for her. He'd always loved her, for sure, but now he really loved and appreciated her as never before—her dedication to them, her sacrifice, her wisdom, her humor, her love for God and His creation. *Wow*, he thought, *this must be how God feels about His kids.*

"Mom?"

Looking up from the computer, and smiling at him, she said, "Yes?"

"I just want you to know that I love, and appreciate you."

"Aww, Brad, thank you. I love and appreciate you too."

She watched as a blush made it's way to Brad's face.

All of a sudden, tears formed in his eyes, and he started crying, gut-wrenching sobs, which took Christina by surprise. She was immediately on her feet and next to his bed.

Handing him a wad of tissues, concern filling her voice, she asked, "What is it, honey? Are you sick? Hurting?"

He shook his head. After the emotional storm had passed, and he had regained control, he said, "Geeze, that took me by surprise."

She nodded. "Me, too. I admit you kinda scared me."

Grinning, and wiping away tears and snot, he said, "All of a sudden, I had this overwhelming jumble of emotions; sadness, compassion, and love for everyone and everything. I think God gave me a little taste of what He feels. He doesn't want any of us humans to be separated from Him, but because of our free will and stubbornness, many will be. It breaks His heart. And now mine."

Christina reached down, and pulled him into a hug and kissed the top of his head.

"Oh my goodness, Brad, I can see why God chose you. You have such a sensitive spirit."

"Only because God gave it to me. I'm pretty self-centered most of the time, but I think that's gonna change. I can feel my heart and mind switching gears. It's not all about me anymore." Putting one hand over his heart and the other pointing up, he said, "It's about Him and what He wants."

That evening, as bedtime approached, Brad insisted his mom go home, and get a good night's sleep.

"Mom, I'm fine, really. Remember, God healed me. You, on the other hand, look a little worn out. I bet you'll sleep like a log in your own bed."

Scrunching her face, debating the issue of staying or leaving, she decided he was right. She was exhausted, and the idea of a soft bed with her own pillows and blankets was appealing.

"Alright, I'll call Grandpa to come get me."

CHAPTER 76

Tuesday morning, one week before Christmas, the Sanders family woke to an inch of unexpected snow. Ice had been predicted, but much to their delight, snow came, instead. Nicky and Stacey were so excited, they rushed through breakfast and headed outside with their grandpa, to make the first snowman of the season.

"Do you think we'll have a white Christmas?" Nicky asked, as he pulled on his hat and gloves.

Leaning against the kitchen counter, holding a mug of coffee, watching her children prepare to tackle the one inch of snow, Christina said, "Maybe, Texas weather is just as unpredictable as Michigan weather this time of year. I've been here when it's been as high as seventy-five degrees and as cold as ten degrees on Christmas day."

Zipping her jacket, Stacey said, "I can't imagine seventy-five on Christmas day. That would be just too weird!"

Ruth, a native Michigander, said, "I agree, Stacey. That would be weird!"

Dan asked, "What's the thermometer read?"

Christina glanced at the thermometer outside the kitchen window. "32."

"Probably will warm up pretty quick, so we'd better hurry."

While the kids and their grandpa busied themselves building a decent snowman with the dusting of snow, Christina and Ruth enjoyed a few minutes together.

Ruth asked about the envelope.

Christina smiled and nodded.

"It was a copy of the check and bank deposit statements from the law office....and a letter explaining the transaction. They won't be contacting me any more unless I have questions."

"Wow! Do you have any immediate plans for the money?"

Christina scrunched her face, and shaking her head, said, "Not really. I've opened savings accounts for each of us, and until I can decide what to do with it, it'll draw interest."

Nodding, Ruth said, "Good. I know you'll be wise with your investments."

"I hope so, because what I *want* to do, is go to Disneyland, then to the Bahamas!"

Ruth chuckled. "I'm right there with you!"

"Mom!" She heard Nicky call from the front yard. "Come look at our snowman!"

She and Ruth donned their jackets, and went to see the not so marvelous, quite pitiful looking, two foot tall snowman, who was probably more grass than snow.

Looking around at the bare yard, Christina said, while stifling a laugh, "Wow! I didn't think it was possible to make a snowman out of such little snow, but y'all pulled it off."

Smiling, nodding, and winking at Dan, Ruth said, "Well, will you look at that!"

"Mom, take a picture of us!" Nicky called, as he proudly stood by the sad looking creation.

"Sure, everyone stand by the snowman."

With silly grins and poses, the moment was immortalized, which was a good thing, because when the sun came out, Frosty was no more.

Standing in front of their deflated-looking pile of snow and grass, Stacey said, "I'm glad we got a picture."

Giggling, Nicky said, "Yeah, Brad wouldn't have believed that we were able to build a snowman." They high-fived each other and headed back indoors.

Entering the front door, they heard the toot of a car horn. It was Margaret, delivering Elijah.

CHAPTER 77

Samara was awakened by her mother's squeal of excitement.

"Samara! You have to come see the snow! It is so beautiful!"

Samara, who's hair was askew and pj's rumpled, joined her mother at the living room window. Her eyes grew large, as she took in the beauty of snow-covered branches and lightly dusted landscape.

Whispering in reverence, and concern for waking Ed, whom she thought was sleeping on the couch, Samara said, "Wow! It is pretty. I like how the sun reflects off the snow. Kinda looks like sparkly diamonds."

Ed stood in the doorway, holding his cup of coffee, quietly observing the two ladies, standing side by side, with arms encircling each other, oohing and aahing at the beauty before them. It was then and there, that his heart swelled, and he knew beyond a shadow of a doubt that he wanted them to be a permanent part of his life. His mind and heart had been dancing around the issue of commitment for the past couple of weeks, and he had pretty much examined and put to rest any arguments and doubts, but, still, that fear of being bound to, not one, but two women, had kept him at bay. Now, however, watching their interaction with each other, he couldn't deny his feelings.

Clearing his throat to alert them of his presence, he set the coffee down and joined them at the window, encircling both women with his big arms.

"I thought you were still sleeping," Cindy said, looking over at the rumpled bedding on the couch.

Gently placing a kiss on top of each head, he said, "What? And miss all this?"

Samara, still whispering, said, "Isn't it gorgeous, Ed? I wish there was more and it would last longer, but I guess this is all we get for now."

"Looks that way. You want to go build a snowman?"

Cindy and Samara looked at each other and giggled. "You think there's enough snow?"

Chuckling, he said, "I doubt it, but we can try."

Samara squealed. "Okay, let me get dressed and I'll meet y'all back in here in a few minutes. Is it okay if I bring Sasha?"

Cindy said, "She'd like that. I'll just throw a jacket over these sweats. Should be warm enough."

Zipping up his jacket, and throwing open the front door, Ed called, "Last one out gets a snowball in their face!"

Unfortunately for Samara, she got double slammed by snowballs from two different directions as she sat Sasha on the ground.

"Hey! That's not fair!"

"Sorry, babe, snowball fights are about each person defending themselves against further attack!" With the word attack, Ed lobbed another snowball in her direction, which missed and hit her mom instead.

Cindy was so focused on making a snowball, she didn't see it coming, and raised her head in time to get a face-full. Sasha ran around in circles, from one adult to another, yipping and trying to catch the snowballs in her mouth.

The three of them squealed, laughed, and lobbed snow, until the yard and surrounding surfaces were empty.

"Hey," Samara said, looking around, "Guess we won't make a snowman this time." Pointing a finger at Ed, and making a pouty face, she said, "I hope it snows again this winter, 'cause you owe me a snowman."

Laughing and pulling her into a hug, he said, "I'll talk to the man upstairs, and see if we can arrange that."

She gave him an eye roll.

Cindy called from the doorway, "Hey, why don't I cook us up some pancakes and bacon?" Watching as her man and daughter interacted so comfortably with each other, she couldn't help but smile.

Ed and Samara looked at each other and grinned, saying in unison, "Yum, bacon!" Running to the door, and trying to shut it before Ed came in, Samara was easily pushed out of the way. Her petite, ninety-eight pounds were no match for his hulking mass. He growled like a bear, which sent her to her room squealing, and Sasha barking and nipping at his ankles.

Samara ran out, scooped up the dog, and returned to her room, with a slamming of the door. Ed and Cindy burst out laughing.

"You think I really scared her?" Ed asked, when Samara didn't return after a few minutes.

"Nah. I think she's just playing scared."

A few minutes later, Samara stuck her head out, and whispered to her mother, "Where's Ed?"

Her mom nodded towards the living room, where Ed was sprawled on the couch, watching the morning news.

Samara held up the water pistol for her mother to see. Cindy's eyes grew round in surprise, and she put her hand up to her mouth to stifle a giggle.

After filling the gun from the bathroom sink, Samara ever so carefully and quietly, tiptoed down the hall to the living room, and jumped out yelling, "Surrender, you scallywag!" and shot her pistol of cold water at...an empty couch. When she realized her mistake, and turned to retreat, Ed whipped his own water pistol out, and proceeded to soak her face. Squealing, yelling, laughing and barking filled the little house. Sasha, worried about her mistress, clawed at the bedroom door barking and howling, until Cindy released her. Not wanting to miss out on any of the fun, Cindy turned off the stove, found a squirt bottle, filled it, and added her own liquid to the battle. When she joined the fray, Ed and Samara looked at each other, grinned and unloaded the rest of their water on Cindy, who kept screaming, "Not fair!," in a vain attempt to defend herself.

Samara's little gun was depleted first, and as she fell on the floor laughing and trying to catch her breath, Cindy and Ed brought the battle to an end.

Looking at her soaked clothing, and hair, Samara said, "Oh, man! I can't believe you did that!"

"What? You didn't think I'd notice that you were gone a while and wouldn't think you were up to something?"

"Well, no. I thought I was being pretty sneaky. How'd you know I'd have a water gun?"

"I didn't, but I wanted to be prepared for any kind of attack."

Putting her hands on her hips, she asked, "Where' did you get that pistol anyway?"

Ed looked at Cindy, who said, "Oh my. I need to get those pancakes finished."

"Mom!" Samara called out as Cindy disappeared into the kitchen. "I thought I was your favorite kid. How could you betray me?"

Cindy peeked around the corner, "You are my favorite kid, but Ed is my favorite boyfriend, and it didn't seem like a fair fight for you to be the only one with a weapon."

Samara grinned, did an eye-roll and said, "Okay, I guess you're right." Giggling, she said, "It *was* fun, wasn't it?"

Ed held his arms open. "We still friends?"

"Of course," she said as she walked into his arms and poured the remaining few drops of cold water down his back.

"Gotcha!" She said, turning and running to her room.

Grabbing the towel Cindy was holding out to him, and after wiping his face and neck, he said, "I didn't know she was such a little spit-fire." Looking at Cindy, he added, "Just like her mama."

Cindy feigned shyness and, batting her eyelashes, said in her best Texas drawl, "Why, Mr. Florres, why would you ever think such thoughts about little ole' me?" Sashaying over to him, she took the towel, threw it on the counter and said, as she ran her fingers up and down his arm. "A big strapping man like yourself, having trouble handling two little wild fillies?"

He laughed, scooped her up and swung her around the kitchen.

Samara, hearing her mother squealing and Ed's deep voice laughing, peeked around the corner and witnessed their shared tender moment. Smiling, she turned and quietly retreated to her bedroom. She hated to admit it, but she hoped her mom would marry Ed. He'd be fun to have around.

CHAPTER 78

Brad stood at his hospital room window on the second floor, looking across the flat Texas plain, admiring the beauty of the snow covered landscape. He had never witnessed snow in Texas before now, and was impressed with how beautiful everything looked. Maybe it was because he was high enough to see for miles, and the reflection of the sun and the light breeze seemed to cause the flakes to sparkle and dance, as if they were hearing a minuet, and felt compelled to join together for the enjoyment of the moment—as if they somehow knew their time was limited.

He felt a smile creep across his lips as he imagined the scene in an animated form. *Add some other characters, like woodland creatures or dancing plants, and real music, and voila', a movie that could rival any Disney one, for sure!*

It was then that the longing in his heart had begun. He missed his life in Michigan: his friends, his school, his church, his house, the little town they lived by, the seasons, the snow, and everything else that had been a part of his life for the first fifteen years.

Mostly, though, he missed his dad, and the fun times they had shared. His death had been so sudden and unexpected that, even after two years, Brad was still having difficulty processing the finality of it. There were times, he knew he heard his dad's laugh, or his voice or saw his face in a crowd, or out of the corner of his eye. Now, after seeing him in Heaven, he ached to see and hug him again, knowing that he wouldn't want to let go.

Oh the frustrations of being human!

As he stood there, letting his mind and heart remember what was, and could have been, he could feel a heavy blanket of despondency being draped across his shoulders, and he physically slumped from the weight of it. He imagined a dark spider of despair probing at his heart and mind, with it's long legs, trying to find a chink in his armor, so it could burrow in and make a nest, slowly consuming any hope or joy he had there.

He heard his dad's voice say, "Brad! Only *you* can stop this blackness trying to get into your soul. Remember the promise that God made to you. He has great plans for you. Don't let this evil in!"

As if coming out of a trance, Brad took a deep breath, and shook his shoulders and head, as if to dislodge the blanket and spider that were beginning to settle in. He immediately felt peace and joy return and had to chuckle, then giggle, then laugh out loud. He knew he was called for something greater, and was determined to figure out what it was and how to achieve it.

Argus looked at David and smiled. "That was a close one. Father must have known he would resist, or He wouldn't have allowed the test."

David nodded and returned the smile. "I'm thankful He let me speak to Brad, to remind him of the promise."

"Isn't your job assignment to be an encourager?"

David grinned and patted Argus on the back. "Yes, yes it is."

Grinning, he waved and was gone in a blink, leaving Argus to stand guard over Brad.

"Hey, Argus, you there?" Brad whispered. Argus reached out and touched Brad's shoulder. No words were spoken. They didn't need to be.

CHAPTER 79

Dr. Carmichael sat on the side of Brad's bed, and after examining him once more, and finding him perfectly healthy, began asking probing questions concerning his out-of-body experience.

Brad, sensing there was more to these questions than a psychological evaluation, asked, "Dr. Carmichael, do you believe in life after death? Do you believe in an actual heaven and Hell?" *Wow, it seems I'm asking that question a lot lately,* he thought as he waited for Dr. Carmichael's answer.

Dr. Carmichael stood, furrowed his brow, then stroked the goatee on his chin as he thought about how to answer Brad's questions.

Nodding, he said, "I believe there is a life after death, and I want to believe in an actual Heaven and Hell, but because of my upbringing, I wrestle with the whole Heaven and Hell concept. My parents are both believers in re-incarnation—that when this body dies, we are somehow transformed into a different form, so we can experience that way of life and either move up or down."

"What is the highest form you can achieve? And, how do you know when you've achieved it?" Brad asked, genuinely curious.

"Well, being human is the highest form, and just being good, honest, hard-working, and generous is enough to transport a person to a better, higher level."

"If being human is the highest level, how can one go higher? Does the soul start over? What is the first form? An amoeba?"

Dr. Carmichael shook his head and smiled. "So many questions! If one has enough good Karma, then I suppose being human could be the highest level. As far as what comes after that, I'm not sure. Maybe that's the last form and then the person's soul is no more. And to be quite honest, I'm not sure what the first form is. I always assumed it was an ant, or one of the other tiny creatures." Stroking his goatee again, he said, "I never really thought about it until now. Your questions have me questioning my own belief system."

Brad continued questioning, as if he couldn't stop. "So how do you know if you have enough good karma? For that matter, how does an animal know right from wrong? And how do they get good or bad karma? Who or what determines that?"

Dr. Carmichael pondered these questions before answering.

"The law of Karma states that all our actions in this or previous lives, have inevitable consequences. Whatever we send out returns to us. Positive karma returns in the form of happiness and good fortune—negative karma in the form of tragedies and hardship."

"Kinda like the saying, "What goes around, comes around?"

Smiling, and nodding, Aaron said, "Yeah, that's right."

"Well, that makes some sense, but again, how do you know if you're good enough or have gained enough good karma? Who or what determines that? Who sets up the cycle of who or what you come back as? And what about bad things happening to good people?"

Patting Brad's leg, Dr. Carmichael said, "You know, I'm going to ponder these questions, and I want to get back to you to discuss them further, but I need to get going. I have a tonsillectomy to perform in an hour."

"Oh, okay." Brad said, reaching out his hand and saying, "I just want you to know that I don't know very much about reincarnation, so I'm going to do a little research myself."

Dr. Carmichael nodded. "I'm looking forward to our next chat. Maybe before you leave this afternoon."

Brad smiled. "So I *am* leaving this afternoon?"

"I don't have any reason to keep you here, unless you just want to hang out with the toddlers."

Grinning, Brad said, "As much fun as they are, I'd rather go home...but thanks for the offer."

Smiling and shaking his head, Dr. Carmichael said, "See you later, Brad."

"Later!" Brad called out.

Sitting on his bed, Brad closed his eyes, and just listened to the cacophony of noise outside his room. He rarely did that—just listened. Life was so full of busyness and noise that his brain tuned most of it out, and he wondered how many times he had missed something because he just didn't listen. He was reminded of the verse in the Bible that says, "Be still and know that I am God." It was difficult to be still, but if he wanted to know God better, he should follow His advice. He heard one of the children crying down the hall and his mother speaking softly, the ding of the elevator announcing someones arrival, the public address system announcing they needed Dr. Meils to call line two, the murmuring of nurses and visitors, the opening and closing of cabinet doors, the flushing of toilets, the running of water, the crinkle of paper towels, the clack, clack, clack of uneven tires on the laundry cart being pushed down the hall, the music, talking and laughing coming from the TV sets, and the light rapping of someone knocking on a door. *Oh wait, that's my door being rapped on.* He opened his eyes to see the lab tech standing in the doorway with the tools of her trade, reminding him of a picture in one of his story books about a little girl named Red-Riding Hood, who had a basket of goodies for Grandma. Unfortunately for him, these goodies weren't edible.

Glancing down at the clipboard balanced on top of her basket of colorful vials and syringes, she said, "Excuse me, Mr. Sanders?"

Smiling, because it was just weird being called, "Mister", Brad said, "Yes?"

"I'm here to draw some blood before you're discharged."

Brad made sure his sweatshirt sleeve was pulled up, and presented his arm for the sacrificial blood-letting.

As the tech drew his blood, and he watched the dark liquid fill the syringes, he was reminded of how truly amazing the human body is. It wasn't as if he never thought about his body, and how marvelously it functioned, but now that he had met the Creator Himself, he was even more cognizant of every cell and its purpose. Blood, for instance, is such a vital substance for human existence. Without it, the body ceases to function. It carries oxygen, fluid, nutrients, antibodies, waste products, and a myriad of other substances he didn't know the names for, but was determined to learn.

The tech, whose name tag identified her as Dana Andrews, smiled pleasantly and placed a cotton ball and band-aid on the distended vein she had just punctured. "Thank you, Mr. Sanders."

"You're welcome, Dana." He said with a smile as he bent his arm at the elbow, exerting more pressure on the bandaged area.

He turned the TV on to catch up on the latest news. Every channel had some kind of special about the twin towers, and how their demise had affected the Christmas spirit around the world. He remembered asking God why He had allowed that to happen and God's reply was, "It's not for you to understand."

What did that mean? He had so many more questions, but had a feeling that even if he asked, he'd get a similar answer. Sighing, he thought, *God is God, and I am a human—incapable of understanding my Creator.*

As he watched interview after interview of people whose lives would be forever changed because of the misguided view of a few people who believed in a god of unholy vengeance, he couldn't help but feel gut-wrenching sorrow for all involved: the instigators, who truly felt they were right, and the victims, injured, dead or left behind who didn't understand how fellow human beings could be so cruel. He felt tears sting his eyes and escape down his cheeks.

Clinching his fists, he felt a wave of anger wash over him, bringing with it a desire to retaliate on behalf of the innocents. As his mind began to travel down that path, he felt as if a hand had been placed on his shoulder, and a calming voice say, "This is not your battle."

Muting the TV, he laid his head back and closed his eyes, asking God to take care of all the hurting families of the 911 incident. He may not be able to physically do anything at this time, but he *could* pray.

CHAPTER 80

In preparation for Brad's homecoming, and the Christmas celebration scheduled for the next day, the family, busied themselves in food and gift preparations.

Stacey and Nicky helped their grandparents bake and decorate cookies, while Christina prepared the Christmas feast of ham, sweet potatoes, turnip greens, green beans, cornbread and two different fruit salads.

Even though her kitchen was small in comparison to the one she left in Michigan, they all managed to mill about without too many incidences of bottom bumping, or pan banging.

"Mom?" Stacey said, as she took a batch of cookies from the oven.

"Yeah, babe."

"I was just thinking how sad it is for some of those families that were hurt or killed in the whole 911 thing."

Everyone stopped what they were doing, and silence ruled the kitchen as all eyes turned to Stacey.

Drying her hands on a dish towel, Christina walked over and pulled her daughter into a hug. "Oh, honey."

Stacey continued her train of thought, "Here we are, so happy and fixing food and carrying on, and yet so many families lost moms and dads and kids. I can't even begin to imagine how awful that would be. It's bad enough knowing we almost lost Brad, but what if we really had? What about those people killed just the other day out on I-35? I wonder how they're doing." Putting her hand to her chest, she said, "My heart hurts when I think how sad they all must be. Christmas is supposed to be a happy time, but geeze, so many awful things have happened this year, it's really hard to stay in a festive mood."

Christina looked around the room at the sympathetic faces. She rested her chin on the top of Stacey's head and sighed.

"I know, honey. My heart hurts, too. It certainly has been a challenging few months. I don't know how people get through times like this without faith in God. That's the only thing that keeps me on track, sometimes."

Nicky walked over and stood between his grandparents, who embraced him. Silence ruled once more as emotions ran the gamut in their minds and spirits.

Nicky said, "It's like the whole world changed in a few minutes, and I don't feel safe anymore."

Dan led everyone into the breakfast nook and they all sat around the table.

"I'm not sure if I have any great words of wisdom or special insight," he began, "but I do know this, God is still in control. Whatever has occurred over the past several months, or years, for that matter, is what He has allowed. It wasn't a surprise to Him. I'm sure it grieved Him to allow some of these choices to be brought about, but with every sacrifice, big or small, there has been some kind of redeeming quality that has come forth. Sure, there will be many instances in which we want to scream and shout and shake our fist at Him and ask why. Our human brains can't make any sense of it, but when the dust all settles, it comes down to giving man a free will, and allowing him to choose which path he will take. God will win in the end, and that's our hope. What we as believers have to hang on to. Unfortunately, we may witness more of this kind of behavior as the enemy tries to destroy God's creation."

There were audible gasps.

"I don't want to scare you or worry you, but you do need to understand and be prepared in your mind and spirit." Looking into each face, he added, "I believe God is allowing this family to be tested and tried for a greater purpose."

Nicky whispered, "What kind of purpose?"

Shaking his head, Dan said, "That, I don't know, but because of the events that have occurred over the past few months, and seem to be continuing, I feel the enemy is trying to steal our joy, our faith, our peace and our security. If he can do that successfully, we become ineffective and unable to carry out God's plan, which is to know Him and make Him known."

"What's so special about us?" Stacey asked.

All eyes turned to Dan, who seemed to be chewing on his words before speaking them.

"I don't think any one of us is any more special than any one else, because I believe God loves us all the same, but I do think we each have a role to play, a task to do, that has been specifically designed for each one of us." Leaning forward and resting his elbows on the table, he continued.

"Remember when Jesus said we can't all be eyes, or ears, or hands? How could the body function without each individual part doing their job? Well, that's how it is in the body of Christ. Each believer is given a talent in some area of their life, and it's up to them to develop that talent."

Stacey smiled and said, "Like, if I can sing, I should be singing to glorify God?"

Dan nodded and tousled her hair. "Exactly."

Cocking his head, Nicky asked, "Or if I can draw, I should do it for God?"

"Right. So many people are given gifts and talents and don't use them properly and get lost in them or lose them all together."

Stacey crinkled her brows. "What do you mean, get lost in them?"

Dan cleared his throat. "Well, think of all the talented young actors, singers, dancers and such, who started out so pure and noble and have ended up in all kinds of trouble because of the bad choices they made, when their talents were used for fame and money, instead of for praising God."

Chewing on her bottom lip, Stacey said, "Yeah, but so many of the Christian singers, and actors don't become very famous."

"And what is your definition of fame?" Dan asked.

"Well, being on TV, and in the movies, and in the magazines, and everyone knowing your name."

"And making lots of money." Nicky added.

Nodding and smiling, Dan said, "Well, you're right. That's what the world says fame is, but do all those things really bring peace and happiness?"

"I think it does for a while." Stacey said, adding, "But, I don't think it lasts, because so many of them end up doing more and more crazy things."

"Exactly. Everyone has a God-shaped hole in their heart, which only God can fill. People try to fill it with other things...like, fame, money, drugs, people, material possessions, but they are never satisfied. They are always trying to find the next thrill or challenge or thing to fill that void, but just can't seem to get it. We, as believers, understand that, even though all that stuff is nice to have, it won't give us the peace and true joy of experiencing God's love. So, to bring us back to our purpose in life, if we truly want joy, peace, and security, we need to seek God and honor Him in all we do and say."

"Sounds like we have to be perfect," Stacey whispered. "I don't think I can do that all the time."

"Oh, honey. God doesn't expect us to be perfect all the time—or for that matter, any of the time. He created us with a mind and will of our own, and knows that we are incapable of perfection. He just wants to know that we desire to please Him, in any possible way we can. He just wants our heart, our love and devotion. He will take care of the rest."

"That's a lot to think about," Nicky said with a grimace. "I have no idea what gifts or talents, or even what I like to do best from one day to the next. How am I ever gonna figure out what He wants?"

Christina spoke up.

"Right now, Nicky, I think God just wants you to enjoy being a kid, and He will reveal to you what His plans are as you mature."

"Yeah," Stacey added, "Even Jesus didn't do much 'till he was grown."

Ruth reached over and patted Stacey's hand.

"That's right, the first time He did something amazing was when he was around twelve, and He was talking to the religious leaders. Otherwise, the scriptures are pretty silent about his activities. As far as anyone knew, he was just a normal little Jewish boy, helping his dad build furniture."

Dan said, "Before your mom leaves to get Brad, why don't we pray for the families around the world that were affected by the 911 tragedy." They joined hands, bowed their heads and Grandpa Dan asked God to please let something good come out of these tragic events.

CHAPTER 81

Realizing there was nothing of interest on TV, Brad turned it off and looked around the room for something to read. He smiled when he spotted his mother's computer, and reached for it. *I can do some research on reincarnation*, he thought, as he switched it on.

The activity around him seemed to dim as he focused on the information before him. When the aide took his lunch tray, he was surprised, as he didn't remember eating the soup and sandwich. He must have, though, because the tray was empty and his stomach felt full.

Weird, he thought as he turned his attention back to the computer.

Two hours later, Dr. Carmichael came to his door.

"Hey, Brad. You up to continuing our conversation?"

"Sure." Closing the lap-top, and placing it on the bed-side stand, he said, "I was just reading about reincarnation. Fascinating stuff."

Dr. Carmichael nodded, pulled a chair by the bed-side, and sat.

"How are you feeling?"

Chuckling, Brad said, "Actually, I feel great! No headache, no dizziness. Ready to go home."

Dr. Carmichael patted Brad's leg. "Soon."

Clearing his throat, Dr. Carmichael said, "Tell me again about your out-of-body experience."

Brad spent the next several minutes retelling what he saw, heard, and felt.

"I see."

"Dr. Carmichael, are you a practicing Islamist?"

"What? No." Shaking his head, and rubbing his eyes, he added. "My parents weren't either. I think they believed the way they did out of convenience."

Brad cocked his head. "How so?"

"Well, my mom's family is from Lebanon, and most of the folks there are Islamic. When she moved to the United States to attend the University of California, and met my dad, she had pretty much walked away from those practices. My dad believed in a supreme being of sorts, because he wasn't an atheist, but he didn't practice any religion either. When my siblings and I came along, they didn't want us to be totally heathen, so they gave us a rudimentary belief in reincarnation and karma. You know, 'what goes around comes around' kind of thinking."

Nodding, Brad said, "Well, there is some merit in that kind of thinking. If it keeps people from doing bad things to one another, then that's good, right?"

Smiling, Dr. Carmichael nodded in agreement.

Brad cocked his head. "So, do you have a question for me?"

Dr. Carmichael leaned back in his chair, rubbed the whiskers on his chin, then leaned forward again. "I'm not sure how, or where to begin. I know you're only sixteen and may not have the answers I seek, but I feel you are wise beyond your years, and may have some insight that may help me."

Brad shrugged. "I'll do my best."

Dr. Carmichael began by telling Brad of his wife's accident and death, and ended with admitting his struggle with the whole 'life after death' question.

Brad nodded and said, "So, what you want to know is...?"

"Is there really life after death? Is there really a Heaven and Hell? Where do you think my wife is?"

"Dr. Carmichael, all I can tell you is what I believe the Bible teaches. There is life after death—there is a Heaven and Hell, but as far as where your wife is, only God knows that. Only God can judge the heart of man, or woman, in her case. As believers in God and Christ, we are promised eternal salvation when we cross over, but no one knows where your wife stood on that, except God. We are only responsible for our own relationship with Him. His word says that if we confess with our mouths and believe with our hearts that Jesus is Lord, the son of God, then we'll be saved."

"Saved? From what?"

"Saved from eternal separation from God. From Hell."

"So how does one become a believer?"

Brad smiled. "I'm glad you asked. I can show you what God's word says about that. Got a few more minutes?"

Dr. Carmichael looked at his watch. "Yes, I do. I'm curious to know."

Brad reached for his Bible on the bed-side table and turned to John 3:16, then to the book of Romans, and proceeded to go through the verses he had learned in his discipleship program, for such a time as this.

CHAPTER 82

Janet felt exhausted in mind, body and spirit. She had worked seven straight days, and it was taking a toll on her. Rubbing her eyes, she thought, *I'll be so glad when Christina comes back to work. Barring any complications, she should be back to work on Friday, then I can have at least one day to rest up, before having to work the weekend. If all goes as planned, I'll have Christmas Eve and Christmas Day off.*

She was thankful the unit only had two patients. Everything was quiet, for the moment, and she decided to lay her head down and close her eyes.

She was jolted awake by a voice whispering in her ear, "Janet, stop running from me."

"What?" She sat up and looked around. No one was there.

Rubbing her eyes, she muttered, "I must have been dreaming."

Sally Jean walked up to the counter.

"You okay, Janet? You look like you saw a ghost."

Janet frowned. "I'm fine. Did you get the vitals on the patients?"

Sally smiled. "Yes, ma'am. Got them right here." She handed a slip of paper to Janet who read them, nodded, and pulled the charts out to document the information.

Sally Jean leaned on the counter, watching her co-worker.

Irritated that she was standing there, Janet said, "Do you need something?"

Sally shrugged. "No, not really. Just noticing how tired you look. Bet you're ready for a vacation."

Janet sighed and pinched the bridge of her nose. "Yeah, I'm not used to working so many days in a row. It's starting to wear me down."

"Well, I think it's nice that you are working Mrs. Sanders' shift, too. I'm sure she appreciates it. What about the other RN that fills in sometimes?"

Janet sighed. "Irene Taylor?"

Sally nodded.

Rubbing her neck, Janet said, "I asked Mrs. Ferguson about that, and she said Irene just had a baby, and hasn't returned to work yet."

"Any idea when she'll return?"

Janet shrugged, then said, "Well, I appreciate the extra money I'll be getting, especially with the holidays and all."

Sally Jeans eyes brightened.

"So, what are you getting your daughter for Christmas? I remember when I was thirteen. That was the year I switched from wanting toys to wanting clothes and CD's."

"Yeah, Linda's at that stage, too. I've bought her a couple of sweaters and jeans, but I plan to go Friday, and do the rest of the shopping. I had her make a list of things she would like to have because, quite honestly, I haven't a clue as to what she likes. Her tastes seem to change from week to week."

"Janet, if you could have anything in the world, what would it be?"

Janet leaned back in her chair. "Interesting question. I guess I would have to say, I would like for someone to love me and Linda, just the way we are, without trying to change us into what they want."

Sally Jean raised her eyebrows. "Unconditional love."

"What?"

"Unconditional love. When someone loves us no matter what we've done or who we are, or what we might do."

Janet nodded. "Yeah, like that. I wonder if there's anyone out there like that?"

Sally shrugged. "Maybe." Putting her hand over her heart, and closing her eyes, she said, "I'm looking for my Prince Charming to come sweep me off my feet, give me a magical kiss, and take me to live with him in his castle on a hill."

Janet chuckled. "Well, at my age, I'd be glad if he came in a battered pick-up truck, pecked me on the cheek, and took me to his double-wide on some back road—as long as he truly loved me."

"Aww. That's sweet! I don't think I'd like a double-wide though. Maybe a log cabin."

Janet chuckled. "Nah, me either. I'd definitely prefer a log-cabin."

A bell rang and Sally Jean said, "Be back in a jiff."

Walking down the hall to tend to the patient, Sally Jean thought, *I've never seen Janet smile or chuckle like that. Maybe there is hope for that poor woman.*

As Janet reflected on Sally Jean's question, and her answer, her mind took her back to a time when she thought she had found her Prince Charming.

It was the summer of her seventeenth year and, after traveling around Texas with her dad and brothers, doing what-ever odd jobs were available to keep food in their bellies and clothes on their backs, they had ended up in the little town of San Saba. While the males of her family cut cedar for firewood, fencing, and to clear the land for the cattlemen in the area, she worked in a little restaurant, serving the local ranch hands.

On a beautiful clear, hot day in June, Pedro Mendosa, and several other migrant workers from across the border, walked into the restaurant. When she looked up from the counter she had been wiping, and their eyes met, she knew in that instant, he was her soul-mate. He must have felt it as well, as he gave her a wink, and a smile that made her heart flutter, and her knees feel like melted butter. She had to hold on to the counter for support. Reigning in her emotions, she took her pen and pad of paper, and walked over to take their order. She stood on the opposite side of the table so she could get a better look at him. His looks were captivating. Never had she seen eyes so dark, teeth so white, dimples so deep, and a body so tanned and toned. He was a smokin' hot representation of the male species, and she wanted him for herself.

After the initial meet and greet, he began coming into the diner more often—sometimes with his buddies, other times by himself. As their friendship blossomed, and they became more comfortable with one another, he asked her out for dinner and a movie. By the end of summer, they had declared their mutual love for one another, and by the end of his six month work visa, she announced she was pregnant—a bitter sweet turn of events.

She and Pedro had to keep the pregnancy, and their plans to escape, a secret from her father for as long as possible, for if he discovered that she and Pedro had been together, they would be in danger. He had a fiery hot temper, and wasn't concerned about showing it to anyone who crossed him—even his children. He would be furious with her, not only for being involved with a Mexican, but also because he would be losing a fourth of their income.

Knowing Pedro had to return to Mexico, she kept her secret bound tightly in her heart, as the details of their escape were finalized. Pedro would return to Mexico, then send her money to join him once he had settled. She would sneak out, catch a bus to Mexico, and leave a letter for her father and brothers.

When the day came for Pedro to leave, and she knew she had to remain behind, her heart felt as if it had shattered into a million pieces. Weeping as they shared a last good-bye kiss, and with the promise to send for her as soon as humanly possible, Pedro rode out of sight, in the back of his father's beat-up, red Chevy pick-up. She stood in the center of the road, waving until nothing was left but a cloud of dust. Every day, for weeks, she eagerly awaited word from him, while promising her unborn child a better life. When six weeks had passed, without a card, call, or any form of communication, she came to the harsh realization that he would never send for her. She grieved so deeply her body rejected the one thing that had brought her joy. All alone in her father's trailer, begging God, her baby, and any other powers around, to stop the inevitable. She screamed and wailed, as her tiny baby girl left her protective womb. She lay for what seemed like hours, holding the precious little body, until it grew cold and stiff. Not wanting her father or brothers to discover her secret, she cleaned up the mess, and wrapped her daughter in a handkerchief and placed her in a shoe box. She then stripped the linens off the bed and put them in the washer. There was so much blood. As they washed, she took the box and buried it under a pecan tree at the back of the property.

Returning from the awful task of saying good-bye to her baby, she checked the sheets, and found them still stained. After putting them back through the wash a second time, with extra bleach, any evidence of a miscarriage had been obliterated.

Over the next several months, Janet rarely smiled or laughed, as she silently grieved the loss of her baby girl, Pedro, and her innocence. No longer would she trust her heart to feel affection towards another pursuing male, for fear of being rejected and abandoned. Her father and brothers, not understanding the change in her, began avoiding her. She couldn't blame them—she didn't like being with herself either.

When summer came around again, she began working at the local Wal-Mart. As she tallied up purchases, she was shocked to look up and see Pedro's brother, Juan.

"Janet?"

Feeling faint from her racing heart, she whispered, "Yes."

The young man began speaking quickly.

"Oh, my goodness! I was afraid I'd never see you, again. I have to talk to you."

Still in shock, and batting her eyes to ward off tears, she looked at her watch, and said, "I have a break coming up in five minutes. Can you wait for me?"

Nodding and smiling, he said, "Sure. Come outside when you can. I'll be in the red Chevy truck."

Nodding, Janet whispered, "Okay."

After what seemed like an eternity, Janet left the register, and headed outside. Spotting the truck, but leery about approaching it, for fear of seeing Pedro, she walked cautiously towards it. *I'm not sure I could survive an encounter with him.* Her heartstrings were wound so tightly, she was sure they'd break.

Juan exited the truck, and approached her. No Pedro. She looked around, but he was nowhere to be seen. No one else was in the truck.

Spotting a bench by the entrance, Juan pointed to it, and asked if they could sit.

Feeling anxious and afraid of the news she may hear, she sat and held her breath.

Juan reached out and took her hand, causing her to relax a bit.

He sighed, then began his dialogue.

"As I said earlier, I thought we'd never meet again. We've been in town for a month or so, and I looked all over town trying to find you. Seemed like no one knew of your whereabouts."

She bowed her head and sighed. "I don't have any friends."

Nodding and frowning, he continued. "I know you're wondering about Pedro, why he never wrote, called or came back for you."

She nodded slightly.

Sighing heavily, he said, "On our way home, as we approached the border, a group of men attacked our truck. They took all our money we had just earned, stabbed, and beat us. Pedro fought as mightily as he could, but a couple of the men grabbed him and stabbed him in his gut."

She gasped and put her hand up to her mouth. Juan wiped tears from his eyes, as he continued his story.

"We were helpless, as we were all pretty beat up, ourselves. When they left, my papa went to Pedro and held him, until an ambulance came. He died in Papa's arms." Catching his breath, wiping his eyes, and letting out a sigh, he concluded.

"I heard Pedro say, 'Tell Janet I love her and always will. I'm sorry I can't be there with her and our baby.' When they cleaned out his pockets at the hospital, they found this letter." He pulled a folded piece of paper from his back pocket. Handing it to her, he said, "I'm so sorry, Janet. I wish it could have turned out differently. By the way, did you have the baby?"

Shaking her head, Janet began to sob, as a whole year's worth of pent-up emotion broke through the barrier she had constructed around her heart. Like a dam bursting, the tears flowed.

Holding the letter, unable to open and read it yet, she said, "All this time I thought Pedro had rejected me. I thought he didn't love me or our baby anymore. I missed him so much." Wiping her eyes, and between sobs, she said, "I lost the baby a few weeks after he left."

Juan's eyes widened, and he reached for Janet's hand.

"Oh, Janet. I'm so sorry. We couldn't get back over the border until the beginning of the summer. I wish we'd known how to get in touch with you sooner. I only knew that you lived somewhere in this town. I didn't even know your last name, and as I said, no one else seemed to know where you were, either."

She reached out and patted his hand. "It's okay, Juan."

"I have another envelope for you, as well. When the robbers came, Pedro had enough time to slip his envelope with money between the seats. The men didn't bother looking in the truck, which was a good thing. I, too, had put my envelope with his, so at least we had a little money to take home."

Janet frowned, and shook her head.

"Some people are just so mean."

Nodding, he said, "Yes, they are." Pulling the envelope out of his shirt pocket, he said, "Anyway, here it is. I know Pedro would want you to have it."

Janet frowned as she took it. "What is this?"

"It's money from Pedro's last pay check. It isn't much, but, hopefully, it'll help."

Janet opened the envelope, and inhaled sharply as she pulled out five one-hundred dollar bills. Shaking her head, and wiping the tears with a tissue she had retrieved from her purse, she said, "Oh, Juan, I can't take all this."

He smiled and shook his head. "Yes you can. It's what Pedro would have wanted. I know it doesn't make up for his loss, but maybe you can use it to get something special."

Smiling, and wiping her eyes and nose, she said, "I could use a car. I wonder what I can get for five-hundred dollars?"

Chuckling, Juan said, "Not much."

Even though she was grief-stricken, it was a relief to know that Pedro had truly loved her, and would have sent for her.

When she turned eighteen, she was making enough money to live on her own, and she and her family parted ways. She remained in San Saba a few more years, and earned her nursing degree.

As the barrage of memories began to fade, she placed her hand on her belly and said quietly, "I'm sorry, baby. I wish I could have known you."

Sally Jean returned a few minutes later, reporting that Mrs. Bledsoe was complaining of a headache. Janet stood, rubbed her eyes, stretched, checked Mrs. Bledsoe's chart to see which pain relievers she had ordered, and headed to the elderly woman's bedside.

After checking her blood-pressure, pulse, and temperature, and finding the readings within normal parameters, she gave the woman two Tylenols.

"Those should take effect in about fifteen minutes, Mrs. Bledsoe. Is there anything else I can get you?"

The woman was in her eighties, thin, pale and very frail looking. Janet sensed she didn't have many more days left here on earth.

"Thank you, dear. Could you please close the curtain? I think I'd like to take a little nap."

"Sure." Janet glanced out the window before closing the curtain. It was sunny, and all the snow was gone. She hoped it would snow for Christmas. There was just something magical about a white Christmas. Maybe it was because of the song, 'I'm Dreaming of a White Christmas,' or because one of her fondest memories as a child was of a snowy Christmas. Whatever the reason, she always hoped for a white Christmas.

CHAPTER 83

"So, let me get this straight," Dr. Carmichael said, leaning in, and resting his elbows on his knees, "You're saying that all we need to do to get to Heaven is believe in Jesus, as God's son?"

Brad shrugged. "Pretty much. We're all sinners, saved by grace. Not one of us can get to Heaven by our own merit, our own good deeds. That's why God sent Jesus. He took on all our sins, sicknesses, and failures, when He went to the cross, so we wouldn't have to. Because He did that for us, we need to just acknowledge that, be thankful, and declare our love for Him and God. As I said before, God wants our heart, our will. He will take care of the rest."

"So you don't think we keep coming back to get better—to make up for past mistakes?"

"If I understand our scriptures correctly, there is no mention of coming back for a do-over. I'm not going to put God in a box and say He wouldn't allow it in certain circumstances, because He can do anything He wants, but as a general rule, once we leave this life, we cross over into Heaven or Hell and live there eternally."

Pausing and taking a sip of water, he said, "Again, my question would be, how would we know if we did better or worse? Would we even remember what we had done, and wouldn't Jesus' sacrifice be for nothing?"

"What about all the people that lived before Jesus?"

Brad sighed. "I've wondered about that myself, but really, that is no concern of ours. God will take care of them, in His way. We are responsible for our own actions—whether we trust and believe in Him."

Dr. Carmichael sat back and closed his eyes a moment, as he considered Brad's argument.

"So, is there some kind of special ceremony, prayer, or something I need to do to let God know I believe in Him and Jesus?"

Brad smiled and shook his head. "All you need to do is tell Him you're sorry for your mistakes, and ask His forgiveness, then tell Him you want Him to be Lord over your life."

"But what if I keep making mistakes, and doing and saying the wrong things?"

"Like I said, no one is perfect. If we waited 'till we were perfect to come before God, we'd never get there. He wants you just the way you are. He made you, so He already knows everything about you—past, present and future."

After a pause, Brad said, "If you want, I can pray with you right now."

Dr. Carmichael considered this a moment, then said, "I'd like to think some more about this."

Brad nodded. "Dr. Carmichael, do you have a Bible?"

"I'm pretty sure I do, on the bookshelf in my study."

"Is it okay if I write down some scriptures for you to look up and read?"

"Sure. That would be helpful."

As Brad wrote down scriptures, Dr. Carmichael stood, walked over to the window, and looked out over the flat Texas plain. For the first time, since his wife's death two years ago, he marveled at what he saw. His eyes stung with tears, as he felt an indescribable feeling of love enfold him. *Could that be God?*

CHAPTER 84

Sheriff Clifton sat in front of his computer, reading through the previous years' police reports laid out in front of him. He sat up straighter when he began to see a pattern of petty thefts emerging. He called in his secretary.

"Loraine, could you look in the files from the past three years, and bring up any reports of petty thefts in the area?"

"Sure, do you want me to send what I find over to your computer?"

"Yes, thanks."

A few minutes later, he began receiving several reports, indicating that things had been reported missing, but then had mysteriously reappeared elsewhere in the house. Gradually increasing from once every month or two to two or three times a month, for the past couple of years.

He leaned back in his chair, and pondered that for a few minutes.

There were too many incidences—around fifty—to chalk up to mere chance or coincidence. A thief with a conscience? Why would someone risk getting caught stealing, if they planned to return the objects anyway? That would be a double risk. The thrill?

Imagining himself in that situation, he could understand how it could bring on an adrenalin rush. He figured it must be a kid or teen. He doubted an adult would bother returning anything. An adult would go for something more valuable and sell it, as soon as possible. As with most criminals and adrenalin junkies, however, the thrill never lasted, and they would start increasing the episodes and become bolder, as indicated with the frequency of reports. It was just a matter of time before this person would graduate from petty theft to more valuable items, and increase his risk taking, which could lead to lives being threatened—the thief's as well as the victim's.

He called in his four other deputies, and they discussed the case and their options. One of the men suggested they use his son, who was a senior at Alva High School, to keep his eyes and ears open for anyone who may let it slip that they had been involved in the fire at the school, or with the petty thefts. Kids who did this kind of thing rarely kept it a secret. They would feel a need to brag about their conquests, thereby gaining them recognition and status, among their peers.

After considering it, Sheriff Clifton decided that it would be an acceptable option, at the present. In the meantime, he'd do a little more investigating to see what other patterns and information he could gain. He had a couple of weeks before the kids returned to school, to set everything in motion.

CHAPTER 85

On their way home from the hospital, Brad said, "Mom?"

"Yes?"

"I had an interesting conversation with Dr. Carmichael today."

Glancing at him, she said, "Really? Tell me about it."

As she drove, he told of Dr. Carmichael's family and their beliefs.

Christina couldn't disguise her surprise.

"Dr. Carmichael was Islamic?"

"Well, according to him, not a practicing one."

Brad continued telling of Dr. Carmichael's curiosity concerning Christianity, and life after death.

Christina nodded. "So what do you think will happen next?"

Brad shrugged. "I'm praying he develops a relationship with God. I think he'll want to talk some more, but I'm going to encourage him to talk to our pastor. I'm not sure I'm qualified to answer any more than basic questions."

"Maybe that's all he needs."

Shrugging, he said, "Maybe, I'll do my best, but I'm still just a kid and learning as I go."

Wanting to change the subject, he asked, "So what's everyone else doing?"

Christina smiled, "They're getting ready for your homecoming."

"And what does that mean?"

"You'll see soon enough."

Nodding and grinning, he said, "Okay."

Pulling into the driveway, Brad noticed the extra cars along the curbs, then the "Welcome Home, Brad" banner hanging above the garage opening. He looked at his mom, shook his head, and said, "Really?"

She shrugged.

Entering the back door, he was met with balloons and confetti and shouts of "Welcome home, Brad!" One would have thought he'd been off fighting a war somewhere, instead of in a hospital bed for three days. He felt he should be sporting a uniform and duffel bag, instead of wearing a sweat suit and carrying a backpack.

The kitchen was filled with a cacophony of noise and bodies, as hugs, kisses, and pats on the back were distributed. Benji, who was determined to get his fair share of attention, wriggled his way to Brad, who knelt and instantly got a face full of doggy kisses.

Standing and wiping his face, he looked around and said, "Wow! This must be how Lazarus felt when he walked out of the tomb." Everyone chuckled.

Blushing, he said, "Thanks."

Eric, who was leaning on the cabinet next to Brad, said, "So, your mom says your heart stopped for a few minutes, and you saw God. Tell us what that was like."

Brad shrugged and said, "Okay. Why don't we go in the family room, where it's not so crowded?"

He led the way, as his grandparents, Eric, Samara, Cindy, Ed, his siblings, and mom followed.

They all found a place to perch, and were captivated as he recounted his encounter with God, his dad, and the angels.

As questions were raised concerning the description of Heaven, he closed his eyes, and was surprised at the clarity of his memory—as if he were right back there, seeing it for the first time.

Opening his eyes once again, and looking around, he said, "That's all I've got for now. It's like every time I retell it, God gives me more to reveal. I guess, my mind can only handle so much at a time."

Cindy, whose eyes were as big as saucers, said, "Wow! I guess I've never given God, or Heaven, or any of that spiritual stuff much thought. Sure makes me re-consider some of my opinions. I always pictured Heaven as some sort of giant amusement park."

Samara gave her mom an eye roll.

"What?" Cindy said, looking around. "You can't tell me that idea didn't cross anyone's mind, at some point in their life?"

Nicky spoke up. "I kinda pictured it like that."

Cindy gave her daughter a look that said, *"See? I'm not the only one."*

Everyone chuckled.

Christina said, "Hey, we baked some cookies, and I have coffee, tea and hot-chocolate, if anyone would like some."

The group began dispersing, as a few headed for the kitchen, and others began their own separate conversations.

When the last guest left, Christina asked, "Okay, who's ready to open gifts?"

She was answered with a unanimous, resounding, "Me!"

Grandma Ruth and Grandpa Dan gave each child a gift certificate for a new top-of-the-line bicycle from the local bike shop, which they were to pick out the next day.

Brad had hoped for a car, but was pleased he could get a better bike, as his was beginning to show wear and tear, from his many trips to school, work, and back home.

Stacey and Nicky were excited about getting new bikes, as they had always settled for second-hand ones.

Christina presented her in-laws a collage of photographs, documenting their arrival in Alva, to Brad's arrival home a few hours earlier.

Noticing the last picture, Ruth asked, "When did you put that one in?"

"When Brad was telling his story, I slipped up to his bedroom and printed it off. Pretty cool, huh?"

Shaking her head, Ruth said, "I'll say. We love it! I love the candid shots of the kids. Who took these pictures at the Thanksgiving get together?"

"My friends, Donna and Lisa, took a few, and I also gave cameras to the kids, and asked them to take a few. It was fun going through them and picking the best ones."

"Wow! I'm impressed." Looking at Dan, she said, "As far as we're concerned, you can give us something like this every year. We're at a point in our lives where we don't really need anything, and these pictures are priceless!"

Dan smiled, and nodded in agreement.

When the last gift had been opened, Nicky said, "I'm starving!"

"Me, too," added Brad and Stacey.

"Then, let's eat!" Christina said, as she and Ruth headed to the kitchen to bring the meal to the dining room. Christina gave her mother-in-law a hug.

"Thanks, mom, for preparing this meal for us. With everything that went on today, I wouldn't have had time."

Ruth said, "It's just pot roast and biscuits. Nothing fancy."

"Well, it's fancy enough for us." Christina said, as she finished setting the plates and flatware on the table.

The ladies grinned, as they heard comments and laughter coming from the family room, as Dan and the kids studied the photographs.

Nicky said, "I can't believe Mom put in a picture of Madeline picking her nose!"

Stacey giggled and said, "She'll hate that when she get's older."

"Yeah," agreed Nicky, "but at least she's not eating the buggers!"

Making a face, Stacey said, "Eww, that's so gross! I hate when kids do that. Makes me gag!"

Brad said, "Yeah, well, I remember you both doing that when you were young, and Mom slapping your hands and handing you tissues. Guess all kids do it at one time or another. Mom says it helps build their immune systems."

Stacey and Nicky made disgusted faces.

Dan muttered, "Kids are generally nasty, gross little creatures. It's a good thing they're so cute and loveable!"

He reached over, grabbed Nicky and gave him a noogie on his head.

Giggling and squirming, he said, "Grandpa!"

"Remind me, sometime, to tell you of a few disgusting things your dad and uncle did when they were young."

"Okay!" Nicky said, pulling free, and smoothing his hair.

"Dinner's ready!" They heard Christina call from the dining room.

Dan reached out, shook Brad's hand, and pulled him into a hug.

"I'm so proud to call you my grandson."

He then walked into the dining room with his arm around Stacey's shoulder, after kissing the top of her head and whispering, "I'm glad you outgrew that nose-picking stage, and are growing into such a lovely young woman."

She giggled. "Thanks, Grandpa."

CHAPTER 86

After putting Sammie to bed, Dr. Carmichael looked through the bookshelf, found the Bible belonging to his wife, blew the dust off, and took it to his recliner. He pulled the slip of paper, which Brad had given him, out of his pants pocket, opened the Bible, and began locating the scriptures—reading them for the first time. He had been taught that the Christian Bible is heresy, and the Qur'an is the true word of Allah, and felt a twinge of guilt in his spirit as he read, but his need for understanding overcame his concern of retribution. He thought about what Brad had said. *"According to the Bible, all humans, because of their imperfect nature, were incapable of meeting the requirements of a perfect God. They needed a champion—a Savior—someone to take their place, and plead their case. They had laws and rules to follow, and for the most part did well, but even that proved inadequate, as they got ignored, twisted, and became overwhelming. God, seeing the plight of His people, sent His son, Jesus, to be that champion—that intercessor—that Savior. Unfortunately, many couldn't accept what was before them, and rejected Him, and eventually crucified Him."*

Dr. Carmichael pondered that for a moment. *Because of my upbringing and belief system, I would have been right there, in that crowd, calling for His crucifixion.* He shuddered. He was a healer, not a murderer. But he probably would have crossed that line, all in the name of religion—like so many before him, and after him, and even now—recalling the 911 event.

He continued reading, putting the puzzle pieces together in his mind and spirit. Brad had said, "All God really wants is our heart." *How hard would that be?*

Thoughts of his child, career, money, possessions—objects of his affection—flooded his mind. *Does that mean He wants all that, too? Can I really give those things up to Him? He already took my wife. Could I risk Him taking my child, too? She's my responsibility. Can I trust Him to take care of her?*

He heard a whisper. "No, she's *my* responsibility."

His breath caught, and he felt a sob work it's way up from his inner core as tears stung his eyes. *What?*

The voice continued. "Aaron, everything you are, and everything you have, is because I, *God*, chose you. All you need to do is acknowledge that, and give your heart to me. I will do the rest. I will fulfill my promises to you. Trust Me. If you reject my call, you will be in the enemy's hands and will suffer, until you decide to call on me. I will always be here."

"God, is that really you talking to me, or am I just imagining this?"

He waited for an answer. Getting none, he figured it must have been God, because he would have never said those things to himself.

Taking in a deep cleansing breath, and blowing it out slowly, he said, "Okay, God. I'm not sure how to go about this, but I'm gonna give it a shot. Brad said all I have to do is admit I'm a sinner, ask Your forgiveness, and say I want You to be my Savior. So, here goes."

When he said, "Amen," he felt a tingling sensation from the top of his head to the bottom of his feet—like he was being sprinkled with a light shower—a cleansing of sorts. He smiled, then chuckled, then laughed out loud, and said to the empty room—which really wasn't empty at all, but filled with angels rejoicing, "Wow! That's amazing! I feel like a huge weight has been lifted off my shoulders!"

Since Tabitha's passing, it was if a part of his senses had been anesthetized. He felt as if he was merely existing, not living life to the fullest, just doing what needed to be done without any real emotion. He knew now what he had been missing—joy. He had had moments of elation, and happiness, but not real joy—not that inner peace and contentment.

That night, as he slept, he dreamed of Tabitha, and was blessed with his own view of Heaven, and what she was experiencing. He felt a peace so vivid, he knew without a doubt, that Heaven was real as well as what he had committed to. Now he understood the phrase "the peace that passes understanding." Because, at this moment, he couldn't understand or explain it. He just knew it.

CHAPTER 87

Wednesday, the whole Central Texas area was blessed with sunshine, clear blue skies as far as the eyes could see, and temperatures in the mid fifties. By nine that morning, stores were beginning to fill with shoppers, gearing up for Christmas the next Tuesday. Christmas decorations and items were being discounted to encourage consumerism. Music, from the classic rendition of songs reminding the shoppers about sleigh rides, snow, and Santa, to carols and more modern hip-hop versions of the classics, played through the speakers, putting people in a festive spirit.

The outlet mall parking lot was filling up, as well as the local businesses. It seemed the residents of Alva and the surrounding areas, were out and about on this beautiful day.

The Sanders family had a leisurely breakfast, and planned out their day. The elder Sanders would be leaving for the airport the next morning, and they wanted to enjoy their time together, before heading out.

Dan said, "So, kids, you want to go to the bike shop, and pick out your new bikes?"

He received an excited, "Yes!"

Nodding and chuckling, he said, "Allrighty then, how about we plan to leave around ten, then we can go to the outlet mall, or somewhere else. I'd like to go to that steak house out on I-35 for lunch or dinner." Looking at Christina he asked, "What's the name of that place?"

"Oh, you mean Zimmerman's?"

"Yeah, that's it. I love their steaks!"

Ruth said, "Me too! Except they give us way too much food. Anyone want to share a chicken-fried steak with me?"

Stacey and Nicky spoke up. "I will!"

Ruth giggled. "Well, there'll probably be enough to split it three ways."

Christina asked, "Nicky, have you seen Elijah?"

"Yeah, he came out to eat some breakfast. He actually let me pet him, but when he finished eating, he went back behind the couch in the front room.

Chloe hissed at him. She's not very happy about having another cat invading her space."

Christina nodded. "It'll take a little while for them to adjust to each other. How's Benji handling him?"

Nicky giggled. "Well, he sniffed Elijah's bottom, which the cat didn't appreciate, and he growled, hissed and swatted at Benji, who barked and backed away. It was pretty funny."

"Maybe, while we're out, we should get another litter box, and we'll need to get more litter." Looking at Nicky and pointing a finger, she said, "With two cats, we'll be going through it faster, which means you'll have to change it more often."

Nicky grimaced. "Oh, yeah. Eww!"

Stacey asked, "Do we need to get more cat food too. I doubt if Chloe will want to share hers."

"Well, Margaret did leave a bag, so I think we're okay for a little while. Hopefully, he'll get acclimated soon, and will start coming around more often."

Ruth said, "As old as he is, I doubt he'll interact with you much. Cat's aren't pack animals as a rule, and are fine off by themselves."

Christina sighed. "Yeah, you're right. We'll just have to see how it all plays out."

Glancing at her watch she said, "If we're gonna get out of here by ten, we best get going."

CHAPTER 88

The bike shop was located in downtown Alva between a tattoo parlor and an antique mall. Christina had never been inside the building before, and was surprised at the vast array of riding equipment offered. There were various bikes, tools, parts, clothes, bags, and even camping equipment—anything a biker would need for a day or extended trip. The aisles were long and wide enough for the kids to take a bike or two on a test run, which Nicky enjoyed. Brad picked a sleek black ten-speed with a cushioned seat. Stacey picked a purple five-speed with a flowered cushioned seat, and Nicky picked an orange and black ten-speed, off-road bike.

Dan pulled out his credit card, and gladly paid for the purchase with a promise of coming back later to pick them up. The owner said he would be able to deliver them free of charge.

"That would be great!" Dan remarked. "I was wondering how we'd get them in the back of the van, without having to make multiple trips."

"We'll close up shop here around five. How about I bring them by after that?"

Dan looked at Christina, who nodded her approval, saying, "We should be back home by then."

The Sanders family spent a couple hours wandering in and out of shops downtown, before heading out to Zimmerman's. The ladies went in to visit Cindy at Mary's Clothes Garden, and make a few purchases, while the guys went to the hardware store.

Returning home with full tummies and bags of leftovers, the family was just exiting the van, when a pick-up truck, loaded with bikes, pulled in behind them. Nicky and Stacey squealed and ran to greet the driver.

Brad and Dan helped unload the bikes, as Nicky and Stacey began tearing the protective plastic and paper off. Christina pulled out her camera, and took a couple of pictures, as Ruth stood back, enjoying the commotion. This was definitely one of those Kodak moments, which would be forever seared in their minds. Anxious to show his bike to Danny, Nicky begged his mom to let him ride down, with a promise to be right back. Since this was the first time he had asked to go anywhere alone, since his abduction, she thought it would be a step in the right direction in his healing process.

"Sure, you can go, but it's getting dark, and I want you back here within the half hour."

"Thanks, Mom! I'll be right back!"

She watched as he sped away, and felt anxiety fill her heart. Ruth stepped over and put her arm around Christina's waist.

"He'll be okay. It's only five houses down."

Christina sighed. "I know, but that mama bear in me can't help but be a little anxious. This is his first time to venture off alone since he was kidnapped."

Stacey and Brad rode their bikes up and down the driveway a couple of times, and commented how they could hardly wait to really put them to the test.

Returning the camera to her jacket pocket, Christina said, "If it's as nice tomorrow as it is today, maybe we can all go to the park and ride around. I'll take your old bike, Brad."

"That'd be awesome!" Stacey interjected. "Could I invite Carmen or Linda to come along?"

Christina considered that. "Sure, if they're available."

True to his word, Nicky returned a few minutes later, and announced that Danny wanted to come over and go bike riding the next day. Stacey told him of their planned trip to the park, after their grandparents left for the airport.

"What time do y'all have to leave, Grandma?" Brad asked.

"We need to be out of here around nine. Our flight leaves at one."

Brad said, "I'm sorry we weren't able to spend as much quality time with you, as we had planned."

Reaching out, and pulling Brad into a hug, Ruth said, "Oh, Brad, honey. We're just so thankful we were here during this crisis. I'd hate to think you guys would have to go through something like this alone."

Wiping his eyes, Dan added, "We're just glad everything worked out as well as it did. I don't even want to think how things could have turned out."

Shaking his head, Brad said, "It all seems so surreal. I know it happened, but yet it almost feels like a dream. It's just weird. I can't really put into words how it makes me feel."

Christina asked, "Hey, who's up for a card game?"

"I'll get the pack of cards." Stacey said.

Nicky said, "I need to take care of the animals, then I'll be in."

"I'll put the bikes away," Brad volunteered.

Dan and Ruth looked at each other. "I guess we can put the leftovers away, and get some snacks together."

Christina nodded. "I'll get us drinks. Y'all want hot or cold?"

Ruth and Dan wanted hot tea, and Christina and the kids settled for cold juice. As Christina prepared the drinks, she realized the anxious feeling she had been harboring all day was beginning to lift. Now that the day was ending, and nothing catastrophic had happened, like a plane falling from the sky, or another explosion, she felt relieved.

After three games of Spades, with the guys winning the final one, the group decided it was time to call it a day, and headed to bed. As much as Brad enjoyed his grandparents, and gladly volunteered his room for them to use during their stay, he had to admit that it would be nice to be back in his own bed. The couch was better than the floor, but his lower back was beginning to protest as he struggled to drop off to sleep.

He thought about his conversation with Dr. Carmichael, and wondered if he had followed through with reading the scriptures. Hopefully, he'd have an opportunity to speak with him, again, before too long.

As the residents of Alva slept under a cool, cloudless, star-studded sky, dreaming of upcoming Christmas events, they were totally unaware of the turmoil taking place in the spiritual realms.

CHAPTER 89

Around two o'clock, Al Conger, woke from a fitful sleep. He sat up and listened intently. *Did I hear something? What woke me? A bad dream? A full bladder?* Slipping on his robe and slippers, he decided he should use the toilet, then take a walk around the house to check the windows and doors once again, even though he had done that before heading off to bed.

He had been diagnosed with dementia, with paranoid tendencies, a couple of months earlier, and had been taking a new medication, which seemed to help clear his mind during the day, and keep him asleep at night. This was the first time he had been up during the night, in quite a while, so he wasn't sure what to think of that. He didn't bother turning on any lights, as he knew the layout of the house, and if someone were in it, or on the outside, he would have that element of surprise on his side. He grabbed the hammer he kept by the bedside and went hunting. Seeing no one inside, he decided to turn on the porch and barn lights. Nothing. The night sky was clear, and the moon was bright enough to see the yard and fields. Nothing ominous presented itself, but yet he felt as if something weren't right. For a split second, he was back in Viet Nam, wondering if the enemy was sneaking in through the trenches. As quickly as the thought presented itself, it dissipated, leaving him feeling a bit disoriented. *That's odd,* he thought, as he switched the lights off and headed back to bed. Tomorrow he would call his daughter, Eleanor. Her former husband, Tom, and his partner, Ed may be able to check things out more thoroughly, and calm his anxiety.

When the teen was sure the old man was back in bed, and could hear his sonorous breathing, he crawled out from behind the couch. *Whew!*

That was close! The way the old guy was looking around, I thought surely he would discover my hiding place. Lucky for me, the guy didn't look there. I wonder what woke him? I was being super careful and quiet. Well, whatever it was, it was too close for comfort.

Running his shaking hands through his hair, he thought, *I'll have to admit that was quite an adrenalin rush. I'm still shaking. I don't know if I'll risk coming back here, though. I think if the guy caught me, he'd kill me for sure.* Returning to the basement, and grabbing the bag of items he had collected, he crawled onto the workbench, and out the poorly latched window. Being small in stature had its advantages.

CHAPTER 90

The next morning, after a light breakfast, the elder Sanders loaded up their rental car, and headed for the airport. The clear blue sky held promise of a pleasant flight to Detroit.

As they waited to board the plane, Ruth and Dan discussed the week and marveled at how many life-changing events had occurred in such a short amount of time. It seemed surreal to think that their grandson had actually met and talked with God.

Ruth said, "I find myself feeling a bit jealous. I wish *I* had been chosen to visit with God and David."

Dan smiled, nodded, and patted her hand. "I know. As Brad described Heaven, I felt a twinge of that myself, but at our age, we're getting closer to the real thing, as each day passes."

Leaning her head on Dan's shoulder, Ruth said, "That's true. I hope we live long enough to see what God has in store for Brad."

CHAPTER 91

After returning home from their bike trip to the park with their friends, in which the Sander's kids tested the limits of their new bikes, Nicky asked his mother for a shoe box, in which he could pack a few items for Ruby.

"Could we ride our bikes to the post office to mail the box?" Nicky asked, as he wrapped the lavender scented soap, shampoo, conditioner, body wash and lotion in multicolored tissue paper. Not wanting to forget Sweet Pea, the guinea pig, he added a little bag of dried fruit and nuts.

Nodding, Christina said, "I guess so. Danny and Carmen need to ask their moms though."

Adding the last piece of tape to the box, he asked, "You think Sweet Pea will like the fruit and nuts?"

"Absolutely! Remember the little guinea pig Stacey brought home from school for the weekend years ago?"

"Stacey brought a guinea pig home from school? When? I don't remember that."

"She was in first grade so you would have been around four at the time. I guess you wouldn't remember that. Anyway, that little thing ate any kind of food scrap we put in the cage."

Stacey, followed by Carmen, came into the kitchen, and dug around in the refrigerator for a couple of apples. Handing one to Carmen and biting into the other one, she asked, "What are y'all talking about?"

"Nicky was adding dried fruit and nuts in his package for Ruby's guinea pig and asked if I thought it would like them. I asked if he remembered the guinea pig you brought home for the weekend when you were in first grade."

Scrunching up her face, she searched her memory bank. "Oh yeah!" She said excitedly. "I remember him. Smelly little thing. Cute, but smelly. I didn't like cleaning out his cage, and swore I'd never have one as a pet." Taking a bite of apple, she added, "I think his name was Rex."

Brad walked in and poured a glass of juice. "Rex, the guinea pig?"

"You remember him?" Stacey asked.

Making a face, he said, "How could I forget? The house smelled like cedar and guinea pig for about a week, after he left."

Christina chuckled. "Yeah, y'all had begged for a hamster, or guinea pig before that weekend, but never asked after that. I always wondered why." Shaking her head, she said, "That was a good learning experience for us all."

Rolling her eyes and shuddering, Stacey said, "Carmen has a pet ferret. That thing creeps me out. Looks like an over-grown rat. I don't want one of those either."

Carmen rolled her eyes and said, "My ferret isn't creepy. He's adorable."

Christina said with a chuckle, "Well, maybe to you. There are limits to my whole animal rescue and adoption standards. If it doesn't meow or bark, or have human DNA, it may *not* take up residence here."

Brad sighed and said, in as convincing tone as he could muster, "You would have to throw that human DNA qualification in. I was hoping maybe some day to have a spider monkey. I always wanted a little spider monkey. Did you know they can be trained to do most things a three-year-old can do?"

It was Christina's turn to do an eye-roll.

She said, "Let me put it this way. When y'all move out on your own, you can have any pet you want, or ones your spouses will *let* you have."

Nicky grinned and said, "I'd like to have a spider monkey."

Stacey said. "First of all, spider and monkey shouldn't even be in the same sentence, much less a name for something. And secondly, you still gotta clean up their mess. I hate cleaning up messes."

Nicky gave his sister a look. "You never clean up the cat or dog mess. I do."

"Exactly. That's what little brothers are for."

Frowning, he asked, "What if I wasn't here?"

"Then Brad would do it, or we just wouldn't have an animal that needs mess cleaning."

Christina bit her bottom lip to keep from laughing at this exchange.

Making sure Nicky's box was taped well, Christina asked Brad, "You want to ride with the kids to the post office?"

He grinned and nodded. "Really? I could use more practice changing gears. These gear changes are smoother than my old bike, and it's gonna take some getting used to."

Christina said, "Carmen and Danny, you need to call your moms to see if it's okay to ride to town with Brad."

Stacey and Nicky gave each other high fives. "You're gonna let us ride to the post office alone?" Stacey asked.

"Not alone. Y'all will have each other. Besides, it's only a few blocks away, and it's such a beautiful day. I don't want y'all growing up so paranoid, you can't enjoy a little independent bike riding. I used to ride my bike all over town, by myself, when I was a kid. Makes me sad that times have changed, so a kid can't even feel safe in their own town anymore."

After calling their moms, Carmen and Danny were given permission to ride into town with the promise to return home soon after.

As they mounted their bikes, Christina ran through a mental check list.

Helmets—check

Phones—check

Jackets—check

"Alright, you five, looks like you're ready to go. Have fun, be careful, watch out for traffic, and each other. If you decide to stop at a store for a soda along the way, call me."

"Yes, ma'am." They all answered in unison.

"Then, off you go! See you in a while." Stacey took the lead, then Carmen, Nicky, Danny and Brad—keeping the youngest in the safest spot, like most animal species would do.

She and Benji watched, until they turned the corner at the next block and disappeared from sight.

Reaching down and patting the whimpering dog's head, she said, "I know, boy. Maybe, next time you can go with them." As they headed back to the house, she asked, "You want a cookie?" He knew the word "cookie," and responded by jumping in circles and woofing.

About the time she was stuffing a load of sheets into the dryer and another load in the washer, her phone rang. Brad's number appeared.

"Mom, we're at the corner store across from the church. Gonna drink our sodas, then head on back."

She smiled. Four blocks from home. *Nothing can happen to them that close to home, right?*

Jamie sat on his bike across from the store, and watched the Sander's kids drink their sodas, and joke around with each other. Their voices and laughter floated on the air, and reaching him, touched a spot in his heart. He felt jealousy rise within his spirit. *How come some people have such good lives, such good families, and others of us don't? It's not right, and it's not fair! Why did I get stuck with a mom who didn't love me enough to stay, and a dad who doesn't care*

if I live or die? I wonder if I could somehow get adopted into their family? I think I need to spend more time in their house, getting to know them better. Maybe I can figure out how to insinuate myself into their lives.

He followed the kids home, and riding by, waved as they were heading into the house from the garage.

Glancing over, and seeing the teen riding by and waving, Nicky said, "Hey, Brad, isn't that the kid who delivers pizzas?"

Brad caught a glimpse of Jamie's back. "Yeah, I think so. I wonder what he's doing in our neighborhood."

"Delivering pizza?" asked Stacey.

Brad shook his head. "Nah, he's on a bike. He usually drives a car to deliver pizza."

Cocking her head, she said, "Yeah, it would be hard to balance a pizza, and ride a bike. Maybe he lives around here?"

Sighing, Brad said, "I don't think so. Oh well, let's go tell Mom we're home."

Carmen and Danny said their good-byes and headed home as promised.

The pizza boy was soon forgotten, as the Sander's family prepared for their evening routines.

CHAPTER 92

Steven held the envelope in his hand, and had a mental argument with himself. *Should I open it, or just toss it and let bygones be bygones?*

The return address showed it was from Anika Marouf, his former girlfriend, who was now living in New York City. He let his mind wander back to the last time they had spoken.

He'd received a call from her at the end of October, stating the moving van would be there the next morning, if he wanted to come by for one last visit. A month earlier, Steven had thought their relationship was heading in a more permanent direction, but things had taken a totally opposite direction. Her excitement about moving in with her girlfriend and setting up a counseling center near ground zero in New York, was contagious as they loaded her meager possessions into the back of a small rental van.

After placing the last item in the vehicle, they shared a long embrace, then said their good-byes. He hadn't communicated with her since.

Looking at the envelope once more, he decided to open it. *What could it hurt?* That chapter in his life had been written and was completed. He found a Christmas card containing a form letter, telling of her work at the clinic. Her last sentence touched his heart.

Even though it is difficult watching the clean up crews day after day, and knowing there are people still missing, it is a comfort to know we are making a difference in people's lives. It is well worth any sacrifice we make.

Sighing, he folded the letter, and returned it to the envelope. Setting it aside and mentally closing the door to that period of his life, he began perusing a magazine featuring the latest in cardiac procedures to identify pre-existing cardiac anomalies.

Every few minutes, his mind wandered to thoughts of Christina. *Why, after all these years, has she reappeared in my life? Where is this relationship headed, and do I want it to continue on this path?*

Closing the magazine, he laid his head back, closed his eyes, and let his mind explore the possibilities of a life with Christina and her children.

CHAPTER 93

When Janet returned home, she went immediately into the shower and stood under the hot water until her tension abated. She then donned her pajamas and went to the kitchen to prepare dinner.

Linda, who had been in her room drawing, while listening to a CD, didn't hear her mother come in, but did hear the shower running, which was a bit unnerving. Usually, her mom let her know she was home. It was weird that she didn't even say "hi", when she left the bathroom. A few minutes later, she heard her mother in the kitchen.

"Mom?"

"Yes?"

"Can I help you fix dinner?" She asked warily, not sure how her mom would react.

"Sure, come on in."

Linda walked over and put her arms around her mother's waist. Janet turned and pulled her daughter into a hug.

"You okay, Mom?"

Sighing, and turning her back to Linda, Janet said, "Yeah, just have a lot on my mind, plus I'm exhausted. When we're done eating, I'm going to bed. I feel like I could sleep a week."

Picking up a head of lettuce and tearing off leafs, Linda said, "It'll only be six o'clock. You sure you want to go to bed so early?"

Janet gave Linda an exasperated look, and said tersely, "If I didn't have to fix dinner and eat, I'd be in bed right now."

"Oh, okay."

The rest of the meal preparation and consumption was done in silence.

Janet took her dishes to the sink, and Linda said, "I'll take care of the kitchen, you go on to bed."

Janet nodded wearily, went to her room, and shut the door.

As she took her own dishes to the sink, and prepared to wash them, Linda thought, *Geeze, that was weird. Mom's never acted like that before. I hope she's not sick.*

There had only been a few times in her life that Janet had been so utterly exhausted—usually because of physical or emotional illness. *What is different now? Could it be because I'm getting older? Forty isn't old! Guess I'll go for a check-up next week if I'm still feeling this way.*

As soon as her head hit the pillow, she was asleep.

Linda quietly opened her mother's door, and peeked in. Janet was curled on her side, snoring. Linda whispered, "Good night, Mom."

CHAPTER 94

Janet was drifting on a raft in the middle of an ocean. The sky was the same color as the water, making her surroundings blend, so it was difficult to tell where one began and one ended. She turned in a circle. There was nothing but water and sky as far as she could see. "How did I get here?" She asked, as she noticed the raft she was in. It, too, was the same color as the water. Everything was a monochromatic gray. There was no breeze or sound of any kind.

"I am totally alone—on a raft—in the middle of an ocean."

She reached into the water, and found it to be warm. She then made circles in the water with her finger tips and watched as they dissipated.

Drawing in a deep breath, she yelled, "Hello? Anyone out there?"

No answer. *Surely this is a dream. No way could I really be here!* She willed herself to wake up, but to no avail.

After a time, she began crying. "Why? Why am I here?"

Still no answer. "I want to go home! I want to wake up!"

Still no answer. "God, is this some kind of joke? It's not funny!"

Silence. More time passed as she drifted lazily in circles.

Am I dead? Surely this can't be Heaven. There are no angels. Maybe it's Hell. Or purgatory.

She became angry and stood, shaking her fist towards the sky.

"God, if you're out there, talk to me! Let me know you're real! How can I believe in someone or something, if I can't see them? Oh, God, I don't want to be alone anymore! Please help me!"

Sitting once again in the raft, she wailed, and screamed, and cried and the boat rocked with her anguish. Once she was all cried out, she sat in silence, wondering if she would be in that void forever. Then she woke up.

Sitting up in bed, realizing her covers were all on the floor, and her pajamas were drenched with sweat, she took a minute to get her bearings. She was *not* in a raft, but in her bed. *It was only a dream,* she thought as she stumbled to the bathroom. Changing her pajamas, and re-arranging her bed covers, she crawled back in bed, and immediately fell back to sleep.

She wasn't in a raft this time, but she *was* in the middle of a desert. Sand everywhere, and not a soul to be seen.

Not again! Why am I here? Recalling her last dream, she didn't feel the need to panic, yet. *This is a dream, right?*

She wasn't sure if she should stay put, or start walking. There were no plants, animals, or humans as far as she could see. *Why am I having these dreams? Am I destined to be alone, and this is the universe's way of preparing me?* She sat in the sand and waited. For what, she wasn't sure. Maybe she'd just wake up, like before.

In the distance, she could see someone, or something, coming towards her. Putting her hand up to block the sun's rays, she was able to make out the shape of a man. She stood and started walking towards him—feeling no fear. As he came closer, she could see he was dressed in what appeared to be a white gown. He was carrying something in his hands. When he finally reached her, he held out a canteen and said, "Drink."

She did. It was the coldest, purest, sweetest water she had ever tasted.

Looking up into his green eyes, she felt as if she should know this man, but didn't.

He smiled and said, "Janet, stop running from me."

She was confused. She wasn't running, and hadn't even run to meet him. What did he mean by 'stop running?'

In a whisper, she said, "I'm not."

He smiled again and said, "Yes, you are, and you need to stop."

She handed the canteen back, and turned to walk away.

"Janet, I'll be waiting."

Janet woke in her bed, once again—her bed covers intact, and her pajamas dry. *What is going on? First, I'm in the middle of an ocean, then I'm in the middle of a desert. What next? Antarctica?* She looked at the ceiling and giggled, saying, "I didn't mean that!"

She never knew what 'powers' may be listening.

She went to the toilet, then returned to bed, fearful of what may be awaiting her when she gave in to sleep. Finally, unable to keep her heavy eyelids open another minute, her body and mind drifted off into a quiet, peaceful slumber. No trips to Antarctica.

Janet wasn't the only one having nightmarish dreams. All across Alva, sleepers were dreaming similar ones. Like Janet, they were alone somewhere, and a man dressed in white approached, warning them to stop running from him.

After talking to several of the guardians, and hearing of the strange dreams, Jarrod and David came to the conclusion that God was planning something big for Alva. What, they weren't sure. It could be a natural disaster, a terrorist attack, a plague, or a spiritual awakening. Whatever was planned, it would be epic. David couldn't help but wonder what role his family would play in the event.

CHAPTER 95

Thursday morning, as she was enjoying her coffee in a perfectly quiet house, Christina's phone rang. *Who would be calling me at this hour?*

"Hello?"

"Christina, it's Aaron."

"Oh, hi Aaron."

"I apologize for calling so early, but I wanted to talk to you before I went on rounds."

"Okay, so what's up?"

"Well, first of all, did Brad tell you about our conversation the other day?"

"The one about God?"

Chuckling, he said, "Yes. That one."

"Well, yes, he did. He said you had a lot of questions about Christianity."

"And I still do, but that's not why I'm calling. I wanted to let you know that I did pray and ask God to save my soul."

"Oh, Aaron! That's wonderful!"

"I would like to tell Brad personally, being he was the one to instruct me on how to go about it."

"Of course. He's asleep, but when he gets up, I'll have him give you a call. Would it be better to speak to him in person?"

"I'd like that. When he calls, I'll set up a meeting time. Christina, please don't tell him about my decision."

"I won't, Aaron. I'm so happy for you. If you have any other questions that Brad can't answer, maybe I can, or I can point you to someone who can."

"Thanks, Christina. I look forward to sitting and discussing this with you. I need to go on rounds right now, but maybe we can meet for lunch or dinner soon?"

"That sounds nice, Aaron. I'll see you soon, then."

Setting the phone on the table next to her chair, she shot a quick prayer up to Heaven, thanking God for Aaron's salvation.

She heard the toilet flush and knew that at least one of her kids was up. A few minutes later, Stacey appeared in the doorway.

"Mornin', Mom." She said as she walked over to give Christina a hug.

"Mornin', Babe. Did you sleep well?"

"Sorta. I had a weird and kinda scary dream, though."

"Do you remember it?"

Sitting on the couch across from her mom, she said, "I dreamed I was up on a hill, standing on the edge of a cliff, looking across a valley full of trees. Like I picture Colorado to look like. Anyway, I heard a voice say, "Step off the edge, Stacey. Trust me. I'll catch you." She paused a moment with her eyes closed, reliving the dream.

Standing and spreading her arms open wide, she continued, "Anyway, I put my arms out, like this, closed my eyes and started to step off. That's when I woke up." Sitting back down, she made a face and said, "Weird, huh?"

Christina nodded in agreement, asking, "What do you think it means?"

Stacey shrugged. "I don't know. Maybe it's a test to see if I really trust God to take care of me."

Nodding, Christina said, "Yeah, that sounds feasible. As I've said before, sometimes God relays messages to us in our dreams."

Cocking her head, Stacey said, "It seems like He's been doing that a lot lately. I wonder what He's planning?"

Christina nodded. "Yeah, it seems as though He's preparing His people for something. Maybe it just seems like He's speaking to us more, because we're more sensitive and open to His promptings."

Stacey gave her a confused look.

Christina continued, "Our family has been through a lot of trials in the past couple of years, and because of our concern over what may happen next, we're more apt to seek comfort in our faith and seek God's presence. I think He honors our desire to be close to Him. There's a verse in the Bible that says, 'Draw close to God and He will draw close to you.'"

Stacey smiled. "When I think of that verse, I picture myself crawling onto God's lap, and Him wrapping his arm around me. Like when I was a little kid and would crawl up in daddy's lap when I was hurt, or sad, or just needed to feel his love."

Picturing that scene in her mind's eye, Christina's eyes began tearing up, and she blinked rapidly, thinking, *Oh, how I miss David's lap.*

After a few moments of silence, Christina asked, "So, what would you like for breakfast?"

Stacey thought for a minute and said, "You know what I'm really craving?"

"No, what?"

"I'm craving some good ole' biscuits and gravy with sausage."

Christina grinned. "That does sound good. There's a can of biscuits in the fridge, and some sausage in the freezer. I could whip up some gravy to go with them."

"I'll take care of the biscuits," Stacey said, as she headed to the kitchen.

CHAPTER 96

Brad woke and stretched. *What is that smell? Sausage!* He jumped out of bed, donned his sweatpants, and headed downstairs.

"Mornin', Brad." Christina said as she stirred the gravy in the pan.

"Hey, Mom. This smells so good! Makes my mouth water."

Stacey smiled and said, "The biscuits will be done in about five minutes.'

Taking a deep breath, savoring the aroma of biscuits baking and sausage frying, he moaned and said, "I can hardly wait! I'm gonna go to the bathroom, and, hopefully, by the time I get back down here, it'll be ready."

Nicky appeared in the doorway as Stacey was taking the biscuits out of the oven.

She put the biscuits on a plate and carried them to the breakfast nook, as Christina carried in the sausage and gravy. Brad came bounding down the stairs, head wet from the shower he had apparently taken. Rubbing his hands together as he pulled a chair out and sat, he said, "Thanks, Mom and Stacey. This looks and smells delicious! I think I could eat it all by myself."

Nicky looked at his sister and said, "Guess we'd better get our share first, or there may not be any left!"

Passing him the biscuits, she giggled and said, "Yeah."

As breakfast dishes were being cleared from the table, Brad asked if he could spend the day with Eric.

Nodding, Christina said, "Sure. Oh, I almost forgot, Dr. Carmichael called, and wanted to talk to you. Maybe give him a call before you talk to Eric?"

"Did he say why he wanted to talk to me?"

"Well, I think it has to do with the conversation y'all had the other day."

Nodding, he said, "Oh, probably. Can I use your phone?"

"It's in the family room, by my chair."

Brad retrieved the phone, then disappeared upstairs.

Placing his plate in the sink, Nicky asked, "Mom, why does Dr. Carmichael want to talk to Brad?"

"He and Brad had a conversation the other day about God and Jesus, and I think he just wants to ask more questions."

"God? Why was he asking about God and Jesus?"

Christina put the remaining dishes in the sink, and turned to face Nicky.

"Well, Dr. Carmichael grew up in a home where Jesus and God were rarely discussed. He didn't go to Sunday School and church, and never read the Bible, so he never learned about Jesus, God or the Holy Spirit."

Wide-eyed, Nicky asked, "He didn't read the Bible?"

Stacey said, "I can't imagine not knowing about God, Jesus, or the Holy Spirit."

Nicky looked at her and nodded, "Me neither."

"Well, there are a lot of people around the world who've never heard of the trinity." Christina said, adding, "That's why we send missionaries, to teach people about them."

Nicky scratched his head and said, "Maybe when I grow up, I can be a missionary."

Stacey asked, "Where would you want to go?"

Nicky shrugged, "I don't know. Somewhere I could fly a plane."

Christina's eyebrows shot up, "A plane?"

"Yeah, I decided I want to learn how to fly a plane someday."

"When did you decide that?" Stacey asked.

Making a face, he said, "Well, just now, I think."

Christina smiled, "Oh, okay. That's interesting. I never had the desire to fly a plane, but I always wanted to fly. You know, with my own wings?"

Stacey smiled and said, "Me, too! I wish God had given us wings, when He created us."

Nicky nodded. "Yeah, I wonder why He didn't."

Christina shrugged, "I've often wondered that myself."

Brad returned after a few minutes, handed her the phone, and said, "I'm gonna meet with Dr. Carmichael around four o'clock. If the weather stays nice, I'll just ride my bike over to the hospital, otherwise, can I borrow the van?"

Christina nodded. "Sure, did you get in touch with Eric?"

"Yeah, he's gonna come by around one and we'll hang out here until I have to leave. His mom has to run a few errands, so she'll drop him off and pick him up later."

"Okay, that sounds like a good plan. In the meantime, could you run the vacuum in the upstairs rooms and hallway?"

Rolling his eyes, he said, "Okay."

"What? You have something more important to do?"

"Well, I guess playing a video game isn't really more important, but it's what I was planning on doing."

She smiled. "Okay, play your game after you vacuum."

Stacey and Nicky giggled.

Looking at her two youngest, she said, "You two will also be doing chores. Stacey, I need you to vacuum the floors down here, and Nicky, I'd like you to dust the furniture."

"Oh, man!" They said in unison, which made everyone giggle.

As Stacey was dragging the vacuum out of the hall closet, she asked, "Mom, when do you have to go back to work? You've been off a long time."

Christina sighed. "I have to return on Monday, which is Christmas Eve. Then I'm scheduled for Christmas Day, and Wednesday and Thursday, then I'll be off for the weekend."

Stacey made a face. "Oh man! I was hoping you'd be home those days!"

Christina walked over and pulled her daughter into a hug.

"I'll be home by four each day, so we can do stuff in the evening. That tradition won't change."

Stacey sighed and nodded. "I wish you didn't have to work, so you could stay home with us."

"Maybe, someday, I'll stay home, but right now, I need to work."

"Why do you need to work? Don't we have enough money?"

Christina put Stacey at arm's length and looked her in the eyes.

"Stacey, it's complicated, and you probably wouldn't fully understand, but I feel this is where God wants me, right now. Perhaps, some day I won't feel this way, and I can quit and stay home."

Stacey's shoulders drooped and she said, "Okay, but I'm gonna be praying that God let's you quit soon."

Christina shook her head and kissed Stacey on top of hers.

CHAPTER 97

As Christina was dividing up chores for her children, Janet was checking on the two cardiac patients with Dr. Dawson.

"Janet," he said as he wrote in a chart, "I'm going to dismiss Mr. Snyder this morning. He's doing well, and I know he wants to be home, when his grandchildren arrive from Pennsylvania tomorrow."

Nodding as she took the chart, she asked, "What about Mrs. Bledsoe?"

Sighing, Steven said, "Well, I want to keep her here at least a couple more days. She's running a low-grade fever, and I want to make sure it's nothing serious. I'd hate for her to go home, then have to come back, with some kind of infection."

She nodded, thinking, *I was hoping we'd be patient free for the holidays.*

Handing her the second chart, Steven asked, "So, do you have any plans for the holidays? Visiting any relatives?"

Shaking her head, she said, "No, just me and my girl staying home and watching movies."

"Well, that sounds relaxing."

Janet shrugged. "Yeah. So what are you going to do?"

Smiling, he said, "On Christmas Eve, my sister has the family over and we exchange gifts, and play games. It's pretty fun, actually."

"What about Christmas Day?"

"Well, that I'm not sure of. I have to do rounds for sure, then I may just do as you and watch movies or read the rest of the day."

Nodding, Janet thought, *Not spending time with Christina and her kids?*

After signing the discharge papers, he handed Janet the pen.

Walking away, he thought, *Should I have told her I was planning on spending Christmas Day with Christina and her kids? Nah. Some things are best left unsaid.*

CHAPTER 98

The teen lay on his back—thinking. Looking at the clock, he thought, *I should get up. And do what?* He could hear his dad's sonorous breathing through the thin wall that separated their rooms. *Four more days 'till Christmas. Big deal.* Sighing, he thought, *I won't be getting anything, anyway. I haven't for the past several years, so why would this year be any different?*

When his dad was around, the teen acted like Christmas didn't matter, but inside was that little boy who wanted a gift—wanted to be recognized, appreciated and loved. Wiping his eyes, he stuffed those feelings back down deep inside, chiding himself for acting like a baby. He rolled over and crawled out of bed. Feeling chilled, he put on a sweatshirt, and turned on the furnace.

What can I do today? He poured a bowl of cereal and retrieved the local paper from the front door steps. As he read the headline, he dropped his spoon.

"Police Are Narrowing Their Search For Suspected Arsonist." He read the following article, and felt his heart skip a couple of beats and his palms begin to sweat.

"According to evidence found at the crime scene, it was concluded that the arsonist is most likely a teenage boy."

What evidence? He wondered. *I know I was very careful and didn't leave any clues around, so what are they talking about?* As he lifted the spoon to his mouth, he realized his hand was shaking. *I'd better play it cool for a while. See what I can find out. My dad will kill me, if he discovers what I did. He wouldn't want his name or reputation sullied by his wayward kid.*

He thought back over the past few years, and realized that his father's affection for him had been a slow fade.

He had observed other father and son relationships, and had envied them, feeling an ache in his soul. Now, however, he just accepted their relationship as it was. Which in reality, was nothing. They each led their own lives, with very little interaction—except to pass each other in the hall or kitchen. Sometimes, his dad would reach out and punch his arm, or slap the back of his head. After several such incidences, he avoided them by simply staying out of arm's reach.

What is my dad trying to prove? That he is stronger, and in control, or that he is just a mean old jerk. Could it be his sick way of showing affection? If that's the case, I'd rather be ignored.

He had plans to leave home when he turned eighteen, which was in a few months, but he wasn't sure where he would go, or how he'd survive. *Well, I can continue sneaking into people's homes, and take what I need. I could probably find some place to hole up, until I can save enough money to find a decent place. Maybe out in the barn of that old man I visited the other night. I bet he hardly ever goes out there, and, if I'm careful, he wouldn't even know I was there. That actually sounds like a pretty good idea.*

He thought about that awhile longer, and in his mind, watched different scenarios play out. He could probably pull it off, as long as he didn't get caught. If that happened—well, it would probably be in his best interest, if he just put a gun to his head.

First, he'd have to deal with the police, then his dad, and then the other criminals in jail or prison. His small stature wouldn't offer him any protection against the onslaught of cruelty and rage. *Well,* he thought, *I'd better not get caught.*

Putting his cereal bowl and spoon in the sink, he realized the house was absent of the snoring sound. *Uh oh,* he thought, *Dad must be awake. I'd better get moving. If he finds me in here, and not making him breakfast, he'll throw icewater on me, like he did a couple other times I didn't have it ready.*

He heard the bathroom door close, then he heard his dad grunting and moaning—something he did every morning. *I wonder why he does that?*

He turned on the coffee maker, and by the time his dad came in and plopped himself down in a chair, there was a steaming cup sitting on the table. The man grunted as he took the cup. The boy took that to mean "thank you."

"Boy!" The man said, startling the young man.

"Yes, sir." The man never used the boy's name—always addressing him as "boy."

Turning to look at the man, who was his biological father, he wondered if he even remembered his name.

"Here's fifty bucks, and a list of groceries. Get what's on the list, and nothing more."

Nodding, the boy said, "Yes, sir."

"I have to pull a double shift tonight, so I won't be home 'till tomorrow. I don't care what you do, as long as you don't bother me. Are we clear?"

"Yes, sir. I won't bother you." *Not that I ever do anyway*, he thought as he returned to frying the eggs and bacon. Placing the plate of food in front of his dad, he turned and left the room. On his way out, as anger and resentment made their way to the surface, he thought, *I hate you, and I wish you'd drop dead.*

CHAPTER 99

Once Eric left around three, Brad hopped on his bike, and rode it to the hospital, for his meeting with Dr. Carmichael. It turned out to be warm and sunny, and he had to stop half-way there to remove his varsity jacket. Tying it to the handlebars, he continued his trek, and thought about his previous conversation with Dr. Carmichael..

I wonder if he wants to talk more about Christianity? I hope I have the right answers.

As he rode, he prayed for wisdom.

Parking his bike near the front door, he looked around the nearly empty lot.

Muttering to himself, he said, "I don't think I've ever seen it this empty. Maybe because it's so close to Christmas." Shrugging, he entered the hospital, and headed for Dr. Carmichael's office.

Dr. Carmichael must have heard him coming, or he was psychic, because as Brad was ready to knock, the door opened.

"Brad! It's so nice to see you again." He held out his hand for a shake.

Brad asked, "Did you hear me coming or what?"

Dr. Carmichael chuckled, "Actually, no, I was just going to peek out to see if you had arrived yet. And, here you are!"

Brad nodded, "Yep, here I am."

"Come on in and sit. Can I get you anything? Soda, coffee, tea?"

"A Dr. Pepper if you have it, or I can just do water."

"Actually, I do have a can of Dr. Pepper. I've developed a taste for it, and keep it available."

Popping the top, and taking a sip, Brad said, "I never drank Dr. Pepper, until I moved here. I used to drink Pepsi all the time, but now I like Dr. Pepper." Wiping his mouth, he said, "Funny how our tastes change."

Dr. Carmichael popped the top off a can and took a sip as well.

"Mmm. This is so refreshing!"

Brad asked, "So, I don't mean to be rude, but why am I here, besides to share a Dr. Pepper?"

Setting the can down, and leaning forward, Dr. Carmichael smiled and said, "Remember the Bible verses you gave me?"

Brad nodded.

"Well, I looked them up, thought about everything you said, and I decided to ask God to be my Savior. I don't know if I said the right words, but I really meant what I said."

Brad smiled. "What did you say?"

"I said, God, I want to believe in You and your Son, Jesus. Please help me be the man you want me to be. I accept You to be the one true God and one true Savior and please forgive me for any wrongdoing on my part."

Brad nodded, and continued to smile. "That sounds perfect. I don't think it's how we pray, or the words we use, but our motive behind the prayers. It sounds like you were sincere, and I'm sure God honors that."

Aaron nodded. "I hope so. I know when I finished praying, I felt a warm peace wash over me, then I started to laugh." Grinning, he said, "I was so full of joy, that it felt like it was bubbling out of me!"

Brad chuckled, "I've had times like that too, when giggles just bubble out, and I have no control over them. I feel all happy and full of love."

"That's exactly how I felt, too. I wanted to go out and just love on people, even though it was around midnight."

Brad took another sip of his soda, all the while nodding and smiling, then asked, "So, what do you want to do now?"

Aaron said, "Well, I want to know more about what is expected of me as a believer, then I want to read the whole Bible and do Bible studies, then tell people about God and Jesus and Heaven!"

Holding his hands up, Brad said, "Whoa! Okay, I understand your enthusiasm to get going in your God walk, but you do need to take it one step at a time. First, it would be wise to plug into a church. I recommend the one I go to, but there are many different ones to choose from. The main thing is that they preach Jesus and salvation."

"Don't all churches preach that?"

"Many do not. Some don't even use the Bible as their foundation, and they teach that everything is acceptable and that a loving God would not send anyone to Hell. They believe we all go to Heaven, no matter what we believe or what we do."

Aaron raised his eyebrows. "It seems so much easier, and nicer, to believe in a god who doesn't condemn anyone to Hell. No one wants to feel bad about what they're doing. If we're nice and get along with each other, it seems that should be enough. Why would we be condemned for that?"

Brad smiled and nodded. "Yeah, I understand what you're saying, but God doesn't really condemn us. We condemn ourselves by not accepting his son. He gives us that choice. We will stand before God someday, alone, and give an account of our life. We can't blame our decisions on anyone else. That's why we have to be wise, and pay attention to what is being taught, and if it doesn't line up with God's Word, then we'd best go somewhere else."

Leaning back in his chair, Dr. Carmichael thought for a moment before speaking.

"I have so much to learn. I think I would like to try your church."

Brad smiled and nodded, "Okay. That'd be cool. There are two services on Sunday morning. One at nine-thirty, the other at eleven. There's even a children's church if Sammie wants to go."

"I think Sammie will want to stay with me until she feels comfortable. She has a difficult time adjusting to new environments." Pausing a moment, he asked, "What time do you usually attend service?"

"Well, we usually go to Sunday School at nine-thirty, then attend the eleven o'clock service. Would you like us to save y'all a spot?"

Nodding, Aaron said, "Yes, thank you."

They shook hands, then Aaron pulled Brad into a hug.

"Thank you, Brad."

Brad patted him on the back, and said, "You're welcome."

They shook hands once again, and Brad left for home.

As he pedaled his bike, his mind replayed the conversation. *Did I say the right things?*

CHAPTER 100

Friday morning, the Alva residents woke to another dusting of snow with the threat of more to come during the day. The temperatures had plummeted during the night, and a cold front from Canada had blown into Texas, and went as far south as Austin. Because it was dark and dreary outside, and the bed felt so nice and warm and cozy, Christina didn't wake until nine-o'clock. She was shocked when she rolled over and saw the time.

"Geeze, oh Pete! I haven't slept this late in a long time!"

She thought about her plans for the day, and decided they could all wait. She rolled over and fell back to sleep almost immediately. An hour later, she was awakened from a nightmare involving tarantulas, by the ringing of her cell phone.

"Hello?" She answered groggily.

"Christina?" Cindy answered. "Are you alright? You sound terrible!"

Clearing her throat, and rubbing her eyes, Christina said, "Oh, hi, Cindy. I just woke up."

"What? Geeze girl, it's ten-o'clock! Are you sick?"

Shaking her head to clear the cobwebs from her brain, Christina said, "I'm not sick. I just wanted to sleep in." Yawning, she continued, "I'm glad you called and woke me up, though, because I was having a terrifying dream about tarantulas."

"Tarantulas? Those things give me the creeps. Fortunately, I haven't seen any around here, but my mom has seen a couple up near her house in Dallas."

"Eww. I haven't seen any around here either, but I remember taking a trip out to west Texas when I was a kid, and they were all over the road. My dad stopped to take a picture of them. I was so freaked out, I was screaming and crying because I was afraid they would jump up and bite him."

"Well, geeze. I hope they don't migrate here!"

Christina chuckled. "They haven't yet, so, hopefully, they never will."

After a moment's silence, Christina said, "So, Cindy, why the phone call?"

Cindy giggled, "Oh yeah. I called to see if you wanted to go to Waco with me and Samara, today. There's a new mall that just opened up, and I hear it's awesome! We can all go, if you want, or just us girls. What do you think?"

Christina, not having any major plans for the day, except cleaning, said, "Yeah, that sounds like fun. Let me get dressed and ask the kids. What time were you planning on leaving?"

"Around noon. We can grab a bite to eat in the food court."

"Sounds good. I'll call you back in a few minutes."

Christina dressed and woke her kids, and they all agreed that an outing to the Waco mall would be fun. She called Cindy, and asked if it was okay to call Donna, who lived in Waco, and ask if she and her gang could meet them at the mall.

"Of course, it's okay. I would love to see her and the kids! I haven't seen or talked to her since Thanksgiving. It'll be fun having part of our fab four together again."

"I'll call when I hang up. Hey, why don't I take my van? It can hold everyone."

"Sounds good. See you in a few."

CHAPTER 101

Janet had the day off, thanks to Mrs. Ferguson's re-arrangement of the schedule, and while she and Linda ate breakfast, asked her daughter what she would like to do.

"I'd like to go shopping somewhere."

Taking a sip of milk, Janet asked, "Where do you want to go? Around here? Dallas? Fort Worth? Waco?"

Linda pursed her lips and thought a moment.

"Well, I heard there's a new mall in Waco that's supposed to be awesome. It has a splash-pad, with play equipment, a two-story roller-coaster, and other rides for kids and adults. I'd love to check it out."

Janet said, "Wow! I didn't realize it had all that. I had heard about the mall opening, but thought it was just another ordinary mall."

"So, can we go?"

Janet shrugged and nodded. "Yeah, I guess so." Looking at her watch, she said, "How about we leave in the next hour?"

Linda grinned. "I can be ready in less time than that!"

Janet chuckled. "Okay. How about in half an hour?"

CHAPTER 102

Ed and Tom sat across from their boss, Henry Steil.

Leaning forward, Ed asked, "So, what you're telling us, is that there has been some phone chatter about a possible attack in one of the major cities in Texas?"

Henry let out a sigh.

"Actually, there's been chatter about several attacks in several cities across America, but I'm most concerned about any threats pertaining to Texas."

Tom asked, "Any idea which city, or which location?"

"Well, I'm assuming it won't be any schools or universities, since most, if not all, are closed for the holidays. It could be one of the government buildings, but most of them are pretty empty, as well." Pausing, he added, "If I were a terrorist, I'd want to attack where there will be a large number of folks. This time of year, my guess would be a mall."

The three men sat in silence a moment as they considered the possibility of such an attack.

"Has there been any mention of a time the attack would occur?" Tom asked, as he leaned back in his chair.

Henry shook his head. "No, as it is, we're not sure if there will even be an attack. It's all speculation, due to a few key code words that were picked up over the past couple of days."

Ed asked, "What are the plans, if there are any, to keep citizens safe?"

Henry said, "We have people calling malls in all the major cities across Texas, and informing the security staff of the possible threat. Hopefully, they will beef up security through the holiday season, and be able to thwart any potential hazard."

Ed and Tom nodded, then Ed asked, "Is there anything we can do in the meantime?"

Henry pinched the bridge of his nose, and thought for a moment.

"I wish I could tell you there are things to do, but quite honestly, I'm not sure what we can do. There are so many malls across Texas, I'm not sure we will be able to reach them all, and even if we do, I'm not sure we can stop an attack. These terrorists are relentless and devious. If they are determined to do harm, they will find a way to do it. Besides, we're not one-hundred percent sure it will even be a mall."

Tom said, "So, I guess we just have to wait and see what happens?"

Henry sighed and nodded. "Afraid so. I mean, we can do our best to inform and prepare, but there's no guarantee we'll succeed."

Ed grimaced and rubbed his eyes. "I hate this feeling of helplessness! I wish we could just hunt these people down, and be done with them. Let God sort them out!"

Tom shook his head and smiled, patting Ed on the shoulder.

"I'm right there with you, buddy. I have a feeling that these terrorists groups have so many members and branches, we'd never get them all. Even if we cut the head off the snake, so to speak, four more would pop up."

Ed stood and stretched.

"So, I guess I'll head back to my desk and catch up on some paperwork."

Tom stood as well, reaching out his hand to his boss.

"I'm with Ed. I need to do some catching up, too. We'll see you tomorrow, unless something comes up."

Henry stood, and shook hands with both men.

"Yep, I'll keep y'all informed. Have a good day."

As the two men boarded the elevator to the first floor, where their cubicles were located, Ed turned to Tom and asked, "You got any plans for the weekend?"

Tom, nodding, said, "I was gonna pick up Tommy tomorrow morning and go check out that new mall in Waco. I hear it's something to behold. It has a mini-amusement park right smack dab in the middle."

"Really? That's kinda weird." Ed said, cocking his head.

"Yeah, I think it's trying to be another mall of America."

"When did it open?"

"The weekend after Thanksgiving. I heard on the news that it was supposed to open before that, but there was some kind of electrical problem." The elevator door opened and the men stepped through. They were met with a cacophony of noises—phones ringing, voices talking, machines beeping.

Ed patted Tom on the shoulder, and said, "You want to meet for lunch?"

Tom nodded, "Sure. What time and where?"

Looking at his watch, Ed said, "How about twelve-thirty in the cafeteria? That'll give us a couple of hours to work."

"Sure, see you then," Tom said, as he turned to head for his desk on the other side of the large room.

Entering his cubicle, Ed felt his phone vibrate in his pocket.

He pulled it out and checked the caller ID before answering—Cindy.

"Hey, beautiful." He said, smiling.

"Hey, handsome. How's your day going so far?"

"It's good. How about yours?"

"So far, so good. I just wanted to let you know that Samara and I, and Christina and her kids are going to the mall in Waco today. I may not hear my phone, if you try to call me, but I'll check it now and then. If you need to reach me, just text, or keep calling. I'll eventually get back to you."

Ed felt his gut clench. *The mall? Where terrorists could attack?* He wanted to scream, *Don't go!* But knew in his mind that his fear was paranoid, and a bit irrational. *What are the chances that they will attack there? Today?*

He cleared his throat and mind and said, "That's great, honey. Just be careful. There's probably gonna be a lot of people there."

Cindy, in her most serious voice said, "Yes, Dad. We'll be careful, and not talk to strangers, or go with any for that matter."

Ed chuckled. "Okay, smarty pants. I can't help but worry a bit, with the whole 911 thing, and the constant threat from terrorists. Just promise me that, if you sense any danger, you'll leave immediately."

Nodding, Cindy said, "Sure, babe. I'll keep my eyes and ears wide open."

Ed sighed. "Will you at least text me sometime during the day, so I know everything is okay?"

"Yes Sir, I'll either call or text. Have a good day in your tiny cubicle while we go play at the mall!"

"Yeah, go ahead, rub it in!"

Giggling, Cindy said, "Talk to you later!"

Ed laid the phone on his desk, leaned back in his chair and shot a prayer of protection up to Heaven, for Cindy and the gang. His desk phone rang, bringing him back to the tasks at hand.

CHAPTER 103

When Christina entered the mall parking lot, she was astounded by the number of vehicles.

"Oh, my goodness! There must be thousands of cars here!"

Looking around the congested parking lot, Nicky said, "Wow! I hope you don't have to park a mile away."

Christina nodded, "Yeah, me too. Why don't I drop y'all off, and I'll find a parking place, then meet you in the food court?"

Cindy cocked her head, "You sure? We could walk in with you."

"Nah. It's okay. I don't mind."

With that, Cindy and the kids exited the van, and watched as Christina drove away.

Cindy put her arm around Nicky, "Come on y'all. Let's go find Donna and her kids."

As Christina drove down the second isle, a car, three slots from the entrance, pulled out.

"Thank you, God!" She shouted as she pulled into the convenient spot.

Everyone was shocked, when she entered the food court.

"Mom!" Nicky shouted as he ran to her. "I thought you'd be a lot longer."

Hugging her son, she said, "Me, too. I found a spot three cars away from the entrance."

"Oh, that's awesome!" Cindy said, as she walked over to where Christina stood.

"Do you see Donna and her kids?" Christina asked, looking around the crowded eating area.

"Not yet. Oh wait, I think I see them over by the merry-go-round."

Christina glanced in that direction and waved as Donna turned her head and spotted them.

"There they are!" Shouted Nicky, as he ran to greet them.

Christina shook her head, thinking, *He's like a little puppy. So excited to see people he knows.*

Donna and her three boys, Andy, Steven, and Jason, walked over and greeted everyone with hugs and high-fives.

Donna looked around and said, "Oh, my goodness, this place is amazing!"

Cindy giggled. "I know! I'm not sure where to start."

Christina said, "Why don't we start with lunch? I'm starving. All I had this morning was a cup of coffee."

Nodding, Donna said, "Sounds good." After dividing the group according to their food preferences, she said, "We'll meet back here at these tables."

Everyone nodded and headed off in the direction of their favorite foods.

Christina shook her head, and grinned. "You handled that really well, Donna. I'm impressed."

Donna smiled, "Well, with three boys, and three different preferences, one tends to learn how to divide and conquer."

Cindy said, "It's times like this, I'm glad I only have one to worry about."

After everyone returned with their various menu choices, they ate and chatted, catching up on the latest news. The kids, ranging in age from Brad, who was sixteen, down to Jason, who was nine, wanted to know the plan for the afternoon.

Wiping her mouth on a napkin, Christina said, "Okay, kids. I'd prefer if we all stay together, but I know with so many things to see and do, we may get separated, so, why don't we have a buddy system? Everyone gets a partner or two? Jason, Nicky and Steven stick together. Samara and Stacey, then Brad and Andy? If we get separated, y'all have your cell phones. Use them."

"Yes, ma'am." They said in unison.

Grinning, and clasping her hands together, Cindy asked, "Ready to go check out the rides?"

She received a resounding "Yes!"

While at the apex of the roller-coaster ride, Stacey looked out at the crowd of people and spotted her friend, Linda. No amount of waving and yelling out her name caused Linda to look up. Disappointed, but hopeful that she would catch up with her on the floor, Stacey finished the ride with eager anticipation.

As their children enjoyed the roller-coaster ride, the three women sipped coffees, and chatted.

Donna asked, "So Cindy, how are things going with Ed?"

Cindy was just about to speak, when she felt the familiar buzzing of the phone in her pocket.

Putting up a finger, she said, "Just a sec."

There was a text message from Ed which said, "Call me ASAP."

Cindy said, "Excuse me ladies, but Ed just texted me to call him ASAP. So I guess I'd better call him."

Because of the noise level, Cindy walked to the nearest exit and disappeared. Donna and Christina looked at each other.

"I wonder what that's about?" Christina asked.

Donna shook her head and shrugged.

"Guess we'll find out soon. Hope it's nothing serious."

"Yeah, me too." The children came running up to the ladies and begged for one more ride on the coaster.

Donna and Christina looked at each other, shrugged and said, "Why not?"

After a few minutes, Cindy returned with a worried look on her face.

Christina asked, "Hey, what's going on?"

"I talked to Ed, and he said we should leave because someone called in a bomb threat."

"Seriously? A bomb threat, here?" Donna asked.

Nodding, Cindy said, "Yeah, he said there has been some concern that the terrorists may try something over the holidays, but no one knew where or when. Ed said his department thought it could be a mall because of the increased attendance during the holidays."

Looking around, she asked, "Where are the kids?"

Donna said, "They just boarded the coaster, again. I doubt if the guy can stop it in the middle of the ride. Guess we'll have to wait 'till it finishes."

Christina asked, "Did Ed say the threat was imminent?"

"Well, he said the mall security has been notified, and they're sending agents to help search the building. But, yeah, we should be hearing an announcement soon, saying we need to evacuate."

Christina put her hand over her heart, and Donna chewed on a thumbnail. They all looked at the ride, willing it to end.

As the coaster came to a stop, the anticipated announcement came.

"Ladies and gentlemen, may I have your attention, please." A hush descended over the crowd, like a blanket being put on a bed. People stopped where they were, and listened.

"Because of circumstances beyond our control, we are asking for everyone to evacuate the building, in an orderly fashion. Hopefully, we will get the problem resolved, and the mall will open again tomorrow morning at nine. If you are in the middle of a transaction, please finish, then exit the building. I apologize for any inconvenience. Thank you for your cooperation."

"Mom!" exclaimed Stacey, running up to Christina. "What's going on?"

Not wanting to terrorize the kids, she answered, "I'm not sure, but we need to leave."

"Oh, man!" whined Jason. "We just got here! I wanted to ride the merry-go-round."

Donna patted her son's shoulder. "We're all disappointed, but we'll come back again, sometime."

Cindy said, "Yeah. Maybe after Christmas when all the sales will be starting."

Brad pulled his mom aside and whispered, "What's really going on?"

Christina whispered, "There's been a bomb threat, so they're evacuating until it's resolved."

Nodding, he said, "Guess we'd best get going then."

She nodded and said, "Yeah. Can you please help get the kids moving?"

On their way out, Donna said, "Hey, there's an ice-cream place with an inside play-scape not too far from here. Y'all want to meet there?"

Christina looked at Cindy, who shrugged and nodded.

Unlocking the door, and sliding it open, Christina said, "Sure, I'll follow you there."

Donna nodded, and said, "I had to park out quite a ways, so it may take a few minutes."

"I'll drive you to it. I bet we could squeeze y'all in." Christina said, inserting the key into the ignition.

Christina looked back at the kids and asked, "Can you guys make room for Donna and the boys?"

Scooting closer to Stacey, Nicky said, "Sure, Mom."

CHAPTER 104

Janet heard the announcement, and grabbed Linda's hand. They were on the third floor and had to take the stairs, as the elevator was locked down. Standing on the staircase, looking over the crowd of people, Janet thought, *There has to be thousands of people here. It's gonna take forever to reach the ground floor.*

Linda asked, "What's going on, Mom?"

Janet shook her head, "I don't know, honey, but it must be something serious. There are security guards and police everywhere."

As they passed by the store fronts, shop keepers were bringing down the metal security gates, and locking them. Panic gripped her heart.

Janet looked around, wondering what could possibly be wrong? *Terrorist? Fire? A bomb?* None of her ideas put her heart at ease. Another announcement came over the public address system.

"Ladies and gentlemen, please continue in an orderly fashion to the nearest exits. There is no need to panic. There seems to be a malfunction in our electrical circuitry. Our people have everything under control. This situation should be resolved quickly, and we hope you will be able to return shortly. Thank you for your cooperation."

Janet heard a strange sound. At first she wasn't able to identify the whoosh-boom sound, until someone yelled, "A bomb!" Then terror and chaos ruled. People began screaming and running, not caring who they pushed or knocked down. The police and firemen were trying desperately to keep the crowd under control, but to no avail.

Janet continued to hold on to Linda's hand, and both were pushed and bustled on towards the exit. At least that's where Janet hoped they were headed. She couldn't see above the heads or around the bodies of the throng of people. She looked back at Linda and saw fear, panic and hysteria on her daughter's face. She saw her lips move, but couldn't hear what she was saying.

When they had reached the first floor, Janet saw an opening in the crowd, and pulled Linda towards it. She was able to break free, and head towards a hallway that led to the restrooms. At the end of the hallway was a door with an exit sign above it. No one was there. *Why?* She wondered. She looked around and seeing no one, pulled Linda towards it.

"Mom!" Linda protested, trying to pull her hand free. She finally stopped, causing Janet to almost lose her balance.

She whipped around to face her daughter. "Linda, what are you doing? We need to get out of here!"

Linda was crying and holding her hand to her chest. Between sobs, she said, "Mom, I think you broke my hand! It hurts so bad to move it!"

Janet, with panic on her face, reached over and took Linda's hand. Examining it, she said as calmly as she could, "Honey, I think some of the bones are dislocated, but not broken. I know it hurts, and we'll get it taken care of, as soon as we get out of here, but you need to pull yourself together, and come with me now."

Linda wiped her nose, shuddered and nodded. Janet turned and continued down the hall, her mother's heart breaking, as she listened to her daughter's whimpers and sniffles.

Reaching the end of the hallway, she was surprised and pleased, when she pushed on the door handle and it opened. *That's weird*, she thought.

Exiting the building, she and Linda were hit with a blast of arctic air and snow that seemed to suck the breath out of them. It was then that they realized they had left their heavy coats in one of the lockers. All they had on were turtleneck sweaters.

Grabbing Linda and putting her arm around the girl's shoulder, trying to shield her from the wind, Janet led her to the parking lot, where they were immediately surrounded by police, who were bombarding her with questions.

"Excuse me, ma'am, where did you come from?"

"How did you get here?"

"What is your name?"

"Why are you over here?"

She put her hands up, as if in surrender and through chattering teeth said, "Please, I'll answer your questions, but can we get somewhere warm? My daughter is freezing!"

One of the officers led them to a nearby squad car, and helped them into the back seat.

Shivering, Janet said, "My name is Janet Washburn and this is my daughter, Linda. I can show you my driver's license if you'd like."

The officer nodded. "Yes, ma'am. I'm officer Davis."

Nodding, she pulled her wallet out, and found her license, then handed it to the officer. He looked at it and turned to enter the information in the squad car computer. Much to her surprise, a minute or two later, the back door opened, and a young officer handed them cups of hot chocolate.

"Here, ma'am. Maybe this will help warm you up." He smiled and winked before closing the door.

Officer Davis turned to face her and handed her license back.

"So, you want to tell me how you ended up on this side of the mall?"

Janet told of their great escape. He smiled, nodded and said, "That was some pretty good thinking on your part. Most of the people had what we call a mob mentality, and just followed the leader."

"Did everyone else get out okay?"

"Seems so. There were a few with minor injuries, however."

Linda cleared her throat and said, "So, what was this all about?"

The officer looked at her, as if just realizing she was there.

"I'm sorry. I can't tell you. Suffice to say, we think the problem has been resolved."

Linda scrunched her face. "Resolved? As in over with?"

The officer smiled and nodded. "Yes, ma'am."

Noticing the way she was holding and caressing her hand he asked, "Your hand alright?"

"I think it's sprained. My mom was holding it so tight, I thought she broke it, but I can move it now. It just hurts a little."

Nodding, he looked at Janet, who shrugged. "Well, why don't we have one of our EMT guys check it out?"

Linda looked at her mom, who nodded her approval.

He made a call, and a few minutes later, an EMT guy came, checked the range of motion in Linda's fingers and hand, wrapped it in a bandage and pronounced it to be sprained.

Janet asked, "So, when can we go retrieve our belongings from the locker?"

"Well, ma'am, I'm afraid that'll have to happen tomorrow. Given the circumstances, the building needs to be checked thoroughly for any other explosive devises, and it needs to be deemed safe for civilian occupancy."

Janet and Linda said simultaneously, "Explosive devises?"

Janet asked, "So the noise we heard was an explosion? Like a bomb?"

Officer Davis sighed and shook his head.

"I wasn't supposed to let that information out, but since it is, I can tell you that, yes, it was a bomb. As far as how big or how many, we aren't sure yet."

"So, when do you think it'll be safe to return? Our coats are in there."

Sighing and running his hand over his bald head, he said, "I wish I could tell you. I think the mall manager is telling everyone to call tomorrow, and he will have an estimated time for them to return for their belongings."

Rubbing her eyes, Janet said, "Great. I'll have to make another trip down here."

The officer shrugged. "Yes ma'am, seems so. Where are you from?"

Handing him her empty cup, she said, "Alva. So, can we go now?"

Nodding, he said, "Well at least it wasn't further away."

She raised her eyebrows and frowned.

"I guess it doesn't matter where you're from, it's still inconvenient."

She nodded, and cocked her head. "Can we go?"

"Yes, ma'am. You're free to go."

Gathering their belongings, Janet and Linda thanked the officer, and exited the patrol car. The snow had stopped, but the wind was biting, and they huddled together as they headed towards their car, which was on the other side of the building.

Officer Davis, noticing their distress and remembering they didn't have coats, pulled the squad car beside them and said, "Hey, why don't I give y'all a ride to your car?"

Nodding, and with teeth chattering, Janet said, "That'd be great!"

The ride to the car was short and silent. As she exited the patrol car, Janet said, "Thank you."

Smiling and nodding, he said, "You're welcome. I enjoy helping ladies in distress."

Once in their car, Janet cranked the heater to the highest setting, and sat with the engine idling a few minutes before leaving the lot. The area, which had been teeming with Christmas shoppers a few hours earlier, was now filled with emergency vehicles. It reminded Janet of a fireworks display with all the red, white and blue flashing lights.

"Mom?" Linda half whispered.

Turning to face her daughter, Janet said, "Yes?"

"Do you think the bomb was put there by terrorists?"

Pondering the question a minute before answering, Janet replied, "I don't know, honey. I guess it's possible. From what Officer Davis said, it may not have been a real bomb. It could have been some kind of foolish prank instigated by a group of teens to get some kind of thrill."

On a sigh, Linda said, "Well, I hope it wasn't terrorists. People aren't gonna want to leave their homes, if this kind of stuff keeps happening."

Nodding, and moving the gear shift to drive, Janet said, "Yeah."

As they headed home on I-35, Linda asked, "Is it okay if I call Stacey?"

Sighing, Janet said, "Sure, my cell phone is in my bag."

Listening to Linda's side of the conversation, Janet concluded that the Sander's family had been at the mall, as well.

When Linda closed the phone, and was placing it back in the bag, Janet asked, "So, the Sanders were at the mall, too?"

"Yeah, they left before the explosion, though. Stacey said her mom's friend, Cindy, got a text from her boyfriend telling them to leave the mall. Stacey said he works for the government, and knows a lot of stuff about the terrorists."

Janet shook her head in disbelief. "Huh."

Linda continued, "Yeah. Well, anyway, Stacey said they were already leaving when the announcement was made, so they missed all the excitement. I told her about my hand, and the nice policeman who helped us."

Nodding, Janet said, "Yes, I heard."

Stacey said they're at some ice-cream place near the mall and asked if we could join them. I told her probably not."

Nodding still, Janet said, "Well, you're right. I'm not in the mood to talk to anyone right now."

With disappointment etched on her face, Linda said, "Okay."

CHAPTER 105

When Stacey finished her conversation with Linda, she said, "Mom, you won't believe what Linda said."

Christina set her milkshake down, and turned to face Stacey.

"What did she say?"

Stacey recounted her conversation with Linda, as everyone stopped what they were doing and listened.

Arching her eyebrows in surprise, Christina put her hand to her heart and said, "Wow! Unbelievable!"

Looking at Cindy, she said, "I'm so glad Ed texted you, and we followed his advise. It would have been awful to be in the midst of that chaos."

Both Cindy and Donna nodded their agreement.

Donna said, "I wonder how long the mall will be closed? This is an awful time of year to have to close a mall."

"Yeah," agreed Christina. "After this, people may shy away from shopping at the malls."

Cindy said, "Well, I hope they catch the people responsible."

After a few minutes of silence, Cindy asked, "So, everyone ready for Christmas?"

To this, she received diverse responses. The younger kids were more than ready, and the older kids and ladies, not so much. There was still more shopping and gift-buying to be done.

Glancing out the window, and noticing the darkening sky, and wind kicking up leaves, Christina said, "Well, folks, I think it's time we head on home. Looks like another storm is coming in." Everyone turned to look out the window.

Donna said, "I don't think it's supposed to get any worse, according to the weather report this morning."

Nicky said, "Oh, man, I was hoping we'd go shopping somewhere else." Looking at his mom with pleading eyes, he asked, "Do we *have* to go?"

Christina looked at Cindy and Donna. "What do y'all want to do?"

Donna shrugged and said, "Well, there is that mall on the other side of town. It's not as fancy, but it has a few nice stores."

Cindy made a face. "I don't know. I'm still a little freaked out by what just happened. I'm not sure I want to chance another incident."

Sighing, Christina said, "Well, we could do something else, like see a movie."

The kids heard the word "movie" and became quite animated.

"A movie?" Nicky asked.

"Yeah, let's go to a movie!" Jason said, enthusiastically.

Brad said, "All in favor of seeing a movie, raise your hands."

All seven youngsters raised their hands.

Brad grinned. "It's unanimous."

Christina shook her head and smiled. *What could she do now?* Looking at Donna and Cindy, she asked, "So, what can we go see?"

CHAPTER 106

While the ladies and kids were enjoying a movie about a family of spies, Ed, Tom, and the rest of the ATO team were busy making and answering phone calls, and setting up teams for surveillance and monitoring.

Henry Steils, their boss, called Ed and Tom into his office.

After greetings and hand-shakes, he asked, "How would you two feel about taking a trip down to Waco, to check out the mall incident?"

Tom and Ed looked at each other, shrugged and nodded.

"Sure." Tom said.

"What do you want us to do?" asked Ed.

Henry handed them a sheet of paper with questions to ask, and items to check while there.

"I'd like y'all to walk around the mall, and see if anything may have been missed in the investigation. I know the local law enforcement agency has been thorough, but it doesn't hurt to have more eyes and ears on the scene."

"Will other agencies be involved?"

Henry looked at Ed, "By other agencies, you mean the FBI and CIA and such?"

Ed nodded.

Henry rubbed his chin, then said, "Well, probably. We have to be sure it wasn't terrorist related. If it was, then we'll all come together and work on our next plan of prevention."

Tom and Ed nodded.

Tom asked, "So, you want us to leave today?"

Henry nodded. "Yes, sir. The sooner, the better."

Tom and Ed stood.

"We'll take off then. We'll let you know when we get there, and keep you appraised of the situation."

Nodding, Henry said, "Thanks. Be safe."

CHAPTER 107

Entering the elevator, Tom asked, "So, you want to take my car or your van?"
Ed said, "Well, we'd get better gas mileage in your car."
Nodding, Tom said, "My car it is."
Ed asked, "Mind if we stop at my apartment, for a minute? I want to grab a few things."
Exiting the elevator, Tom said, "I'm going to stop by my place, and pick up a bag of stuff I usually take on investigations."
After stopping at their desks, and informing fellow workers of their plans, they met at the back door, and headed for Tom's car.
The drive to Waco was uneventful. Traffic was light, and road construction had ended for the season. The men made small talk.
"How's Tommy doing? Is he excited about Christmas?" Ed asked, taking a sip of coffee.
Tom chuckled. "Oh, man, is he ever excited! It's pretty funny, really. I took him to Toys R Us the other day, just to get an idea of what I might get him for Christmas, and I'll be danged, if he didn't want everything we looked at!"
Ed chuckled. "Well, aren't most kids like that?"
Nodding, and smiling, Tom said, "Yeah, I suppose so. One thing I realized is that I could get him anything, and he'd be happy."
Smiling, Ed said, "Well, at least you don't have *six* kids to buy for. I'm thinking I'll just give all the nieces and nephews money or gift cards. It's too hard to go shopping for them, especially since I don't know what they have."
Tom looked at Ed. "You have *six* nieces and nephews?"
Ed nodded. "Yep, my sisters have been busy making babies."
Tom chuckled, then asked, "What are you getting Cindy and Samara?"
Ed shook his head, "I've been thinking about that, and haven't quite made up my mind yet. There's a part of me that wants to get Cindy a ring, and ask her to marry me, but we've only known each other a few months, and I don't want to rush things. Then there's the other part that wants to throw caution to the wind, and just go for it."

Sighing and running his hand through his hair, he said, "I haven't come to a definite conclusion yet."

Tom nodded and blew out some air. "Yeah, that's a tough decision, especially when a kid is involved." After a moment, he said, "I'm thinking that, if you're not one-hundred percent sure, you should wait. Get them something they could enjoy together."

"Like what?"

"Eleanor liked the spa day gift I gave her last year. She spent the whole day getting pampered. She especially enjoyed the full body massage." Chuckling, he added, "She told me I could get her that kind of gift from now on."

"That sounds like a possibility. Where did she go?"

"There's a nice spa in Dallas. I can get the number for you."

Ed smiled, and nodded. "Thanks."

Pulling into the mall parking lot, the men were surprised at the number of police cars and emergency vehicles.

"Man, it looks like they've called out the whole cavalry." Tom said, stepping out, and zipping up his jacket.

Ed nodded in agreement, as he looked around the lot.

"Guess we'd better find the one in charge of this operation."

After a couple of steps, they were approached by an officer.

"Excuse me, gentlemen, this is a restricted area."

Ed and Tom reached in their pockets and produced their ID's, and asked to speak to the man in charge.

The officer nodded, and led them to a trailer, then said, "You'll want to speak to a Mr. Rick Johnson. He's in charge of all this."

They entered the warm trailer filled with men and women, several of whom were watching monitors. A fifty-ish looking man, in navy-blue pants and shirt with an FBI logo on the back, approached them, holding out his hand.

"Gentlemen."

Ed and Tom introduced themselves, showed him their credentials and shook hands.

Ed asked, "So what's the latest word?"

Pointing at the monitors, he said, "Right now, we're looking at the mall security tapes hoping to spot the perpetrators."

Tom asked, "So, you think it was terrorists?"

Running his hand through his thin hair, Rick said, "Well, we haven't ruled that out, but because the bombs were placed where they were, and the minimum amount of damage they caused, we suspect it was done by thrill seeking amateurs."

"So, where were the explosives placed?" Tom asked.

"There were six of them. Two on each floor of the mall, at opposite ends, placed in waste receptacles."

"Garbage cans? They were in garbage cans?" Ed asked, shaking his head.

Nodding, Rick said, "Yes, Sir, and they were set to go off a few seconds apart from each other, so it would cause more chaos. Even though they were harmless, it was a miracle more people weren't hurt because of the panic."

"How many were hurt?" Ed asked, thinking of Cindy and her friends.

"Only a few. Some young girl who had a sprained wrist, a little old lady who fell on the icy steps, and an older man who fell out of his wheelchair. Then there were a few who had anxiety attacks, and one who had to be taken to the hospital, for chest pains."

For as many people as there were, they handled themselves amazingly well. I think it helped that the mall security was calm and efficient. If they had panicked, well, it probably would have turned out differently."

Nodding, Ed asked, "Mind if we take a look around?"

Rick turned to one of the officers, told him he'd be back in a while, donned his jacket, and led Tom and Ed to the mall entrance.

CHAPTER 108

Once Janet left the Waco suburbs, and was headed North on I-35, she glanced at her daughter, who was looking out the window. She noticed tears streaming down her face.

Reaching over, she patted Linda's leg. "What's wrong?"

Wiping her eyes, Linda turned towards her mother.

"I was just thinking about how things could have turned out. We could have been killed!"

Janet sighed, and nodded. "I suppose so, but we're okay. We were lucky."

"Lucky? I'm not sure luck has anything to do with it. You were amazing, Mom! You got us out safe and sound. I would have never thought about finding another way out."

Janet smiled. *She thinks I'm amazing.* Looking at Linda's bandaged hand, she sighed. "I'm so sorry, I hurt your hand, though."

Linda shrugged. "It's okay. I'm kinda glad you hung on to me so tightly. If I'd gotten separated from you, I think I would have gone crazy!"

Janet nodded. "Yeah, me too." *I think I would die if I ever lost you, my sweet girl,* she thought as she felt a tear escape down her cheek.

After a few moments of silence, Linda asked, "Mom, have you ever thought about what happens after you die?"

Caught completely off guard by the question, Janet inhaled sharply.

"Linda! Why would you ask such a thing?"

Linda shrugged. "I was just thinking. If things had turned out differently. I mean, if one or both of us had died, what would happen next? Is there a Heaven or Hell, like Stacey says, or do we just die and that's it? Or, do we come back as something or someone else?"

Janet frowned, and gripped the steering wheel. *How do I answer these questions when I'm asking the same ones?*

She cleared her throat and said, "I think everyone wants to believe in Heaven: a wonderful place where there are angels, beautiful music, fantastic colors, and where they'll see their loved ones again, but I'm not sure I believe in that fantasy."

Cocking her head, Linda asked, "Why not?"

Frowning, and sighing, Janet said, "Linda, we've talked about this before."

"I know, but that was before we almost got killed! I hope Stacey is right and there is life after death. I hope I can be good enough to go to Heaven. I hope we don't just die and that's it. What if we haven't lived a long life, and done good things? What then? Do our lives just end? Do they? Why are we even here then? What purpose do we have?"

Janet held her hand up. "Whoa! That's a lot of questions."

Linda shook her head and sighed. "I know, I'm just so confused. Stacey tells me one thing, and you tell me another. I just don't know who or what to believe."

Janet nodded, and reached over to pat Linda's leg. "Well, I am your mom, and I think I know what's best for you. You just have to live each day to the fullest, and be the best person you can be. The earth's energies will help direct you."

Linda frowned. "How can the earth's energies help? They can't talk to me."

"Oh, Lee Lee, there are so many things to learn. There are positive and negative energies all around us, and we have to learn to tap into the positive ones. Only then can we truly live life to the fullest."

Linda frowned, not quite comprehending her mother's words.

Janet continued, "I, and the others in our enlightened group, will help guide and direct you. I've learned so much from them this past year, and I'm sure the leaders will be thrilled to help you, as well."

Linda nodded. *Maybe Mom is right, and this life is all we have, but then again, Stacey's beliefs sound true, too. Oh, man, I'm really confused now.*

The rest of the trip home was uneventful and quiet, as each female thought about the day's events and the what ifs.

CHAPTER 109

After the movie, and leaving Donna and her boys, Christina turned her van towards Alva.

Cindy said, "Hey, Christina, could we drive by the mall? Ed said he and Tom were there checking things out."

"Sure, but I doubt they'll let anyone near it. Especially, if there's still an investigation going on."

"Let me text Ed, and see if he can meet us in the lot somewhere."

After a few minutes, Cindy got a return text.

Sighing, she said, "Ed said they're not letting anyone near the mall, and he can't leave right now. He says he'll talk to me later, and let me know what's going on." Sighing again, she said, "So, I guess you don't have to go by after all."

Christina reached over and patted Cindy's shoulder.

"Hey, you'll be one of the first to know what's going on. That's pretty cool."

Cindy nodded and did a crooked smile. "Yeah, it is kinda nice knowing someone in power."

As they left the well lit suburbs, and were plunged into total darkness, except for the lights of the few vehicles passing by, Christina said, "Wow! It got dark fast!"

Cindy frowned and said, "You okay?"

"Yeah, just a little nervous. I drove through this kind of stuff all the time in Michigan, but here, it seems different. More icy."

Cindy nodded. "Yeah, I hate driving in this kind of stuff."

Christina let up on the gas pedal as she watched the car ahead swerve. Her van hit a spot of black ice on the road a second later, and her own van swerved, but she was able to correct it swiftly. All those years of driving in Michigan winters had taught her well.

"What happened, Mom?" Nicky asked from the back seat.

"It's okay. We just hit an icy spot. I'm going to slow down a bit, so it may take longer to get home."

"Oh, okay."

Cindy gave Christina a worried look. Tightening her grip on the steering wheel, Christina said, "We'll be okay. Remember, I've driven through worse than this."

Cindy sighed and nodded.

Pulling into Cindy's driveway about an hour later than planned, Christina heard an audible sigh from the passengers.

She smiled. "See, I told you I'd get you home safe and sound."

"Yeah, thanks." Cindy said, reaching over to hug her friend.

Nicky said, "I counted ten cars and trucks on the side of the road, from Waco to here. I'm glad you know how to drive through that ice, Mom."

Turning in her seat to look at Nicky, she said, "I'll have to admit, there were a few times I was afraid we'd end up like them, but, thank goodness, we were okay."

Samara said, "Well, I wish it'd make up it's mind, whether it's gonna rain, sleet or snow. I hate this mushy, icy stuff."

"I know!" Stacey said, "This stuff is yucky. I'd much rather have snow. At least that's pretty."

Cindy exited the van, and promptly landed on her bottom and disappeared.

Christina shouted, as she opened her van door, "Cindy! Are you okay?"

Cindy didn't answer, and Samara opened the sliding door and looked out. Cindy was half under the van and looked unconscious.

"Mom!" She shouted as she stepped out and slid to her bottom.

The Sanders kids, unbuckled their seat belts and leaned out the sliding door.

"Mrs. Murray?" Stacey called. Cindy didn't respond.

Christina carefully made her way around the van and knelt down beside Cindy. She called her name, and noticed blood pooling under her head.

"One of you call 911!" She shouted as she cradled Cindy's head in her lap.

Samara crawled over to her mom and began crying.

"Mom! Please open your eyes!"

Cindy moaned.

Christina went into nurse-mode.

"Samara, go in and get some blankets. I want to get her off this ice, and keep her warm."

Samara, with the help of Brad, rose to her feet and made a bee-line to the house.

"Mom, is there anything we can do?" Stacey asked, worry etched on her face.

"I think you and Nicky just need to stay in the van, and keep warm. It's very icy here, and I don't want you falling, too."

Stacey nodded, and put her arm around Nicky who was mumbling something.

"What are you saying, Nicky?" she asked.

"I'm just praying."

"Oh, okay. Good idea."

A few minutes later, Samara and Brad returned with arms full of blankets.

"Brad, can you help me lift her, and Samara, will you slide the blankets underneath?"

Brad and Samara both bent down and did as they were asked.

Standing, Brad said, "Mom, you're shivering. Let me get your coat."

"Thanks. I didn't even notice I didn't have it on."

A few minutes later, they heard sirens. By the time the paramedics arrived, Cindy was beginning to stir.

Christina gave them the information about the incident, and as they loaded Cindy into the ambulance, informed them that she would be following them in.

Samara began to sob, and Brad pulled her into a hug and held her, until the emotional storm passed.

She pulled away after a few minutes and wiped her nose on her coat sleeve.

She looked up into his face and said, "Thanks, I'm just so scared. I don't know what I'll do, if she dies."

Brad nodded. "She'll be okay."

She looked into his eyes and frowned. "How do you know?"

"Well, I'm not psychic or anything like that, but my gut feeling is that she'll be okay."

She leaned into his chest once again, as he encircled her with his arms.

"I sure hope you're right."

As the ambulance drove off, Christina turned to Brad and Samara and said, "Okay, you two, let's go."

Around two hours later, after consuming coffee, soda and snacks, Christina and the kids were able to visit Cindy. She was sitting up in bed with an IV in one arm, heart monitor wires extending from her chest to a beeping monitor, and enough bandages on her head to resemble a white football helmet. She was conscious, but groggy.

When Christina and Samara entered the room, she smiled and reached out her hand.

Samara ran to her mother, and practically jumped on the bed with her.

"Oh, Mom! Are you okay? I was so scared and worried!"

Cindy stroked her daughter's hair.

"I'm fine, honey. Just a concussion."

Samara, looked around. "It doesn't look fine. Why all the bandages?"

Cindy smiled. "I hit my head hard enough to split the skin, so I had to have a few stitches. And here, I thought I had a really hard head. At least, that's what people have told me."

A tear ran down Samara's face, as she leaned in to hug her mother.

"I'm so glad you're okay."

Christina walked over and patted Cindy's hand.

"You gave us quite a scare. Just a concussion, huh?"

"Yep. Should be back to my ole' self in a few days."

"How long do you have to stay here?"

"The doc said I could go home tomorrow, if I'm doing okay."

Christina nodded and sighed. "Good. Maybe we can go half and half on a big ole' bag of sand or rock salt for the driveway and sidewalks. I wouldn't want anyone else to get hurt."

"Maybe by the time I go home, it'll all be melted off. This is Texas, you know. Freezing one day, and sweltering the next."

"Yeah, not like Michigan where it's cold from November to April."

Looking around at her kids tired faces, she leaned in, kissed Cindy on the forehead and said, "I need to get the kiddos home. Samara can stay with us tonight."

Cindy sighed and nodded. "Yeah, thanks. I can barely stay awake myself."

Samara hugged and kissed her mom once again, before exiting the room.

Walking down the hall, Samara asked, "Mrs. Sanders, can we go by my house and get a few things, and is it okay if we bring Sasha?"

Christina nodded, and put her arm around Samara's shoulder.

"Sure thing."

As they walked through the icy parking lot of the hospital, Stacey said, "Look, the snow has stopped, and the sky is clear."

Everyone stopped, and looked up at the black sky, dotted with twinkling, diamond-like stars.

"Well, look at that!" Christina said, gazing up in awe. The moon's light reflected off the ice-covered trees and grass, and gave the whole area a surreal, magical kind of look and feel.

"Wow!" Nicky said, turning in circles. "I feel like I'm on some sort of alien planet."

Samara gasped and said, "I've never seen anything so beautiful! I mean, last week when it snowed, that was pretty cool, but this," she said, turning in circles with her arms outstretched, "this is amazing!"

Brad smiled and said, "Yeah, even though I've seen this kind of thing lots of times in Michigan, it never ceases to amaze me. It's like God is giving us a tiny glimpse of Heaven."

Nicky asked, "Did Heaven look this beautiful?"

Brad smiled and closed his eyes, saying, "Nicky, it was even more beautiful than this. Words can't even begin to describe it, but this," opening his eyes and pointing to the area around him, "this is about as close as it can get."

Nicky's eyes widened, as he said, "Awesome!"

Christina cleared her throat and said, "Okay, gang. We need to get going."

Touching Christina's arm, Samara said, "Mrs. Sanders?"

"Yes, Samara."

"Do you think I should let Ed know about my mom?"

Looking at her watch, Christina said, "Well, it's past midnight. Why don't you wait until tomorrow. By then, your mom may have already spoken to him."

Nodding, Samara said, "Yeah, he usually calls her every morning. She can tell him herself."

Samara slapped her forehead. "He can't call her. I have her phone."

"Well, if he calls, then you can talk to him."

"Right, my brain's not working very well right now."

Christina put her arm around the girl's shoulder.

"It's been a long day. I don't think any of us are thinking very clearly, right now. The sooner we get to your house, and pick up your stuff and Sasha, the sooner we can get to bed."

CHAPTER 110

Drifting off to sleep, Cindy felt a presence next to her bed. Thinking it was one of the nurses coming to check on her, she didn't open her eyes, until she felt a warm hand on her forehead. Opening them slightly, she was surprised to see no one there, but yet the pressure of a hand on her forehead was still present. She assumed the drugs were causing hallucinations, and closed her eyes once again, giving in to the beckoning sleep. Drifting, as if on a raft in a sea of blackness, she was once again aware of a presence. Opening her eyes and sitting up, she found herself, not in a hospital room, but on a small island surrounded by water as far as her eyes could see. *What the...? How did I get here? This can't be real.* Slapping her face, she yelled, "Wake up!"

According to her senses, she was awake. She could feel a slight breeze, smell the tangy, fishy odor of the water, feel the sand between her toes, and see a couple of palm trees, blue sky and dark blue water. Walking around the island, which was about the size of her house, and void of any warm or cold-blooded life forms, she experienced a mixture of feelings; confusion, loneliness, fear, and anger.

She sat under a palm tree and cried and screamed, "I want to go home!"

After a while, her mouth felt parched and her stomach growled. *Great!* she thought, *There's no food or water on this island. Guess I'll die of dehydration or starvation.* When her tongue felt like sandpaper, and there wasn't a drop of saliva left, she crawled over to the water's edge. *I know I'm not supposed to drink ocean water, but I'm so thirsty. I'll just wet my mouth and tongue.*

She sat on the sand, cupped her hands and brought the water to her mouth. Amazingly, it tasted sweet and pure. No salt at all. *How can that be? Doesn't matter, I can drink all I want!*

Standing, she looked around the island, wondering what in the world she was going to eat, when she spotted a coconut lying where she had been sitting a few minutes earlier. Running over to pick it up, she realized she didn't have anything with which to open it. Looking around once again, she spotted two large rocks which she didn't remember seeing before. Taking the nut over to the rocks, she split it in half, drank the juice, and ate half the pulp. Feeling satiated, she sat back under the tree. It was then that she noticed the sunlight never waned. She had to have been there for hours, yet the sun never moved. Looking up at the sky, she realized that there wasn't a sun after all. It was just bright all around.

How can that be? She wondered. *Am I dead? Did I get captured by aliens? Am I on another planet? In a spaceship? Where am I?*

Feeling fear and panic clawing their way into her mind, she started hyperventilating, and held her head, which was free of bandages, as dizziness overcame her.

Consciously slowing her breathing to calm herself, she said, "Okay, whoever or whatever has me here, I'm listening. What do you want from me? What do you want me to do?"

Feeling a presence behind her, she turned to see a man dressed in a white gown. Standing and backing away, she realized she had nowhere to run, and stopped. She looked around for some kind of craft, either boat or spaceship, and finding none, asked, "Who are you, and how did you get here?"

The man sat cross-legged on the sand and said, "Come, sit, and talk to me, Cindy."

Warily, she asked, "How do you know my name?"

He smiled, revealing teeth so white, they gleamed.

Cocking his head to look up at her, he said, as he patted the ground next to him. "Come, I will tell you."

She sat across from him, far enough so he couldn't reach out and grab her, and drew her knees up, ready to jump up and fight, or run.

He drew in the sand with his finger as she looked him over. He had to be in his mid thirties, well built, and had a pleasant face. Not drop-dead gorgeous like Ed, but handsome enough. His dark, wavy hair hung to his shoulders, and he had a short beard. His eyes were an emerald green, surrounded by long dark lashes, and arched dark eyebrows. *Middle-eastern?*

He looked up and asked, "Do you know who I am?"

Shaking her head, she said, "No, should I?"

Shrugging, he said, "I know you."

"How do you know me, if I've never met you before?"

Smiling, he said, "I've known you from the beginning."

"The beginning? The beginning of what?"

"From the beginning of time."

Oh, boy, she thought. *He's a nut case. I'm stuck on an island with a lunatic!*

Smiling, he said, "I'm not a lunatic. Although, some people accused me and my followers of being lunatics."

"Followers? Are you like...Charles Manson or something? Do you have a god complex?"

He laughed. A full belly, melodious laugh. "No, nothing like that."

"Then what do you mean by followers?"

"I know this will be difficult for you to comprehend, but people on earth called me Jesus."

Cindy laughed. "Yeah, right! Like the Son of God, Jesus?"

Nodding, and smiling, he said, "Yes, the one and only."

Cindy stood and began pacing, "You mean to tell me that I'm talking to the son of God? Am I dead?"

Smiling, he shook his head. "No, you aren't dead. Just sleeping."

"Am I dreaming?"

He cocked his head to look up at her. "You're in between."

"In between? In between what?"

"You're in between living and dying."

Cindy made a face. "What? How can that be? I'm either alive or dead."

Shaking his head, he said, "Well, I know you can't fully comprehend this, but your body is still in the hospital bed, but your spirit is here with me."

Rubbing her forehead, pacing and mumbling to herself, she stopped and turned towards him.

"Okay, if what you say is true, and I'm not saying I totally believe you, then why am I here?"

Patting the sand, he said, "Sit, and I will tell you."

Sitting Indian style, closer this time, she sighed, as she leaned forward and rested her chin on her knuckles.

"I'm listening."

"Remember when you were six years old, you attended a Vacation Bible School at a church on your street?"

Chewing her bottom lip as the memory surfaced, she nodded.

"While there, the teacher told you about me, and asked if anyone wanted to ask me into their heart, and you raised your hand."

Frowning, she nodded again.

"Well, I honored that prayer and I've been with you ever since."

She shook her head. "Really? Because when I went home and told my mom, she said I was too young to understand what that meant, and so I just dismissed it. We moved around a lot, and she never let me go back to church after that. She said they were filling the kids' heads with a bunch of nonsense."

Jesus nodded and frowned. "Your mom has issues of trust. She's been hurt many times, and, even though she cries out to us for help, she doesn't believe, so our hands are tied, so to speak."

Cindy frowned, "She doesn't believe what?"

"She doesn't believe that she is worthy of our love and forgiveness, and she won't open her mind and spirit to us. We keep waiting, because we want to help, but because Father designed humans with a free will, we can't intervene until they open their hearts and minds to us."

"You keep saying us and we. What does that mean?"

"The Father, Son and Holy Spirit. We are all the same, but have different roles. It is difficult for the human mind to understand, I know, but when a person accepts one, he or she accepts all three of us."

"So when I asked you into my heart or mind or whatever, all three of you came in?"

Jesus nodded.

"Even though I didn't acknowledge you all these years, you've still been here?" She pointed to her heart.

Jesus smiled and nodded. "Your prayer as a child was quite sincere, and we honored that. We knew you would walk away, but we also knew you would come back. Once we fill that God-shaped hole in your heart, nothing else can come in, at least not permanently."

Cindy cocked her head. "Huh? I don't understand. God-shaped hole?"

Jesus chuckled. "It's like this. When your physical body was created in your mother's womb, your spirit was also created, and Father made it so it would desire a relationship with Him. Well, sometimes, because of free will, humans choose not to fill that desire with Him. They know they're lacking something, but they don't know what it is. They keep trying to feel fulfilled with everything else, but to no avail. Their life becomes a series of broken relationships, failed jobs, and loss of self esteem. Because of their misery and hopelessness, many end their lives. It hurts our hearts to see that happen. We try desperately to give them chances to turn to us, but they won't."

"What kind of chances?"

"We put people in their paths to show them the way, remove people and things that would keep them from turning to us, and sometimes we cause events to happen to turn them around, but again, because of their free-will, we can't force them to choose us."

"But if God can see the future, doesn't He know that they'll reject Him? Why bother giving them a chance?"

Jesus smiled, "That's a good question. Many have asked it before you, and my answer is that God is God, and His ways are not understood by humans. His desire is for everyone to have a relationship with Him."

Cindy chewed on her thumbnail, "So, why am I here? What do you want from me?"

Jesus reached out and took her hands.

"Cindy, we want a relationship with you. You've blocked us out long enough. There are going to be some events that will test your endurance, and we want you to trust us to do what is best for you in the long run."

Panic filled her face. "Events? What about Samara? She'll be okay, right?"

Jesus patted her hands and sighed.

"Cindy, Samara hasn't acknowledged us yet. When you wake up, you will want to tell her about this encounter. She will have to make her own choice as to what she will believe. Right now, my concern is with you. Will you recommit your life to us?"

Closing her eyes and nodding, she felt a warm tingly feeling from the top of her head to her toes. When she opened them, she was back in her hospital bed.

"Oh, man." she whispered. "What just happened?" Rubbing her eyes, and noticing her hands were shaking, she took in a lung full of air, and blew it out.

Surely, that was a dream!

Reaching over for the call button, she pressed it.

"Yes, Mrs. Murray." A disembodied voice said through the box on the wall.

"I need to use the restroom."

"Okay, I'll be right there."

When the nurse came in, Cindy said, "I had the weirdest dream."

As she helped Cindy into the bathroom, she said, "Really? Tell me about it."

Cindy told of her encounter with Jesus.

Tucking her back in bed, the nurse said, "Wow! That is weird. But, maybe it wasn't a dream. Maybe, it was a true encounter with God."

Cindy frowned. "Well, it certainly felt real."

The nurse patted her hand. "Sometimes God speaks to us through our dreams."

Before the nurse left, Cindy asked if she would bring her a pen and paper.

"I want to write this down, so I don't forget it."

The nurse smiled. "Good idea. I'll be right back."

CHAPTER 111

Saturday, three days before Christmas, the Alva residents woke to a crystal clear, blue sky. Ice still covered the foliage and ground, and the sun's reflection made it sparkle like glitter.

Christina stood in awe as she sipped her coffee, and took in the beauty of the ice-covered landscape. Knowing it wouldn't last, she found her camera and stepped into the back yard to take a few pictures.

David had bought her the digital camera with various lenses the Christmas before he died, and even though she didn't use it often, she had been impressed with the quality of the pictures taken. She zoomed the lens in on the ice crystals on the window pane, and was thrilled with the minute details. She continued to walk around the yard, snapping pictures, as Benji followed, sniffing and marking his territory. That's where Brad found her when he came downstairs.

"Mom? What are you doing?" He called from the back porch.

She turned and showed him the camera. "I'm taking pictures of this beautiful ice."

As if seeing it for the first time, he looked around and nodded. "Yeah. It is beautiful. With the sun so bright, I don't think it will last long."

"Yeah, that's why I'm taking pictures now."

Nodding, he said, "I'm gonna stay in here where it's nice and warm and watch TV."

She smiled. "I'll join you in a minute, but I have to work today, so I'll need to get ready."

Stomping her feet, and removing her ice-covered slippers, she said, "I bought some new cereal the other day. It's granola with dried cherries. Tell me what you think of it."

Brad, who was sitting on the couch watching the news said, "I'm eating some now, and I like it. Not too sweet, but crunchy. I like the cherries."

Christina headed to the stairs. "Good, I was getting tired of the other stuff."

"I thought you didn't have to work 'till Monday."

"I thought so too, but Mrs. Ferguson called, and reminded me that I had signed up to cover another nurses' shift today. I'm glad she called, 'cause I completely forgot about it."

As she was walking up the stairs, Stacey was walking down, rubbing her eyes.

"Hey Mom."

"Hey, babe. Why are you up so early?"

"I don't know. I just couldn't sleep any more. I kept thinking about Linda, and what happened at the mall. I'm gonna call her in a little while."

"Good, I'd like to know all the details as well."

"Do you have to work today?"

Christina sighed. "Yes, my vacation is over. It's going to be hard getting back in the swing of things."

Stacey nodded. "Yeah, I dread going back to school in a couple of weeks. I like sleeping in, and doing whatever I want to do."

Christina smiled and nodded. "Yes, me too, but duty calls."

CHAPTER 112

Arriving at the hospital a few minutes early, Christina went to check on Cindy.

Entering the room, and seeing Cindy sitting up in bed eating a bowl of oatmeal, she said, "Hey girlfriend."

She smiled and put her spoon down. "Hey, yourself!"

Christina walked over and hugged her, asking, "So how are you? Did you sleep well?"

Cindy put her hand up to the bandages on her head.

"I still have a little headache, but otherwise I'm okay. I slept pretty good, except I had the weirdest dream." Pausing to wipe her lips, she said, "I have to tell you about it!"

Christina looked at her watch and frowned. "I wish I could stay, but I need to get upstairs."

"Oh, I didn't realize you were working today. I'm sorry I kept you up so late last night."

Shaking her head, Christina said, "Yeah, I forgot I had to work. Thank goodness Mrs. Ferguson called to remind me. Amazingly, I'm doing okay. I woke up early, and was even able to take a few pictures of the beautiful ice, before coming here."

"Really? I figured you'd be exhausted."

"Yeah, me too, but I feel okay so far. Now, I might crash after lunch."

Looking at her watch again, she said, "I hate to leave, but I really do have to go. I'll stop by during my lunch break, and you can tell me about your dream."

"Well, I'm hoping I can go home today, so I may not be here."

Christina sighed. "If the doctor releases you, why don't you wait until I can take you home when I get off work—around three thirty?"

Cindy nodded. "Okay, I'll see what the doctor says. Now that I think about it, I don't have a ride home, unless Ed comes to get me."

Christina leaned in for another hug, then left her friend, and headed up to the CCU.

In the quiet of the elevator, she revisited the previous day's drama, thanked God once again for protection at the mall and drive home, and asked for healing for Cindy's head injury.

Exiting the elevator, and heading to the nurse's lounge, she was greeted by Sarah.

"Hey, stranger!" Sarah said, reaching out for a hug. "It's so nice to see you, again. I was wondering if you'd ever come back to work."

Christina returned the hug and said, "It does seem like a long time since I've been here, but it's been only a week or so."

Giggling, Sarah said, "Yeah, but it was a long week!"

Smiling and shaking her head, Christina said, "You'll have to tell me about your week. Hopefully, it'll be an easy day, and we can sit and chat a bit."

Sarah said, "Well, there's only two patients on the floor right now, and they're stable, so I think we'll have plenty of time to catch up."

Donning her lab coat, Christina said, "Good, I could use a stress-free day, after yesterday."

Sarah frowned, "What happened yesterday?"

Christina sighed and said, as she closed the locker door, "I'll tell you later."

Raising her eyebrows, Sarah said, "I can hardly wait!"

After morning rounds with Dr. Dawson, assessing the two patients, and charting, Christina sat at the station perusing the two charts, when Sally Jean approached.

"Hey, Christina, I'm glad you're back. How's Brad doing?"

"Hey, yourself, Sally Jean. It's nice to be back." Looking around, she said, "Amazingly enough, I've kinda missed this place."

Sally Jean cocked her head, waiting for an answer to her question.

"Oh, and Brad is doing well. Seems to be completely recovered."

The aide smiled broadly. "I'm glad to hear that. He seems like such a nice boy." Pausing, she added, "I kinda wish I was younger."

Christina chuckled. "Funny, after meeting you, he said he wished he was older."

Giggling, the girl said, "Oh, that's sweet!" Hearing the dinging of a call bell, she turned and headed back down the hall, calling over her shoulder, "Tell him I said hi."

Christina smiled and nodded.

Sarah came around the counter and sat next to Christina, who looked up from the chart she was reading.

"So how are our patients doing?"

Sighing, Sarah said, "Well, I just helped Mr. Abner to the bathroom, and he seems to be stronger and steadier than yesterday. Did Dr. Dawson say when he might be going home?"

"He said probably tomorrow if he continues to improve. Dr. Dawson is trying to get everyone out and home for Christmas."

"Then what will we do if there aren't any patients?"

"Well, I wish we could all stay home, but unfortunately, we still need to be here."

"Are you working Christmas Day?"

Christina sighed and nodded, "Yep, and Christmas Eve. Janet has been covering my shifts and hers, while I was on vacation, and it only seems fair that I take those two days. After Christmas, we'll get back to our normal schedules."

Sarah nodded. "Well, I guess we'll be here together. I signed up to work both days because I don't like to be home alone during the holidays."

Christina cocked her head, "You don't have any family around to visit?"

Sarah shook her head and sighed. "No, my husband was an only child, and his parents are gone, and I have a sister in Arizona, but, other than her family, I'm pretty much alone."

Christina reached over and patted her hand. "I'm sorry. It must get pretty lonely at times."

Sarah nodded. "Yes ma'am, but I keep busy with work here, and volunteering at the local animal shelter."

"Alva has an animal shelter? Huh. Guess I never thought about that."

Sarah smiled. "Yeah. It was built about five years ago. We take in all strays or drop ins, spay or neuter them, get them healthy, and try to find them homes."

Sally Jean approached the desk, and asked Christina, "Is there anything else you want me to do?"

Christina cocked her head, "I don't know. What have you done so far?"

Sally went through the list of things she had done for the two patients.

"Well, since you've given them baths, changed their beds, and given them fresh water, maybe you could clean up in the nurses' lounge. I noticed a few dirty coffee cups and stray papers."

Sally Jean smiled. "I can do that!" She turned and headed to the lounge area.

Sarah whispered, "She's such a sweet girl. Always willing to help."

Christina smiled and nodded. "Yes, she is."

Turning her attention back to Sarah, Christina asked, "So, are you planning on spending any time with Mr. Wilson?"

Sarah blushed and shook her head. "He has family out in California he plans to visit, but he did ask me out for New Year's eve."

Christina smiled and said, "Well, that's something to look forward to!"

Grinning and nodding, Sarah said, "Yes, it is."

After a moment's silence, Sarah asked, "Are you and Dr. Dawson doing anything special on New Year's?"

Cocking her head, Christina said, "I don't know. We haven't discussed any plans." Shrugging, she said, "It's okay. I'd be happy sitting at home with the kids, watching the ball drop, and bringing in the new year with them."

Nodding, Sarah said, "That sounds nice. Maybe Dr. Dawson will be there with y'all."

"Maybe."

CHAPTER 113

Jamie sat on the couch, listening to a reporter giving details about the garbage can bombs found in the Waco mall. He sat forward, spilling milk from his bowl of cereal onto his jeans. Ignoring the wet spot, he set his bowl on a nearby table, reached for the remote and increased the volume.

He was feeling restless. It had been a couple of days since his last break-in, and he needed a fix.

"Geeze, that sounds exciting," he mumbled. "I'd love to be able to pull off something like that."

When the news switched to another topic, he turned off the TV set, and sat for a few minutes, contemplating his next move.

I bet I could do something like those bombers, and not get caught. I've been breaking into houses for years and have avoided the law, so... He smiled, as ideas began taking shape in his mind.

CHAPTER 114

Samara was awakened by the ringing of a phone. Remembering it was her mom's, she jumped off the couch, and ran to her jacket, followed closely by Sasha. Digging into the pocket, she retrieved it on the last ring.

"Hello?" She said breathlessly.

"Samara?" Said a male voice on the other end.

Recognizing the voice, she answered, "Yeah, Ed, it's me."

"Why are you answering your mom's phone?"

"Hang on." She found a chair to sit in, and patted her leg as an invitation for Sasha to jump up. Once the dog was settled, she spoke again.

"Oh Ed, Mom's in the hospital."

"What? Hospital? Why?"

"She slipped on some ice last night, and hit her head."

"Hit her head? Okay, Samara, start from the top and tell me what happened"

She spent the next ten minutes recalling the details.

"So, she's in the hospital in Alva?" He asked

"Yes, sir."

"Can you give me her room number?"

"I'm not sure of her room number, because when we left, she was still in the emergency room.

"Okay. I'm going to call the hospital, then I'll come down this afternoon. I have a few loose ends to tie up here at work. You'll be okay?"

She nodded, then said, "Yes, sir. I'm staying with Mrs. Sanders."

"Good. Is she around?"

"No, she had to work today."

"Alright. I'll see you later then."

They said their good-byes, and Samara put the phone on the counter. Hearing the TV on in the family room, she was curious to know who was up.

As she entered the den, carrying Sasha, Brad looked up and said, "Hi."

Brushing hair out of her face, she said, "Hi."

"Did you sleep okay on that couch in the front room?"

"Yeah, it's not too bad." Smiling, she said, "As tired as I was last night, I think I could have slept on a bed of nails."

Chuckling, he said, "Yeah, I think we all felt that way."

She took Sasha to the back door and let her out to do her morning business, then she plopped down in his mom's easy chair. He watched as she rubbed her eyes, and ran her fingers through her hair.

"So, would you like some cereal? My mom got this new granola stuff. It's pretty good. It has cherries in it."

She smiled and his heart did a triple beat.

"What I'd really like is a cup of coffee."

"You drink coffee?"

"Well, let's put it this way, I like a little coffee with my cream and sugar."

Grinning, he said, "My mom drinks it like that. She says she likes the idea of coffee."

Nodding, Samara said, "I like that. I guess I like the idea of coffee too." Making a face, she said, "I certainly don't like it black, like my mom."

Shaking his head, Brad said, "Me, neither. I haven't developed a taste for it. I suppose I will someday. Don't most adults drink coffee?"

"Seems like it. At least all the adults I know."

Standing, Brad said, I'll go pour you a cup of coffee, but you'll have to add the cream and sugar."

Rising and stretching, she said through a yawn, "Sure, I can do that."

Sitting back in the family room, both sipping on pale, sweet coffee, Brad said, "So Samara, how's school going so far?"

Shrugging, she said, "It's okay."

"Have you thought about what you want to do with your life once you graduate?"

Making a face she said, "Well, not really. I was thinking that when I start high school next year, I'll give it more thought."

Brad said, "I think I'd like to go into computer programming. That's what my dad did."

Nodding, she said, "That's cool. I don't know much about computers."

Stacey entered the room, followed by Benji. "Hey, you two. What are y'all talking about?"

Samara said, "We're talking about our futures."

Stacey made a face. "Your futures?" She went to the back door and let Benji out. Sasha ran in and jumped in Samara's lap, whimpering and shivering.

Wrapping the dog in a blanket, Samara said, "Oh, baby! I forgot about you! I'm so sorry."

Looking out the window at the blue sky, Stacey said, "Looks like it's gonna be a beautiful day."

Samara said, "Brad wants to do computer stuff and I'm not sure what I want to do when I grow up."

Stacey sat on the couch next to Brad. Nodding, she said, "Yeah, I'm not sure either." Hearing Benji bark, she rose and went to the door. Continuing her train of thought she said, "Well, at least we have a few years to decide."

Brad asked, "So, Samara, what do you think of Ed? You think he and your mom will get married?"

Smiling, she said, "I like him a lot. He's fun to be around. I wouldn't be surprised if they get married, because they sure seem to like each other."

Standing and stretching, Brad said, "That's cool. He seems like a nice guy." Reaching for Samara's coffee cup he asked, "You want anymore?"

Shaking her head, she said, "No, one cup is enough. I do want to try that new cereal you were talking about though."

"Sure. You want to get it, or I could bring you some."

Standing and stretching she said, "Nah. I'll get it. Thanks though."

"Well, I need to go upstairs for a few minutes. I'll be back down in a while."

He turned and headed towards the stairs.

Stacey whispered, "I think he likes you."

Samara made a face, "Really? I like him too, but kinda like a big brother."

Looking at her watch, she said, "I'm gonna call my mom, then I'll get some cereal."

Stacey nodded and stood. "I'm gonna find something to eat."

Walking up the stairs, Brad thought about Samara. He liked her, even though she was a couple years younger. He knew he couldn't pursue any kind of relationship because of her age, so he decided he would just treat her like a sister, and maybe in a couple of years, they could date. He smiled.

CHAPTER 115

Stacey took her peanut-butter toast into the family room and turned the volume up on the TV. There was a news bulletin about the homemade bombs found in the six garbage cans at the mall. She was surprised to see Ed's face appear on the screen. She called Samara, who was in the front room talking to her mom.

"Hey, Samara! Ed's on TV!"

Samara came in, holding the phone up to her ear.

"Hey, Mom, turn on your TV. Ed's being interviewed."

They sat in silence, and watched as a reporter asked him questions about the bombing.

Samara said, "Mom, I'll call you later. I want to hear what he's saying."

Nicky joined them on the couch.

"Hey, it's Ed."

Both girls shushed him.

He made a face. "Sorry."

The woman who was interviewing Ed asked, "So, Mr. Florres, what you're saying is that the bombs look like the work of an amateur?"

Ed nodded. "We don't believe they were planted by terrorists. Because of the nature of the bombs, and their placement, we feel it was done by one or more people seeking thrills. They were placed in secluded areas, and they were too small to cause much damage."

"So, no one was hurt?" She asked.

"Well, there were a few minor injuries, but none caused by the explosives."

"What kind of injuries are you talking about?"

"A few bumps and scrapes caused by people evacuating the building. We commend the mall security in keeping the crowd calm and under control, or it could have been worse."

The reporter nodded, and turned to face the camera, saying, "There will be more information on the ten-o'clock news. This is Louise Bastrop, reporting for the channel four news."

The screen went to a commercial about a new brand of cat food, and Stacey turned down the volume.

She said, "I need to call Linda, and see how she's doing."

"Yeah," said Samara. "I wonder how much she saw."

Leaving Samara and Nicky, Stacey headed upstairs to retrieve her phone. Lifting it off the dresser where it had been charging all night, she almost dropped it, when it began ringing.

Caller ID said it was Linda.

"Hey, Linda, I was just about to call you."

Linda giggled. "Great minds run on the same track. What are you doing?"

"Well, I *was* watching TV. Ed was being interviewed."

"Ed, as in Mrs. Murray's Ed?"

"Yep, the very one."

"Why was he being interviewed?"

Stacey explained Ed's involvement in the Anti-terrorist organization, and why he was at the mall being interviewed."

"Wow, that's cool."

"Yeah, I know. Hey, did you hear about Mrs. Murray?"

"Uh, no. What about her?"

Stacey told her about the accident and subsequent hospital stay.

"Oh!" Linda exclaimed. "Is she going to be okay?"

Stacey sighed. "As far as we know. Samara is staying with us until her mom gets out of the hospital."

"I don't know Samara very well. From the few times I've been around her, she seems nice enough."

"Oh, she is. I think Brad has a crush on her."

Both girls giggled. The girls talked a while longer about school, boys, and Christmas, then Stacey asked Linda to tell her all about the previous night's events.

"Don't leave anything out."

CHAPTER 116

Jamie lay on his back, with his hands under his head, staring at the bedroom ceiling, thinking about something spectacular he wanted to do. His mind played through several scenarios—poking and prodding each one to find and eliminate any potential flaw. Just thinking about causing chaos, fear, and awe, made his heart rate accelerate. After a little while, he knew what he wanted to do. He giggled as he thought about how surprised the residents of Alva would be.

Leaning over the side of the bed, he reached for the gallon jar of money stashed there. It was quite heavy, since he'd been saving the change from the money his dad had given him for groceries over the past couple of years, and his tip money from delivering pizzas. He dumped the contents of the jar on his bed and began counting. Two hours later, he came to the last coin. He sat back and smiled.

He had a little over three-hundred dollars, and figured he could spend about one-hundred to get the equipment he needed to pull off his plan. The rest would go back in the jar, to be spent on a vehicle, or place to live, once he graduated. He was tired of riding his bike everywhere, especially since the cold weather was setting in. *Maybe I can get a small used car, like the one I drive for the pizza deliveries. Maybe the owner would even sell it to me. I'll ask him today when I go into work.*

Stepping into the hot shower, he let his mind return to his previous ideas of chaos, and continued working out any potential flaw.

CHAPTER 117

True to her word, Christina went to visit Cindy, during her lunch break. Leaning in for a hug, she asked, "So, what did the doctor have to say?"

Making a face, Cindy said, "He said he wanted to run a few more tests, so I can't go home yet."

"What? What kind of tests?"

"He said my white blood count is elevated, which could mean an infection or something."

"Did he say how elevated it was?"

Shaking her head, she said, "No, and even if he did, I wouldn't know what it meant."

"Who's your doctor?"

"Dr. Harrison. He said he knew you."

Nodding, Christina said, "Ah, yes, he's the doctor that took care of me, when I had my bleeding episode."

"He seems nice and thorough."

"Oh, he is. One of the best internists in the area."

Straightening her blanket, Cindy asked, "So what do you think it means, when one's white blood cell count is elevated?"

Christina thought: *anemia, infection, trauma, cancer.* She said, "Well, it could mean different things, but I bet it's because you are recovering from the injury you sustained, when you fell."

Cindy made a face, "Well, geeze, I hope it isn't something more than that. I'd like to get out of here as soon as possible. This bed is not very comfortable and the sheets are rubbing my heels and elbows raw."

Christina patted her friend's hand. "I know. I remember feeling all raw and sore after being in one of those beds. They probably use some pretty strong chemicals to clean and purify the linens."

Cindy said, "I'd like to walk down the hall. My bottom's getting numb from sitting here."

Christina chuckled. "Sure, I'll help you."

Together, arm in arm, they walked to the lounge area at the end of the hall. Cindy said, "I have to tell you about that dream I had. It was weird and scary."

They sat in chairs next to each other, and looked out the large window, thankful they were inside, out of the blowing, frigid air.

Cindy recalled the dream in vivid detail, which left Christina baffled.

She said, "So, it almost sounds like you had an out-of-body experience."

"Yeah, like Brad. I was asleep, but fully alert, at the same time. Do you think God or Jesus was really talking to me?"

Christina chewed her bottom lip and twirled a ringlet of hair around her finger, as she contemplated the question.

She turned the question back to Cindy. "What do you think? Do you feel it was God trying to get your attention?"

Making a face and rubbing her forehead, Cindy said, "It was so real, Christina. I mean, I felt the breeze, smelled the water, touched the sand, and ate and drank from a coconut. When I awoke, I could still taste the coconut on my tongue. Plus, this man knew things about me that I had totally forgotten, like when I was a little girl." Realization hitting her, she gasped and asked, "Do you think I'm dying, and this was my mind's way of telling me I'd better get my life in order?"

Christina reached out and took Cindy's hands. "I don't think you're dying, but I will say that sometimes God *does* talk to us in our dreams. I've had a few encounters with Him in my dreams, over the years."

Christina paused a moment, then said, "So, let's say it was God or Jesus speaking to you, what do you think the underlying message was?"

Shaking her head and frowning, Cindy said, "I think He wants me to come back to Him."

Christina nodded. That was the impression she had.

"So," Christina said, hesitating, "what are your plans?"

Shrugging, Cindy said, "I've run so far away from God, I'm not sure I know the way back, and besides, why would He even want me back? I'm a mess."

Christina smiled and patted Cindy's hand.

"You know, God can use messed up people, just as well as He can use those who aren't. He loves us, just the way we are. He created us and He knows how flawed we are, yet He still loves us, unconditionally."

"I don't even know where or how to start."

"Well, you start with baby steps. I can help if you want me to,"

Cindy made a face. "I don't know if I'm ready yet. I'd like to think about this some more."

Disappointed, but not wanting to pressure Cindy, Christina nodded and said, "Sure, when you're ready to talk about it, or have questions, I'll be available."

"Thanks, especially for not pressuring me."

Christina reached over and hugged Cindy. "Hey, this is something you and God have to work out."

Nodding and standing, Cindy said, "Yeah. Hey, I'd best get back to my room or someone will be sending out a search party."

Christina chuckled. "Yes. I need to get back to the floor as well."

They walked back to Cindy's room, and Christina tucked her into bed, gave her a hug, and left to finish her shift.

Cindy reached for the phone to call Ed, just as he walked in the room.

"Hey, beautiful," he said as he walked over and kissed her on the forehead.

She smiled and shook her head. "I'm certainly not feeling so beautiful. I was just going to call you. I have a lot to tell you."

Smiling, he said, "I also have a few things to tell you." Looking around, he asked, "Where can I put these flowers?"

He pulled a beautiful mixed bouquet of flowers from behind his back.

Cindy gasped. "Wow, those are beautiful! Let me call the nurse. She can help us find something to put them in."

Sipping on cups of coffee, they talked about the events of the past couple of days.

Ed said, "So, after reviewing the mall security tapes and getting eye-witness accounts, we have pretty much ruled out a terrorist attack. The mall should re-open tomorrow, just in time for any last minute Christmas shoppers."

Cindy said, "Well, I'm glad it wasn't terrorist related. People are paranoid enough." Setting her coffee cup on the bedside table, she said, "I have something to tell you."

She proceeded to tell him of her dream.

Rubbing his chin, Ed said, "Wow, that sounds interesting."

"Have you ever had any dreams like that?" She asked, reaching for her coffee cup.

Shaking his head, he said, "Can't say that I have. So what do you make of it?"

Scrunching her face, she said, "I'm not sure yet. I've never been one to get all hyped up about religion or anything, so I'm not sure what this means.

Maybe it was a message from God, maybe it wasn't. Maybe it's because I have an overactive imagination."

Rubbing his chin, Ed said, "Well, I guess if you have any more like that, you should consider that it is a message from God."

"And if it is, what then?"

Shaking his head, he said, "Well, that's between you and Him."

"That's kinda what Christina said."

"If God's got a message for you, I don't think He'll quit reaching out to you."

Shrugging, he said, "Guess you'll just have to wait and see."

Looking at his watch, he said, "Babe, I want to stop by the sheriff's office, before he heads out. I'll be back in a little while."

"Okay, tell Larry hi for me."

Standing, he leaned over and kissed her cheek. "See you in a little while."

"Thanks again for the beautiful flowers." She said, as he left the room.

CHAPTER 118

Sheriff Clifton sat at his desk, thinking about the 911 incident, and the subsequent threats and activities around the world. *If any attack happened in Alva, would their police and fire department be ready and able to handle it?* He played different scenarios in his mind, and came to the conclusion that, if his town became a target, they would not be prepared. They'd have to call in help from neighboring communities.

He thought back to when the courthouse burned, and the tornado hit the trailer park outside of town. The Alva residents pitched in and helped as much as they could, but fire and rescue departments from Waco, Dallas, and Fort Worth were also on hand, to add their equipment and assistance.

Rubbing his eyes and pinching the bridge of his nose, he whispered, "I hope nothing happens in Alva." He knew that by the time outside help arrived, significant loss of property and life could occur.

Loraine, his secretary, knocked lightly on his door.

"Yes?"

Poking her head in, she said, "Sheriff, Mr. Florres is here to see you."

Standing, he said, "Send him in."

Ed walked over and shook the Sheriff's hand.

"So, what brings you in today, Ed?" The sheriff asked, motioning for Ed to sit, and then sitting in his own chair.

"I wanted to come by and discuss the incident in Waco, then assess your emergency protocols, in case something like that happens here."

Nodding, Larry said, "That's interesting. I was just thinking about all that. Here's what I think..." He proceeded to tell Ed about their departments and how inadequate he felt they were.

Sighing and shaking his head, he said, "If a significant event occurs, I know we'd have to call for outside help."

They continued discussing options, and began formulating a plan of action.

"I think you should call a town meeting and ask for volunteers to be ready in case of an emergency. We can send folks here to train *your* folks in basic first aid and disaster help. I hope y'all never have to use them, but I've always felt it's better to live on the side of caution."

Sheriff Clifton nodded. "That's a great idea. How about I get the word out, and we plan a meeting in a couple of weeks?"

"I was thinking sooner, but I guess a couple of weeks would be okay. I know our Homeland Security Department wants to train as many people as possible across the nation in disaster relief. We don't feel the threats will just go away. The terrorists have an agenda, and it involves killing as many infidels or Americans as they possibly can. Our job is to be on guard and nip their plans in the bud, while keeping collateral damage to a minimum."

Larry sighed. "We're living in uncertain times, that's for sure."

Changing the subject, Ed asked, "So, how's it going with the investigation concerning Christina's tormentor and the school fire?"

"Somehow, I feel they are connected, but I haven't gotten any solid leads to prove it. At this point, it's just a gut feeling."

Nodding, Ed said, "Well, I wouldn't rule out gut feelings. They're usually right to some degree."

"I've gotten several reports of break-ins over the past few months, along with Christina's incidences. Seems there may be a pattern developing. I just find it strange that some of these have come about, since Christina and her kids moved back to Alva."

"What kind of break-ins?"

"This is the odd thing. Seems like whoever breaks in, takes something, usually an insignificant item, then returns it, at a later date. I also got a call from the local vet, who stated that he's had several owners bring their dogs in because they were acting odd. He said, when he ran a blood chemistry on them, there were barbiturates present. I compared the break-in times with the vets report, and low and behold, they match up. Which brings me to the conclusion that whoever is breaking in comes prepared with drugged treats for the dogs."

"So it sounds like these were pre-meditated break-ins. How many are you talking about?" Ed asked, leaning forward in his chair.

"Over the past few months, there have been a dozen or so. Averages about once a week. According to my records however, I've had reports of break-ins dating back a couple of years."

"That's well before Christina and the kids came back." Ed said.

"Yes, but the increase in reported cases, and all the other incidences occurring in the past few months, leads me to think this is all related, somehow."

"How so?"

Larry chuckled, "Well, like I said, I don't have any substantial proof, but the timing just seems too coincidental."

"You could be right. Any word from your high school guy?"

Shaking his head, Larry said, "No, since school is out for the holiday, he hasn't had much contact with the students. I'm hoping by the time they return to classes, this will all be resolved." Pausing and pinching the bridge of his nose, he added, "At the rate we're going, I don't see that happening unless the perpetrator makes a mistake along the way."

"Well, if it's a kid, he probably will."

"We can always hope."

Larry asked, "How's Cindy doing?"

Smiling, Ed said, "She's okay. Just a concussion."

"She coming home today?"

"I think so. She said the doctor wants to run a couple more tests, however, because her white cell count was up. I'm not sure what that means, if anything. I plan to ask Christina about it."

Nodding, and rubbing the whiskers on his chin, Larry said, "Hopefully, it's nothing serious."

"Yeah."

CHAPTER 119

"Mom?" Linda called from the living room.

"I'm in the laundry room." Janet called back.

Linda found her mother folding clothes. Standing in the doorway she said, "Stacey just called and asked if I could come over for a while. Can I?"

Clenching her teeth, and gripping a towel she had in her hands, because she didn't want to take her daughter over to see Stacey, she forced herself to calmly ask, "Did she say what time?"

"No, but I imagine it's anytime. I can call and ask if you want me to."

"Well, why don't you call her back and ask? I want you to clean and organize your room and put your clothes away. When that's all done, if it's not too late, I'll take you." *If I'm lucky, you'll take all day and you won't have time to go.*

Smiling, Linda said, "Okay, I'll call her."

Janet stood in front of the dryer absently folding clothes while her mind recalled the mall incident. She had watched the news that morning, and was relieved to know the incident wasn't terrorist related. She thought about Jamie and his involvement in the school fire. When she hired him to break into Christina's house, she had no idea he would take his thrill seeking further, and endanger other people. The few times she had noticed him at church, he seemed like a nice enough kid. A little creepy, for sure. *What kid in their right mind broke into people's houses to steal something and then return it later on? Maybe I should break off my ties to him. If he does make good on his threat about doing something more risky, I don't want to be a part of that.*

She finished folding the towels, put another load in the washer and dryer, then went to find her business phone.

After an hour, Linda announced that her room was clean and she was ready to go over to Stacey's. Janet shook her head and sighed. Luck didn't seem to be on her side.

CHAPTER 120

Jamie felt the phone vibrating in his pocket. Retrieving it, he answered, "Hello?"

Taking a deep breath, and releasing it slowly to calm her nerves, Janet said, in a Mexican accent, "Jamie, I've been thinking, and I've come to the conclusion that I don't want to have any further contact with you. Your behavior has not only put yourself at risk, but others as well. It's one thing to break into people's houses, it's another thing to start a fire and endanger others."

"Who is this?" he asked, panic gripping his heart. "How do you know my name, and how did you get this number?"

"It doesn't matter who I am. The point is, I hired you to do a specific job, but you seem to have taken things into your own hands, and that has caused me to re-evaluate our business connection."

Silence ruled the moment, as he thought about the implications of what had been said.

"So, you're the lady that hired me to break into the Sander's house?"

Silence.

"Well, what makes you think I did the school thing?"

"Did you?"

"Why is that any of your business?"

Before speaking, Janet thought, *What if I've jumped to the wrong conclusion?* "Look, if you did set the fire at the school, you need to stop and think about your actions. You may think that kind of behavior is fun and exciting, but people got hurt, not to mention the thousands of dollars worth of damage it caused."

Jamie let out a loud sigh, and said, "Well, I will certainly take into consideration what you said. I will make no promises, however. This town needs some excitement. It needs waking up."

"Look, you need to be careful. I know who you are, and I can easily turn you over to the police if anything suspicious happens again."

"Lady, whoever you are, you need not concern yourself with what I do or don't do. If you want me to continue breaking into the Sander's home, I will, if not, it's no sweat off my brow. By the way, you still owe me for the last time."

Janet thought for a moment. "Why don't you cool it for now. If I decide I want you to re-start, I have your number. I will put the money in our usual spot."

"Today?"

"Yes, in about an hour or two."

"Okay."

Janet disconnected, and felt her heart race around her rib cage, as if doing a marathon in her chest. Her hands were shaking, as she put the phone back in the bottom of her purse. *When I drop Linda off at Stacey's, I'll go to the bank, drop the money off for Jamie, and dispose of the phone. Then I'll be done with this mess.*

Jamie put the cell-phone in his pocket, and let his mind revisit the conversation. He'd been hired by this mysterious voice over the phone a month ago, to invade the Sander's home. He had no idea why, but for fifty dollars a visit, he figured it was easy money. *Why have me stop now?* The whole school thing must have really made her paranoid, even though the two were unrelated. He had an idea as to whom was responsible for that.

He hadn't planned on revisiting the Sanders, until sometime in January, so he wasn't bothered that much with the request. He just wondered about the motive behind it.

Even though he wouldn't be receiving the extra money, he could still carry out his plan to surprise Alva on Christmas eve.

I wish I knew who the lady is behind this. Sighing, he returned to the task at hand, which was folding and stacking pizza boxes.

He had bigger plans to work on, and the less distractions, the better.

CHAPTER 121

When Christina finished her shift, she headed down to Cindy's room, and was surprised to see her fully clothed, and sitting in a chair, instead of the bed.

"Hey, girlfriend!" Cindy said as Christina walked in the room.

"Well, you certainly sound and look perky. What's the word from the doc?"

"He said my white blood cell count is still up, and my red blood cell count is low and that concerns him, but because everything else looks okay, he will send me home, but wants me to come back in for more blood work next week. If the numbers are still off, he may send me to some kind of specialist."

Christina nodded. "Well, hopefully this is just a fluke and you'll be back to normal soon."

Cindy nodded. "Yeah, I don't have time to be sick!"

Christina chuckled. "I know, with Christmas in a couple of days, who has time to be sick?"

"So, you think you can take me home?"

"Sure," Christina said. "Are you ready?"

"Yes, ma'am. I was just waiting for you to come down." She reached for the call button and a nurse appeared.

"Mrs. Murray, here are some last minute instructions. No heavy lifting or operating any machinery, and no driving for a few more days. The doctor would like to see you next Wednesday, to check your wound, and do more blood work. You need to call his office and make an appointment."

Cindy said, "Yes, ma'am."

"Okay, then, I need you to sign these papers, and you are free to go. I'll send an aid in with a wheelchair."

"That's okay, I can walk."

"I know, but it's hospital policy to take the patients to their car in a wheelchair."

Cindy made a face. "Well, that's weird, especially if they're okay to walk."

The nurse shrugged. "I know, but rules are rules."

Cindy rolled her eyes. "Okay."

Christina said, "I'll go pull the van up to the entrance, and meet you there."

Once Cindy was situated in the van, Christina said, "I was thinking that maybe you should stay with us tonight. Just to make sure you're okay to be on your own."

Cindy made a face. "Thank you for the offer, but I'd really like to go home and sleep in my own bed tonight. I'm feeling alright. No headache or dizziness to speak of, and Samara will be there, so I won't be alone."

Christina nodded. "I understand. We need to go by my house to pick up Samara and Sasha, so if you'd like to come in for a few minutes for a cup of coffee..."

Rubbing her eyes, Cindy said, "Any other time, I'd jump at the offer, but I'd really like to go home, take a long, hot shower, and get into my warm pajamas."

Christina reached over and patted Cindy's arm. "I do understand. I remember when I left the hospital, all I wanted to do was go home and relax and sleep in my own bed. Did Ed come by?"

"Yes, and he brought me this beautiful bouquet of flowers."

Christina smiled. "They are beautiful. Is he coming back by?"

"I think so. He said he had some business to take care of and he'd see me later, so I'm assuming he'll come by later."

After dropping Cindy, Samara and Sasha off, Christina went to Wal-Mart to get a few grocery items and check out their sale items. While debating whether she wanted a red or green tablecloth for the dining room, she looked up to see Mr. and Mrs. Conger, Eleanor's parents, standing a few feet down from her.

They glanced over at her and smiled.

Walking over and pulling Christina into a hug, Mrs. Conger said, "Christina, it's so nice to see you again." They hadn't seen each other since their last encounter at a restaurant in July.

Returning the hug, Christina said, "Likewise. How are you two doing?"

Smiling, and glancing over at Mr. Conger, Mrs. Conger said, "We're doing well. Al is on a new medication, which seems to be helping with his dementia, PTSD, and paranoid symptoms. How are the kiddos?"

"We're doing okay right now. Looking forward to Christmas."

"I heard about the school fire and your son's injuries. So, he's doing alright now?"

Christina nodded. "Yes, he gave us a bit of a scare, but he seems to be recovering nicely."

"Well, I'm so glad. Tom keeps Eleanor informed about events, and she keeps us informed, otherwise we wouldn't know what's going on. We hardly ever watch the news, and living so far out in the country, we don't talk to too many folks, so it's nice having someone keeping us up to date on issues."

Smiling and nodding, Christina asked, "So, will Eleanor and Tommy be over on Christmas?"

Nodding, she said, "Yes, they plan to come stay a couple of days."

After a few more moments of conversation, the three people said their good-byes, and Christina headed to the register to check out.

Christina had no idea that Mr. Conger had been behind the kidnapping incident involving her son. In fact, the only ones who knew, were Mrs. Conger and Eleanor, and they weren't talking. Mr. Conger had no recollection of the event, due to his dementia.

Standing in line, she overheard a couple of ladies talking about the bombings in Waco.

One woman, with a toddler on her hip, said, "I just hope no one does anything like that at our outlet mall, or anywhere around here for that matter."

The woman standing behind her, nodded and said, "Amen to that, sister!"

Christina thought, *I doubt if anyone would target Alva. Maybe in one of the major cities, where there are more businesses and people, but Alva? Highly doubtful.*

She had no idea that two rows over, a young man was purchasing items to do the very thing everyone feared.

CHAPTER 122

Christina was grateful that she didn't have to work on Sunday—thanks to one of the part-time nurses. As she and the children were listening to the announcements of upcoming events in the church, they were joined by Aaron and Sammie. Christina knew he had expressed interest in attending their services, but wasn't sure if he would be able to follow through. When he slid in beside her, her heart did a drum-roll.

She glanced in his direction, occasionally, during the pastor's sermon, and noticed he was hanging on every word. At the end of the service, when the congregation was invited to stand and sing the Hallelujah chorus from Handel's Messiah, she noticed him wiping tears from his eyes. Her heart was touched beyond words.

After the final prayer and dismissal, several people came up and welcomed him and Sammie. As they were leaving, he invited Christina and her children out to lunch.

"There's a new restaurant downtown, that just opened this weekend, called The Thunderbird, and I'd like to try it. Sammie and I would love it if y'all joined us."

Christina glanced at her children, who were all nodding their approval.

"We'd love to. Where is it located?"

"It's on the south-side of the courthouse. You can't miss it. It has a big Thunderbird logo on the overhang."

Brad said, "Yeah, I remember seeing the sign the other day, when we went to the post office. It looks pretty cool from the outside."

Smiling and nodding, Christina said, "Okay, we'll meet y'all there."

Sammie squealed with delight, which elicited a chuckle from everyone.

Christina had to park her van a block away from the entrance. They weren't the only ones willing to try out the new restaurant.

The wait for a seat was well worth it. There was a nice variety of food to choose from, and each one in their party chose something different, so everyone could have a sample of various entrees.

After trying a bite of Christina's steak, and Brad's garlic mashed potatoes, Stacey said, "Oh! This is all so good!"

As they were enjoying their meal, and each others company, Christina looked up to see Janet and Linda being seated at a table nearby.

She leaned over to Stacey and whispered, "Linda and her mom just walked in."

Stacey looked around, spotted them, and said, "I'm gonna go say hi."

When Linda saw Stacey approaching, she stood and reached out for a hug. Stacey pointed out where they were sitting, and Janet looked over and did a finger wave, surprise registering on her face.

Why is Dr. Carmichael there with them? It's not enough that she stole Dr. Dawson from me, now she's trying to steal any chance I may have with Dr. Carmichael? Why are these men attracted to her? What could she possibly have, that I don't?

Reaching over, and touching Janet's arm, Linda said, "Mom?"

"What?" She responded harshly.

"You okay?'

Janet nodded, and noticed the waitress standing beside Linda with a notepad and pen in her hands.

Mother and daughter placed their orders, and try as she might, Janet had trouble focusing on what Linda was saying. She found her eyes wandering across the room, wondering what was being said at Christina's table.

CHAPTER 123

During the drive home, the Sander's children discussed their impression of Dr. Carmichael and Sammie.

Stacey said, "Sammie is such a cutie."

Nicky added, "Yeah, she didn't make any noise during the service. I was afraid she'd get bored, and start complaining or something, but she didn't."

"Mom?"

"Yes, Brad."

"Did you notice how emotional Dr. Carmichael got when we sang the Hallelujah Chorus?"

Nodding, Christina said, "Yes, he said he'd never heard the Hallelujah chorus before, and that's what he pictures Heaven to sound like."

Nicky asked, "So Brad, did Heaven sound like that when you were there?"

Brad chuckled. "No, not really. I remember, when I was in God's throne room, hearing something like millions of whispering voices, but when it was just the two of us, it was pretty quiet."

"Wow!" Nicky said in awe. "I wish I could visit Heaven."

"Hopefully, not any time soon," said Stacey.

"Yes." Christina agreed. "One trip to Heaven is plenty enough for this family to handle."

Nicky shrugged. "Well, I'd want to come right back, like Brad did."

Christina smiled and shook her head.

"Okay, change of subject. I have to work tomorrow, and on Christmas Day. Do y'all want to do anything special on those two evenings?"

After a few moments of silence, Brad said, "Well, we already opened our gifts with Grandma and Grandpa, so I'm not sure what else we could do."

"Would y'all be interested in watching a couple of the old classic films about Christmas?"

"Like that one with Scrooge?" Stacey asked.

Christina nodded, "And White Christmas, and possibly a couple others."

Nicky leaned forward in his seat and asked, "Haven't we already seen those films? Seems like we watch them every year."

Christina nodded, "Yes Nicky. We watch a few of them every year. That's why they're called classics."

Brad said, "Could we rent a couple of different movies to watch during the day while you're at work, then we can watch those classic movies with you in the evening?"

Christina smiled and nodded. "Okay, I'll drive over to the movie rental place and y'all can each pick a movie."

CHAPTER 124

Driving home from the restaurant, Janet was so preoccupied with thoughts of Christina and Dr. Carmichael, that she drove right through a stop sign, and into an oncoming truck. Her last conscious thoughts were; *Why is Linda screaming?* And, *I forgot to get rid of that phone!*

Christina had just pulled onto the street from the movie rental building, when she had to stop suddenly, as an ambulance and police car whizzed by.

Pulling out after them, she said, "Geeze, I wonder where they're going?"

A few blocks later, she knew.

"Mom!" Stacey screamed, "That's Linda's car! That's her standing by the ambulance! Stop, Mom!"

Before Christina had come to a complete stop, Stacey was out of the van, and running towards her friend.

"Stacey!" Christina called, to no avail.

Brad and Nicky threw open the van door and ran after their sister. Christina parked her van by the curb, and headed in the direction her children had run.

Looking around, she spotted the ambulance her children had made a beeline for. Emergency vehicles, with their multicolored lights flashing, lined the street, and police cars blocked the cross streets, as officers re-routed vehicles. EMTs, firemen, and police milled about, as a crowd of people gathered along the sidewalks, and in nearby yards, to get a glimpse of the two-vehicle accident.

As she approached the distraught girl, Christina noticed she was holding her right arm, and had blood running down her face. The EMT was trying to assess her injuries, but she kept trying to run towards the automobile smashed against the truck. Brad, Stacey and Nicky were talking to her, and assisting the EMT in holding her still. Christina followed Linda's line of vision and inhaled sharply. Janet's car, which was barely recognizable, looked like a pop can that had been stepped on. The EMTs and firemen were working frantically to remove the metal trapping her.

"Oh, my goodness!" Christina said, as she felt her knees buckle. She reached out and steadied herself against a nearby ambulance. *There is no way anyone can survive that!* Taking in a deep breath and releasing it slowly, she forcibly calmed herself, and went into nurse mode. She spotted the chief of police, and walked towards him.

"Larry, is there anything I can do?" She asked calmly, glancing over at the driver of the truck.

Surprise registering on his face, he asked, "Christina, what are you doing here?"

She explained how and why she was there, then asked, "Is she alive?"

Larry shook his head and sighed. "It doesn't look good, Christina. She's alive, but I don't know how much longer. Thankfully, she's unconscious. The firemen have been working for several minutes to cut through the roof and door. All we can do is pray."

Christina nodded. She could do that. Taking a few calming breaths, she forced herself to push her emotions aside, and tackle the crisis at hand.

Walking over to the ambulance, she was almost knocked over by Linda, who came running into her arms, the EMT and Sander's children following close behind.

Screaming and crying hysterically, Linda said, "Please tell me my mom's not dead!"

Christina held her close and whispered, "She's not dead."

Forcing her back, to get a close look at her face, Christina said, "They'll get her out, and take her to the hospital. Right now, we need to get you to the hospital, to be checked. I'll come with you in the ambulance, if you'd like." Looking at Brad, she said, "Will you please take Stacey and Nicky home?"

She was met with protests from all the children. Holding her hand up, she said, "Alright Brad, y'all can come to the hospital, for a little while."

The Sanders kids nodded, and after giving Linda hugs, headed to the van.

Christina climbed in the ambulance, took Linda's hand, and held it during the ride to the hospital.

What will happen to this child if her mother dies? She wondered. Then she began to pray.

Once the EMTs were able to start an IV in Linda's arm, they gave her a sedative, to calm her enough for them to assess and begin treating her injuries. It was evident that she had a large, deep gash on her forehead, caused from hitting the window, and a broken arm, caused by hitting the door handle. Those were the obvious injuries. Internal injuries were always a possibility.

Christina felt a strange disconnected calmness enfold her. Everything seemed to be moving in slow motion, until they arrived at the hospital, then she was slammed back into reality, and all her senses were on high alert.

She exited the ambulance, and reassured Linda that she would be waiting for her when the doctor was finished assessing her injuries.

Walking into the waiting area, she was met by her three children.

"Any word on Linda?" Brad asked.

Christina shook her head. "It may be a while."

Stacey, wiping her eyes asked, "Has Linda's mom arrived yet?"

"Not yet. Hopefully, she'll be here soon."

Nicky asked, "How bad was Linda hurt?"

Christina led her children to a waiting area, and they all sat. Sighing, she said, "Well, it looks like her arm is broken, and she's got a big gash on her forehead, but I don't know if there are other injuries. I'm sure Dr. Carmichael will do some x-rays and other test, to determine if there are more."

Stacey asked, "What will happen to Linda, if her mom dies?"

Shaking her head, Christina said, "I don't know. I don't know Janet well enough to know if she has relatives. If she doesn't, well, I hope we can keep her."

"You mean, like adopt her?" Nicky asked.

Christina twirled a ringlet of hair, and said, "Maybe, but I was thinking I could just be her guardian. I'd have to ask a lawyer about that."

Brad asked, "Do you know any lawyers?"

"I know the one in Dallas. I don't know if he handles that kind of stuff, but he probably knows someone who does. We'll have to cross that bridge when, or if, we get there."

Christina stood and walked towards the emergency bay, as she heard the ambulance arrive. She inhaled sharply when she saw Janet's bloodied, swollen, unrecognizable face, as the ER staff whisked her into a cubicle, and closed the curtain. Christina listened, as orders were being shouted.

Turning, she almost ran into Dr. Carmichael.

"Christina, I'm surprised to see you here."

She explained her presence.

Looking around the room, he asked, "Is there anyone here for Linda or Janet Washburn?"

Christina shook her head. "I don't think Janet has any relatives around here. So far, we're the only ones here for her and Linda."

Scratching his head, he said, "Well, I guess I'll just have to go ahead and treat Linda, without her mother's consent."

"If I may ask, what are the extent of Linda's injuries?"

Shaking his head, he said, "She has a broken arm, a gash on her forehead and some internal bleeding, probably from the seat belt. I'll need to do surgery to assess the amount of internal damage."

"May I see her, before you take her in?"

Nodding, he said, "I don't see why not. She's in one of the treatment rooms down the hall. The surgical team is preparing her."

Reaching out to touch his arm, Christina said, "Thanks, Aaron. I know she's in good hands."

Christina told her children she'd be right back, and headed towards the cubicle Linda was in. The girl looked small and fragile lying on the gurney. Several nurses were present, preparing her for surgery. Christina walked over and took Linda's hand. With tears running into her ears, Linda said, "I'm scared, Mrs. Sanders."

Christina patted her hand. "I know, honey, but you're in good hands, and you'll be out and about, before you know it."

Shaking her head, she said, "I'm not scared for me, I'm scared for my mom. What if she dies? What am I going to do?"

"Oh, Linda. I'm sure she'll be okay. You just concentrate on your own healing. In the meantime, we'll be praying for you both."

She whispered, "Thank you," as she gave into the sedation being administered through her IV.

Returning to her children, Christina said, "I think it's going to be a long wait before we can see Linda or Janet. Why don't I run y'all home, and I'll come back?"

Glancing at the wall clock, Brad said, "It's almost seven. Can we go somewhere, and get a bite to eat, on the way home?"

Glancing at the other two children, who were nodding, she said, "Sure, what do y'all want?"

Stacey said, "How about Pizza Hut?"

"Yeah!" The boys said, simultaneously.

Stacey added, "We haven't had pizza from there in a while."

After sharing a slice of pizza with the kids before dropping them off at home, Christina returned to the hospital waiting room, and was approached by the sheriff.

Removing his hat, running a hand through his hair, and replacing it, he said, "Hi, Christina. What are you doing here?"

She said, "Janet and Linda Washburn don't have any relatives that I know of, so I wanted to stand in that gap for them. I'm sure Linda would like to see a familiar face, when she wakes up."

Nodding, he motioned to a group of chairs. They sat.

"Well, that's very nice of you. From what I've heard, you and Janet aren't on the best of terms."

Christina sighed. "Janet is a difficult person to know on a personal level. I believe she has trust issues, and is very cautious about what she says. Very rarely do we talk about anything but work, and then it's about our daughters."

"Your daughters?"

"Linda and Stacey have developed a friendship this year, and even though it's been rocky these past few weeks, I think they still like each other."

Rubbing his chin, he said, "Well, I had Mrs. Ferguson, the nursing supervisor, look at Janet's employment application, and there was no mention of family, other than Linda—not even a name of a contact, in case of an emergency. Looks like y'all may be the only ones who care about them."

Christina rubbed her forehead. "That's sad. I don't know what I'd do without my friends and family. I can't imagine having neither."

Larry stood. "I guess I'd better get back to the station, and begin filling out paperwork."

Christina reached out and touched his arm. "Wait, can I ask you a few questions first?"

He sat again. "Sure, shoot."

They discussed the school fire, the shenanigans pertaining to her family, the bombing at the mall in Waco, and the possibility of anything like that occurring in Alva.

Larry removed his hat and held it in his hands, twirling it as he spoke. "Well, I wish I had better news for you," he began, "but, unfortunately, I don't. We don't have any suspects in the fire or the break-ins, and according to Ed, they're closing in on suspects for the bombing in Waco. As far as anything like that happening here, well, I guess it's possible, but highly improbable."

She nodded and sighed. "It feels like we're living from one crisis to the next, with hardly a break in-between."

"Yep, seems that way. Something's gotta break soon, I think. I'm not a very religious man, myself, but I know of many folks who are praying for God's intervention."

Christina smiled. "Well, I do believe in the power of prayer. It seems that God doesn't allow injustices to go on forever. There is always a day of reckoning. Maybe not as soon as we'd like, but in His time."

Nodding, he said, "Yeah, that does seem to be true."

A nurse from the ER approached. "Sheriff Clifton?"

He stood. "Yes, ma'am?"

"When Mrs. Washburn was brought in, I went through her purse to see if there was any medical information there, and I didn't find any, but I remembered you saying that you wanted to go through her purse to see if there was any information about her family. I just remembered and thought I'd better bring it to you, before you left."

She handed the purse to the sheriff.

"Thank you, ma'am."

He sat again, and opened the bag.

Christina asked, "Do you want me to leave?"

He looked up and shook his head. "Nah, you can stay."

Remembering scenes from a police show drama, she asked, "You don't need a search warrant or something?"

Shaking his head, he said, "In some cases, but since Janet is incapacitated, I can go ahead and take a look."

She watched, as he emptied the contents on the chair next to him.

He sorted through several items: gum wrappers, loose change, pens, scraps of paper, receipts from various stores, make-up bag, and her wallet. In it, he found various credit cards, health insurance cards for her and Linda, pictures, license, receipts and a key. Removing the key, he looked it over. It was small, and had a number imprinted on one side—A04.

Setting it aside, he continued his search. He found a bank withdrawal receipt for fifty dollars, dated for yesterday. He set that aside with the key.

Christina watched with growing curiosity, as he continued looking through the wallet. He found another slip of paper with names and phone numbers—he added that to his small collection. Finding nothing else of interest in the wallet, he sorted through the pile and came across two cell-phones. "Now why would she have two cell-phones?" he mumbled.

Christina said, "Maybe one belongs to Linda."

Nodding, he set them in his growing pile.

Not finding anything else of interest, he returned the contents to the purse, and put it aside. He then focused his attention on the pile he had set aside.

Scrolling through one cell-phone, he concluded it was her personal one, containing numbers and texts from Linda and co-workers. The next phone, however, piqued his curiosity. It contained one phone number and a few texts. He read them and said, "Well, this is interesting."

"What?" asked Christina leaning over to get a glimpse of the screen.

Scrolling to the top, he began reading each sent and received message. He pulled out a notebook from his pocket, and wrote down the dates the messages popped up on. Carefully reading each one, he shook his head and whispered, "Janet, what have you got yourself involved in?"

Unable to read the texts, Christina asked, "What do you mean, Larry?"

Closing the phone, he shook his head and said, "I think I'll have to do some digging into Janet's life. I can't go into detail now, as this is becoming a police investigation."

Christina, expressing surprise, said, "A police investigation? Why?"

Putting the remainder of the contents back in the purse, he stood and said, "I'm going to take these with me and do a more thorough search through them. I'll go inform the ER nurses that I'm taking the purse."

Christina stood. "Can you explain any of this to me?"

Shaking his head, the police chief said, "Sorry. I may be able to, once I understand it myself. Suffice to say, Janet may be involved in some shady business."

Christina put her hand to her mouth. "Oh my goodness!"

CHAPTER 125

"Hey Jamie, come over here."

Jamie finished folding a box and walked over to his boss, who motioned for him to enter his office.

"Yes, sir?"

"I've been thinking about what you asked me the other day. About possibly buying the Pizza Hut car."

Jamie nodded.

"I've observed that you ride your bike in, no matter the weather."

Jamie shrugged and nodded.

"You've been an excellent employee, and I've never heard a single negative word about you from our customers."

Jamie bit his bottom lip, wondering where this was going.

"That being said, I've decided to give you the Pizza Hut car."

Jamie's jaw dropped, unsure if he heard the man correctly.

"Excuse me, sir. Did you say "give", as in I don't have to pay for it?"

The manager chuckled and patted Jamie on the back.

"Yes, son. I'm going to give you the car."

"Why?" Jamie had never been given anything, since his mother had died five years ago. He wasn't sure he could truly trust this man's word. He had learned through the years that there was always a catch. He waited for the, "if, and, or but" that usually followed such a declaration. He didn't hear it, so he asked, "So, what's the catch, if I may be so bold in asking?"

Again, the man chuckled. "There's no catch, son. When you asked me the other day, I said I needed to think about it, and I did. I also prayed and talked to my wife about my decision. I feel God wants me to give you the car. It's beginning to show a little wear and tear, and I think a new one for the business would be a good investment."

Jamie couldn't help but grin. He reached out and shook his boss' hand.

"Thank you so much, sir. I can't believe it! I was just thinking today that I may have to quit, because it is getting too cold to be out on my bike. I've been saving money, but It'll be a while before I can actually purchase a car."

The owner smiled. "Well, son, I was concerned about that as well, and being that I don't want to lose such a wonderful employee, the motive behind this may be a bit selfish."

"How do we go about this, sir?"

"I've already drawn up the paperwork, so all you need to do is sign them."

"Really? That's it?"

Nodding, the man turned a pile of papers around for Jamie to read and sign.

"You understand that you'll be responsible for the gas, maintenance and insurance?"

Jamie nodded. "As I said, I have some money set aside, but I may have to pick up more hours."

"Right, I've also decided to give you a dollar an hour raise. I know that doesn't sound like much, but if you work more hours, and get more tips, you should be able to make a fair chunk of change."

"Yeah, thanks." *How am I going to explain this to my dad? He probably won't believe me, and think I stole the car.*

"Sir, could I get copies of these papers? My dad will want to look them over."

"Absolutely. You think your dad would want to come in and talk to me?"

"Maybe." *Highly doubtful.* "I'll ask."

After signing the last paper, his boss said, "I'll get these processed, and then you can take possession of your car."

"How long do you think it'll take?"

"With the holidays upon us, a few days. Probably between Christmas and New Year."

Jamie nodded. He could wait.

Lying in bed that night, recounting his day, Jamie realized that he'd forgotten to go to the post office. *Tomorrow,* he thought, as he drifted off to sleep.

CHAPTER 126

Sheriff Clifton entered his office and shut the door. Pouring the contents of Janet's purse on his desk, he searched through them once, again, more thoroughly. Not finding anything different, he sat back in his chair and steepled his fingers, thinking.

Picking up the small key, he pocketed it, stood, donned his jacket and told his secretary he'd be back soon.

Arriving at the post office, he found the mailbox that went with the key. Opening it, he found an envelope containing five tens. There was no name on the envelope and no note in with the money.

"Huh, I wonder who this is for?" He mumbled.

Placing the envelope back in the box, he thought about hanging around to see if anyone came to claim the money. Deciding he didn't want to tie up his day, he radioed one of his deputies, and appraised him of the situation.

Before signing off, he added, "So, when you see someone arrive, follow them in. If they go to the mailbox in question, bring them in for questioning. In the meantime, I will send a text telling this person that the money is in the box."

Arriving back at the precinct, he went to his office, found the phone and sent the text. He thought about calling the person, but was concerned about spooking him or her. He decided to wait, until they had someone in custody, then make the call. If that person's phone rang, he'd know they had the right one.

Then what? He wondered. He couldn't very well question Janet, at least not yet. He felt in his gut that he was on the right track—to where, he wasn't exactly sure.

CHAPTER 127

Christina stood when Dr. Carmichael entered the waiting room, wearing his surgical scrubs and hairnet. He motioned to the chairs and they sat.

"How's Linda doing?" Christina asked.

"The surgery went well. She had a small tear in her bowel which was easily repairable, and I ended up giving her a unit of blood. I've started her on IV antibiotics, to counteract any infection in her gut."

Christina nodded as she processed the information.

"May I see her?"

"She's in recovery now, but when she wakes, I'll have her moved to the Pediatric floor, and you may see her then."

"How's Janet doing?"

Sighing, he said, "Last I heard, she was still in surgery."

"She must have been injured pretty severely."

Nodding, he said, "Seems so. I sure hope she pulls through, for Linda's sake. From what I gather, they only have each other."

"Yeah, I don't know her very well. She doesn't share much at work."

Standing, he said, "Well, I need to get back and check on my patient. Are you planning on staying the night?"

Shaking her head, Christina said, "I don't think so, but if Linda wakes and wants me to stay, I will. I'd hate for her to be alone."

Nodding, he said, "I don't think she'll be aware of much. I've got her on some heavy duty meds that will keep her sedated 'till morning."

"So, she may not even be aware of my presence?'

Shaking his head, he said, "Probably not."

Standing and stretching, she said, "Well, I'd still like to see her. Sometimes, when people are heavily sedated, they can hear, they just can't respond. I want her to know that I'm available."

"That's nice of you, Christina."

"I hope if my kids are ever in a similar situation, someone will be around for them."

Nodding, he said, "Yes, I'd feel the same way, if it was Sammie." Checking his watch, he said, "I really need to go. I'll see you around."

CHAPTER 128

Sheriff Clifton jumped when he heard the buzzing of the confiscated phone. Picking it up, he read the text message. *Thanx. wl get aftr wrk.*

Smiling, he said, "Gotcha!"

He radioed his deputy, and told him he'd received a text back, and the person in question should be picking up the envelope soon.

"Let me know, as soon as you have that person in custody."

Leaning back in his chair, the sheriff thought about Janet and the possibility of her involvement in Christina's misfortunes.

He had heard rumors concerning Janet's resentment of Christina because of the job situation. She felt she had been unjustly passed over for the nursing position, when Christina was hired.

Huh, I wonder if she is still harboring those feelings? If so, would she act on them? When she was at the Thanksgiving dinner at Christina's, she seemed fine. Maybe she's just a good actress.

He scrolled through the text messages, again, and had the feeling that she and the unknown recipient were working together to somehow rattle Christina's emotional security. *The one text mentioned taking a picture and vase. Christina mentioned a picture being taken and returned. I should ask her about a vase. Why would Janet hire someone to break in and take things, only to return them later? Come to think of it, Janet could have also planted the heparin bottle and note in the locker. She certainly had motive and opportunity.*

He scrolled back through to the very first message sent on Thanksgiving day, and was shocked at what he saw. *Oh, my goodness! She did send Christina that threatening message on Thanksgiving!* He rubbed his eyes and massaged his forehead, as he thought of the implications.

He called Christina.

She heard her phone ringing in the bottom of her purse. Digging through it, she answered on the last ring.

The sheriff introduced himself, and asked if she was missing some kind of vase.

"Well, that's a weird question. Why are you asking?"

"I need to know."

She thought for a moment, then said, "As a matter of fact, I am. I noticed it missing when I was cleaning up after Thanksgiving. I just assumed one of the kids had taken it. I never gave it another thought. Why are you asking about that?"

"I can't go into detail, but it has to do with the recent break-ins. I think whoever took your stuff has been breaking into other people's homes. Seems he or she takes an item, then returns it at a later date. Weirdest thing I've ever heard of."

"That is weird. What purpose would that serve?"

Sighing, he said, "I guess it's just a thrill seeking act. Most thieves keep whatever they've taken. This person is taking a double risk of being caught by returning it." Pausing, he said, "I guess I could see how that would pump up one's adrenalin."

"Well, now I want to know if my vase has been returned. I'm going to call Brad and have him look."

"You know Christina, you mentioned that your dog had been acting funny off and on the past couple of weeks. I was wondering if his sickness corresponded with the times your items went missing, and were returned."

"Do you think those are related?"

"I talked to the local vet, and he said there were several folks who brought their sick animals in, and after doing blood work, found barbiturates present. Those appointments correspond with the dates of the break-ins. I think the perpetrator drugs the pets, mostly dogs, so the owners won't be alerted."

Christina put her hand to her chest. "That sounds possible. Benji's been acting weird off and on lately. Let me check through my journal and I'll let you know."

Clearing his throat, he said, "Well, I need to make more calls, so why don't you think about that and talk to Brad? I'll call you back in a little while."

Nodding, she said, "Sure, I'll talk to you later."

Hoping to catch her before she disconnected, he said, "Wait, how's the girl doing?"

"She's in recovery right now. I hope to see her in a little while, before I head home. Janet is still in surgery, as far as I know."

"She's still in surgery? What's it been? About three hours now?"

Sighing, she said, "Yeah, her injuries must have been pretty serious."

"Well, considering the condition of the car, and how long it took them to get her out, I can see how it could be serious. I just hope she pulls through."

Christina blew out air and said, "Yeah, thank goodness for airbags. They both could have been killed."

Larry said, "I'm surprised the girl wasn't hurt worse than she was. It looks like Janet turned the car so she got the full impact of the collision, thus minimizing the damage on the passenger side."

Imagining how Janet must have reacted right before the collision, Christina said, "The protective maternal instinct is strong."

"Yes, it is, even on a subconscious level."

After a pause, Larry said, "I'm surprised the driver of the truck was so lucky. He just got a few cuts from the flying glass, and he was bruised from the seat belt and air bag, but other than that, he walked away."

"Yeah, I heard his truck was totaled, though. Who was at fault?"

Larry sighed. "I hate to say it, but, Janet ran right through the stop sign."

Twisting a ringlet of hair around her finger, Christina said, "Oh, man. I'm so glad no one was killed."

Nodding, Larry said, "Yes, I'm thankful for that." After a pause, he said, "Well, I'll call you later."

"Right, talk to you later."

As she sat waiting for permission to see Linda, Christina closed her eyes and thought back to when Benji had acted strangely. She was so focused on remembering, that she jumped when her phone rang.

Pulling it out of her pocket, she saw that it was Cindy.

"Hey, Cindy."

"Hey, yourself. What are you doing?"

Christina brought her up on the news about Linda and Janet.

"Are they going to be okay?"

Sighing, Christina said, "Well, I'm pretty sure Linda will recover because she wasn't injured as severely, but I don't know about Janet. She's been in surgery going on four hours now."

"Geeze, how long are you staying at the hospital?"

"I plan to visit Linda when she wakes up, then probably wait and see how Janet's doing, then I'll head home."

"That could be hours."

Nodding, Christina said, "Yeah, I hope not, but I don't feel right about leaving. They have no one else here for them. Besides, I kinda promised Linda I'd be here when she woke."

"Is there anything I can do? Want me to come sit with you?"

Christina smiled. "Thanks, but you just got out of the hospital, yourself. I think it best, if you just stay home and continue to heal."

"I feel fine. In fact, I was thinking about going in to work tomorrow. Mary will be swamped with last minute Christmas shoppers."

"I don't know if that's a good idea. But you know yourself better than I. Just promise me that, if you get tired or develop a headache, you'll go home."

After a pause, Cindy said, "Alright, but I think I'll be okay."

Christina said, "I just remembered that you have that big ol' bandage on your head. What are you going to do about that?"

Giggling, Cindy said, "I have a Santa hat that fits perfectly over it. No one will even know I have a bandage."

Sighing, Christina said, "Cindy, you're something else."

As she was saying her good-bye to Cindy, a nurse approached and asked if she was waiting to see Linda Washburn. She nodded.

"She's awake now, if you'd like to see her."

Putting the phone in her purse, she grabbed her coat and followed after the nurse, who led her to the recovery room. Pulling the curtain back, Christina stepped over and took Linda's hand. Linda opened her eyes, and focusing on Christina, smiled.

"You're still here?" She whispered.

Christina nodded, fighting back tears. "I told you I'd be here when you woke up."

"How's my mom?"

"The last I heard, she was doing okay."

Linda nodded. "I hope I can see her soon."

"I'm sure, when she's awake, y'all can see each other. Right now, you just need to focus on healing."

Linda yawned and nodded. "I'm very sleepy."

"The doctor wants you to sleep so your body can heal quicker."

Nodding and closing her eyes, Linda said, "Okay."

Christina stood by the bed a few more minutes as Linda gave in to a drug induced sleep.

As she turned to leave, she almost ran into Dr. Carmichael.

"Oh, excuse me!"

Surprise registering on his face, he asked, "Christina, why are you still here?"

"I didn't want Linda to wake up, without a familiar face close by. I think that would be very scary for a child."

Nodding, he said, "Well, I'm glad you stuck around. Even though she may not remember much, she'll know that you were here for her."

Christina smiled and nodded.

Walking over to his patient, Dr. Carmichael said, "She was one lucky little girl, even with the broken arm, and small tear in her bowel. It could have been so much worse."

Nodding, Christina asked, "So, have you heard anything about Janet? Is she out of surgery yet?"

Shaking his head, he said, "When I finish here, I'll check. I'd like to know as well."

After checking Linda's vital signs, he went to the nurses' station and made a phone call.

Smiling, he said, "Well, she's out of surgery, and headed to recovery."

"How is she?"

"Dr. Harrison said it will be touch and go for the next twenty-four hours."

Christina sighed and shook her head. "This poor family. Guess they'll be spending Christmas in the hospital."

"Yeah, seems so."

Rubbing her eyes, Christina said, "I have to work on Christmas, so I'll come by and spend some time with them."

Nodding, Dr. Carmichael said, "Once they're both out of danger, I'm going to put them in the same room. If possible, they should be together on Christmas."

Smiling and nodding, Christina said, "That'd be awesome! I just hope they're alert enough to enjoy the day."

"Well, it's Sunday night, so hopefully, by Tuesday, they'll be more alert."

Looking at the sleeping child, Christina said, "I guess we'd better do some heavy praying."

Patting Linda's hand, Dr. Carmichael said, "Yeah, I know I will be."

Gathering her belongings, Christina said, "I'm gonna head on home. I have to work tomorrow."

"You're working Christmas Eve?"

"Yep, lucky me." She said with a grin. "By the way, Aaron, what are you and Sammie doing for Christmas?"

Leaning against the wall, he said, "We're going to spend some time at my folks, then head over to spend time with Tabitha's folks. What are you and your kids planning to do?"

Sighing, Christina said, "Well, since I have to work both days, we'll probably watch movies in the evenings. Even though we opened gifts, when my in-laws were here, I have a few surprises left for the kids."

"That's nice. Holidays are kind of bittersweet for me. I miss my wife, but I have Sammie, so I have to put on a happy face for her."

Christina nodded. "Yeah, I know that feeling."

"Of course you do. I'm sorry. I forgot you lost your husband a couple of years ago as well."

Leaning against the bed, Christina said, "You know, people say as time passes, it gets easier emotionally, but after two years, I haven't found that to be true. I miss David as much now as I did last year." Shrugging, she added, "I guess it will get easier and less sad as time passes, but I don't think that longing, that yearning, for their presence ever diminishes."

Nodding, Dr. Carmichael said, "My feelings exactly. I guess we can gain some comfort in knowing that they're in Heaven waiting for us."

"Yeah, there is that."

CHAPTER 129

Walking in the backdoor, Christina was met by Stacey, who inquired of Linda and Janet's condition.

"When I left Linda, she was sleeping. Dr. Carmichael thinks she will recover from her injuries. As far as Mrs. Washburn, I don't know."

"Why?" Stacey asked, worry etched on her face.

Sighing and shaking her head, Christina reached out and pulled her daughter into a hug.

"She was just wheeled into the recovery room when I left."

"Wow! She must have been hurt pretty bad, if she just got out of surgery."

"Yeah, she was in surgery at least five or six hours. Sometimes, when there are broken bones to set, internal injuries to repair, and all the blood tests and x-rays and such, a person can be in surgery around ten to twelve hours."

Stacey's eyes filled with tears.

"Oh, my goodness! Those doctors and nurses have got to be exhausted! And Mrs. Washburn. How can she be under anesthetic so long? Wouldn't that be bad for her?"

Christina hugged Stacey and stroked her hair.

"Bless your heart, for being so concerned. The doctors and nurses usually have a second shift come in, after about five hours, and the anesthetic they use these days is much safer than what was used years ago. There are so many monitors and such, that it's rare for anyone to suffer long term effects from being under so long."

Stacey nodded and pulled away. Wiping her eyes she asked, "Can we go see Linda tomorrow?"

Christina nodded. "I have to work tomorrow, but when I get off, I'll come get y'all. Hopefully by then, she'll be more alert and her mom will be out of danger."

Stacey hugged her mom again. "Thanks, Mom."

"For what?"

"Oh, for just being you. I'm so glad you're my mom."

"Oh, honey. I'm thankful to have you for a daughter."

Nicky walked into the kitchen, and noticing his mom and sister, cleared his throat, and asked, "Am I interrupting something?"

Stacey pulled him into the hug. "Nah," she said, "we were just having a hug."

Grinning, he called Brad. Brad came sauntering in, and the two siblings pulled him into the hug. "Now," Nicky said, "we can have a real family hug."

After a minute, everyone disengaged. "Well, that was unexpected." Brad said, causing everyone to giggle.

CHAPTER 130

Lying in bed, thinking about the day and how it had turned out so differently than anticipated, Christina heard a light rapping on her door.

"Yes?" She called out.

Stacey opened the door and stuck her head in.

"Mom, can I come in?"

Christina patted the spot next to her on the king-sized bed.

"Sure, Babe. Come on in."

Stacey crawled up next to her mom and stretched out beside her, resting her head on her chest.

"What's wrong, honey?" Christina asked.

Stacey sighed. "I can't help but wonder what'll happen to Linda, if her mom dies. What if she doesn't have any other family? Will she have to go into foster care?"

Kissing the top of Stacey's head, Christina twirled a ringlet of hair, as she contemplated her answer.

"I don't know the answers to those questions. I would hope she can stay with us, while her family is sought. I just don't know how the system works. I just pray her mom survives, and we won't have to cross any of those bridges."

Stacey wiped her eyes and sighed. "I wonder why God allows things like this to happen?"

Christina nodded. "Yeah. Me too." Looking at the clock, Christina asked, "You want to sleep with me?"

"Could I?" Stacey asked with a smile.

Christina lifted the covers, and Stacey crawled in. Within a few minutes, she was deeply asleep, as Christina lay awake praying for Janet and Linda.

CHAPTER 131

Jamie sat on the floor of his bedroom, surrounded by the paraphernalia he needed for pulling off his big Christmas surprise for the folks of Alva. If he played his cards right, no one would ever suspect him of being the perpetrator. As he assembled the items, he recalled the events of the day.

He could hardly believe his boss had offered him a car. *How am I going to explain that to my dad?* The man firmly believed that no one gave anyone anything without some kind of string attached. The man was so distrusting, he wouldn't believe the truth, if it came and slapped him in the face. He could picture his dad storming into the Pizza Hut, and confronting the manager, without any regard for the customers or other employees. *I'm gonna have to warn my boss about the inevitable confrontation.*

Feeling exhaustion creeping in and sapping his energy, he pushed the finished items deep under his bed. His dad never came into his room, but one couldn't be too careful. He had watched enough TV shows to know that. How many times had a person thought he had gotten away with something, only to be caught because of a careless oversight? He knew his dad would jump to conclusions, and quite honestly, he wasn't in the mood for a beating. There was no reasoning with the man once the yelling and hitting began.

As he was dropping off to sleep, he heard the familiar door slamming, grunting and coughing noises his dad did every time he returned from work. Jamie wondered for the thousandth time if all that noise was really necessary. *Maybe the man just wanted to make his presence known, without having to speak a word. If so, he certainly accomplished that. His noises would wake a sleeping grizzly, for goodness sakes!* Jamie rolled over and put the pillow over his exposed ear. It didn't completely muffle the sounds, but at least they were less irritating. Somewhere between the snorts and flushing toilet, Jamie fell asleep. He didn't hear his dad open the door and peek in.

CHAPTER 132

Christina woke to the sound of Christmas music on her clock/radio. She usually had it set for buzzing, but being it was Christmas Eve, she wanted to wake in a festive spirit. Smiling, she reached over and turned it off. Next to her, Stacey stirred and mumbled something. She turned to look at her daughter, who had curled up in a ball, and was visiting dreamland, by the sound of her deep sonorous breathing. Christina reached over and pulled the blanket up to her daughter's chin, then crawled out of bed.

The floor felt cold on her bare feet. Finding her slippers and robe, she donned them and quietly headed downstairs. She turned on the coffee maker, then let Benji out, and shuddered as she felt the finger numbing cold bite at her bare hands.

Urging Benji to finish his business, she wrapped the robe tighter around her waist and stuck her hands in her armpits. He woofed as he ran to her, and sprinted through the open door. Shaking himself, he ran into the kitchen and stood in front of his empty bowl.

"Geeze, Benji, let me get my coffee first. I promise you won't starve in the next couple of minutes."

He looked up, then back to his bowl. He wasn't thoroughly convinced.

Once Benji's and the two cat bowls were filled, she took her cup, and headed for the den. Grabbing the hand-crocheted afghan her mother had made for her wedding, she wrapped it around her feet. Benji, being satiated for the moment, jumped up beside her. With a "hmph" he laid his head across her lap. She closed her eyes a moment and let herself float on the silence. She even held her breath a moment, as she listened to the quietness, except for Benji's breathing, and let her mind wander. She breathed in and out slowly, allowing her body and mind to relax and brought up memories of the Christmas Eve before David had passed. She smiled, as she remembered him snuggling up to her and whispering in her ear that it was Christmas Eve, and he wanted her to stay in bed because he planned to fix her breakfast and bring it up to her. Of course, she couldn't go back to sleep, so she toileted, made herself presentable, and wrote in her journal, until he came back in, with a tray containing an omelet, coffee and toast. They sat and shared the breakfast, laughed and teased and held each other, until they heard the children stirring.

Tears stung her eyes as she recalled the sweet tenderness of their time together. If someone had told her she would be spending the next Christmases without him, she would have protested and deemed them insane for having any such thought. Rubbing her eyes, she asked once again, "Why God? Why David? Why us? We were so happy. I don't know if we can ever be that happy again." And again, as always, there was silence.

She blew out a lungful of air, startling Benji, who jumped, and bumped her hand with the half-full coffee mug.

"Oh, man, not on my white robe, again!" She yelled, as she tried to disentangle herself from the frantic dog, afghan, and chair. Once free, she ran to the laundry room and put detergent and stain remover on the quickly spreading brown spot, and threw it in the washer, with a few other items.

"Geeze, I hope I caught it in time!" She realized she was shivering and ran upstairs to find another robe. Looking at the clock, she realized she had time for a nice, hot shower.

Standing under the pelting, hot stream, she couldn't help but giggle when she thought of poor Benji's reaction to the whole coffee fiasco. "Poor guy. He had no idea why I was acting so crazy."

Once showered, dressed and downstairs for a second cup of coffee, she was surprised to walk in the family room and see Nicky and Benji, in her easy chair, curled up in the afghan, and watching cartoons.

Looking confused, she asked, "Hey, why are you up so early?"

Shrugging, he said, "I had another nightmare and couldn't go back to sleep. I heard you in the shower, so I came down to wait for you."

"Well, you think you could scooch over and let me sit with you?"

"Sure," he said with a grin.

Benji, deciding the chair wasn't big enough for three, jumped down and with a huff, curled up on his bed and went to sleep.

Sipping her coffee, and absently twirling a ringlet of Nicky's hair, she said, "Do you remember what your dream was about?"

Sighing, he nodded and said, "Yeah, it was another scary one, where I'm being chased by a demon dog thing and I can't find you or Dad, and then I hear a big explosion, and see fire and people running and the dog thing disappeared, and I saw you and Stacey and Brad, but not Dad. Y'all were running away from the fire." Sighing and shrugging, he said, "I woke up then."

Raising her eyebrows, and pulling Nicky into a hug, she said, "Wow, that sounds awful! I'm glad you woke up when you did."

"Yeah, me too."

After a moment, she asked, "Could you tell where the explosion was?"

Shaking his head, he said, "Nah, just some tall building."

"Interesting."

Looking at her watch, she said, "Hey, babe, as much as I enjoy this, I gotta go."

Looking up, he smiled. "I like these times. I'm glad you got such a nice big chair, too, or we couldn't fit."

"Hey, are you saying I'm fat?"

He giggled, "No way. I'm just getting bigger and, well, you know."

She gave him a look of mocked surprise. "Why Nicky, are you insinuating that I'm spreading out?"

He snorted, "Well, like you say, 'If the shoe fits.'"

She gave him a light shove and said, "That's it buddy. No more chair sharing with you!"

Giggling, she disentangled herself a second time, and headed upstairs to finish preparing for work. Nicky patted the empty spot beside him and Benji instantly filled it.

CHAPTER 133

Dr. Harrison looked down at his patient, and sighed. She was so battered, bruised, broken, and barely recognizable. Checking her vitals once more, and recording them in her chart, he took her hand. Bowing his head, he asked God to please heal her body, mind and spirit. He knew she was an unbeliever and had many emotional issues, and would have a long healing process ahead. She would need more than just physical help and healing in the days to come. She would never be the same. Her beautiful face would be severely scarred, even though the finest plastic surgeon from Dallas had driven in to work on the repairs. It would be a miracle if all the broken bones healed properly, and she wouldn't be left with a limp, or limited use of her limbs. He hoped, for her sake, that time was on her side—she was only forty, and under normal circumstances, had a long life ahead of her. She stirred and moaned, mumbling Linda's name.

He'd forgotten about the child. He'd have to go check on her. Hopefully, God would be merciful and wake and reunite them both for Christmas Day tomorrow, even if for a few minutes.

He patted Janet's hand once again, and left to check on her daughter.

CHAPTER 134

Linda woke with a start and looked around, confused as to where she was. She had expected to wake up in her bed, but, instead was in a hospital room with all kinds of tubes snaking in and around her body. She whimpered, and tried to sit, but every inch of her hurt. Tears filled her eyes as she called out for her mom. All that came out was a whisper. Looking around in a panic, the reality of what had happened slammed into her like a train and she tried to scream.

The nurse in the ICU station noticed Linda's monitors spiking, indicating that something unusual was occurring. She put down the chart she had been reading, and went to check on Linda, who was wild with fear and panic. She was trying to remove the IV and leads to the heart monitor, and was crying and moaning and trying to get out of bed. The nurse went to her and laid a calming hand on the frantic child's arm.

"Linda, honey, you need to calm down, and I'll tell you what happened."

Linda, with tears and fear in her eyes, stopped moving and focused on the nurse.

"My name is Angela, and I'm a nurse here in the ICU unit. You were in a car accident and were injured. You had to have surgery on your abdomen. That's why it hurts when you try to sit up. Everything else is here to help us know how you're doing."

She smiled pleasantly as she checked the IV and other monitors and replaced missing cardiac leads that had been ripped off.

Linda whispered. "Why does my throat hurt so much?"

Patting the girls' hand, Angela said, "The doctors had to place a breathing tube down your throat, when you were in surgery, and it's probably irritated from that. It'll feel better in a day or so."

Linda nodded, looked around and asked, "Where's my mom?"

Sitting next to the bed, the nurse, still holding Linda's hand, asked, "Honey, do you remember what happened?"

Linda closed her eyes and nodded.

"Mom didn't stop at a stop sign and ran into a truck. I remember screaming, then everything went dark for a while, then I remember seeing Mrs. Sanders, and riding in the ambulance." Opening her eyes and sighing, she said, "Everything after that is a blur, or dark."

Angela nodded. "Well, your mom was hurt pretty bad, and had to have surgery to fix a few broken bones and such. She's in the room two doors down."

Trying to sit up, Linda said, "Is she okay? Can I see her?"

The nurse looked around and assessing her patients' status said, "Tell you what, I'll get the other nurse and we can transfer you to a wheelchair, and take you over, but only for a minute or two."

Linda frowned.

"Trust me, you won't want to be up for more than that."

Linda nodded and whispered. "Okay, thanks."

After a few minutes, two nurses returned.

Angela introduced the other nurse.

"This is Carla. She and I will help you up. If at any time you feel sick or in too much pain, let us know. You just move as slowly as you need to."

Linda nodded and gritted her teeth, as the ladies prepared her for the transport.

Once settled into the wheelchair, after a few tears and a lot of sweat, Linda nodded for them to get moving.

"Now, Linda," Angela said, "Your mom is going to be pretty bandaged up and she may not look like herself. There will be lots of wires, tubes and such, as well."

Linda looked up and frowned.

Carla who was older and heavyset, said, "It'll be okay, sweetie. She'll look a lot worse than she is. We just don't want you to be scared when you see her."

As they entered the room, Linda looked at the woman in the bed and shook her head.

"That's not my mom," she whispered. The woman in the bed couldn't possibly be her mother. Her head was wrapped in a huge helmet-like bandage, her arm and both legs were in slings, there were tubes and wires snaking under the sheets and blankets, and monitors were beeping and shushing. Linda motioned for Angela to wheel her closer.

She whispered, "Mom?"

The woman on the bed didn't move. Tears filled Linda's eyes.

Taking her mother's free hand, except for an IV, Linda kissed it and whispered, "Mom, please come back to me." She laid her head on the bed and let the tears and sobs overtake her. The two nurses looked at each other, and shook their heads.

After a moment, Angela whispered, "Honey, it's time to get you back to bed."

Linda nodded. Holding her arms tight across her abdomen, she said, "My tummy hurts."

Carla said, "I'll run and get you some medicine for that, while Angela takes you back to your room."

Linda nodded and wiped the tears and snot from her face with the hem of her gown. Angela handed her a tissue, which Linda promptly blew her nose in.

As Angela hung the IV bags back on the poles and straightened the bed covers, Linda asked, "Is my mom gonna die?"

Angela stopped and turned to face the girl. She didn't believe in sugar-coating the truth, especially with children. They could usually see right through the deception, and when reality didn't line up with what they had been told, feelings of confusion and betrayal ensued. She felt children, especially Linda's age, should be trusted with the truth, even if it may be harsh.

Leaning her backside against the wall, she said, "Linda, as you know, your mother is in pretty bad shape. I can't tell you for sure, if she will live or die. There are so many factors involved. I've seen people with far less injuries die, and I've seen people worse off than your mom make a full recovery." Shrugging, she added, "Our team of doctors and nurses will do their best to help her have a fighting chance, but honestly, there are some things that are just out of our control."

A tear ran down Linda's face. Nodding, she said, "Okay."

Carla entered the room, injected the IV line with a sedative. Linda rolled on her side, shut her eyes, and was asleep almost immediately.

"You think she'll be okay?" Carla asked, as she gathered a pile of dirty linen, and dropped it in a receptacle.

Sighing, Angela said, "I think so. She seems to be a fighter. I think she'll *force* herself to be okay, so she can take care of her mom."

Nodding, Carla said, "Poor thing."

"Speaking of her mom," Angela said, "I need to go check in on her."

CHAPTER 135

When Jamie had arrived home that evening, after a busy day at work, he nearly bumped into his dad, who was leaving for a late shift at the cotton processing plant outside of Alva.

Surprise registering on his face, he said to his son, "Hey, I won't be home tonight. One of the guys called in sick, and I volunteered to cover for him."

Nodding, Jamie said, "Alright, by the way, Merry Christmas."

"Oh, yeah."

Jamie waited for his dad to say it back, but after a moment of awkward silence, he said, "Okay, then, I guess I'll see you whenever."

Nodding, his dad said, "Right."

Jamie clenched his fists, and fought the urge to shake his dad for not even acknowledging Christmas. *The man is hopeless,* he thought as he entered the dark little house.

Setting his backpack on the couch, and hanging his coat, gloves and hat in the closet, he headed to his room, failing to notice the tiny little Christmas tree on the kitchen counter.

He was tired after delivering pizzas all over town, even to the Sanders family, that he almost gave in to the urge to lie down for a few minutes. He headed to the bathroom to splash cold water on his face, and as he reviewed his plan for the night, felt his heart kick it up a bit, re-energizing him.

Returning to his room, he pulled the boxes out from under his bed, and riffled through them, making sure every wire, fuse and item was properly connected. He'd hate to get everything set up and ready to go, just to be thwarted by a stray wire.

Running out to bring the car his boss had given him up closer to the house, he slipped on an icy spot and went down hard on his knees.

Catching his breath, he swore and stood slowly, making sure nothing had broken. Limping the rest of the way, he brought the car up to the back door and loaded the boxes.

Looking up at the clear sky and noticing there was no breeze, he smiled and thought, *What a perfect night for what I have planned.*

While parents tucked their children into bed, and hurried to assemble last minute gifts, in anticipation of the big day, Jamie was setting up his equipment by the courthouse.

Before leaving home, he had called in a bomb threat at the high school, knowing the police and fire department would be busy investigating that, thus freeing him up to do what needed to be done.

He wore a black snow suit, gloves, and a face-covering stocking cap. Not even his grandma would know it was him. He chuckled. The night air was biting cold, and when he had to remove his gloves to connect wires and such, his fingertips numbed immediately.

"Man, it's cold! One would think we were in the North Pole!"

He looked at his watch. *Right on time. Ten more minutes, then boom! Surprise!* He giggled, thinking, *No one will even know who did this.*

CHAPTER 136

Christina turned off the TV, and said good-night to her children, as they all went to their separate rooms. Feeling restless, though tired, she decided to pull out her journal, and read the entries concerning Benji's odd behavior.

If they did correspond to the times of her items disappearing, and re-appearing, then that meant that their home *had* been invaded.

Benji had been the victim of some misguided thief. *Did that mean the person would be back? The vase re-appeared yesterday, so is he finished with our house? Will he return? Are we safe? Should I get my locks changed? Yes! Hopefully I can have someone out on Wednesday.*

She listened as the house noises settled into a peaceful quietness. She listened, as Brad said something to Benji, who had decided to go with him, instead of her. She knew the dog would pick someone other than herself to sleep with on occasion, just to reassure them of his love, she presumed. She would miss his warm doggie presence, at the foot of her bed.

She wrote about the kids plays, and Brad's heavenly experience, as well as Cindy's accident, and encounter with Jesus, then Janet and Linda's car accident. She had to stop occasionally and massage her hands. *You know,* she thought to herself, *it would be a lot easier and quicker if I'd put this on the computer. Okay, starting next year, I'll do that. As for now, I'll just keep writing.*

She wrote for another hour or so, and between tired eyes and hands, and feeling the warm blanket of sleep beckoning her to give in, she laid down her pen, and journal and scooted down under the nice warm covers. Looking at the clock, and making sure the alarm was on, she turned out the light. 11:45. *Tomorrow's Christmas, and I have to be up by six, so I'd best get to sleep.*

CHAPTER 137

As the twelfth ring echoed from the courthouse clock, and before it had completely dissipated, the first of Jamie's explosions rocked the town of Alva, followed quickly by several more.

Those who were awake, stopped and listened in shocked silence, then headed outdoors, or to windows, to see what had caused such a ground shaking noise.

The chief of police, who had been searching lockers at the high school, stopped in his tracks and thought, *Oh, have mercy! Someone is bombing Alva!*

He shouted for his men, and ran to his police cruiser.

By the third explosion, house and car alarms were going off, dogs were howling, and people were yelling and screaming, thinking their town was under attack.

As all the chaos was occurring, a strange thing happened at the hospital. Janet, who had been sleeping deeply, sat up in bed and yelled, "No, Jamie, don't do it!"

CHAPTER 138

Cindy was jolted awake from a nice dream involving Ed, when her daughter Samara jumped on her bed and yelled, "Wake up, mom. It sounds like a bomb went off somewhere!"

Cindy sat up, and grabbed her head, as the sudden change in position caused a throbbing sensation.

"Ow!" She said, as she became fully conscious. "A bomb? Are you sure? Where?"

Samara, helped her mom out of bed, as Cindy was still recovering from the concussion she received the previous week.

"I don't know if it was a bomb, but it was a loud boom and it woke me up."

Just as she said this, another explosion rocked the town.

Now fully awake, Cindy said, "What in the world?"

She and Samara went to look out the front window and were shocked to see the southern sky—right behind the courthouse—lit up. They grabbed their coats and headed outside with the rest of the Alva residents, to see what was causing such a display.

CHAPTER 139

Jamie lay on the ground, well hidden under a bush, and undetectable in his black apparel, watching and listening as the downtown area began filling with cars, emergency vehicles and people—all making some kind of noise. He giggled, and shook his head, thinking, "Merry Christmas, Alva!"

As he gathered his equipment and put it In the car, leaving no trace of his presence, he thought about people's reactions and what they would say: "Hey, remember that Christmas night, when the sky lit up?"

Too bad no one would know he was behind it all. He shivered and cranked up the heat as he felt the wind kicking up the dusting of snow on the ground. Taking one last look around, he pulled away from his hiding place, right as the police chief and his deputies arrived.

Sitting at the stop sign, he felt a buzzing in his pocket, and pulled out his cell phone. Not recognizing the number, he pulled up the message, and was instantly fearful and confused, and had to pull his car over. He began hyperventilating as he read the text.

Hey, Jamie. I like your display, but check this out!

As soon as he read the last word, another set of explosions rocked the north end of town. Looking out the window of his car, he could hardly believe what he saw.

Jamie's amazing firework display was forgotten, as folks turned their attention to the orange sky at the opposite end of town.

Driving slowly through town, so as not to draw any attention to himself, he heard someone yell, "It's the old oil refinery!"

Once past the city limits, he sped up and drove his car in that direction, knowing who was behind this.

"Oh, man, Jimmy, what have you done?"